I0740507

David D. Porter

Incidents and Anecdotes of the Civil War

David D. Porter

Incidents and Anecdotes of the Civil War

ISBN/EAN: 9783337224790

Printed in Europe, USA, Canada, Australia, Japan

Cover: Foto ©Andreas Hilbeck / pixelio.de

More available books at **www.hansebooks.com**

INCIDENTS

AND ANECDOTES

OF THE

CIVIL WAR.

BY

ADMIRAL PORTER,
AUTHOR OF "ALLAN DARE AND ROBERT LE DIABLE," ETC.

NEW YORK:
D. APPLETON AND COMPANY,
1, 3, AND 5 BOND STREET.
1885.

CONTENTS.

INCIDENTS AND ANECDOTES OF THE CIVIL WAR.

CHAPTER I.

REJOICINGS IN WASHINGTON AT THE SECESSION OF SOUTH CAROLINA.

DURING the Presidency of James Buchanan, and just previous to the inauguration of Mr. Lincoln, I was ordered to the command of the Coast-Survey steamer Active on the Pacific coast.

I could not conceive why I was thus ordered, except that ships and officers were at that period being sent out of the way. This, too, at a time when the Southern States were threatening to secede, and it seemed probable the Government would require the services of all its officers to maintain the integrity of the Union.

At that moment I was in a despondent frame of mind, and troubled with the most gloomy forebodings. I felt that a crisis was impending that might influence all my prospects in life and cast me upon the world without resources and with a large dependent family.

I sought consolation by visiting the houses of Southern members of Congress in Washington whom I knew, but obtained little satisfaction from the sentiments I there heard expressed.

One night in December, 1860, on my way home from a visit to Congress, where I had listened to a great deal of incendiary language from Southern members and plenty of vituperation from Northern ones, a gentleman met me in the street and informed me of the secession of South Carolina.

The news, though not unexpected, was startling, and, viewing the matter in the most philosophical light possible, I proceeded homeward to carry the unpleasant intelligence.

On my way I had to pass the house of a distinguished Southern gentleman whom I knew well and for whom I entertained a high regard. I had always heard him discuss the questions at issue between the North and South in the most dispassionate manner, whatever may have been his course in Congress.

There were a dozen carriages standing before the door, and the house was all ablaze with lights, making the interior look cheerful enough, while a drizzling rain rendered everything gloomy without. Those were not the days of well-lighted streets and asphalt pavements. Washington was a city of muddy highways, and corporation moonlight was more frequent than convenient.

As I entered the mansion the lady of the house, in bonnet and shawl, was descending the stairs. She was a magnificent woman, greatly esteemed in Washington society for her genial manner, and admired for her wit and intellect. Had she aspired to do so, this lady might have been the leader of fashion in the Federal capital, but I do not think her ambition ran in that direction. She had a small and select circle of friends, mostly Southern people, and chiefly affected politics.

Her heart was fixed on what she called the emancipation of the South from Northern thralldom, and with her handsome person and dignified bearing she seemed worthy to occupy the loftiest position.

As this lady saw me she exclaimed, "Ah, captain"—for so she always called me—"I am so glad to see you! I want you to escort me to the White House. The horses are sick, and I am going to walk over."

"It is impossible for you to walk," I replied, "through the rain and mud ; but there are ten or twelve hacks at the door, and I will press one of them into your service." So saying, I called a carriage, helped the lady in, and got in after her.

"I was under the impression," I said, as we started, "that you were having a party at your house, seeing it so brilliantly lighted up, and I thought I would venture in uninvited."

"No, indeed," she replied, "but we have received glorious news from the South, and my husband's friends are calling to congratulate him. South Carolina has seceded, and, O captain !" she continued, with increasing fervor, "we will have a glorious monarchy, and you must join us !"

"Yes," I said, "and be made Duke of Benedict Arnold."

"Nonsense!" she exclaimed, "but we will make you an admiral."

"Certainly," I replied, "Admiral of the *Blue*, for I should feel blue enough to see everything turned upside down, and our boasted liberty and civilization whistled down the wind."

"What would you have?" she inquired. "Would you have us tamely submit to all the indignities the North have put upon us, and place our necks under their feet? Why, this very day my blood fairly boiled while I was in Congress, and I could scarcely contain myself. That old Black Republican, Mr. ——, was berating the Southern people as if they were a pack of naughty children. However, I was indemnified in the end, for Mr. Rhett took the floor and gave the man such a castigation that he slunk away and was no more heard from. We can stand these outrages no longer, and will take refuge in a monarchy—a glorious monarchy!"

"Of course you will be queen," I said. "Well, I should be happy to serve under such a beautiful majesty, but somehow I like this homely republicanism under which I have been brought up, and so I will stick to it; but don't repeat to others what you have said to me, for it might compromise your husband."

"Ah," she exclaimed, "he thinks as I do!"

Just then we reached the White House. I helped the lady from the carriage and escorted her into the great hall. I proposed to take my leave, but she insisted on my remaining, saying, "I want to tell the President the good news."

Heavens and earth! thought I, what will happen next? "No, thank you," I said, "I will take some other opportunity to see the President," and, taking my leave of the lady, I went out and never saw her afterward.

I rode back to the house to return the borrowed carriage, and, when I reached the door, heard sounds of merriment issuing from the mansion, and was induced to step into the parlor.

As I entered I was welcomed with boisterous shouts by a dozen gentlemen, only two of whom I had ever met before. They embraced me, and insisted on my drinking with them, but this I declined, thinking there had been too much drinking already.

I can only compare the scene to Pandemonium.

> "The people all acted like the jacks at the Nore,
>   And ran the Palmetto flag up to the fore,
>   Where all ranted and raved, and their language, O dear!
>   Was so full of billingsgate 'twas shocking to hear.

> Cooney and lawyer, politician and sage,
> And the craziest men of the palmetto age,
>> With defiant looks,
>> Full of crotchets and crooks,
> Were chafing and swearing and scowling so black
> As hosts sometimes do when the dinner's put back.
> Yet few of the folks at that chivalric fair
> Seemed willing to think—nor a curse did they care—
> That a sword hung over them just by a hair.
> *Old Clootie* was there, and said all was right;
> 'Twas he held the bottle, and urged on the fight,
>> And stood up in his place,
>> With his stoical face,
> His hands meekly folded, as if he'd say grace,
> While Rebellion was moving at an awful fast pace."

The only person who seemed to preserve his equanimity was the master of the house, who sat, calm and smiling, conversing with an uproarious friend who had partaken deeply of the flowing bowl.

When I had an opportunity I asked the host quietly if there was anything in this excitement, and if it could be possible that the Southern States would secede. "What more do they want?" I inquired. "They have a majority in the Senate and in the House, and, with the Supreme Court on their side, they can make laws to suit themselves."

"Yes," he replied, his bright eye almost looking through me, "most people would be satisfied with that.

> "'Better to suffer from the ills we have,
>> Than fly to others that we wot not of.'

"But you will join us," he continued, "and we will make you an admiral."

"Thank you," said I, "but I am going to the California gold-mines, and when the South and the North have done quarreling, and all you seceders have come back and taken your seats in Congress, I will join the navy again."

"You must join *us*," he said, "for we will have a navy to be proud of."

A few weeks later my friends left Washington for the South, regretted by all who knew them. Their house had been the rendezvous of the most brilliant and refined persons at the capital. The clever women of the South met there to discuss the prospects of a Southern confederacy or monarchy, and to urge on their slow-moving husbands in what they considered the path of duty.

These ladies saw in the distance the gleam of the coronets that were to encircle their fair brows, and certainly none were more fitted, by the graces of mind and person, to wear them than the beautiful Southern women who formed the bright galaxy of stars in Washington society.

As to the lady whom I accompanied to the White House, she shone, like Venus, brighter than all the other planets, and her departure cast a gloom over the firesides of the friends she left behind in Washington, soon to be overshadowed by the stirring scenes at the outbreak of the civil war—the tramp of legions of soldiers through quiet streets where, since the rebuilding of the Capitol, had been heard nothing more stirring than

"Sounds of revelry by night,"

or the simple pageants which accompanied the President to and from the Capitol at the quadrennial inauguration.

No wonder the capital and its surroundings seemed stupid to these vivacious Southerners, and that their hearts were not satisfied with our plain republican trappings.

An opera-house or two, half a dozen fine theatres, and a court, or the semblance of one, at the White House—something more in the style of the present day—might have prevented the catastrophe which overwhelmed both North and South.

The Romans understood these things better than we. They omitted nothing to keep the people amused; they even had the street fountains at times run with wine, and the investment was worth the money spent.

But what could one expect at a court presided over by an old bachelor whose heart was dead to poetry and love; who sat at dinner with no flowers to grace the festive board, and never even wore a *boutonnière* on his coat-lapel; who eschewed everything like official state, and was content to live out his term of office in plain republican simplicity?

What was there to attract charming women to an administration like that of Abraham Lincoln, conducted with even more simplicity than that of his predecessor, and only to be appreciated by sturdy republicans that despised all the vanities of a court and took no stock in monarchy?

Barren and dreary as the fair Southerners left the city of Washington—to which they intended to return when a Southern court should be established—it has since risen from its ashes like a Phœnix, and blooms as it never did before.

The angels of heaven smile serenely over the happy meeting of those who did all they could to imbrue their hands in each other's blood, but she who once moved radiant amid the throng is still absent from the Federal capital.

> "She was superb—at least so she was thirty summers ago—
> As soft and as sallow as autumn, with hair
> Neither black nor yet brown, but that tint which the air
> Takes at eve in September, when night lingers lone
> Through a vineyard, from beams of a slow-setting sun;
> Eyes the wistful gazelle's, the fine foot of a fairy,
> A voice soft and sweet as a tune that one knows.
> Something in her there was set you to thinking of those
> Strange backgrounds of Raphael, that hectic and deep
> Brief twilight in which Southern suns fall asleep.
> Thou abidest and reignest forever, O Queen
> Of that better world which thou swayest unseen."

It is not my intention at this late day to reflect upon the motives of those whose acts brought about such desolation. Let them rest in peace, and may the future bring back to us those who once formed the most refined and delightful society at the capital.

They will find the Federal city improved and beautified, ready to receive them with warm hearts and friendly greetings. The capital will smile as of yore when the bright galaxy of Southern ladies which once illumined its halls again take their places in a society they are so well fitted to adorn.

And those clever men of the South—the successors of the great statesmen who played such a prominent part in our early history—may they realize the task before them of reconstructing their several States and making their people feel that we all belong to one country, which, if united, can be made the grandest in the world.

CHAPTER II.

PLAN TO SAVE FORT PICKENS—DISLOYALTY IN THE NAVY DE-
PARTMENT—STEALING A MARCH ON THE SECRETARY OF THE
NAVY.

MR. LINCOLN had been installed in the Presidential office, and
the subject of relieving Fort Sumter was under discussion. A
small squadron was being fitted out for the supposed purpose of
relieving the fort, the final action of which was to be guided by
Mr. G. V. Fox, afterward Assistant Secretary of the Navy.

My orders to California were still hanging over me, and I had
even engaged my passage in the steamer from New York, and was
taking my last meal with my family, when a carriage drove up to
the door.

It brought a note from the Secretary of State (Mr. Seward), requesting me to call and see him without delay ; so, leaving my dinner unfinished, I jumped into the carriage and drove at once to the
Secretary's office.

I found Mr. Seward lying on his back on a sofa, with his knees
up, reading a lengthy document.

Without changing his position he said to me, " Can you tell me
how we can save Fort Pickens from falling into the hands of the
rebels ? "

I answered, promptly, " I can, sir."

" Then," said the Secretary, " you are the man I want, if you
can do it."

" I can do it," I said, as Mr. Seward rose to his feet.

Those familiar with the history of that period will remember
that Lieutenant Slemmer was holding Fort Pickens with a small
force and had refused the summons of General Bragg to surrender,
and all the naval guns and munitions of war that had fallen into
the Confederates' hands were being placed in position behind earth-
works, preparatory to opening on the Union lines.

It was to save Slemmer and the Union works that made Mr.
Seward so interested in this affair.

" Now, come," said Mr. Seward, " tell me how you will save
that place."

I had talked with Captain (now General) Meigs a few days before about this matter. That officer broached the subject to me, and it appears first suggested the matter to Mr. Seward, and the latter, being anxious to show the Southerners that the Government had a right to hold its own forts, and seeing the likelihood of our losing Fort Sumter, listened very kindly to Captain Meigs's suggestions.

Our plan was to get a good-sized steamer and six or seven companies of soldiers, and to carry the latter, with a number of large guns and a quantity of munitions of war, to Fort Pickens, land them on the outside of the fort under the guns of a ship of war, and the fort would soon be made impregnable—that was all.

I repeated this to Mr. Seward, and said to him, "Give me command of the Powhatan, now lying at New York ready for sea, and I will guarantee that everything shall be done without a mistake."

Mr. Seward listened attentively, and, when I had finished what I had to say, he invited Captain Meigs—who had come in in the mean time—and myself to accompany him to the President.

When we arrived at the White House, Mr. Lincoln—who seemed to be aware of our errand—opened the conversation.

"Tell me," said he, "how we can prevent Fort Pickens from falling into the hands of the rebels, for if Slemmer is not at once relieved there will be no holding it. Pensacola would be a very important place for the Southerners, and if they once get possession of Pickens, and fortify it, we have no navy to take it from them."

"Mr. President," said I, "there is a queer state of things existing in the Navy Department at this time. Mr. Welles is surrounded by officers and clerks, some of whom are disloyal at heart, and if the orders for this expedition should emanate from the Secretary of the Navy, and pass through all the department red tape, the news would be at once flashed over the wires, and Fort Pickens would be lost for ever. But if you will issue all the orders from the Executive Mansion, and let me proceed to New York with them, I will guarantee their prompt execution to the letter."

"But," said the President, "is not this a most irregular mode of proceeding?"

"Certainly," I replied, "but the necessity of the case justifies it."

"You are commander-in-chief of the army and navy," said Mr. Seward to the President, "and this is a case where it is necessary to issue direct orders without passing them through intermediaries."

"But what will Uncle Gideon say?" inquired the President.

"Oh, I will make it all right with Mr. Welles," said the Secretary of State. "This is the only way, sir, the thing can be done."

At this very time Mr. Welles was—or supposed he was—fitting out an expedition for the relief of Fort Sumter. All the orders were issued in the usual way, and, of course, telegraphed to Charleston, as soon as written, by the persons in the department through whose hands they passed.

Mr. Seward was well aware of this, and he wanted to prevent such a thing happening in this instance.

Mr. Welles, no doubt, had the Powhatan on his list of available vessels, and may have relied on her to carry out his plan for the relief of Sumter. Orders had been sent for the several vessels to rendezvous off Charleston on a certain day, but, strange to say, no orders had been issued for the Powhatan to join them, for reasons that will appear in the course of my narrative.

I observed one thing during this interview, and that was that the best of feeling did not exist between the heads of the State and Navy Departments. Mr. Seward doubtless thought that he had not been as much consulted as he ought to have been in the fitting out of the expedition for the relief of Sumter. He looked upon himself as Prime Minister, and considered that the Secretary of the Navy should defer to him in all matters concerning movements against those in rebellion, in which opinion Mr. Welles did not concur. Mr. Seward was by nature of an arbitrary disposition, and wanted everything done in his own way—not a bad quality on occasions, but apt to create confusion if persevered in in too many cases.

In this instance it was eminently proper that the Secretary of State should take the initiative.

In the course of the conversation Mr. Lincoln remarked : "This looks to me very much like the case of two fellows I once knew : one was a gambler, the other a preacher. They met in a stage, and the gambler induced the preacher to play poker, and the latter won all the gambler's money. 'It's all because we have mistaken our trades,' said the gambler; 'you ought to have been a gambler and I a preacher, and, by ginger, I intend to turn the tables on you next Sunday and preach in your church,' which he did."

It was finally agreed that my plan should be carried out. I wrote the necessary orders, which were copied by Captain Meigs and signed by the President, who merely said as he did so, " Seward, see that I don't burn my fingers."

The first order was for me to proceed to New York and take command of the steam frigate Powhatan, proceed at once to Fort Pickens, run across the bar and anchor at all hazards on the inside, where I could cover the fort and co-operate with Captain Meigs while he was landing the troops, which were to go in a steamer chartered for the occasion.

The second order was for the commandant of the New York navy-yard, directing him to fit out the Powhatan with all dispatch and with the greatest secrecy, and under no circumstances to inform the Navy Department until after the ship had sailed.

The third order was to the commanding officer of the Powhatan, informing him that circumstances required that the utmost dispatch and secrecy should be observed in fitting out the ship, and that it was necessary for the President to confide the execution of his plans to some one who understood them thoroughly, in order that they might be carried out ; that for this reason he was compelled to detach Captain Mercer from the command of the Powhatan, but that, having the highest confidence in his abilities and patriotism, the President gave him the option to select any other ship in the navy, etc.

Armed with these documents, I bade the President good-day, and, in company with Captain Meigs, proceeded to the headquarters of the General-in-Chief, General Scott, then the military oracle, without whose authority no troops would have been granted.

Lieutenant-Colonel Keyes was at that time General Scott's Military Secretary, and when we called on the general he showed us into the anteroom, where Meigs unfolded to him our plans and instructions, requesting that the general would grant us an audience as soon as possible.

When Keyes delivered the message, General Scott gruffly inquired what we wanted, and, when informed, said, " Tell Captain Meigs to walk in ; I won't see any naval officer ; *he* can't come in."

The fact was, the general at that moment was suffering from a severe attack of gout, which made him unwilling to see anybody outside of his military family.

Captain Meigs shortly rejoined me in the anteroom. With the aid of Keyes, he had succeeded in getting the general to give him the desired force of troops for the relief of Pickens, and we therefore departed to carry out the plans.

Next morning at nine o'clock I was at the New York navy-yard, and found that Commodore Breese, the commandant, was absent on a two weeks' leave, and that Captain A. II. Foote was in command. This was a fortunate circumstance, for if I had to deal with Commodore Breese I should have experienced no end of trouble in keeping the expedition secret. Breese was a particularly "cautious man," a by-word in the navy to express a lack of the higher qualities, and he would have eventually let the cat out of the bag, or insisted on telegraphing to the Secretary of the Navy for orders, notwithstanding the President's instructions. It is hard to get an old officer out of a groove in which he has been running for many years, and this way of carrying on operations would have seemed altogether wrong to a man of Commodore Breese's way of thinking.

As it was, I had trouble enough with Foote to bring him to reason, and it was only after three hours' earnest conversation that I convinced him I was not a rebel in disguise plotting with the Powhatan's officers to run away with the ship, and deliver her over to the South.

"You see, Porter," he said, "there are so many fellows whom I would have trusted to the death who have deserted the flag that I don't know whom to believe." He read my orders over and over, turned them upside down, examined the water-mark and Executive Mansion stamp, and surveyed me from head to foot. "How do I know *you* are not a traitor ? Who ever heard of such orders as these emanating direct from the President ? I must telegraph to Mr. Welles before I do anything, and ask further instructions."

"Look at these orders again," I said, "and then telegraph at your peril. Under no circumstances must you inform the Navy Department of this expedition. Now give me a cigar, let me sit here in quiet, and you may take an hour or two to look over those letters if you like ; but if you telegraph to Mr. Welles the President will consider it high treason, and you will lose the best chance you ever had in your life. If you must telegraph, send a message to the President or Mr. Seward."

"Yes," replied Foote, "and what would prevent you from having a confederate at the other end of the line to receive the message and answer it—there is so much treason going on ?"

I burst out laughing. "What would you say," I inquired, "if

2

I were to tell you that Frank Buchanan, Sam Barron, and Magruder were going to desert to the rebels ? "

Foote jumped from his chair. "God in heaven !" he exclaimed, "what next ? You don't expect me to trust you after that ? How do I know you are not in league with the others ? But, man, that can't be, for I saw by the morning papers that President Lincoln was at a wedding last night at Buchanan's, and Buchanan had the house festooned with American flags, and all the loyal men of Washington were there."

"So they were," I replied, "but, nevertheless, they will all desert in a few days, for their hearts are on the other side. Ingraham is going also—his chief clerk has already preceded him, and carried off the signal-book of the navy."

"Good Lord deliver us !" exclaimed Foote, piously. "I must telegraph to Mr. Welles. I can't stand this strain any longer. It will kill me. You sit smoking and smiling as if this was not a very serious matter. Here "—to his chief clerk—"bring me a telegraph blank."

"Before you send that message," said I, "let me call your attention to a paragraph of the President's order : 'Under no circumstances will you make known to the Navy Department or any one else the object of this expedition, or the fact that the Powhatan is fitting out.' Just think," I continued to Captain Foote, "of the President taking you into his confidence so early in these troubles ; think what a high position you may reach before the trouble with the South is over if we succeed in carrying out this expedition successfully. Then, again, think what a tumble you will get if you disobey a positive order of the President. He will believe rebellion rampant everywhere, and won't know whom to trust. Think of Captain Foote being tried and shot like Admiral Byng for failing to carry out his orders."

"Hush, Porter !" exclaimed Foote, "hush at once ! I believe you are a rebel in disguise, for after Frank Buchanan, Barron, and Magruder preparing to desert, and Ingraham, too, with his Kosta record, I won't trust any one. Where are your trunks ?"

"At the Irving House," I replied.

"Send the postman here," said Foote. When the man came he said to him, "Go to the Irving House, pay Lieutenant Porter's bill, and take his trunks to my house and tell Mrs. Foote to prepare the best room.—There, my boy, I have you now. You shall stay with me, and I will be ready to arrest you the moment I find there is any treason about you. After all," continued Foote, "you have come on a wild-goose chase. The Powhatan is stripped to a girt-line. Her engines are all to pieces, her boilers under an order of survey, her boats are worn out, and the ship wants new planking all over. Her magazines are too damp to keep powder in, and we are pulling them all to pieces. She wants a new fore-yard and painting throughout. In fact, the ship is worn out, and I gave orders to haul her into dock this morning preparatory to thorough repairs."

"So much the better," said I ; "she is just the ship I am looking for. Never mind paint, never mind repairing the boilers, never mind new spars, or repairs to magazines. I will take her as she is ; only set your people to work and put everything in place, and we can get off in four days. I want a ship that can be sunk without any great loss."

"But," said Foote, "all the Powhatan's officers have been granted leave, and her crew transferred to the receiving-ship."

"Telegraph the officers to return at once, and send the crew on board to rig and equip her," I replied.

"I can't do that," he said, "unless I telegraph to Mr. Welles."

I repeated from the order of the President, "Under no circumstances will you make known to the Navy Department the object of this expedition."

Captain Foote was puzzled. At last, after considering the matter, he said, "I will trust you, though I am utterly nonplussed ; it's such a doubtful business. I will set to work immediately, and by night we will have the spars up and by noon to-morrow I will have all the officers back. Come home with me now and take lunch, and I will give the sentry at my house orders to keep an eye on you when I return to the office."

"And I will return to the office," I replied, "and watch you to see that you don't telegraph to Mr. Welles. I want to save you, if possible, from the fate of Admiral Byng."

Foote laughed heartily now that the weight was off his mind, and he had determined to carry out the President's instructions. A double set of men were put on board the Powhatan with orders to work day and night that the ship might be ready in three days.

Captain Foote and myself sat up nearly all that night talking over this adventure, for Foote had now as much interest in the matter as I had, and was very enthusiastic over the anticipated success of the expedition.

It was cold weather, and a fire was burning in my room. To make things comfortable, I said, "Suppose you send for a kettle of water, some lemons and sugar, and let us have some hot punch."

Foote, although a teetotaler, had every kind of liquor in his house for the use of his friends. "If you ever tell anybody, you bad fellow," said he, "that I sat up with you after midnight brewing punch, I'll never forgive you."

But in ten minutes I had brewed some whisky-punch which I thought admirable. "Let me make you one," I said.

"Well," he replied, "if you will take some hot water, lemon and sugar, and mix them together, and put in a very little whisky 'unbeknownst' to me, I will keep you company."

So there we sat during the long hours of the night, discussing the future prospects of the navy, and before daylight the captain had given up all idea of telegraphing Mr. Welles.

Next morning I accompanied Foote to his office. Captain Mercer was sent for and the President's letter read to him, and he was enjoined to secrecy. Captain Meigs also came over and explained the part he was to bear in the expedition, and informed Foote that he had transcribed all the orders in the President's presence ; this settled all Foote's qualms, and the work on the Powhatan proceeded rapidly.

The boilers and machinery were put in pretty fair order, and the officers returned in obedience to the telegrams. Captain Mercer took nominal command, and my presence in the navy-yard caused no comment, as I never went near the ship.

On the fourth day the ship was all ready for sea, with steam up and the pilot on board, and Captain Meigs had informed me he would sail in the Atlantic at 3 P. M. with the troops under command of Colonel Harvey Brown.

My luggage had been sent on board the previous night, and I was in Captain Foote's office, having a last talk with him, when a telegram came from the Secretary of the Navy : "Prepare the Powhatan for sea with all dispatch."

Foote handed the telegram to me, quite dazed. "There," he said, "you are dished !"

"Not by any means," I replied ; "this telegram is all right, only the President has got uneasy about the ship not sailing, since he was under the impression that she was ready for sea at a moment's notice, and has made a confidant of Mr. Welles. Let me get on board and off, and you can telegraph that the Powhatan has sailed."

"No," said Foote, calling for pen and ink, "I must telegraph to Mr. Welles."

"Don't make any mistake," I said. "You must obey the Commander-in-Chief of the army and navy in preference to all others," and I quoted the President's order : "Under no circumstances will you make known to the Navy Department the object of this expedition."

Foote threw down his pen. "Porter," he exclaimed, "you will be the death of me ; but I will send for Mercer and Captain Meigs to join our conference."

Both these gentlemen were soon at the office, and both urged Foote to obey the President's order, which he concluded to do.

I afterward ascertained that other telegrams had been sent to Captain Foote, while I was staying at his house, by the Secretary of the Navy in relation to the fitting out of the Powhatan, but he never mentioned the fact to me—a circumstance for which I can not account.

"Now go right on board, my boy," said Foote to me, "and get off, and as soon as you are under way I will telegraph the Secretary that you have sailed." So, bidding Captain Foote good-by, I slipped on board the Powhatan, unnoticed amid the crowd, and locked myself in the captain's state-room.

Captain Mercer was to remain in command until we got to Staten Island, when he was to go ashore and the ship proceed down the bay in charge of the first lieutenant. After the ship passed the bar and the pilot had left, I was to appear.

The moment the ship turned her head down stream Foote telegraphed her departure to the Secretary of the Navy.

We met with many obstacles in our progress down the East River, and did not have steam fairly up for an hour after leaving the navy-yard. We were an hour and a half in reaching Staten Island, and consumed another hour in landing Captain Mercer, as the old boat nearly filled with water going on shore, and kept half the crew bailing her out.

Just as the boat was hoisted up and the order given to go ahead, the quartermaster reported, "A fast steamer a-chasin' and signalin' of us, sir, and an officer wavin' his cap !"

Perry, the first lieutenant, did not know who was captain or that I was in the cabin, so he stopped until the steamer came up, although she would have caught us anyhow, for Foote had chartered the fastest little steamer out of New York, and kept her with steam up, ready to start after me the moment the expected telegram should arrive.

The steamboat was soon alongside the Powhatan, and Lieutenant Roe came on board and delivered a telegram. Perry walked into the cabin, and, to his astonishment, found me there and handed me the dispatch. It read as follows :

"Deliver up the Powhatan at once to Captain Mercer.

"SEWARD."

I telegraphed back :

"Have received confidential orders from the President, and shall obey them.   D. D. PORTER."

I then went on deck and gave orders to go ahead fast. In an hour and a half we were over the bar, discharged the pilot, and steering south for an hour, and then due east, to throw any pursuers off our track (for I was determined to go to Fort Pickens). At sundown I steered my course.

When my answer to the Secretary of State was handed to Captain Foote he was astonished. "He's clean daft!" said he, "or has run off with the ship to join the rebels. They would have tried him by court-martial anyhow. Well, I'll never trust any one again, for I have lost faith in human nature. Porter would have been such a help to our side, whereas if he can get a fast vessel he will be the most destructive pirate that ever roamed the seas."

We often laughed together afterward over this episode, but Foote always ended by saying, "You ought to have been tried and shot ; no one but yourself would ever have been so impudent."

Mr. Seward, however, was of a different opinion, and chuckled over the success of his pet scheme and at the idea of circumventing Mr. Welles. The President smiled complacently when he read my telegram, and said, "Seward, if the Southerners get Sumter we will be even with them by securing Pickens." I made a warm friend in each of them, and Mr. Lincoln and Mr. Seward both stood by me during the war whenever Mr. Welles—who was not partial to me—was disposed to be annoying.

When Mr. Welles received Captain Foote's telegram announcing the departure of the Powhatan, he hurried over to the White House, where he found Mr. Seward with the President, and forthwith protested against the interference of the Secretary of State in the affairs of the Navy Department, demanding the restitution of what he termed "the stolen ship," and informing the President that on the Powhatan depended the success of the relief expedition to Fort Sumter, as she carried the large boats necessary for that occasion—when in fact the Powhatan would not have been of a particle of use, as she drew too much water to cross Charleston bar, and the boats in question were good for nothing, as they had been so long exposed to the weather without paint that they filled with water as soon as they were lowered overboard.

If Mr. Welles had reflected a little he would have discovered that the Powhatan could not have reached Charleston in time to be of any use, for his order to prepare the ship for sea did not reach New York until the morning of the 1st of April, 1861, and if the vessel had not been taken in hand when she was, she would have been on that date in dry-dock, pulled to pieces, and with half her boilers on shore. As it was, the rebels opened fire on Sumter from their heavy earth-works as soon as the vessels composing Mr. Welles's expedition approached the bar, and they could not have done a particle of good. Had they tried to succor the people in the fort, they would have been sunk in a very few minutes. A more foolish expedition was never dispatched, and Mr. Lincoln remarked, when the news was brought to him, "It's a good rule never to send a mouse to catch a skunk, or a polywog to tackle a whale."

The attempt to relieve Sumter was a curious muddle, and had, from the first inception of the design, no chance of success. Mr. Seward was evidently opposed to it, feeling sure that it would be a failure, and so he got up the expedition to Pickens, certain that it could not fail to be successful. The Secretary of State wished to show that he was a better sailor than Mr. Welles.

We reached Fort Pickens the day after the Collins steamship transporting the troops, although she sailed after we did. I ran in for the harbor, crossed the bar, and was standing up to Round Fort, when a tug put out from Pickens and placed herself across my path. Captain Meigs was on board the tug, waving a document, and, hailing, said he had an order from Colonel Brown. It was to the following effect : "Don't permit Powhatan to run the batteries or attempt to go inside. It will bring the fire of the enemy on the fort before we are prepared."

I felt like running over Meigs's tug, but obeyed the order. The stars and stripes were hoisted, in hopes the enemy would open fire, but they did not, nor do I believe they had any intention of so doing.

The people in this part of the country were not in the same state of excitement as the Charlestonians, and would have been more careful about firing the first gun. Besides, I do not think they were prepared for hostilities, for they had mounted a number of guns all *en barbette*, and did not seem to have any intention of using them.

The Powhatan had her ten ports on the port side filled with nine-inch guns, and there was one eleven-inch pivot. All were loaded with grape and canister. Besides, there were twelve howitzers placed in different parts of the ship and loaded with shrapnel. With our trained gunners we could have swept the raw soldiers from the rebel batteries.

It was therefore unfortunate that Captain Meigs interfered by presenting the order. A fine opportunity was lost for the Government to demonstrate its power and determination to maintain its authority at all hazards.

Mr. Welles claimed that this expedition to Pickens was useless, as he "had already instructed the commanding officer of the forces off Pensacola Bar to send re-enforcements to Fort Pickens in case it was attacked." (!) But that prudent officer lay at anchor five miles from the fort, where he could be of no manner of use in case of a surprise.

General Bragg had a large force of troops in and around the navy-yard, and the second day after our arrival a number of tugs and schooners, filled with soldiers, came down from Pensacola and approached Fort Pickens, whether with the intention of attacking it or not I don't know. They no doubt took the Powhatan and the Collins steamer for store-ships, and thought it a good time to commence operations and secure "loot," but I changed the programme by sending an eleven-inch shrapnel among them, which, bursting at the right time, threw up the water in all directions.

The flotilla scampered off in quick time, and left us to quietly prepare the fort for any emergency, and it remained in our possession during the whole of the civil war.

At that time the news that Sumter had been fired on had not reached us, and we were under the impression that our shot was the first that had been fired.

When I left Washington it had seemed to be the leading idea that nobody should get hurt, and that the sensitive feelings of our Southern brethren should not be ruffled ; but when I beheld Bragg's transports approaching, I thought it high time to try the persuasive power of an eleven-inch shell.

My sentiments at that moment were like those of an old fellow they tell of at Bunker Hill, who was much amused at the repeated volleys of musketry poured out by the advancing British until a ball struck him in the fleshy part of the leg, when he roared out to his son, who stood near him, "Dang it, Jim, they're firin' bullets; we must fire back at 'em!" I thought it time to be firing bullets.

The above is the way Fort Pickens and the gallant Slemmer and his men were saved from capture.

If the commanding officer of the naval forces off the bar had been left to his own discretion, Slemmer would have had but a poor show in case he had been attacked, although Mr. Welles no doubt thought everything was being done to guard the fort against surprise. The commander of the squadron, however, assured me that he was so tied down by instructions *"not to commit any overt act"* that he would not dare to undertake anything without specific orders. He thought me very reckless in firing a shell among General Bragg's vessels, as, "after all, they perhaps meant nothing, and were merely going to land stores at the navy-yard!" It seemed to me shameful, with such a force as this officer had under his command, that the rebels should be holding the navy-yard at all.

There was a great want of discretion among some of the leading officers of the squadron. As an example, I will mention that Lieutenant Renshaw, who had deserted his flag, went out from Pensacola in a sail-boat, and, after spending some time in the cabin of the flag-ship, came out with a boy carrying a large bag of ship's biscuit, which was passed into his boat.

The sailors gathered at the gangway to witness this novel proceeding, and many a hearty curse did Renshaw receive as he slid down the man-ropes into his boat. The general expression was, "Double-dyed traitor!" yet the same captain who had entertained Renshaw told me I would probably be tried by court-martial for firing at Bragg's men, who I had every reason to suppose were trying to capture Fort Pickens.

I must leave the reader to judge what were Mr. Seward's motives for making this movement on Fort Pickens, and whether or not it was a good one. Without doubt the Government vindicated its authority, and maintained possession of its own property.

————

CHAPTER III.

INCIDENTS AT PENSACOLA — TWO DISTINGUISHED TRAVELLERS WHO PROVE TO BE OLD ACQUAINTANCES — A MEMORABLE BREAKFAST.

WHEN one takes a retrospective view of the events which occurred twenty-four years ago, he can not help but admit that this is a progressive age ; and when he sees a building burn down he may console himself with the idea that he will live to see a finer one springing up from its ashes, particularly if the old one has been well insured. There may be pleasant recollections associated with the original building, for the loss of which we can never be repaid ; but time heals all things, and we learn to do without the old associations and form other and dearer ties.

I have often lamented the wicked waste of life and property caused by our civil war ; but I have now learned to look upon all these matters philosophically, and sometimes think it was intended the nation should pass through such an experience, as children go through with their various diseases, by way of preparing them for the greater trials of life.

If we take this view of the matter, we may find some consolation for the events of a fratricidal war which should never have taken place.

It seems difficult, however, to find any compensation for the numerous blunders that were committed by those in authority. Our house has indeed sprung from its ashes more beautiful than ever, but how much better it would have been to have saved it from the fire by using proper precautions !

When I look back to the time when it was considered so important to secure Fort Pickens and the Pensacola navy-yard, I have often wondered why our vessels did not go in and take possession, since it was easy enough to do so, and, in all probability, no one would have been hurt ; but our Government was so exceedingly sensitive about wounding the feelings of the seceders that although we had the force at hand no steps were taken to prevent General Bragg from fortifying the navy-yard and the approaches to Pensacola. Fort Pickens after it was re-enforced could have knocked all Bragg's batteries to pieces in half an hour ; or a single frigate under cover of the fort could have driven the enemy away and recovered a large amount of valuable public property.

But no; the officers of the army and navy were obliged to look quietly on the unceasing labors of the Confederates, apparently waiting the completion of works that they would then proceed to knock to pieces, at the same time destroying the public property which it was their duty to preserve.

After Fort Pickens was fully manned, the Union squadron hauled in closer and looked placidly on, while the people of Mobile were supplying the rebel army with everything they wanted by means of tugs and schooners.

At first the Confederates were cautious how they sent in supplies; but, finding that they were not molested, or even questioned, they began to send them openly by sea in large quantities.

Vessels loaded with lumber departed daily from Pensacola harbor, and others entered, but not a boat was sent from the flag-ship to inquire what were the cargoes and for whom intended, and Bragg and his officers lived quietly in the navy-yard houses, no doubt wondering why they were permitted to enjoy themselves so pleasantly, and hoping the truce would last an indefinite period.

I went on board the senior naval officer's ship several times to try and get an explanation of this very peculiar method of carrying on war, but the only satisfaction I received was the information that the commanding officer's orders were to "commit no overt act." These orders were the last communication received from the department some thirty days previous.

I asked the senior officer to let me take the responsibility of blockading the port of Pensacola, but he objected to my doing so. There was in all this business an inanity of which I had never conceived. The commanding officer of Fort Pickens had no orders at all that I am aware of, except to hold the fort, and not draw the fire of the Confederates.

One day the commander of the squadron signaled me to meet him at the fort for a conference, and I at once repaired there.

The Confederates had hauled the dry dock out of the basin at the navy-yard and anchored it about two hundred yards from Fort Pickens. There were a number of men on the dock, and four heavy anchors were hanging from its ends.

When I reached the fort the senior naval officer was there in consultation with the commanding officer of the troops. They had written to Bragg to ask what were his intentions with regard to the dry dock.   Bragg replied that the dock got adrift and that he would restore it to its place.   About four hours afterward it *accidentally* sunk in the middle of the channel!   Of course, nobody believed that this was really an accident, but our senior officers thought they had done their duty by inquiring of Bragg what he intended to do, and, after having seen him carry out his intentions, they sat down quietly to dinner.   Colonel Brown filled up some more sand-bags, and Bragg mounted an extra gun; they were like two boys daring each other to knock off chips from their shoulders and playing a farce of war.

Next day the smoke of two steamers was descried to the westward, and I signaled for "permission to chase," which was granted. In an hour I came up with two large river boats loaded with provisions for General Bragg's army, of which they made no secret.   I put each vessel in charge of an officer and prize crew, and escorted them to the flag-ship, where they were anchored.

These vessels had on board some $375,000 worth of stores, and the captains made many silly threats because they were interfered with—enough in fact, to make the senior naval officer think he had committed an "overt act"!   So he was willing to compromise, and let the steamers off, provided they would return to Mobile, which they were very glad to do.   I was ordered to escort them back to the place where I had captured them, and one of the steamers attempting to run into Pensacola, I sent a nine-inch shell after her, which burst over the vessel, whereupon she turned and preceded me toward Mobile.   A nine-inch shot is a terribly effective argument in such a case.

I convoyed the vessels some miles down the coast, and, disgusted with such humiliating duty, I told the steamboat captains to get ready to go on board and take command of their vessels again, saying, as I did so, "Now let me give you a piece of advice.   Don't try this again; if you do, and come within reach of my guns, I will sink you.   I have a great mind to do it anyhow."   They never tried it again.

If permitted, the rebels would have gone on committing infractions of the mutual truce which seemed to have been tacitly established, until finally they would have demanded Fort Pickens, and I am not sure but what it would have been considered "an overt act" to have refused them.

I returned to my anchorage completely disgusted, and went immediately to call on the senior officer and to protest against my officers and ship being employed on such humiliating duty. I demanded permission to blockade the port of Pensacola and stop the supplies that were being constantly taken in to Bragg's army. Much to my surprise my demand was granted, provided everything was done on my own responsibility and that I should commit no "overt act." That seemed to be the stumbling-block in the senior officer's way. The quotation appalled him.

Next day I established a rigid blockade of the harbor with my boats and a small pilot-boat of which I had obtained possession, and Bragg got no more supplies by water, for not even a canoe was allowed to pass in or out. My communications with the senior officer ceased altogether, and for a week I did not see him.

Ever since the re-enforcement of Pickens I had been made to "eat dirt," as the Turks say, and I began to fear there would be no end to our humiliation; but, thank Heaven, it was over at last, and I had the satisfaction of hoping that Bragg and his men would occasionally be short of rations, although he could get provisions by hauling them over the sand from Mobile.

Amid the most serious events there is often something calculated to bring a smile to the face. Much stupidity was practiced by the United States forces at Pensacola, and a good deal of cunning and zeal shown by the Confederates. I changed the aspect of affairs and made things lively for the first few days. When I got hold of the pilot-boat I put Sailing-Master George Brown in charge of her, and with the boats of the Powhatan operated very successfully. There was no prize-money made, but we caused a deal of disappointment to the enemy.

On the third day of the blockade a thick fog set in, giving blockade-runners a fine opportunity to get in and out of Pensacola.

Of course everybody in the Southern States knew the condition of affairs at Pensacola, and how easy it was to get away from there or to enter through the unguarded gates of Fort Pickens. A number of people were picked up and sent back in both directions.

On the third morning one of our boats returned alongside the ship, towing a good-sized sail-boat with two persons sitting in the stern dressed like travelers, each with a traveling-bag by his side.

The moment I saw these persons I recognized them and told the officer of the deck not to give them my real name, but to show them to the cabin and say that "the captain would be on board in half an hour and expected them to breakfast, etc." I wanted to have a little amusement out of this incident.

When the travelers mounted the side and found themselves standing on the deck of a large ship bristling with guns, they both looked exceedingly disturbed, and, though muffled in heavy overcoats to keep out the chilling fog, they trembled perceptibly.

One of the men, a bluff Briton, in rather an arrogant manner asked the officer of the deck who was the captain of the ship, and by what right he dared to detain one of her Majesty's subjects while in transit from one country to another. If he was not at once allowed to proceed, and an apology made for his detention, he would lay the whole matter before her Majesty's Government and claim heavy damages.

"You will have to wait," said the officer of the deck. "Captain Jones will be here in half an hour, and he expects you to breakfast with him, as you must feel quite exhausted after your long journey from Montgomery."

The two travelers started, and the one who had not before spoken said, in an agitated voice, "Bless my soul, there must be some mistake; we don't know Captain Jones, in fact never heard of him. We are simply travelers getting out of that nasty place where you can't get a decent cup of coffee or a glass of wine. My name is Wilkins; my friend here is Mr. Blarney."

"*Barney*, if you please," interrupted his companion.

"Yes, bless my soul," said Wilkins, "you're right. I'm a little confused this morning. Here are our cards."

The cards read, "Mr. Barney, British Legation," and "Mr. Wilkins, Commissioner of Agriculture, Berlin."

"Please walk into the cabin, gentlemen," said the officer of the deck, "and wait the captain's coming. I will have your greatcoats dried by the galley fire."

While this conversation was going on I had directed the steward to set the breakfast-table for three persons, and to give us the best breakfast possible, not forgetting claret and Rhine wine, and some hot pickled peppers. The cards had been handed to me through my state-room window after the gentlemen were shown into the cabin.

Both looked surprised when they saw the table set for breakfast. "Egad!" said Wilkins, "we're in for a lark, old boy; this is better than sailing about in a fog."

I could hear every word they said, and, by moving the slats in the blinds of my state-room, could see the puzzled faces of two old acquaintances, who had no idea I was within a thousand miles of them.

"By George! old fellow," said Wilkins, "the captain does expect some one to breakfast, sure enough; and just look at this old Lafitte and Rhine wine; why, this Jones must know how to live; and, by George! if he hasn't some *chilé colorado* in that pickle-dish—napkins, glassware, silver; why, Barney, old boy, we are in clover; I hope Jones will invite us to stay a week."

"The chances are," said Barney, in a melancholy voice, "that this is all a mistake, and that we will be turned out in half an hour to mess with the crew, or tarred and feathered and sent back to Dixie, as those blasted fools on shore call it. But if this Captain Jones takes any liberties with me, one of her Majesty's squadrons will come down here and open this port in short order."

"Bosh!" said Wilkins. "Devil take me, old boy, if I am going to quarrel with Captain Jones, Brown, or Smith, or whatever his name is, as long as he sets as good a table as this. Ah! my lips smack at the thought of getting some of that Lafitte. You Britishers are so stupid about your dignity! Why, I don't believe Queen Victoria would care a snap if these fellows were to swing you up at the yard-arm to-morrow. She wouldn't trouble herself to send any squadron to look after you, old boy. Come, get in a good humor— God bless the old lady, rule Britannia if you please, but don't let's lose a good breakfast by your stupid English ways."

At that moment, through the blinds of my state-room came the sounds, "Pretty Poll! Polly have a pepper?" as natural as life.

The travelers started, then looked around. "D—n that Poll parrot; this don't speak well for Jones. No one but an ass would keep a parrot. However, his Lafitte seems to be all right."

"Polly, put the kettle on! Britannia rules the waves," yelled the parrot, winding up with a demoniac laugh.

"Well," said Barney, "the parrot isn't as big a fool as its owner, for he knows who rules the waves."

"Bosh!" exclaimed Wilkins, "didn't the Yankees thrash you in the year 1812?"

"Ha! ha!" shouted the parrot, "Yankee Doodle came to town and whipped the British nation!"

"I'd wring that parrot's neck if I had him," said the Englishman; "he's a bigger fool than your friend Jones."

"Don't abuse Jones," said Wilkins, "until we find out what kind of a cook he has."

At that moment the supposed parrot sang out, "Fie! fie!

fic! Sam, does your mother know you're out? Polly wants a cracker!"

Wilkins jumped from his chair. "Did you hear that?" he said.

"Yes, I heard it," replied Barney. "Don't pay any attention to that infernal bird; you will make as big an ass of yourself as Jones, who must be hard up for amusement to keep a parrot."

"Watch your bag, Sam," sang out the parrot. "Contraband! contraband! Spy! spy!"

Wilkins rushed for the state-room door; it was locked on the inside. "I'll wring the d—d parrot's neck," he shouted. "What does this mean?"

"'Conscience makes cowards of us all,'" replied the other. "It's only parrot's nonsense. I knew of one once that could repeat words as fast as he heard them uttered."

"Cowards of us all!" yelled the parrot; "I belong to that ass Jones!"

"That's the devil," said Wilkins; "I wish I could throttle him."

"Ha! ha! ha!" laughed the parrot. "O Sam Ward, Sam Ward, Sam Ward! ha! ha! ha! Polly wants a cracker!"

Wilkins turned pale, seized his traveling-bag and rushed to the cabin-door, but, on opening it, was met by the orderly, who informed him that he could not pass out.

"What!" inquired Wilkins, "am I a prisoner?"

"My orders are, sir," replied the orderly, "that you gentlemen must remain in the cabin until the captain comes on board."

The parrot laughed and sang out, "Sam Ward a prisoner! fie! fie! fie! Sam! fie! fie!"

Wilkins rushed again to the state-room door, which he tried in vain to open, while the parrot inside sang out, "Sam Ward!"

Wilkins sank exhausted on the sofa. "I'll give this Captain Jones a piece of my mind for teaching his rascally parrot such twaddle. I wonder where he could have heard of me."

Just then the parrot shouted, "Walk in, Captain Jones; Sam Ward says you're an ass!" and I opened the state-room door and walked into the cabin.

If a thunderbolt had fallen, Sam Ward, *alias* Wilkins, could not have been more astonished.

"In the name of Heaven," he exclaimed, "where did you come from? Do you belong to this ship?" and he seized me by the hand and almost shook my arm from its socket. "Do you know Captain

Jones ? He owes me an apology for teaching his parrot a lot of infernal nonsense about me."

"Fie ! fie ! fie ! Sam Ward !" exclaimed a small messenger boy, sitting demurely on a camp-stool ; said boy having been brought in to personate a parrot—which bird he could imitate to perfection—"Polly wants a pepper."

"Good gracious !" exclaimed Sam Ward, "that was your nonsense, then ? — and I might have known it the moment I saw you. I haven't forgotten your tricks and jokes when we went through Magellan Straits in the old Panama ; but what are you doing here ?"

"I am Captain Jones," I replied. "I suppose I have as much right to an *alias* as you have."

"Well, thank Providence, I am sure of a good breakfast ; but let me introduce you to my friend Mr. Barney, who is traveling with me ; we won't be sent to Fort Lafayette, will we ?"

"How do you do, Mr. R—— ?" I said, addressing the *soi-disant* Barney. "I knew you through your full whiskers, and congratulate you upon being under a real flag once more. I don't think her Majesty will send a squadron to break up the blockade, but we will get some breakfast and then talk business."

Sam Ward said he had got caught in the South, and he and R—— had to get out of the country the best way they could. Hearing that Pensacola was not blockaded, they came there, and, hiring a boat and a man to manage it, were coming out under cover of a fog when captured. "Thank fortune, I smell the coffee," said Sam, "and know that breakfast is coming."

R—— also became quite communicative, told me he had traveled South to see how things were going, and was glad enough to get out of the country.

That was a pleasant breakfast. Sam Ward, as usual, took charge, called for all the sauces in the pantry, and paid his best respects to the Lafitte and Rhine wine.

Sam Ward talked Union like a man ; R—— was evidently bitten with the secession mania. He said we should have a long and bitter war, and could never restore the Union unless we granted the Southern people all they asked for.

That night I sent my guests off in the pilot-boat with their own boat in tow, with directions to take them to the entrance of Mobile Bay and let them go.

The last thing Sam Ward did was to extort from me a promise

3

never to tell that parrot story, and I only do so now that he has gone to his long home, where, if he takes cognizance of what is occurring here below, he will not be displeased at my bringing in an old friend in connection with this little incident of the war.

I had my suspicions about the two travelers, and thought possibly they might have been messengers from the Southern cabinet to friends in the North, but I was not going to raise a question that might have vexed the Secretary of State and burned my own fingers. I took their word as gentlemen, and dismissed them after they had enjoyed my hospitality.

When I knew how loosely the blockade of Pensacola had been maintained, and how the Confederates had been encouraged to mount guns, complete their defences, and bring in provisions and stores for their troops, I thought it would be idle for me to interfere with the movements of two gentlemen who claimed to be running away from the South and trying to reach the flesh-pots of the Yankees. They could not do much harm, I thought, and I have always been glad that I had it in my power to contribute to their comfort in their journey through the lines.

Four days after the above episode Captain McKean arrived in the frigate Niagara. I went immediately on board and informed that officer, in as few words as possible, how matters stood, and how badly affairs had been conducted.

He signaled at once for all commanding officers to repair on board the Niagara, and, when we were all in the cabin, Captain McKean addressed us as follows :

"Gentlemen, these are ticklish times, and it is necessary for the senior officers of the navy to set an example to the younger ones. What I propose will keep people to their duty ; but if the officers present have any conscientious scruples about taking an oath of allegiance, they can state them or for ever after hold their peace. I propose that we all do now take the oath of allegiance to the United States, and sign a paper to the effect that we will serve the Government until death do us part and, forsaking all others, cleave unto her our natural mother."

The old gentleman was deeply religious, and had evidently been reading the marriage ceremony, but his remarks were forcible and to the point.

The officer, whom I have before mentioned, declined point-blank to take the oath—and it was not an "iron-clad" affair either —whereupon I stepped forward and said, "I think every man should be obliged to take that oath, for I have seen more treason in the last ten days than I ever supposed could exist in the United States Navy." So I signed the paper, and Captain McKean administered the oath to me.

Captain McKean looked coolly at the captain who had declined to sign. "Now, captain," he said, "will you sign this paper and take the oath of allegiance or not?"

"I solemnly protest against it," replied the other; "you have no authority to require it of us. We took our oaths when we entered the navy."

"Yes," said the old captain, "so did many others, and they violated them. You must either take the oath or suffer the consequences for not doing so."

"I will sign the paper under protest, and take the oath with a reservation."

"I don't care *how* you do it," said Captain McKean, "but do it you must."

The officer sulkily signed the paper, took the oath, and, turning on his heel, left the cabin without saying "Good-morning" to any one.

"I fear I have made a mistake," said Captain McKean, "in not arresting that officer."

"Yes," replied I, "you never made a greater mistake in your life; but he will keep his oath with a reservation never to fire a shot at the South in anger," and so it turned out.

In a few days Captain McKean scattered all the vessels in different directions, leaving the above-mentioned officer in charge at Pensacola Bar, with orders to maintain a strict blockade and not let even a canoe pass in or out.

Months passed away. Bragg built his fortifications and never molested Fort Pickens. Colonel Brown piled up sand-bags and never troubled Bragg. Neither of them committed an "overt act." A more innocent war was never carried on.

CHAPTER IV.

DELAY AT PENSACOLA—ATTACK ON FORT MORGAN—PENSACOLA ABANDONED — A REMARKABLE SPECIMEN OF A SOUTHERN UNIONIST.

I HAD at last the satisfaction of seeing Pensacola fall into the hands of the Union forces.

I was sent in the Powhatan to blockade the southwest pass of the Mississippi, and while there recaptured the brig Mary Bradford, the first prize taken by the rebel privateer Sumter.

I obtained from the crew of the brig information of the Sumter's movements, and went on board the Niagara, which had come in that day, and asked Captain McKean's permission to go in pursuit of that vessel. Captain McKean was no longer senior officer, and did not feel justified in permitting me to go. Commodore Mervine had assumed command of the squadron, and was then off Pensacola in the flag-ship Susquehanna, and Captain McKean gave me permission to go there and see the commodore, two hundred miles away.

There was a fascination about Pensacola Bar that kept the commanding officers there day after day gazing at the harbor and fancying, perhaps, that they were acquiring experience in the art of war.

I arrived at Pensacola Bar the next night, found the Susquehanna at the usual anchorage, and briefly stated to the commodore my reasons for visiting him.

"Why, man alive," said Mervine, "I was just going to send for you to come up and help me capture Ship Island. The enemy have mounted six guns and are assuming a threatening attitude. I think our two ships can clean them out."

"Yes, sir," I replied, "either one of them could do it; but I consider the capture of the Sumter of vastly more importance than an old six-gun battery on a sand island that can do us no harm or the Confederates any good. Here is Pensacola," I continued, "that seems to me to have taken a *very* threatening attitude for a long time. I wouldn't mind losing the Sumter if you would let me accompany you in and drive Bragg out."

"But," said the commodore, "such a movement would draw the fire on Fort Pickens, and that would never do, for the place is not yet fully manned and fortified."

I had left Pickens about three months before, and since that time several schooners had arrived from the North loaded with cannon and all sorts of ammunition. One of these vessels even went inside the port to the main wharf and unloaded its warlike cargo without molestation from the Confederate batteries. Bragg sent a letter once to the commanding officer at Fort Pickens and informed him that he considered such proceedings improper, and that he must land his guns on the outside.

The reply of the commanding officer was that it was very inconvenient to do that, as there was no wharf or crane outside, and that the vessel would sail as soon as she had unloaded.

This explanation seems to have been entirely satisfactory to General Bragg, and so this new method of carrying on hostilities was persevered in to the end. Perhaps Bragg was waiting until the fort was filled up, when he intended to invite the commandant to hand it over to him.

Some months after this Bragg did send an expedition to Santa Rosa Island and captured General Vogdes, some of Billy Wilson's zouaves, and an old white horse; and that, I believe, was the principal event of the campaign.

There was no doubt of old Commodore Mervine's bravery, but he had, somehow or other, got it into his head that to make any movement on Pensacola would be to commit "an overt act." I managed, however, to get his permission to go in search of the Sumter, and was off before he had a chance to change his mind.

This detention, however, at Pensacola caused me to lose the prize. I wasted more than two days in going to Pensacola and back again to Cape Antonio, besides using up coal. I arrived at Cienfuegos only sixteen hours after the Sumter had sailed; had I found her there, I should have taken her at all hazards.

I chased the vessel to St. Thomas. She left only a few hours before I entered the port. I followed her to Curaçoa, Maranham, Parana in Brazil, and thence to the equator, where Semmes sank a vessel within thirty miles of us. Had he burned her, we would have seen the smoke and captured the Sumter.

I now steered for St. Thomas to get coal, sighted a supposed Sumter just before dark, overhauled her rapidly, but lost her in the gloom of night. After chasing the Sumter ten thousand miles I returned in disgust to Key West, and thence went to New York, the vessel all broken down, so that we had to proceed mostly under sail.

I subsequently assisted in the capture of the forts at New Orleans, and at that time, a year after the relief of Pickens, Pensacola was still intact! Fort Pickens was full of men and guns, while Bragg and his army were waxing fat on the hog and hominy sent to them from Mobile, and, although Bragg and the commander of the fort wrote no more letters to each other, the *entente cordiale* still existed, and both sides had plenty of time to study Jomini if so disposed.

As to the navy, it is said the several commanding officers grounded on the beef-bones thrown overboard from their flag-ships, but this I do not believe.

There was certainly something in the air of Pensacola that affected the army and the navy, and even the Confederates seemed loath to change the condition of affairs. If the war throughout the country had only been carried on in this fashion, what a blessing it would have been, how many lives would have been saved, and how much hog and hominy would have been eaten!

I think the fall of Pensacola is a piece of unwritten history. There were so many important events occurring at the time that its occupation was hardly noticed. The people of the country only knew that an important place was once more in Union hands.

After the capture of New Orleans I was ordered by Flag Officer Farragut to proceed to Ship Island, in Mississippi Sound, with all the vessels composing the Mortar Flotilla, and await him there, but in the mean time to undertake no expedition without orders. Farragut said that he would join me in five days, when we would sail into Mobile Bay and attack the forts.

This was different from the programme laid down by the Navy Department, as Farragut was ordered, after capturing New Orleans, to proceed up the Mississippi, capture Vicksburg, and, if possible, open the river in its entire length.

Had Farragut attacked Mobile at that time he would have obtained an easy victory, and would not have acquired the renown he subsequently gained in his capture of that place, which I think one of the most daring feats of the war, requiring the greatest coolness and skill against superior force.

I remained three weeks at Ship Island, hearing nothing from Farragut, and began to think he had forgotten me. I afterward learned that he was operating against Vicksburg.

My officers and men grew restless at our inaction, and one fine morning, when the wind was fair, I made signal to the mortar schooners and steamers to get under way for Mobile, determined to attack the forts. I forgot all about Farragut's orders.

When we arrived within eight miles of the place the wind suddenly chopped around ahead, with indications of a gale. I pushed on with the seven steamers of the flotilla, signaling the mortar schooners to beat up to the anchorage, which I supposed they could do in two or three hours.

I found the steam frigate Colorado, Lieutenant-Commanding Davis, off the bar, and, obtaining a pilot, proceeded inside to within gunshot of Fort Morgan. The Morgan and Selma, two Confederate gun-boats, were lying in the harbor.

We had some heavy rifled guns in the flotilla steamers and several eleven-inch Dahlgrens, and I thought we might as well practice a little on Fort Morgan until the mortar schooners came up.

We opened fire, and had it all our own way. Our shot struck the fort every time, knocking stones and bricks about in a lively fashion. There was no reply, nor could we see any people moving about the enemy's works.

We had fired some twenty shot and shell when it came on to blow heavily. One of the enemy's gun-boats was seen to leave the anchorage near the fort and start in the direction of Mobile, crowded with people. I could not understand the movement, but supposed the fort had no guns that would reach us, and the Confederates were trying to draw us farther in.

The gale increased and I became uneasy about the mortar schooners, and sent the steamers to get them safe into Ship Island again. I remained at anchor in the Harriet Lane within gunshot of the fort, thinking that perhaps in the morning one of the enemy's gun-boats might offer me battle.

That night the wind blew so hard from the northward that the Harriet Lane dragged out to sea and had for a time to ride out the gale head-to.

Next morning at daylight a boat containing four deserters from Fort Morgan went alongside the Colorado. They informed Lieutenant Davis that the fort was garrisoned partly with a Mobile fire-company of seventy-five men ; that a good many of these men had insisted on going up to the city in the gun-boat, leaving not more than one hundred and thirty remaining in the fort. This news came too late. Davis could do nothing, as his ship could not cross the bar.

In the mean time I was heading the sea in a northeast gale and slowly approaching Pensacola. Had it not been for the untoward events of the day, Fort Morgan would have fallen into my hands without a struggle, but it was some time afterward before I learned all this.

We had worked along to within about twelve miles of Pensacola, when I was informed that large fires were burning at that place, and that shells could be seen bursting in the air.

It seems that when the Confederates in Fort Morgan saw the mortar flotilla approaching, they telegraphed to Pensacola, "Farragut is coming to attack us with his whole force."

The Confederate commander at Pensacola knew that his position was untenable with Farragut's fleet so near, and he fully expected that Farragut would pay him a visit as soon as he finished with Fort Morgan ; so, in half an hour after receiving the news from Mobile, the navy-yard, naval hospital, and all the other public buildings were in a blaze, and by daylight next morning the Confederate army which had lain inactive so long was in full retreat from Pensacola.

The moment the flames appeared in the navy-yard, Fort Pickens opened fire on the retreating foe with all the batteries, and it was the shells from the fort and the burning navy-yard that we saw at midnight from the deck of the Harriet Lane.

We put on as much steam as the gale would allow and forced the vessel along—bows under half the time—toward the scene of conflagration, and just before daylight reached the dock at Fort Pickens, where I found that the commanding officer of the fort had not a boat to send over to try and extinguish the flames. After a year's hard labor in preparing Fort Pickens to resist Bragg, it had never occurred to any one that the Confederates might some day set fire to Uncle Sam's valuable property and decamp for parts unknown.

I made a temporary ferry-boat of the Harriet Lane and landed about four hundred soldiers at the navy-yard to try and put out the fire, but it was too late ; the mischief had been accomplished, and the Confederates had left nothing but desolation behind them. All that was movable they carried off, but, as if in mockery, left the commandant's quarters standing for the next commandant to occupy.

The Confederates pretended that the shells from Fort Pickens destroyed the navy-yard, and they probably did assist in its destruction. The rebel batteries turned out to be mostly shams, as I had suspected.   A few old thirty-two pounders were mounted in conspicuous positions, where they could do no harm, and many formidable-looking casemates had no guns in them.

When one looks back he can not but smile at the folly committed at Pensacola on both the Union and Confederate sides.   The finale left on my mind the impression that the Confederate cabinet also contained some old women.

Another amusing episode was to come.   I offered to go with General —— to Pensacola to receive the keys of the city from the municipal authorities, thinking what a triumph it would be to receive the surrender of this ancient burgh and figure in history in connection with so glorious an event ! How the loyal people of the North would rejoice over the capture of this stronghold, which had defied for more than a year the combined efforts of our army and navy !

As we approached the landing in the Harriet Lane my heart palpitated, for I saw a crowd of Union people assembling to meet us and to restore once more that loyal city to its allegiance.

But when we landed, our pleasant anticipations were changed to surprise at finding, instead of loyal citizens, a crowd of ragged negroes grinning from ear to ear and turning somersaults to testify their delight.   Amid all their squalor and ignorance shone out a true affection for the old flag which they could never feel for the new one that had been made and presented by the ladies of Pensacola to General Bragg on his assuming command.   The negroes kept their eyes on the flag flying at the peak of the Harriet Lane, and shouted for Mr. Linkum's gun-boats until they were hoarse.

We saw but one white man, but he was a host in himself, and indemnified us for the absence of his fellows.

The gentleman in question was attired without regard to expense.   He wore a blue coat with brass buttons, a white vest, and yellow nankeen trousers.   His huge shirt-ruffle—or, as the sailors termed it, his head-sail—stuck out a foot at least, while his shirt-frills were fastened by a big diamond.   His hat was nicely brushed, and his boots shone as if a dozen darkies had exercised their skill upon them.

He advanced toward us, hat in hand, and, bowing low, exclaimed : " Welcome once more, my glorious old flag and my beloved fellow Union-men.   I feel now that I shall receive protection from the laws of my country.   I am Mr. B——m, gentlemen, a leading citizen of Pensacola, who for the past year have dwelt beneath the folds of an alien flag and who have been despoiled of my goods and chattels worse than the Egyptians were of old. I welcome you to this loyal city, where I hope the tramp of the rebel hosts will never more be heard, and that we may never again be deprived of that dear flag which has sheltered me from boyhood, and of which I have dreamed every night since it was replaced by that meaningless rag which no one could respect, much less revere. There are a thousand, aye, ten thousand associations—"

There is no knowing how long this eloquent gentleman would have continued his patriotic harangue had not General —— interrupted the flow of his eloquence by inquiring why the municipal authorities were not present to surrender the city.

"Ah!" replied Mr. B——m, "the city is at your feet—a child that has been wronged, asking a mother's protection. When Rome governed the world, it was only necessary to say 'I am a Roman citizen' to insure every consideration. Will not our great Republic—"

"Where are the Mayor and City Council?" interrupted the general.

"I am truly sorry to say, sir," replied Mr. B——m, "that the fleeing rebels have taken the Mayor's teams into their service to carry their spoils to Mobile, and the City Council, poor fellows! were all pressed into the rebel army, and are now—Heaven help them!—shouldering a musket under a government they abhor, for they are all, I assure you, sir, devoted to the Union. In the absence, then, of municipal government," continued Mr. B——m, "let me extend to you the liberty of the city and welcome you to our once hospitable but now deserted halls."

At this moment an old negro touched my elbow. "Massa Capen," he said, "can't you gib an ole darkey a quarter? I ain't seen no Union silber fo' mo' dan a year."

I dropped back to give the old fellow a quarter.

"It ain't zactly because I want a quarter so bad, Massa Capen, dat I spoke ter yer, but because I wants a chance ter tell yer about dat Mr. B——m. He's de biggest ole rebel in all dese parts. I hearn him talk wen Gen'ral Bragg come here, an' he say mo' about de new flowery kingdom an' glory halleluyah dan he done say to-day by a jugful. Mrs. B——m she done make de rebel flag what floated over de heads of de soldiers, an' she sent General Bragg a dozen fresh eggs every mornin' for he's breakfast, and I'll bet a water-million she'll tell you Union gemplimen dat she ain't seen nary a egg since dem rebels come to dese parts and robbed her hen-roost. Don't mind what dat lady will say. Wust ob all, Mr. B——m done got fifty tousand dollars congealed in his cellar way down under de foundation to keep de rebels from gobblin' it, and to keep you from knowin' he had it. Dat's de kine ob Union man he is. I bress de Lord," continued the old darkey, "dat Mr. Linkum's gun-boats is come ; but don't breave a word ob what dis nigga tole you. If de rebs was to fine it out dey'd bile dis ole man in de coppers."

"Don't be afraid," said I as I gave the old Unionist a half-dollar, which he tucked into his shoe and made off.

Mr. B——m then invited us all to his house. The general had his staff with him, consisting of seven officers, and I had with me the captain of the Harriet Lane and his aid.

When we arrived at the house and were shown into the parlor we were introduced to Mrs. B——m, a stately lady, who smiled pleasantly and received us most graciously.

"Gentlemen," said Mr. B——m, "you see before you in Mrs. B——m the personification of a Union woman—one who not merely loves but adores our glorious old flag. She has undergone every privation on account of her devotion to that banner under which she was born. For years past she has owned twenty niggers, and they have all been employed at the navy-yard at a dollar a day each, thus giving her an income—not exactly net—of six thousand dollars per annum. How could she help loving that dear old flag ? She has borne like a heroine the insults heaped on that flag by the enemies of our great Republic, knowing that the day would come when, like the Phœnix, it would rise from its ashes, every star in its glorious galaxy brighter and more beautiful than ever. She succeeded in obtaining a small fragment of the flag which was lowered by traitor hands when the navy-yard was surrendered to unlawful authority (Mr. B.'s son-in-law was one of those who surrendered it), and she has preserved it to this time, when she can joyfully bring it to the light of day.—Bertha, where is that precious relic ?"

Mrs. B——m produced a piece of red and blue bunting very much soiled.

"There," continued her husband, "there's loyalty for you ; she has carried that relic in a bag on her arm ever since the fateful day when the stars and stripes were trailed in the dust in the navy-yard. Now, when the flag is again hoisted, she will reap her reward, and her faithful servants will once more be paid their dollar a day, and she receive the income she has so well deserved by her fidelity to the sacred Union.   And now, Mrs. B——m," he continued, "can't you manage to give these gentlemen some breakfast ? They must be hungry after such early rising."

"I am very sorry, love," said Mrs. B., "that I can not provide for so many, but I can take care of the general and the two navy captains.   You know we had but a small quantity of tea and coffee left and a few pounds of sugar after the rebels rifled our house, and I have saved it for this very occasion, which I knew would come sooner or later."

"Thoughtful woman !" exclaimed Mr. B——m ; "what loyalty ! and to think she has denied herself and family at times when we were starving ; but the joy of this occasion is her reward."

"But I am sorry, my dear," continued Mrs. B., "that there are but two eggs in the house, and only one loaf of bread and a small piece of butter."

"Ah, that is unfortunate," said her husband.   "You see, General, we used to have plenty of eggs, but our hens would not lay under the rebel flag.   Oh, sir, the suppressed loyalty in Pensacola is most wonderful ; our cow has not given anything like the quantity of milk she once did under the old flag."

I thought this was not surprising, as Mrs. B.'s supply of bran and meal for the cow was doubtless limited since the old flag was hauled down.

Mr. B——m pondered a while, and Lieutenant-Commanding Wainwright whispered to me, "Perhaps if they take the cow down to the dock and let her look at the old flag her milk will come down and we will get a good breakfast after all."

"Well," said B——m, "I have arranged it for all.   The general and captains will do us the honor to breakfast with us, and I will have the other gentlemen shown to the hotel, which of yore has entertained many a gallant Union officer, and will be most happy to do so again.   The proprietor is Union to the core, and no doubt can supply all the gentlemen's wants.   I will go with you and introduce you myself," and with that he led the way. followed by the hungry party, much disappointed at not getting breakfast where they first stopped.

In the mean while the general, Wainwright, and myself were entertained by Mrs. B——m, who was very discreet in her replies to our questions.   We could get nothing beyond the prices of provisions and the difficulty of procuring employment for the twenty negroes from whom she derived her income.

Mr. B——m soon returned, and we sat down to breakfast—two eggs, toast, radishes, tea, and coffee.

"This is glorious," said our host, "to sit once more under the folds of the star-spangled banner. May our Federal Union be for ever preserved from the wild fanatics who would pull it from the proud pedestal on which it was reared by Washington, Adams, and Jefferson! Secession, gentlemen, can not hurt the Union. It is but an incident in the life of a mighty nation like ours, a fungus that clings to the great oak doing little injury to the monarch of the forest."

"You had better drink your tea, Mr. B——m," interrupted his wife, "before it gets cold, and it will make you still more eloquent," she said, with a grim smile.

Then the general broke in. "Secession, sir," said he, "is the craziest scheme that was ever promulgated, and had General Jackson been President he would have hung all the leaders in the movement to a lamp-post."

"It would have taken a strong lamp-post to hold them all," said Mrs. B——m, tartly.

"Oh, my dear," said her husband, "the general is only speaking figuratively."

"No," said the general, "I mean exactly what I say; but," he continued, "this unhappy war is nearly ended. The strength of the Union is manifested in every quarter. We have whipped the rebels at Donaldson, Fort Henry, Island No. 10, and Memphis; we have them on the run. The navy has been successful at Hatteras, Port Royal, and New Orleans. That last affair broke the backbone of the rebellion. Our little Monitor defeated their great Merrimac. We have all the Southern ports blockaded, and not a traitor of them all can escape from the country."

There is no knowing how long the general would have continued in this strain if attention had not been drawn to Mrs. B——m.

Her eyes gleamed like those of a tigress, her face was red with anger, her lips were compressed, and the tea-pot which she held trembled violently in her hand.

"I suppose you whipped us at Shiloh?" she hissed, looking fiercely at the general; "at Bull Run, too, didn't you? The Congress and Cumberland sunk the Merrimac, didn't they? You caught Semmes, and he didn't destroy fifteen millions of your miserable

Yankee commerce ! You mounted a hundred guns on Fort Pickens to batter down the old straw forts Bragg put up to frighten you with ! We will march into Washington yet before we are done with you, and we'll see who will hang at a lamp-post ! "

By this time the lady was so excited that she had risen from her chair, tea-pot in hand, scattering its contents on all around. " Drat you all ! " she exclaimed. " I don't care if I scald every one of you. Here, Mr. B——m, take the tea-pot and pour out. You are only fit to wear petticoats. I leave you to entertain your Union friends. I wish you gentlemen to understand that I am a Southern woman and B——m is a sham ! "

With that she flounced out of the room and was seen no more. Mr. B——m was stupefied, the general looked surprised, while I laughed heartily.

" This episode makes this otherwise joyful occasion sad to me," said B——m. " My loyal wife has been taken with one of her nervous attacks, and her mind has become unhinged through excess of joy. The sight of our old flag floating over our lovely bay has been too much for her, and her unsettled mind imagines that she is on the Confederate side. Give her time, gentlemen, to take an ano-dyne, and she will be herself again. Heavens, what a mind she has ! "

But Mrs. B——m returned no more, and we ate our break-fast in quiet. All the eloquence had departed from B——m, and his shirt-ruffle hung limp as if it had been dipped in water.

In a short time he went out, for the purpose, I suppose, of ap-peasing his better-half. High words were heard up-stairs, and, as he re-entered the room, a shrill voice cried out, " I'll see you scalded first ! "

After breakfast we departed for the boat, Mr. B——m accom-panying us and never ceasing to eulogize his loyal wife and the dear old flag. At the landing my old negro friend again accosted me.

" What I done tole you, massa, about dem B——ms ? You foun' 'em out a sham ? No ? Well," he continued, " dat lady is a screamer an' no mistake, an' if she don't wallop Massa B——m fo sundown den dis ole nigga don't know nuffin."

B——m was loyal to the last, and joined the negroes in their cheers as our boat shoved off from the dock, and swung his hat as long as we could see him.

Before the war was ended I met many such " Union people " as the B——ms.

A few days after this I had all the mortar vessels at Pensacola, so that their crews could get fresh provisions. By this time all the people were Unionists except Mrs. B., and I think she would have been also had the Government re-established the navy-yard and employed her twenty negroes.

Five days later I received an order from Farragut to repair to Vicksburg with the vessels under my command, and thus ended my dream of capturing Mobile, which at that time would have been an easy matter to accomplish. The Confederates afterward fortified it strongly, planted torpedoes, and added to their defenses the formidable ironclad Tennessee.

CHAPTER V.

THE ATTACK ON NEW ORLEANS—SURRENDER OF THE FORTS— THE IRONCLAD LOUISIANA.

ONE of the most brilliant events of the civil war was the passage of Farragut's fleet by the Forts Jackson and St. Philip, and the consequent capture of New Orleans. It was altogether a naval enterprise, for, although an army was sent out under Butler to hold the city *after* its capture, that army had nothing whatever to do with the preceding active operations.

Everything relating to the capture of New Orleans must always be interesting. I do not propose to give a history of the passage of the forts, but merely a short account of the surrender of the defenses of New Orleans. Remarkable scenes were enacted there of which, I believe, no one has yet written a full and accurate account.

I had in the flotilla under my command twenty-one mortar vessels and six steamers. The duty of the steamers was to look out for the mortars and tow them from point to point.

On the night when it was planned to pass the forts, the steamers of my flotilla were ordered to take position opposite the water-batteries of Fort Jackson and as close to them as possible, and open fire with grape or canister and shrapnel while the fleet passed by.

This was done effectually, and by the time Captain Bailey, who took the lead, had got abreast of the forts and the enemy opened fire on him, we opened on Fort Jackson with the mortars and twenty guns from five steamers.

The steamers lay close in to the bank—only about two hundred yards distant from the works—and, although the vessels' hulls were protected by the levees from the casemated pieces, yet the barbette-guns opened rather lively. The first man killed in the fleet was on board the Harriet Lane.

In fifteen minutes after the steamers opened fire on the seven heavy guns of the center battery it was silenced and did no harm to the passing fleet. In fact, only twenty shots struck the hulls of the fleet on their port sides, which shows that the fire of the mortar flotilla was very accurate. Farragut calls it "the mortar steamers taking the forts in flank," which was a very good explanation of the movement.

As the fleet passed by me up the river I could, while standing on the bridge of the Harriet Lane, see every movement that was made. The whole extent of the river for a mile above the forts was as light as day, owing to the enemy igniting several fire-rafts, which illuminated the fleet and forts as if in a diorama.

When the last vessel had passed by, Colonel Higgins, who commanded Fort Jackson, exclaimed, "Shut up shop; the old navy is too much for us; good-by, New Orleans." He told his men they might as well stop firing the few guns that could then be brought to bear, and get under cover from the mortars.

I lay alongside of Fort Jackson fifteen minutes after Farragut had passed up, throwing in a fire of grape and shrapnel, to which there was no reply.

At daylight next morning I dropped down to the mortar schooners to tell them to stop firing, as the work was done. I met the sloop of war Portsmouth coming up in tow of a steamer. The forts opened on her feebly, but did no damage. The soldiers had lost heart, and, as I afterward learned, declined to be exposed uselessly to a heavy fire from the mortars.

It had been a heavy fight for the mortar vessels and for the poor fellows in the forts, who had borne for six days and nights the heavy pelting on their casemates of nearly seventeen thousand thirteen-inch shells, to say nothing of the fire of the gun-boats detailed daily to cover the mortar vessels from the fire of the forts.

Everybody on both sides was tired out, and many dropped in their tracks and went to sleep. As for myself, I had had scarcely any sleep for seven days and nights.

After we had breakfasted and refreshed ourselves I sent Lieutenant-Commanding Guest to the forts with a flag of truce and a polite letter to the commanding officer, advising their surrender to me in order to prevent the further effusion of blood—an invitation which he as politely declined, and said that he could do nothing until he heard that Flag-Officer Farragut and his fleet had arrived at New Orleans. I had, therefore, no alternative but to open again with the mortars on Fort Jackson and make it as unpleasant as possible for the Confederates; but by four o'clock all the mortar-shells were exhausted, and the schooners being now useless, I sent them down to Pilot Town to fill up with ammunition and six of them to appear in the rear of the forts, where they had few or no guns mounted.

What was the surprise of the commander of Fort Jackson when he saw in thirty-six hours several mortar vessels anchored in his rear and others in the distance approaching!

The result was, the soldiers in the forts mutinied and insisted on a surrender, so that, however unwilling, the officers were forced to comply.

That night General Duncan sent an officer in a boat to say to me that he would surrender the forts next morning under honorable conditions, which were granted; for if ever there was a brave defense, it was that of Fort Jackson, which got all the hammering from the mortars and most of the fire from the ships.

Here was to be a meeting of old shipmates who were serving on either side, and who, after messing together many years under the old flag, had been trying for the past week to inflict every sort of injury on one another that ingenuity could devise.

There was an actual desire on the part of some to meet their old acquaintances and talk over the events of the siege, for the surrender was to include all the naval officers and whatever vessels yet remained afloat. This had been stipulated by Lieutenant-Commanding Guest when he called on General Duncan about the surrender.

There was quite a large number of naval officers employed in the Confederate river flotilla, in the rams, and the ironclad Louisiana, and a corresponding number on our side.

I was determined that the Southerners should see no diminution of discipline in the old navy, and that when we went to take possession of the forts we would go dressed up for muster, or, as they say in the navy nowadays, dress parade.

On the morning of the surrender, signal was made for the crews of our vessels to dress in white mustering suits, and the officers in frock-coats and white trousers, everything looking as neat as possible. I was determined that the Southern fellows of the old navy should see that we had not gone to the devil, but still wore clean shirts under the most adverse circumstances; that we were not only true to our flag, but to our old traditional neatness, even after a hard-fought battle of a week's duration.

Flag-Officer Farragut, after passing the forts, had gone on up the river to New Orleans, carrying everything before him and scattering the troops in the defenses along the river like sheep; but he had left behind him some rather ugly customers, among them the Louisiana, a huge ironclad mounting sixteen nine-inch guns, four or five of them rifled, and impervious to any shot we had.

Fortunately, her machinery was out of order, and she could not move without the aid of tow-boats; but had her officers possessed sufficient energy they might have captured or destroyed everything on the river after our fleet passed on up.

Farragut showed his confidence in the mortar flotilla by leaving us to look after the ironclad and her three consorts, and perhaps, had the Louisiana come down and attacked us, we might have managed to dispose of her?

Our little squadron of steamers now comprised nine vessels— three of them gun-boats that had failed to pass the forts with the fleet, not from want of gallantry, but from various causes. Fragile as our little vessels were, they made an imposing sight as they steamed up to the fort in line and anchored *en échelon* across the river.

The huge Louisiana was secured to the bank about four hundred yards above, and it could be seen that her iron sides had not even been indented by the shot poured into her as the vessels of the squadron passed by. I thought what an addition she would be to our force, for with her guns we could batter down any forts the enemy might erect along the river. In my mind's eye I could already see the fortifications at Vicksburg succumbing to this powerful vessel, and I thanked my stars that she had not been used as she might have been and driven us all out of the river.

There she lay, a huge leviathan among minnows, her flag flying and three gun-boats near by. I was not certain but what some act of treachery would be attempted before the capitulation of the forts was accomplished.

When our vessels were all at anchor, ready to receive the officers of the forts, a barge was sent on shore for them, while the officers and crews of the steamers were kept at quarters, ready for any emergency.

When the Confederate officers came down to embark, Colonel Higgins, formerly a lieutenant in the navy, who commanded Fort Jackson, paused for a moment and said to the commanding officer, General Duncan : ''Look at the old navy ! I feel proud when I see them. There are no half-breeds there ; they are the Simon-pure. With fellows like those to back us, Farragut would never have passed the forts.'' What he meant will appear directly.

The Confederate officers were received at the gangway by myself and officers, and, when they stepped on board, one would have supposed they were foreigners paying us a visit of ceremony. They were fine-looking men in the prime of life, and showed no depression. Their bearing was manly without haughtiness.

Although I knew some of them, I did not think it necessary to recognize them at the moment beyond a bow when General Duncan mentioned each one's name. I then invited them to the cabin, where the terms of capitulation were lying on the table. The Confederate officers were all seated on the port side, while I took the head of the table and my officers the starboard side. Colonel Higgins could not help saying, as he descended to the cabin, '' Captain, this is a man-of-war and no mistake.''

I felt much disposed to recognize Higgins, but I buried all my old friendships with naval seceders when they deserted their flag. In my opinion, no naval officer should have been influenced by State-rights sophistry to forsake the flag under which he was born, and which had been to him a source of honor and emolument.

If he could not give the Government active support, he should at least have declined to raise his hand against it.

But, after all, these are matters of conscience, and no man can tell how far he may be carried in a popular excitement until he is tried.

I only know that I would never join a State, because I happened to be born within its limits, in opposition to the legally constituted Government of my country.

Therefore, when I first met old friends whom I thought had wandered from their plain duty, I could not gush over them, though careful to show them as prisoners every kindness.

I felt as Franklin did, who, on receiving a letter from an old friend in England during the Revolution, answered : '' We were once friends; we are so no longer.   You are an enemy to my country; you are mine also."

At the same time I could not help admiring in their misfortunes those brave men who were about to sign a capitulation which would deprive them of the forts they had so confidently and gallantly defended, and who, when all was over and no more could be done, gave up without brag or bluster, and made no excuses for their failure.

I can not help admiring bravery even in a bad cause, and when I went over the works and saw to what a dreadful hammering the Confederates had been subjected, I thought it not without honor for any one to have fought at their side.

I laid before the officers the papers of capitulation.   "General Duncan," I said, "read them carefully."

"I will," he replied, "but I am confident you would offer us no terms that it would be dishonorable to accept; one brave man would not wish to humiliate another."

I acknowledged the compliment so delicately expressed.

"I am satisfied with the terms," said the general, "and speak for the rest of the officers."

The terms were that officers and men should sign a parole not to serve against the United States Government until regularly exchanged, the officers to retain their side-arms and be transported to New Orleans in a United States vessel.

The Confederates were to turn over to the United States all ordnance, ammunition, stores, and small arms, as far as practicable, uninjured—a stipulation which was religiously observed.

I said to General Duncan, "Where is the commanding naval officer and his staff ?   I shall include the vessels in the surrender; are they not under your command ?"

"Yes," replied the general, "at least they are supposed to be, but I know nothing about them.   The naval officers were duly notified what was to take place.   They failed in their support; otherwise matters might have turned out differently."

This was rather perplexing, and I was inclined to postpone the capitulation until the commanding naval officer could be sent for, since under present circumstances the Confederate navy might open fire upon us, on the ground that they were not a party to the agreement drawn up.

We were relieved from this difficulty, however, by Lieutenant-Commanding Wainwright coming into the cabin and reporting that the officers and crew of the Louisiana were leaving her in a gunboat, after setting fire to the ironclad ; that the latter's fasts had been cut, and she was drifting rapidly down upon the line of steamers.

"This is sharp practice, gentlemen," I said, "and some of us will perhaps be blown up ; but I know what to do, for it is now plain sailing. If you can stand what is coming, we can, but I will make it lively for those people if any one in the flotilla is injured."

"We do not consider ourselves responsible for anything the naval officers may do," said Duncan. "Their course has been a remarkable one throughout the bombardment. They have acknowledged no authority except their own, and, although I am commanding officer here, I have no power to coerce them."

I told Lieutenant-Commanding Wainwright to hail the steamer next him and tell her captain to pass the word to the others to veer out all their riding chain to the bitter end, and stand by to sheer clear of the burning ironclad as she drifted down. I then sat down to the table and said, "Gentlemen, we will proceed to sign the capitulation."

I handed the paper to General Duncan, and looked at the Confederate officers to see how they would behave under the circumstances of a great ironclad dropping down on them all in flames, with twenty thousand pounds of powder in her magazine. For myself, I hoped the fire would not reach the powder until the ship had drifted some distance below us. My greatest fear was that she would run foul of some of the steamers.

While I was thinking all this over the officers were sitting as coolly as if at tea-table among their friends.

Just then there was a stir on deck, a kind of swaying of the vessel to and fro, a rumbling in the air, then an explosion which seemed to shake the heavens. The Harriet Lane was thrown two streaks over, and everything in the cabin was jostled from side to side, but not a man left his seat or showed any intention of doing so.

I was glad that I had signed before the explosion took place, as I would not have liked my autograph to look shaky.

When Lieutenant-Commanding Wainwright came back to the cabin he reported that the Louisiana had blown up about a hundred yards above the Owasco, that no one was hurt, and that no vessel had left her anchorage.

I told the Confederate officers that I had no doubt the ironclad had been prepared to blow up right in our midst, for the purpose of destroying us all, to which the reply was, "We are not responsible."

The Confederate officers soon after went on shore, hauled down their flag, took an inventory of all property remaining in the forts, mustered their men, and prepared to depart from what they had once deemed impregnable works.

As soon as they left the Harriet Lane the signal was run up, "Prepare for action!" and I steamed toward the rebel gun-boats, which were fastened to the shore above, with all their flags flying. A rifle-shot was fired at Commander Mitchell's flag-staff, and all their flags were at once lowered.

Thus in the end the Confederate navy had to submit to force, when they could have gracefully surrendered and had all the benefits enjoyed by the army.

I was so indignant at having the ironclad Louisiana thus slip through my fingers that I could scarcely refrain from running the Confederate flag-ship down and sinking her. The ironclad would have been a great help to Farragut in his operations on the upper Mississippi, and would have been a match for the great ram Tennessee, which was at that time being prepared at Mobile.

Look at the destruction of the vessel by Mitchell's orders in any light you may, it was unfair. That was my opinion at the time, and I have never seen any reason to change it.

When I came alongside the Confederate vessels, I found them huddled together and crowded with men. I hailed and asked them if they had surrendered. They answered in the affirmative, and I sent Lieutenant Wainwright to take possession. He was directed to receive only an unconditional surrender, as I would grant no terms.

Commander Mitchell, the senior naval officer, met Wainwright at the gangway and extended his hand. "No," said Wainwright, "you are a prisoner."

"Am I not to have the same terms as the army officers?" inquired Mitchell.

"No," replied Wainwright, "you must surrender unconditionally, and be taken North as a close prisoner. Deliver up your sword."

As Mitchell had no sword, he was obliged to borrow one for the occasion from an officer who stood near by.

I kept my word and held no terms with the naval officers. I

felt sorry for them, for among their number were some fine young fellows whom I had no reason to think were aiders and abettors in a scheme to destroy a vessel which rightfully belonged to us, for, although not actually surrendered, she was virtually so, being included in the terms of capitulation.

There was nothing to justify the destruction of the Louisiana, and I was much disappointed at seeing those who had once belonged to the United States navy excelled in matters of honor and propriety by the officers of another corps.

Suffice it to say that the Confederate naval officers were all sent North by Farragut as close prisoners. They made statements, however, which in the end procured their release; but while the authorities were satisfied, I never was. I could never get over the fact that, when I went below with the Confederate army officers to sign the capitulation, the Louisiana was lying at the river-bank, in all her strength and grandeur, all ready, as I supposed, to be turned over to me. When I came on deck again the vessel had disappeared. The disappointment was great, and no doubt those Confederates chuckled with delight over it.

However, it didn't really make any difference in the final result, and furnished an interesting incident of the war, although the "incident" came near closing the career of all those present at the capitulation of Forts Jackson and St. Philip.

What else relates to this matter will be found in the official reports of the day, as it is not my intention to write a history of the war, but merely to mention such incidents as I think will interest the general reader.

It is astonishing that the Confederates should have had at the defenses of New Orleans such a powerful vessel as the Louisiana, while Farragut had nothing but fragile wooden vessels, that could be pierced by any ordinary smooth-bore gun; and it was only owing to the circumstance that the Louisiana disabled her machinery while coming down the river, and could only move about in tow of another vessel, that a disaster did not befall the Union fleet.

As the fleet passed up the river the Louisiana occupied a prominent position tied to the river-bank, where the light from the fire-rafts showed her as plainly as if it had been daylight.

Every vessel in passing poured in her shot at close quarters, doing the Louisiana no more harm than so many popguns. It is fair to presume that with her powerful battery she inflicted some of the damage done to the squadron. It can be easily imagined what terrible havoc such a vessel would have made among a lot of wooden vessels had her motive power been in good order. The ships scattered about the river could have offered no effectual resistance to her without firing into each other.

How fortunate, then, it was that Flag-Officer Farragut advanced up the river the night he did, when the ironclad was tied up to the bank and could not use her guns effectively !

Only one projectile did any harm to the Louisiana. It was either an eleven-inch or a mortar shell that knocked off part of a light gallery in which riflemen were stationed. Her commanding officer was mortally wounded, and a few of her men were disabled.

How is it, I would ask, that such a vessel could be built in New Orleans with the comparatively meager resources of the Confederates ? The Merrimac built at Norfolk, two heavier ships than either the Merrimac or Louisiana building at New Orleans, four heavy ironclads building up the Yazoo River, and the Tennessee building at Mobile, while the most in this direction that the North had accomplished was the construction of the little Monitor, designed by Ericsson, which was derided while building, was looked upon as a doubtful experiment, and finally saved the honor of the nation.

Where was our boasted energy when we could not build two or three ironclads while the Confederates were building eight ?

With our resources we should, in the time from the breaking out of the Rebellion to the expedition against New Orleans, have been able to supply Farragut with half a dozen heavy ironclads. It was fortunate indeed for Farragut that the Louisiana was not in good working order, for, although there was no end of skill and bravery shown by our gallant commander, his wooden ships were but fragile things to operate against heavy forts on the banks of a swift-running river, and against an impregnable ironclad, besides a dozen gun-boats throwing in shells, a formidable ram that was plunging about in every direction and rending the sides of the heaviest vessels, and packs of fire-rafts scorching the very sides of the ships and causing almost inextricable difficulties.

It was a time to try men's souls, and the fact that almost every ship got by the forts is a proof that the commanding officers knew their business, and performed their duty with the utmost coolness.

Farragut was justly lauded for this remarkable and glorious victory, but neither the Government nor the people ever gave him half the credit he deserved. An English officer who had achieved

so much would have been loaded by his government with no end
of rewards.

The capture of New Orleans broke up the principal stronghold
of the Confederacy.   It virtually gave us control of the Mississippi
River, and was really the insertion of the wedge which finally split
the backbone of the Rebellion.   When the Mississippi was opened in
all its length, the contest was virtually settled.

I know all the difficulties with which Farragut had to contend
—difficulties greater than ever beset British admirals in their most
famous battles ; difficulties, in fact, that many of them would have
thought insurmountable.   The rank of rear-admiral, and finally
that of admiral, when he was broken in health, was all the reward
he ever received, and his rank of admiral carried with it no authority or consequence to make him feel he was of that importance to
his Government which his services merited.

It is only in the present year (1881) that the survivors of the
battle of New Orleans received the final share of prize-money gained
by them in 1862.

The great merit in giving rewards is to give them promptly ; it
can not be considered generous when they are doled out too carefully.

<hr>

CHAPTER VI.

ERICSSON AND THE MONITOR.—AN INTERVIEW WITH THE GREAT
ENGINEER.

GREAT ideas lie dormant in the minds of men until some important event occurs to bring them to light, as the sun causes the
seed to germinate.

Newton, although he had certain theories in his mind in relation to the forces which govern the motions of the heavenly bodies,
never fully comprehended the matter until he saw an apple fall from
a tree.   By so trifling an occurrence as that the philosopher at once
comprehended the principle of gravitation.

So it was with John Ericsson, the distinguished inventor, who,
although he had stowed away in his mind certain theories which
were to radically change the system of naval warfare, never had an
opportunity to put them into practice until a revolution took place

in the country of his adoption, and he saw a chance of making the great talents God had given him useful to the Union cause.

Had Ericsson been listened to on the first breaking out of the war, and his plans adopted, the United States Government would in one year not only have been able to take possession of all the Southern ports, but to have bid defiance even to the great fleets of England and France in case either nation felt disposed to meddle in our affairs.

But who was going to believe that "an iron pot" would float, even if empty, much less when loaded down with guns, ammunition, machinery, provisions, and men ? Mr. John Lenthall, the oldest and ablest constructor in the navy, scouted the idea. "How is the Monitor to ride the sea with all that weight in her ?" he inquired.

"The sea shall ride over her," replied Ericsson, "and she will live in it like a duck."

"The man is crazy !" said Lenthall, and he turned his attention to the model of a wooden double-ender he was about to construct—one of those remarkable vessels of which President Lincoln said, " I have often heard of a vessel with two bows, but I never before saw one with two sterns."

Mr. Lenthall was a man of great ability, but he had been too many years engaged in modeling sloops of war and frigates, and was of too cautious and conservative a temper to be diverted from his course by what he considered visionary ideas. He had hardly patience to examine the plans or calculations on which depended the efficiency of "Ericsson's iron pot," as he called it.

Had he taken hold of the subject with enthusiasm, his mind would have grasped the situation, and the Monitor would have been at Hampton Roads months before she actually arrived there, and a great catastrophe would have been averted.

As it was, only one person in the Navy Department believed in Ericsson's plans from the first, and that was Commodore Joseph Smith, a plain, practical man, who thought he saw in the invention what was worthy of encouragement.

At length it was agreed that Ericsson should build, at his own expense and at a private ship-yard, an iron-turreted vessel, which the Government would accept, provided it fulfilled in all respects the promise of the inventor.

Had the extensive iron-works and machinery at the New York navy-yard been put in operation, the Government could have built in the same time half a dozen vessels of the Monitor pattern, and of much greater power, which would have assured us success all along the coast and made us infinitely stronger abroad.

As soon as the success of Ericsson's Monitor was assured, the Government proceeded to follow out the idea, and the Monadnock class were then constructed on the plans of Chief Constructor Lenthall, who, with the means at his disposal, was able to turn out what were then the most powerful vessels in the world.

While I was fitting out the mortar flotilla, "Ericsson's iron pot" was approaching completion, and I received orders from the Navy Department to make a critical examination of the vessel and report my opinion of her capabilities. After this duty was accomplished I was ordered to proceed to Mystic, Conn., and examine the Galena, a wooden vessel sheathed with iron plates, building there under the supervision of Commodore Joseph Smith.

Arriving at New York, I called on Mr. Ericsson and showed him my orders. He read them, looked at me attentively, and said : "Well, you are no doubt a great mathematician, and know all about the calculations which enter into the construction of my vessel. You will have many papers to examine ; help yourself, and take what you like best."

"I am no great mathematician," I replied, "but I am a practical man, and think I can ascertain whether or not the Monitor will do what is promised for her."

"Ah, yes !" exclaimed Ericsson, "a practical man ! Well, I've had a dozen of those fellows here already, and they went away as wise as they came. I don't want *practical* men sent here, sir. I want men who understand the higher mathematics that are used in the construction of my vessel—men who can work out the displacements, horse-power, impregnability, endurance at sea in a gale, capacity to stow men, the motion of the vessel according to the waves, her stability as a platform for guns, her speed, actual weight —in short, everything pertaining to the subject. Now, young man, if you can't fathom these things you had better go back where you came from. If the department wants to understand the principles of my vessel, they should send a mathematician."

"Well," said I, as the inventor paused to take breath, "although I am not strictly what you would call a mathematician, I know the rule of three, and that twice two are four."

Ericsson looked hard at me, his hair bristled up, and the muscles of his brawny arms seemed to swell as if in expectation of having to eject me from the room. "Well!" he exclaimed, "I never in all my life met with such assurance as this. Here the Government sends me an officer who knows only the rule of three and that twice two are four, and I have used the calculus and all the higher mathematics in making my calculations. My God! do they take me for a fool?"

"But," said I, apologetically, "I know a little of simple equations. Won't that be sufficient to make me understand this machine of yours?"

"Worse and worse!" exclaimed the inventor. "This beats the devil; it would be better if you knew nothing. Father in heaven, here's a man who tells me he knows a little of simple equations, and they send him to examine John Ericsson!"

I was greatly amused with this remarkable man, and entirely forgave his peculiarities. "Well, Mr. Ericsson," I said, "you will have to make the best of a bad bargain, and get along with me as well as you possibly can. I am perfectly willing to receive instruction from you."

"Ah, ha!" he exclaimed, "that's it, is it? and so you think me a school-master to teach naval officers what I know? I'm afraid you're too bad a bargain for me; you must expect no instruction here. Take what you like best from my shelves, but you can't have my brains."

"Well, then," I said, "show me your plans in order, and, if you won't explain them, let me see what I can make of them."

"Ah, young man!" said Ericsson, "with your limited knowledge of simple equations you will run aground in a very short time. Look at this drawing and tell me what it represents."

"It looks to me like a coffee-mill," I answered.

Ericsson jumped from his chair with astonishment in his eye. "On my word of honor, young man, you are vexing, and I am a fool to waste my time on you. That is the machinery that works my turn-table for the turret. I have spent many sleepless nights over it, and now a man who only knows a little of simple equations tells me it's a coffee-mill! Now what do you think of that?" continued Mr. Ericsson, handing me a small wooden model; "that's my 'iron pot,' as you navy people call it."

I regarded the model with a critical eye, holding it upside down. "This," I remarked, "is evidently the casemate"—passing my hand over the bottom—"and this"—pointing to the turret—"is undoubtedly where you carry the engine."

"O Heavens!" exclaimed Ericsson; "well! well! never did I see such a— But never mind; you will learn by and by the world was not made in a day."

So we went on till at length I informed Mr. Ericsson that I thought I understood all about his "iron pot."

He was not in a pleasant humor, evidently regarding me as an emissary sent by the department to try and bring him to grief. As he did not seem to be in a communicative frame of mind, I took a malicious pleasure in worrying him.

After learning all I could possibly from the drawings and plans of the Monitor, I proposed to the inventor to go and examine the Simon-pure article, and we crossed the ferry to Greenpoint, where, if I remember rightly, the vessel was building.

Taking off my coat, I penetrated to the innermost recesses of the Monitor, followed by Mr. Ericsson, who more than once inquired if my simple equations enabled me to comprehend the mysteries.

"Wait till I am done with you," I said; "then the laugh will be on you, and you'll see what my simple equations amount to."

"No doubt! no doubt!" he replied, "but it will take a big book to hold all you don't know when you get through."

At last, after an hour spent in examining the vessel, I emerged from the hold, followed by the inventor, who looked displeased enough. "Now, sir," I said, "I know all about your machine."

"Yes," he answered, sneeringly, "and you know twice two are four, and a little of simple equations."

"Now, Mr. Ericsson," I said, "I have borne a good deal from you to-day; you have mocked at my authority and have failed to treat me with the sweetness I had a right to expect. I am about to have satisfaction, for on my report depends whether or not your vessel is accepted by the department, so I will tell you in plain terms what I think of your 'iron pot.'"

"Say what you please," exclaimed Ericsson, glaring at me like a tiger ready to spring; "nobody will mind what you say!"

"Well, sir," I continued, "I have looked into the whole thing from A to Izzard, and"—gazing steadily at the inventor, not without apprehensions that he might seize me in his muscular arms and squeeze the breath out of my body—"I will say this to the Government—in writing, too, so that there can be no mistake."

"Go on, sir, go on!" said Ericsson; "you will run on a rock directly."

"Well, then," I continued, "I will say that Mr. Ericsson has constructed a vessel—a very little iron vessel—which, in the opinion of our best naval architect, is in violation of well-known principles, and will sink the moment she touches the water."

"Oh," said Ericsson, "he's a fool!"

"But," I continued, "I shall say, also, that Mr. Ericsson has constructed the most remarkable vessel the world has ever seen—one that, if properly handled, can destroy any ship now afloat, and whip a dozen wooden ships together if they were where they could not manœuvre so as to run her down."

Ericsson regarded me in astonishment, then seized my hand and almost shook my arm off. "My God!" he exclaimed, "and all this time I took you for a d—d fool, and you are not a d—d fool after all!"

I laughed heartily, as did Ericsson, and we have been the best of friends ever since.

I telegraphed at once to the Navy Department, "Mr. Ericsson's vessel is the best fighting machine ever invented, and can destroy any ship of war afloat."

After examining the Galena, I telegraphed, "I am not satisfied with the vessel; she is too vulnerable."

On my return to Washington I met a high official of the navy, who said to me: "We received your highfalutin telegram about the Ericsson vessel. Why, man, Lenthall says she will sink as soon as she is launched. He has made a calculation, and finds she will not bear her iron, much less her guns and stores."

Both Fox and Lenthall soon had reason to change their opinions on this subject; both became strong advocates of Ericsson's system, and in a short time a number of much larger vessels of a similar type with the Monitor were commenced, but were not finished in time to be of use in the most critical period of the civil war, when we came near meeting with serious reverses owing to the great energy displayed by the Confederates in improvising heavy ironclads.

To Ericsson belongs the credit of devising the Monitor class of vessels, which gave us a cheap and rapid mode of building a navy suitable to our wants at the time. Through his genius we were enabled to bid defiance to the maritime powers which seemed disposed to meddle with our affairs, and it was owing to him that at the end of the civil war we were in a condition to prevent any hostile navy from entering our ports.

Ericsson may be said to have at one blow destroyed all the

squadrons of Europe, for after the engagement between the Monitor and the Merrimac it was plainly to be seen that the old-fashioned wooden vessels were useless for war purposes, although we have held on to our old rattle-traps until we are a by-word among the nations—a laughing-stock even to the Chinese !

At the age of eighty-four, Ericsson is now a hale, hearty man, with a mind as bright as it was thirty years ago.

The United States owe him a debt they never have repaid and never can repay.

His latest invention is a torpedo which in case of war will bring the name of Ericsson again before our people and remind them of the man who, in the days of our greatest trial, placed us in a position to bid defiance to foreign and domestic enemies.

Few nations have had so great an inventive genius as Ericsson to assist them with his talents in time of war, and he has also in time of peace produced valuable inventions which have added to his reputation and to the prosperity of the country.

By breaking up the great wooden navies of Europe, Ericsson helped to place us more on an equality with them as a naval power, and the distance is not so great between us but that we may hope to overtake them when the people of this country demand a navy commensurate with our national importance, and when the exigencies of politics can no longer prevent proper measures being taken for the defense of the nation, which should at all times be in a position to protect its citizens at home and abroad.

CHAPTER VII.

PLANS FOR THE CAPTURE OF NEW ORLEANS.—CONDUCT OF THE PEOPLE ON OUR TAKING POSSESSION OF THE CITY.—GENERAL BUTLER'S ADMINISTRATION.

WHILE I was at the entrance to the southwest pass of the Mississippi, I had ample opportunity to find out much that was going on at the forts and in the city of New Orleans.

Upon reaching home in the Powhatan, I proceeded to Washington, and found everything at the Navy Department as calm and quiet as if we had nothing to do but blockade the Southern ports.

I could not obtain an interview with the Secretary of the Navy, and soon found that I was out of favor since I ran off with the Powhatan to carry out Mr. Seward's pet scheme of saving Fort Pickens. Assistant Secretary Fox was not communicative; Faxon eyed me askance; Wise was jocose, but knew nothing; old Commodore Joe Smith said, "Well, you didn't run away after all!" etc.; and I wandered about like a cat in a strange garret.

Presently I encountered Senators Hale and Grimes, standing near the door of the Secretary's room. They greeted me warmly, made inquiries about my cruise, and when I told them that I had come to lay a proposition for the capture of New Orleans before the Secretary of the Navy, they became very much interested in the project.

I explained to them the ease with which the city could be captured, and the advantages that would accrue from it. The senators saw the importance of the matter, and invited me to accompany them to see Mr. Welles.

The Secretary of the Navy, much to my surprise, received me kindly, and listened attentively to all I had to say. When I had concluded he suggested we should all go to the President.

We found Mr. Lincoln at the White House pacing the floor, calm and thoughtful, and to him I repeated what I had told the others, and urged the great importance of the capture of New Orleans. When I had finished, the President said, "This reminds me of a story which I must tell you all.

"There was an old woman in Illinois who missed some of her chickens, and couldn't imagine what had become of them. Some one suggested that they had been carried off by a skunk; so she told her husband he must sit up that night and shoot the 'critter.'

"The old man sat up all night, and next morning came in with two pet rabbits. 'Thar,' said he, ' your chickens are all safe; thar's two of them skunks I killed!'

"' 'Them ain't skunks,' said the old woman; 'them's my pet rabbits; you allers was a fool!'

"' 'Well, then,' returned the old man, 'if them ain't skunks I don't know a skunk when I sees it.'

"Now, Mr. Secretary," said the President, "the navy has been hunting pet rabbits long enough; suppose you send them after skunks. It seems to me that what the lieutenant proposes is feasible. He says a dozen ships will take the forts and city, and there should be twenty thousand soldiers sent along to hold it. After

New Orleans is taken, and while we are about it, we can push on to Vicksburg and open the river all the way along. We will go and see General McClellan and find out if he can't manage to get the troops." Just then Mr. Seward came in, and we all repaired to McClellan's headquarters.

McClellan came down as soon as the President was announced, and recognized me as an old acquaintance. "Why," exclaimed Mr. Lincoln, "do you two fellows know each other? So much the better." And he laid the matter before the general in a lucid manner, for Mr. Lincoln was quick of comprehension, and said, "You must find the troops and a general of good administrative abilities to hold the city of New Orleans after the navy shall have captured it. Now," continued the President, "time flies, and I want this matter settled. I will leave you two gentlemen to arrange the plans, and will come over here at eight o'clock this evening to see what conclusion you have arrived at."

So General McClellan and myself were left alone to talk the matter over, and we soon determined upon a plan of operations. At eight o'clock that evening the President returned to General McClellan's headquarters, and was informed that the general could spare twenty thousand men to accompany a naval expedition to New Orleans, and that they would be ready to embark as soon as the naval vessels could be prepared.

The President then directed the Secretary of the Navy to have the necessary number of ships ready. This duty was assigned to Assistant Secretary Fox, who took hold of the matter with his usual energy, and soon assembled a squadron adequate to the occasion.

Mr. Welles, in an article which he published in a magazine called the "Galaxy," many years after the expedition to New Orleans, states the matter in quite a different light. Of all the actors in the scene I have described, only General McClellan and myself survive, and he can corroborate my statement.

In reference to Mr. Welles's narrative in the "Galaxy," it would be charitable to suppose that age had impaired his memory, although his mind was vigorous to the last.

I know his friends were disappointed when the above-mentioned article appeared. The ex-Secretary evidently wrote under a wrong impression, and was disingenuous, to use the mildest expression.

However, I never noticed the article, thinking myself strong enough to defy such attacks, nor would I let my friends publish

5

the papers in my possession that would have refuted Mr. Welles's statements.

Besides, Mr. Welles had, on the whole, been kind to me, and steadily insisted on my promotion to the rank of rear-admiral and vice-admiral, and I felt reluctant to call in question the word of a man who had served his country in its darkest hour with fidelity and zeal, if not with conspicuous ability.

There were too many officers living at the time who knew what I had done, and I really regretted, for Mr. Welles's sake, that the odium of the article fell upon him.

After settling upon the ships and troops, the next thing to be done was to select an officer to command the naval forces.

Mr. Fox named several, but I opposed them all, and finally urged the appointment of Captain D. G. Farragut so strongly that I was sent to New York to communicate with him on the subject. The result was the acceptance by Farragut of the command—a command assuring his reputation, which no man ever more deserved.

This is the way the expedition to New Orleans originated. It is a piece of hitherto unwritten history. The limits of this work forbid my giving further details.

When Farragut reached New Orleans with his fleet, of course he created great consternation. The people fairly went wild; they set fire to the cotton along the levees, and seemed determined that nothing valuable should fall into our hands. They did not apparently remember that, so far, our navy had respected private rights and protected those made homeless by the actions of wild mobs.

Among the property destroyed were two powerful steamers intended for ironclads. Had these been finished, they would have been strong enough to drive our Union ships from the coast. By the time we could have built the proper kind of vessels to compete with the monsters the Confederates were constructing, the Mississippi River would have been so strongly fortified that it would have taken years to break the backbone of the Rebellion.

Instead of wasting our resources in attacking Hatteras Inlet, Port Royal, and other places of less importance, we should have assailed New Orleans in the first instance with just such a force as was finally sent there. It would then have fallen into our hands without much resistance; but the place for a long time was treated by the Government as if unworthy of notice.

New Orleans was the great Southern emporium, and was filled

with all kinds of naval and military stores, supplied by the rich country which borders on the Mississippi and its tributaries, and having easy communication with Texas, which could supply an immense army with food for an indefinite period.

The ports of Texas were so inadequately guarded that, two years after the commencement of hostilities, blockade-runners went in and out almost with impunity, taking away a large amount of cotton, which supplied the Confederates with funds in Europe with which to buy everything they needed.

These articles were sent into Wilmington, Charleston, and Savannah, and thence were distributed as occasion required.

I was in command of the first vessel that undertook the blockade of the Mississippi, having been sent there at my own request by Captain McKean. commanding the Niagara. I realized from the first the great importance of New Orleans to the Confederates. Perhaps because the entrance to the Mississippi was easily blockaded it made the Government indifferent, or perhaps, to use an old quotation,

> " There were men in high places,
> With smooth, placid faces,
> With hands meekly folded as if saying grace,
> While rebellion was moving at an awful fast pace."

We either sent ships there too large to cross the bar, or else sailing-vessels that were not a particle of use. Those who were on the blockade in that quarter a short time after I left can not have forgotten the miserable fiasco made by a detachment of two or three vessels that attempted to ascend the river as far as the head of the passes, and were obliged to make a shameful retreat, being chased down the river and over the bar by the Confederate ram Manassas.

This event became more notorious from the fact that the sailing-vessel grounded on the bar near deep water, and a river steamer called the Ivy, armed with a three-inch rifle gun, kept the shots whistling in so lively a manner around the heads of our people that the commanding officer became panic-stricken, wrapped himself in the American flag, fired a fuse leading to the magazine, and deserted his ship with his officers and men.

They all repaired on board the senior officer's ship, much to the horror of the latter when he heard that the sloop of war would blow up in a few minutes ; but an hour elapsed, and no explosion took place. The reason of this was subsequently explained by an old quartermaster, who informed the senior officer that just before leaving the ship he had cut off the burning end of the fuse, thinking the captain might change his mind when he no longer heard the whistling of the enemy's shells—a fine commentary on the behavior of his commanding officer.

But to return to Flag Officer Farragut, whom I left at anchor before the city of New Orleans, with a vile mob shouting defiance at him through the streets, and a foolish Mayor aiding and abetting their madness, when one broadside from the Hartford would have scattered the rabble like a flock of sheep and set fire to the place.

If ever Farragut deserved credit, it was for the forbearance and humanity he showed to the crowd of maniacs who defied his authority and did everything in its power to prevent him from taking peaceful possession of the city.

A conqueror is never so great as when governing himself and controlling the passions of those around him, in the moment of victory, who witness their beaten foes still defying those who have it in their power to destroy them.

This was exactly the state of affairs in New Orleans when Farragut arrived before the city.

We had been led to believe that many Union people there were actually pining for the sight of the old flag, and that our forces would receive the warmest welcome. On the contrary, Farragut was met with yells of defiance all along the levee from thousands of people *mad* in every sense of the word.

They acted as if they had just escaped from a lunatic asylum. They ranted, raved, and used such shocking bad language that it pained the ears. Boatmen, politicians, sage counselors, women of the town, and fish-mongers were all mixed up in a seemingly inextricable mass, defying Farragut's ships with their fists as if they would annihilate them. It would have been amusing had not the occasion been too serious, and had not the power of the Government required to have been vindicated.

What a reckless mob it was, to be sure, which one shot from a howitzer would have scattered like sheep! But the maniacs, instigated by those who ought to have known better, trusted to the chivalry of the navy, supposing it would not fire on unarmed people, and resorted to every kind of low abuse the human tongue could utter. The Mayor and City Council never reflected how much better it would have been for them to have surrendered with dignity.

Captain Bailey, accompanied by Lieutenant George H. Perkins, was at length sent on shore, with a flag of truce, to wait on the Mayor and demand the surrender of the city. These two brave officers landed without any support and forced that maddened, yelling crowd to open their ranks and let them pass. The mob hooted and shook their fists in the officers' faces, shouting, "Choke them!" "Give them rotten eggs!" Some even threatened them with pistols, but they did them no injury, for the crowd was awed, if not quieted, by the determined looks of the two officers, who marched on to the performance of their mission as coolly as if on parade.

They performed their duty and returned to the ship, escorted by the same demoniac rabble. It was a perilous undertaking, and had a hair of their heads been injured, the commander-in-chief of the squadron would have opened on the city.

In the days of the French Revolution, when the *sans-culottes* dragged their victims to the shambles, the mob were not actuated by a more devilish spirit than this pleasant party assembled on the levee at New Orleans. Men, women, and children of all classes stayed, mixed up together, till late that night, and with the most discordant shrieks and howls defied Farragut and his officers.

It was a critical moment. The commander-in-chief had imposed upon him a solemn duty to enforce the obedience of a rebellious city, which lay helpless at his feet, yet was dominated by a tumultuous crowd instigated by their leaders to a threatening attitude, doubtless with the hope that Farragut would be provoked to fire into the throng and kill some of their number.

That would have been a great boon to the inciters of the mob. They would have filled the civilized world with their complaints of Union cruelty toward helpless women and children, and made many misrepresentations not easy to confute, as noxious weeds, when once they have taken root, are exceedingly hard to remove.

Fortunately, Farragut was too humane to gratify these desperate people, although they gave him no credit for his forbearance, and only increased their offensive demonstrations.

Some officer suggested a dose of grape-shot. "No," said Farragut, "the wretches are crazy, and I can't fire on howling maniacs."

Captain Bell proposed to the flag-officer to let him land the marines and plant the Union flag on the Government buildings. To this Farragut consented.

There was never a more hazardous duty than that imposed on Captain Bell, and he performed it to the fullest satisfaction of his brother officers. His cool conduct even drew respect from the noisy rabble, who, although they howled and hooted and used the most opprobrious epithets, yet gave way before the steady advance of the handful of marines, and then closed in behind them.

For some time no one could learn the fate of what was thought to be a forlorn hope, but the bearing of Bell and his men kept the crowd in a certain awe.

They knew that the well-drilled men and their sturdy leader meant business, and no one had the hardihood to strike the first blow, although the crowd was so great that they might have closed on this handful of men and torn them to pieces.

At length Bell reached the City Hall and demanded admittance. Amid the howls of the multitude he ascended to the roof of the building, leaving the marines to guard the doors, and in a few moments the star-spangled banner floated from the flag-pole.

At the same instant a cheer from the crews of the Union vessels rang along the levee and up the Mississippi, as if to notify the loyal North that the navy had taken possession of the Government property in New Orleans.

The crowd in the streets was astounded, and for a moment silenced at the sight of our country's flag floating from the staff where lately the rebel ensign had waved. Perhaps they had still a lingering regard for the flag under which many of them had served in days of yore, and to which they had looked for protection. Their silence was but momentary, for presently loud shouts went up: "Pull it down!" "Trample it in the mud!" "Tear the vile rag to pieces!"

"The first man who lays a hand on that flag in my presence," said Bell, "will be shot down."

The crowd knew that he meant what he said, and, although they shrieked and yelled and threatened, they committed no overt act, but satisfied themselves with cursing the flag as if it did them a world of good.

Any one can be gallant in action, when the excitement of battle stirs him up to perform deeds of valor, but when men offer their lives by facing a furious mob, that requires heroism.

There were few men better qualified for such an emergency than Captain Bell—a man without bluster, but with a firm purpose to vindicate the authority of his Government. He led that forlorn hope as he had previously in a little four-gun steamer led his division past the batteries below New Orleans.

General Butler and his troops were in transports at Ship Island until Farragut had passed the forts. After the surrender I sent my steamers down to the bar and towed such of his vessels as I could get hold of up to garrison the two forts. Then I towed as many as I could to New Orleans, and the troops landed at the levee about a mile below the city.

When the troops marched into town they found the mob as quiet as possible, seeming to have no desire to come into collision with those grim Puritans, who were perfectly willing to bayonet any one resisting their authority.

Had Butler's transports been all steamers instead of being mostly sailing vessels, and had he followed the navy closely, he might have reached New Orleans in time to receive part of the honor due for its capture. As it was, General Butler's adherents attempted to monopolize the chief credit of the affair, and, in a work issued under authority of the War Department, as a record of the times, the only reference to the fall of New Orleans is that it was occupied by the troops under command of General Butler, April 30, 1862 (!).

After General Butler commenced to administer affairs at New Orleans, Farragut found himself altogether a secondary person. There was a number of shells in the arsenal which fitted the ship's guns, and Farragut sent an officer to get some of them. But the officer was very rudely told to go away and not meddle with things to which he had no right—that Butler had captured New Orleans, and that Farragut could exercise no authority there.

"Damn the fellow's impudence!" said the flag-officer when this rebuff was reported to him, which was about the severest expression he ever made use of.

The fact is, that not only was New Orleans captured by the navy without any assistance from General Butler or his forces, but it was only through the navy that the general maintained his authority in the city—a fact which he did not seem to appreciate.

Butler commenced his administration in a very vigorous manner, and there was never a conquered city that more needed a firm hand to govern it.

General Shepley, a lawyer of repute and a gentleman of ability, was appointed by Butler military governor of the city, and to him belongs the greater share of credit for the administration of affairs at New Orleans, although his superior officer managed to appropriate it for himself.

General Butler was no doubt very energetic in inflicting punishment, but I am of opinion that, had he left matters altogether in the hands of General Shepley, there would have been a happier condition of affairs, although it is true the people of New Orleans were a stiff-necked community, who seemed to delight in aggravating their conquerors.

Whatever may be said against General Butler's administration, it at least secured good order in a city notorious for the large number of desperate characters it contained; for the first time within the memory of man the city was everywhere clean and healthy.

Any one might walk the streets, by day or night, with perfect safety. At every corner was a Northern soldier, as stern and unyielding as one of Cromwell's Ironsides.

There was a secret police established, if not equal to that of Fouché, yet quite adequate to the occasion.

Commerce again began to show itself along the levees, and the stevedores, but lately part and parcel of the mob which ruled the hour, were tumbling cotton into vessels that had been towed up from the bar; like seabirds, they followed in the wake of the naval vessels to pick up the crumbs.

All was apparently as pleasant as a summer evening, when the moon was at its full and the sea-breeze rippling the water with its cool freshness.

The almighty Union dollar, with its beautiful engraved vignette and its look as if it was the true original, had almost immediately thrown into the shade its humbly dressed Confederate namesake worth about three cents—not enough to buy half a pint of gumbo-soup.

The crowd surged where the Union dollars were most abundant, and in a week, although merchant-vessels were not as plentiful as of yore, still there was an appearance of new life.

The people, however, were sulky, particularly the women, and the ladies would not associate with the Union officers, drew their dresses close to them when they passed a Northern soldier, and some of the less refined spat upon the ground to show their contempt of their enemies, and even mocked when Union soldiers were carried to their graves. However, these cases were exceptions, and General Butler left nothing undone to put a stop to such conduct.

His system was doubtless lacking in tact, and he would have saved himself a deal of trouble by not seeing too much. The most prominent disturbers of the peace were women, some of them supposed to be ladies, who, in their zeal for the Confederate cause, violated the proprieties of life. But it should have been taken into consideration that they were women, that it is the custom in this country to give them great latitude and to make for them every allowance, and that the consideration for them even extends to surrendering our seats in an omnibus!

I would have dealt with forbearance in such cases, except one, having satisfied myself of the expediency of humoring the gentler sex when there was no actual danger in so doing.

General Butler was not popular at New Orleans, although the city was never so clean, healthy, and orderly as under his *régime;* but when Banks relieved Butler the inhabitants soon wished the latter back again. Butler's rule, if severe, was consistent, and everybody knew what to expect, while Banks's administration showed less ability, and his ways subjected him to criticism, which was not wholly undeserved.

Like the Caliph Haroun al Raschid, Butler loved to prowl around at night and see for himself what was going on, and endeavor to entrap the governor, chief of police, or others of his subordinates. He had means of obtaining information that they did not possess, and it gave the general great delight to twit them with news he had obtained in advance of them.

Butler held court daily, and dealt out his sentences with unsparing hand. One day, after the session was over, he beckoned the chief of police to him and said : " Look here, captain, you have mistaken your business. I might as well have a log of wood on the police force. If you ever find anything out, I am none the wiser. I find out everything without your help. "

" I tell you everything of importance," replied the chief of police. " I don't trouble you with every trifle that comes under my notice. If I did, you would think me a gossip."

" Well, sir," said the general, " how are you to find out anything except through gossip ? I don't think you know anything to gossip about."

The captain smiled. " Ah, general," he said, " I know everything that occurs in New Orleans ; everybody's movements ; what more would you have ?"

"Bosh !" said Butler. "I don't believe it ; you had better say you know my movements."

"But, sir," replied the captain, "you are the commander-in-chief, and we don't pretend to know what you do."

"It is your business," said the general, "to know every one's movements. You are a humbug, sir, and I don't believe in you."

"I am sorry, sir, to have lost your confidence," said the chief of police ; "but, if it will afford you any satisfaction, I could tell every movement you have made in the past twenty-four hours."

"Where was I last night at ten o'clock ?" inquired the general.

"At General Shepley's, eating a terrapin supper," was the reply.

"At eleven o'clock ?" continued the general.

"Closeted with your brother at his quarters."

"At twelve o'clock ?" inquired Butler.

"Well, sir, you left your brother's at 11.15, went to No. 1,220 Canal Street, knocked at the door, which was opened by—"

"Shut up, d—n you !" thundered the irate general ; "you are too —— inquisitive. The time you spent in spying after me might have been devoted to some useful purpose. However, I am satisfied. But who shadows you, and who shadows the fellow that shadows you ? That's what I'd like to know."

One day the general was going to his office with only a single orderly following, when he saw two Union soldiers talking in a friendly manner with a man who was leaning on a spade, having evidently stopped work for the purpose of having a chat. The general was in citizen's dress, and therefore did not attract particular notice.

As he passed near the group he heard the man with the spade say, "We rebs gave you Yanks hell at Shiloh, didn't we ?"

The general was horrified to think that any one in his jurisdiction should dare to talk treason openly.

"Bring that man to my office !" roared the general to the soldiers. "I will make him eat his words."

The man with the spade protested that he meant no harm, but, in spite of all he could say, he was marched off to the general's office.

It was after two o'clock before the general got through with the docket of poor devils and had time to turn his attention to the

man with the spade, who, from the severity of the punishment
awarded his fellow-prisoners, began to think he had got into a
pretty bad scrape.

At length the general glared at him fiercely and inquired:
"What did I hear you say to those two soldiers? Tell the truth
now."

"Well, gin'ral," said the man, "I'm willin' yer honor should
know everything I said, an' I'm sure yer honor will agree with me
when yer hear what I really did say. Mike Donovan is not the
man to belie what he says, nivir the bit of it, yer honor."

"Well, then, speak out," said the general, "and tell me what
you said."

"All I said, gin'ral," replied Mike, "to thim two Union boys
wid whom I was talkin' friendly-like, was, 'Didn't we rebs give you
Yanks hell at Shiloh?' an' that's the whole ov it, gin'ral."

"And that speech," said the general, "will send you to work
for the Government with a ball and chain to your leg."

"Oh, howly Moses!" exclaimed Donovan, "an' what'll become
ov me wife and childer? I can't stand the work, and the muskeet-
ers will suck all the blood out ov me a-workin' in the foorts; bitter
the day that I left the bogs of auld Ireland. Forgive me, gin'ral,
for the sake ov me wife and childer."

"You ought to have thought of your family before you made
treasonable speeches under the Union flag," said the general. "You
know the Bible says the sins of the father shall be visited on the
children."

"But, gin'ral, is there nothing I can say," said the man, "to do
away wid your displeasure? I'll worruk the skin off me hands if
ye'll let me sarve out me sintince here an' not sind me to the foorts."

"No," replied the general, "I make no terms with such a traitor
as yourself; however, there is one thing that may save you. Will
you take the oath of allegiance to the United States?" for General
Butler considered the taking of the oath a panacea for all evils;
any one who took it was, as it were, born again.

"Oh, yis, yer honor," said the man, his face brightening up;
"faith, an' I'll take it iron-clad, or copper fastened, or any other
kind of oath to get out of this trouble, an' I'll kape it, too."

The Bible was brought out, and Mr. Donovan took his solemn
oath to be faithful to the Union and serve with heart and soul in
her hour of need, probably with a reservation in favor of the stars
and bars, for which he had lately been so enthusiastic.

When this important ceremony was concluded the newly made patriot turned to the general and said, " Now I'm a Union man and no mistake, ain't I ? "

" Yes, you are," replied the general, " and take care you keep your oath, or I will hang you."

" Divil a bit there's a break in me," said Donovan. " I'm intitled to all the pertection av the Government, ain't I ? "

" Certainly," said the general.

" An' I'm to be pertected in free spache like any other Union man ? "

" Yes, yes," replied the general.

" Well, thin, gin'ral, yer honor, I want to ask yer honor wan question, if yer honor plazes."

" Out with it," said the general, " for I can't stand here all the morning bothering with your affairs."

" Well, thin, gin'ral, yer honor," said Mike, " didn't thim rebs give us Yanks hell at Shiloh ? "

The general collapsed. " Get out of this quick, and don't let me ever hear you say 'Shiloh' again, or you may find your way to the forts yet, notwithstanding your oath of allegiance."

Mr. Donovan did not wait for a second invitation, but slipped off to join his " wife and childer," and the general, although rather amused at the incident, cautioned the police to keep an eye on this newly fledged Union man.

There was no apparent Union feeling in New Orleans when we captured it. There may have been isolated cases of persons who still had a love for the Union of their fathers, but the only person whom I ever knew to extend the hand of welcome to a Union officer was the late William H. Hunt, afterward Secretary of the Navy and Minister to Russia.

He was outspoken in his friendship for the Union men, but it lost him the good-will of the residents of New Orleans, and after the war he was obliged to move North on account of the social pressure against him.

I met people in the street whom I had formerly known intimately, but they passed me as if I were a stranger. Any manifestation of Union feeling would have been encouraging, but there was not enough to raise a flutter.

I had some old friends in the city, with whom I had been accustomed to stay when I was there, and of whom I was very fond.

As soon as I could find time I procured protection papers for these friends—at that period a matter of great importance—and, armed with these, I went in pursuit of them.

I found the house just as when I was last there, a few years before, and in a neighborhood so quiet that it would seem that the sounds of war could never penetrate there.

The blinds were drawn, but I did not think anything of that, as New Orleans ladies are proud of their complexions, and I thought they might wish to show themselves to the best advantage in a subdued light.

There was no answer to my knock at the door, although I knew the family were in the house. I continued knocking until people in the neighborhood, attracted by the unusual noise in that quiet street, began to look from their windows. At last, in despair of getting an answer, I put my hand on the knob, the door opened, and I walked in.

I saw no one in the lower part of the house until I reached the kitchen, where the cook, an old acquaintance, was seated, pipe in mouth, beside the hearth.

"Milly," said I, "don't you know me?"

"No, sar, nebber seed you befo'," was the reply.

"Where's your old mistress?" I inquired.

"She ain't har, sar; she done gone out."

"Where is Miss Mary, then?"

"She done gone out too."

"Where are the rest of the family?"

"Dey is all done gone out, sar, as you kin see fo' yourse'f."

"Where have they gone?"

"Don't know noffin' 'bout it, sar," said Milly.

"And you say you don't know me, Milly?" I inquired.

"No, sar, nebber seen you afore in my born days, do I specs youse one ob dem Union folks what's come here to kill us all."

"Now, Milly," I said, "I believe you are lying, and that the family are at home. Go tell them I am here, and shall not leave until I see them."

"Dey don't know you, sar," said Milly, "kase youse de enemy ob dar country."

"Oh, that's it, is it? Very well, I will sit in the parlor until I see the family if I have to stay there a week," I said.

"Dey is done gone away for two week," said the old darkey, "and won't nebber come back s'long as you is here." So saying, she knocked the ashes from her pipe and disappeared into the wash-room.

At that moment a parrot, from his perch in the kitchen, broke out into a hoarse laugh, whistled, flapped his wings, and yelled out, "*Que voulez-vous?*" That was the straw that broke the camel's back, and I retreated from the inhospitable kitchen and took a seat in the parlor.

For half an hour I waited, but not a sound met my ear. At length a little nigger, with nothing on but a shirt, poked his head in the door, then vanished as if he had seen a ghost.

At the expiration of another half-hour a superannuated dog, whom I had known well in former days and with whom I was once a favorite, looked into the apartment, fixed his blear eyes on me for a moment, dropped his head, and walked away with the hairs on his back bristling up.

Still I sat there; the time passed so slowly it seemed as if I had been there for hours. I picked up a guitar from the corner and played an air well known to the family. I heard a discordant laugh, and, looking up, saw the parrot hobbling in. It sang out, "*Que voulez-vous?*" and out it went again, screaming.

I was in despair. Neither cook, dog, parrot, or little nigger would have anything to do with me.

Presently I heard the rustle of a dress on the stair, and in sailed a graceful woman, once a warm friend. I arose, extended my hand, and exclaimed, "I am delighted to see you."

The lady was as stiff and cold as Lot's wife when turned into the pillar of salt.

"I can't shake hands with an enemy of my country," she said. "How do I know but what one of your bomb-shells has fallen on the head of one of my sons, who are gloriously fighting for their beloved country?"—one boy was thirteen years old and the other eleven!

"How came you to let them go?" I inquired.

"They ran away," she replied, "to the forts, to help keep Farragut's fleet from the city."

"A forlorn hope, my good friend," said I; "but you need fear nothing: boys of that tender age would be well cared for by the officers, and not allowed to expose themselves."

"I am not your *good friend*," said the lady. "I am your enemy, and ma told me to say that if you had come here wounded and dying, she wouldn't have given you a glass of water."

"Shocking!" I exclaimed; "but I don't believe a word of it. If I had come here wounded, your mother would have been the first to hunt me up and attend me.   Now listen to me," I continued ; "all this talk of yours is nonsense and very unbecoming. You are too kind-hearted a woman to express such sentiments. You have committed a certain part to memory like that parrot of yours, and don't mean half you say."

She began to cry.   Get a woman to crying, and her enmity is half conquered.   Tears open the fountain of the heart.   In half an hour we were as good friends as ever.   I pressed upon her General Butler's protection, which I thought the family might need. Although at first she was opposed to touching the papers, yet when I told her they meant safety from domiciliary visits, guardianship of the police, bread and meat in case of scarcity of provisions, etc., she was satisfied.

This lady was the only member of the family who would see me, though I knew they were all up-stairs.

When I went away I said, " We shall not meet again, for I shall not subject myself to another rebuff such as I have this day experienced, and I have no doubt you will all regret your action."

" No," she replied, " we are determined to hold no intercourse with our enemies, no matter what happens, and I know ma will never forgive me for being so friendly with you.   Don't come here again, for it is painful to us all to meet you."

I departed, sad enough to see the minds of people whom I knew to be as good and kind as any in the world so warped by their secession sentiments, about the merits of which they had not the faintest idea.   They were afflicted with a madness for which there was no antidote at hand.

> "Old Clootie was with them ; he said all was right.
> *He* held the bottle and urged on the fight."

I did not see my secession friends for a long time afterward.

Soon after the fall of Vicksburg, on July 4, 1863, I proceeded in my flag-ship Black Hawk to New Orleans, in order that Admiral Farragut might turn over to me the command of the entire Mississippi River and its tributaries.

On the second night of my arrival in New Orleans I was sitting in the cabin, when Fleet-Captain Breese came in and informed me that an elderly lady wished to see me.   "From what I have heard you say," he continued, " I think it must be your old friend Mrs. ——."

I went at once into the forward cabin, and found it was indeed my old friend who a year ago had thought so hardly of me.

As I entered the cabin she rushed toward me, but I stood unmoved, bowed formally, and said, "I am the admiral, madam; can I be of any service to you?"

"Why," exclaimed the lady, "am I so changed that you do not recognize me? Why, I am Mrs. ——, your old friend who always loved you like a son."

"Impossible, madam," I replied. "You can not be Mrs. ——. Why, the last time I was here in 1862 she wouldn't see me, although I called at her house to offer her assistance and protection. She sent me word by her daughter that if I had come to her wounded and dying she wouldn't have given me a cup of water to quench my thirst."

"Oh, no!" she exclaimed, "I never said that—never, never! We are all Union people now; we are no longer Confederates. Pierre has a twelve-hundred-dollar clerkship in the post-office, Walter has a nine-hundred-dollar place in the custom-house, George is in the Commissary-General's office, James is a clerk on the levee to register cargo from Government steamers, and Harry is in the Signal Service. We were never so well off in our lives before. I have my pension, which I couldn't get while the rebels held the city, and Mary and Emma have both a promise for the place of folders in the post-office within the next month. Oh, we are all for the Union and the old flag!

"And then," continued the old lady, "New Orleans is so beautiful now; it is clean as a new pin, there is no sickness, you never see a drunken man, there are no gambling-houses to entice young men from home, the markets are so cheap, and the streets are so orderly that a woman can walk them alone at any hour of the night. Yes, we are all Union. Cousin Le Bert is to be appointed solicitor of something, I don't know exactly what, and uncle La Blas is to be Captain of the Port. Oh, what a happy Union family we are!

"And it is so lovely here now!" went on the old lady. "General Banks is such a handsome man and Mrs. Banks such a lovely woman, and they keep up such style, and ride in a splendid carriage with a body-guard just like royalty. Mrs. Banks has her weekly receptions at the St. Charles, and all the best ladies appear there in laces and diamonds. They say Queen Victoria don't have anything to equal it.

"And then, too, Cousin Le Febre is going to become Union as soon as he can get the position of steamboat inspector, and—"

There is no knowing how long the old lady would have run on had I not interrupted her.

"Well," I said at last, "my dear old friend, since you have become Union and love the flag under which all of us were born, come to my arms. I don't believe you ever said what they accused you of. You can thank your stars that you are living once more under the folds of the star-spangled banner, and that you have a beneficent Government that will provide offices for all the family and secure to you a pension for the services of your gallant husband, who would have died sooner than raise a hand against his old flag."

"Ah, yes," sighed the old lady, "he was Union all over, but there was no craziness in the air then; everybody was happy, everybody had an office, and all the widows had pensions."

"My dear friend," said I, "that's the only way to preserve the Union; give every one a fat office, and they will stick to the flag until it blows away. That was the difficulty with half the people; they had to go out of office and see the other half come in, and, not liking to give up the loaves and fishes, they established an office for each one of themselves. I think your idea of keeping up the Union is the correct one. Still you have been guilty of an oversight in not securing offices for that old dog of yours and that intelligent parrot; they seem to have been left out in the cold."

"Ah, yes," said Mrs. ——, "you remember them, do you? Well, worse people than they have been appointed to office."

"I hope both of them are loyal to the Union," said I.

"Yes," she replied, "the dog will bark at a rebel soldier, and the parrot can say *Vive la bagatelle !*"

Next day my old friend and all her grandchildren, nephews, nieces, sisters, cousins, and aunts dined with me and insisted on having the Union flag festooned over the doors so that they might show their Union feeling by walking underneath. They all seemed contented and happy. I am satisfied that if, at the commencement of the war, every man in the rebel army had been given an office, and all the widows in the Confederacy a pension, the revolution would not have lasted a week.

New Orleans was a prolific field for anecdotes of the war, but my limits will not permit me to linger here any longer, and, as these reminiscences are simply for amusement and not for the purpose of exciting unkind feeling, I will pass on.

CHAPTER VIII.

ASCENDING THE MISSISSIPPI—ODD SPECIMENS OF CONFEDERATES —A PLANTATION MANSION—DOUBTING MOSES.

WHILE ascending the Mississippi on my way to join Farragut at Vicksburg, I had a good opportunity of witnessing the disposition of the people along the river. Notwithstanding our desire to be friends with them, they would have nothing to do with us—they were mad with the secession fever. As to the women, they were very Spartans in the secession cause; in fact, rather overdid the matter.

One day, while turning a bend in the river with two schooners in tow of my vessel, a boat containing two men was seen crossing the river ahead of us. We had just been fired upon by field-pieces from a high bluff, and several of our men had been killed and wounded. I wanted to find out the name of the place, so that I could warn our vessels to be on their guard when they reached that point and have their batteries ready. We, having a mortar-vessel on each side of our steamers, could not respond to such attacks, and had to bear them as best we could.

I captured the boat and brought the two men on board my vessel. Far from showing any fear, these persons were as defiant as possible. They were coarsely dressed in linsey-woolsey, wore slouch hats, and had the appearance of laborers.

"I'd like to know," said one of them, "how you dare captur' a peaceable citizen of the Confed'rit States who ain't done nothin' to you. This is a highway, and I think we have a right to travel it."

"Walk down in the cabin, gentlemen," I said, "and take some refreshments."

"We ain't no gentlemen," said the man, "an' we don't want none of your dam' refreshments. We've got a gallon of whisky good enough for an emperor in our dug-out, an' we don't want any of your molasses and water. Zeke an' I have taken four drinks already since we left the store."

The last statement accounted for their belligerent attitude.

"Well, then, gentlemen," I said, "may I at least have the pleasure of knowing your names."

"I told you," said the man, "that we ain't no gentlemen; we

are Confed'rit citizens; but, if it'll do you any good, my name is Jake Potter, and this other feller is Zeke Opdyke."

"Well, Jake," said I, "you and Zeke are not Confederate soldiers, are you?"

"I'm Jake to my friends," said the man, "but you an' I ain't intimate enough for you to call me Jake. My name's Mr. Potter when you speak to me."

"And I," spoke up the other, "am Mr. Opdyke when I'm taken outer my boat an' my w'isky-jug left in thar for yer dam sailors to suck. I seen one just now pokin' his long nose inter it."

I acknowledged the force of the rebuke. "Well, Mr. Potter," said I, "I suppose you are an out-and-out rebel."

"You bet I am," replied that worthy.

"And me, too," said Mr. Opdyke, "though day afore yesterday I was on the fence."

"And pray, sir, if I may inquire, what caused you to change your sentiments?"

"Well, then, Kurnel," said Mr. Opdyke, "if you must know, the Confed'rit Gov'ment hired my wagon-team at three dollars a day, an' I jined 'em right off."

"They pay you in Confederate money, I suppose," was my next remark.

"What 'n thunder do you s'p'ose they'd pay me in, Kurnel?" inquired Mr. Opdyke. "You don't suppose I'd take that Union trash, worth only eighty cents on the dollar, while ourn is worth a hundred an' twenty, do ye?"

"Well, Mr. Potter," I said, turning to the other man, "where were you born?"

"Now, Kurnel, it strikes me you are gittin' a leetle too inquisitive, but, if it'll do you any good, I was born in East Haddam, Con-.necticut."

"And Mr. Opdyke?" I inquired.

"Well," he said, "not more'n a yard from the same place."

"And you have joined the rebels heart and soul?" I inquired.

"You bet we have," they both replied at once.

"How long have you been South, Mr. Potter?" I asked.

"Wall, I don't know as I'm bound to crimernate myself, but I don't mind tellin' you I've been here goin' on two year. We two come South together, but we ain't a goin' to answer any more questions s' long as we're pris'ners."

"You are not prisoners," I said ; "we don't make war on un-armed men or women."

"The devil you don't," said Mr. Opdyke ; "if some of them bummers of yourn didn't steal all the chickens off Mrs. Clapham's plantation last night, then I'll be fizzled !"

That rather took me aback ; but, quickly recovering, I said, "Can you tell me the name of the vessel that perpetrated such an outrage ?"

"She was called the Sally Brown," replied Mr. Opdyke.   ("It is the Sarah Bruen," whispered one of the officers to me.)

"Yes," continued Mr. Potter, "them fellers on board the Sally Brown tuk a lot of water without askin' fur it, an' now, if you don't call that makin' war on defenseless people, I dunno what you do call it."

"But," said I, "didn't the people in the Sally Brown pay for the chickens ?"

"Wall, yes," said Mr. Opdyke, "sich pay as it was ; they only gin six dollars, an' Union dollars at that, for a dozen chickens, while all along the river they charges six Confed'rit dollars for one chicken."

At this statement we all laughed, much to the annoyance of the Southern sympathizers. "You larf now, Kurnel," said Mr. Potter, "but you'll larf t'other side of yer mouth afore you git to Vicks-burg.   Kirby Smith'll pickle you about twenty miles above here."

"Thank you, Mr. Potter, for your information," I said, "we will try to be ready for him."

"Oh, he'll larf at them ole iron pots of yourn," said Mr. Potter, pointing to the mortars.

"Well, Mr. Potter, please tell me how long you resided in Con-necticut."

"Now, Kurnel," said Mr. Potter, "I don't know as that's any-thing to you, but I don't mind tellin' you I was there, man an' boy, fur twenty-nine year."

"And you, Mr. Opdyke ?"

"Well," he replied, "I lived there twenty-seven year."

"And do you mean to tell me that you two gentlemen, after living in your native State twenty-nine and twenty-seven years, re-spectively, after forming the dearest ties and associations, can come South and in two short years be won over by these people —one of you by hiring his cart, the other for I don't know what ?"

"Wall, Kurnel," said Mr. Potter, "you talk durned well, but

all them hifalutin' words is wasted on me ; if you had married a wildcat widder, with a wildcat darter sixteen years old, an' Jeff Davis a backin' on 'em up, you wouldn't a stood out an hour. I stuck it out for three days an' nights, a sittin' out in the rain, before I became a Confed'rit."

"Yes," interrupted Mr. Opdyke, "the ole woman kep' a double-barrel gun handy for him, an' says she, 'Jake, don't you move till you're ready to become one of us, or I'll work some button-holes in your dam' Yankee carcase !'"

"And what made you surrender, Mr. Potter ?" I inquired.

"Why," replied that worthy, "when Zeke he come over to fetch me some whisky, my old woman she run out and smashed the bottle over Zeke's head, an' then, when I was most starved an' begged for suthin to eat, she sent me a bowl o' hot water with a chicken-feather in it. 'Thar,' says she, 'that 'ere chicken-soup is all you'll git till you h'ist the Confed'rit flag.' So I had to cave in. Zeke can tell you what I went through with ; you wouldn't have stood it half a day, Kurnel, I know it by the cut of your jib."

"But how did you come to marry such a woman, Mr. Potter ?" said I, sympathetically.

"Ah," replied the victim, "the Lord only knows. Zeke can tell you all about it, but it overcomes me to think of it, unless I have a drink of w'isky."

I ordered the steward to bring up what was called on board "vinegar bitters," but which I could not help suspecting was something stronger.

Mr. Potter smacked his lips as he took the medicine. "That there stuff is real ole Union, an' no mistake. It held me back some time afore I'd think of jinin' the Confed'rits, for fear I'd never be able to go back an' have a fling at the old critter. But you can call us Jake an' Zeke now, Kurnel, as much as you please. I ain't a goin' to stand on ceremony with a feller as keeps such likker as that, an' a man as sympathizes with another as you done with me. Why, if I'd a bin yer brother you couldn't a took more interest in my case. Tell the kurnel all about it, Zeke."

"Yes," said his friend, "just as soon as I get a mouthful of them bitters to sustain me while I relate that melancholy story ov your marryin' that durned alligator, as goes cavortin' round the house as if she owned all the guaner islands in the Pacific Ocean.

"Well, you must know, Kurnel, me an' Jake was hired hands on Mrs. Rumpkins's place. We was hired the day old Rumpkins died to help handle the coffin, an' two weeks arter I hearn that gal of hern say, 'Ma, I'm tired a totin' wood an' feedin' the cow, an' we must have a man ter do it.'

" 'Well,' said Mrs. Rumpkins, 'hain't we got two men ? Make one of 'em tote wood ; they kin do it when they comes to their meals.'

" 'I asked one of 'em,' said Belle, 'an' he tole me he'd see me durned first. We don't want that kind of a man, ma ; we want a married man ; we cau do as we please with a good-natered feller like ole Pop, who can't get away if we crowd him. You must marry Jake or Zeke. If you don't I will, an' I'd like to hear him say then that he'll see me durned first.'

" 'You're crazy, Belle,' says the ole catamount. 'Your pop's only dead two weeks, an' you want me to marry agin.'

" 'Well, then,' says Belle, 'say three weeks an' bring him to the halter, for I ain't a goin' to tote no more wood, nor feed no more cow arter that.'

" 'Well, I agree to that,' says old Mrs. Rumpkins.

" 'Cos if you don't,' said Belle, 'I'll marry one on 'em myself, an' we'll see who is mistress then.'

" I wish you could a seen how Mrs. Rumpkins laid out her lines. You seen a cat watchin' a canary-bird, ain't you ? an' how the critter crawls up an' purrs soft as a Jew's-harp, an' then you seen the little bird jumpin' round all in a twitter, an' how at last, when the canary clings with its claws to the wires of its cage, Mrs. Cat grabs him, an' he's a goner.

" That's the way Mrs. Rumpkins done. Says she, ' Belle, I'll take Jake. I don't like that other feller ; he eats too much, an' I'll get rid of him.' So she piled it up sweet on Jake until he didn't know his alphabet from the multiplication table, an' then she lassoed him. You seen 'em catch cattle in Texas ? They have a long lariat, an' throw it over the critter's horns goin' full split, an' bring him up all standin'. Now Mrs. Rumpkins uses her long, oily tongue for a lariat, an' so wound it round poor Jake he couldn't a tole who he was ; then, when he was quiet as an old horse with a cart-load of bricks behind him, she marches him off to Squire Spanker's office.

" 'Here, Squire,' says she, 'is a man wot owes me reparation, an' I'll pay the two dollars fur the marriage ceremony, an' here's the same ring as poor, dear Rumpkins put on my finger, an' I'll use it agin. This 'ere feller is a Yank, an' I want him to see that he can't come down here an' win the affections of a lone widder, an' then go off an' larf at her.'

"'Well, sir,' says the squire to Jake, 'what have you got to say to these here charges?'

"'Donno!' says Jake.

"'Well, then, stan' up an' be married, or else be drafted into the Confed'rit army,' says the squire. So they was married then an' there, an' the widder tuk his arm an' toted him home, au' says she, 'Now, Jake, afore you get a bit of weddin'-cake, tote in the wood for the day, an' mix the feed for the cow.' Jake obeyed orders, an' has been the most successful husband I ever see. The only time he ever showed a disposition to kick was when they wanted him to turn Confed'rit, an' then the ole woman went for Jake with a shot-gun. Now that's the whole story. We are both Confeds, an' you can't help us. Belle's got her eye on me, an' I'd no more dare desert than nothin'!'"

All this time Jake said nothing, but looked very melancholy.

"Well, Mr. Potter," I said, "you must keep up your spirits; worse things have happened to people, and they have lived to get over it."

"Yes," said the victim, "I might a-married 'em both to onct, an' then what would I do but jine the Confed'rit army, an' git a Union bullet through me?"

While all this was going on we had proceeded some distance up the river. I therefore recommended that the two men should go home, for fear Mrs. Potter would come after them. So they bade us good-by, and stepped into their skiff with rather sorrowful faces. Mr. Potter's last words were, "Kurnel, don't forget to say, all along the river, what all-fired rebels we two fellers are. If I warn't afeard the old woman would hear me—for she has ears as long as a telegraph-pole—I'd hip, hip, hurrah! for the old flag; but it can't be did."

Mr. Potter's experience was a sad commentary on the matrimonial state; but Mrs. Rumpkins must not be taken as a representative Southern woman, for the women of the South, though of Spartan character and willing to suffer everything rather than sacrifice their opinions, have generally much gentleness and refinement.

That night we tied up to the bank at —— Landing, where some of the bomb-vessels, alias "bummers," had preceded me.

When I arrived the levee was all lighted up by the bonfires

which the negroes had kindled, which brought out in relief the dusky forms of four or five hundred of the colored population, together with the mansion of the owner of the estate, and the cabins of the negroes.

On the front porch of the mansion were collected the gentlefolks, their faces exhibiting some wonder and alarm.

As soon as the vessels were secured to the bank, we landed about a hundred armed sailors and marched them to the rear of the houses, as a precaution against an attack by guerrillas or light artillery, which had begun to infest the banks of the river.

I sent an officer at once to inform the lady of the mansion—for I was told there were only ladies there—that she need be under no apprehensions, as these were only sentries thrown out to keep the sailors from wandering about her place.

In the mean time the negroes were so jubilant and boisterous that they could not restrain themselves; they danced about like mad, and scattered the fire so that I began to fear the buildings would be ignited from the flying sparks; so I went on shore to have a talk with them. All the negroes rushed up to me like wild men. Some wanted to shake hands, some to sell chickens—"only half dollar 'piece, massa"; some women wanted to know if I had "any clo' fo' wash—only dollar dozen, sah," while the pickaninnies were turning somersaults almost into the fire.

"Look here," I exclaimed, "this won't do. You are disturbing the ladies at the house with your noise, and we can't sleep on board the vessels with all this howling going on."

"Oh, de ladies don't mine de noise, Massa Capen; dis is our night (Saturday), when de work all done," said a dozen voices, "an' we want to ax you, sah, if you won't go coon-huntin'?"

"No, I thank you," said I; "but I'll tell you what I would like : bring your banjos, and sing me a plantation song."

No sooner said than done ; three or four banjos, together with bones and other accompaniments, were produced. I knew if I could get the party to singing they would quiet down in a short time, music has such an effect on them.

I sent for the ship's bugler, and told him to stand by to play "Home, Sweet Home" when I gave the order, the negroes all this time keeping up a great chattering, and seeming unable to agree upon a programme, until a venerable darkey, in a voice of authority, sang out, "Look hyar, you niggers! don' make fools of yerse'fs, an' make dese gentlemen tink yer got no more manners 'an a groun' hog!" at which speech the negroes all yelled, "Bully for you, Uncle Moses!"

At that moment the bugler struck up "Home, Sweet Home," and you might have heard a pin drop. The only music these simple-minded darkies had probably ever heard was that of the banjo. They sat on the ground, eyes and mouth wide open, while old Moses held up his finger, as if to enforce silence.

The bugler played until he was tired, when an unusually soft "Ah!" came from the crowd; the ladies on the porch clapped their hands.

"Now, bucks," exclaimed Uncle Moses, "dat's wot I calls music; better you all shut up shop and put yer ole banjos on de fire dar; yer can't come nothin' like dat ober us. Yer mere infan's, I done tell yer."

"Uncle Moses," said I, "don't discourage the boys. That bugle music is a signal for all the sailors to go to bed and get some rest, for they must work hard to-morrow. They want to hear you sing 'Mary Blane,' and after that you must all go home and keep quiet."

"Dat's de kine ob talk dey wants, Massa Capen," said old Moses. "Now, bucks, sit down and open yer music-boxes, an' grease de cog-wheels afore yer begin."

A hundred voices, men and women, now joined in and sang the negro melody in glorious fashion. It was the music of nature given by these untaught negroes. "Mary Blane" rang in my ears long afterward, and I could not sleep for thinking of it.

After the negroes had finished their song I said to Uncle Moses, "I have heard music in the best opera-houses in the world, but I never heard anything better than that."

"Fo' de Lawd, you done spoil dem niggers, Massa Capen," said old Moses. "Dey was wain enuff befo,' an' now dey'll be greasin' each other's faces an' usin' 'em for lookin'-glasses to see how pretty dey is."

"Moses," said I, "you seem to have great control over these people. Are you going to lead them out of captivity as your name-sake of the Bible led the Israelites out of bondage?"

"Well, Massa Capen," replied the old negro, "dese ere niggers is like de Israelites ob ole in many respecs. If dere is a chicken on a roost anywhere in de country dey will fine 'em out, an' dey is a stiff-neck people, dat goes wrong nine times to one time right. Dey is a great trouble to me, sar. Dey talks about fightin' for de

Unyum an' Massa Abe Linkum, an' dey knows as much 'bout fi'tin' as a mule knows about playin' de banjo. Dey is just fit to fight coons an' 'possums, but if dey was to meet a sojer wid a musket dar shirt-tails would shiver in de wind wid de speed dey'd make. Dey don't know what dey want, an', like de Israelites ob ole, dey is tryin' all kind ob speriments. I wish you'd talk to 'em, Massa Capen, and splain to 'em what dey ought to do. You know, sar, what one ob de pooks say; I hear ole massa often tellin' it: 'Better bear wid a ole coat ef it is full ob holes dan go roun' in your shirt-sleebes in winter-time lookin' for a new one.' When you kin get a dish ob hog an' hominy fer dinner, better not leab it to look for somethin' better. Dat's wot I calls filosophy."

"Uncle Moses," said I, "you are wise beyond your generation. But tell me something about your mistress."

"Well, sar," said Uncle Moses, "she is a uncommon agreeable pusson, though sometimes a leetle aggravatin'. She likes to hab her own way, an' as I hab charge ob all dese bucks, I likes to hab mine; so occasionally we has disputes."

"Dispute with your mistress! why, she has a right to her own way, and you should see that she has it," I said.

"Sartin, sar, so I do; but yesterday missus was real aggravatin'. She say dar was a hole in de fence, an' I say dar was a hole in de fence, an' we 'sputed about it mor'n a hour."

"Why, Uncle Moses," said I, "that was a silly thing to dispute about."

"P'r'aps so, Massa Capen, but it ain't no more silly dan what you gemplems ob de Norf an' gemplems ob de Souf been a doin'. De Souf say dar was a hole in de fence, an' de Norf say dere was a hole in de fence, an' after 'sputin' about it a long time, now dey go to shootin' about it."

"Uncle Moses," said I, "you don't understand it. We are disputing about the great principles of universal liberty."

"Yes," said the philosopher, "I knows dat. I hear 'em talkin' a great deal about de niggers will have suffrins at de poles fo' long, but I seen enough nigger suffrins, an' don't want to see no more of 'em."

"Why, Uncle Moses, you talk doubtfully, and I am really afraid you are not sound on the goose."

"Yes, I know, Massa Capen, dey calls me doubtin' Moses, an' I hab my own 'pinions. If I had my way I'd be on de Canada side: de colored man is safe dar, an' no mistake. As to de equality ob de races I hear 'em talk about, why, some ob our bucks run away an' 'listed board a gun-boat, an' spected to be treated just like white men. Dey put dose bucks to shubbel coal an' workin' before a hot fire, an' didn't eben gib um good hog an' hominy."

"Oh," said I, "that's only a beginning. They'll do better by and by."

"An' in de mean time," said Moses, "dey is to be purified wid fire an' water. Some ob dem fellers from Massa Linkum's gun-boats tells de bucks if dey sabe de Unyum dey'll come out some day in Congress. Yes, I knows, but dey'll be brushin' de white man's coats de same as dey been doin' all dere lives. White man an' colored man two different tings; one eat turkey an' de odder hog an' hominy all he bo'n days. Ole massa was de fust ob our family what went to de war, an' he fout de enemy to de las', but a rifle kill him."

"A rifle, Uncle Moses?" I inquired.

"Yes, sah," said Moses, "a demijohn ob rifle w'isky what was made on dis place. Ole massa taught me a good deal; he was a poeck, he was."

We now walked toward the house. Uncle Moses stepped to the door and announced me.

I heard a pleasant voice say, "Ask the gentleman in, Moses," and I entered.

Before me was a stately lady of perhaps forty years of age, still handsome, with large black eyes and dark hair.

I excused myself for intruding upon her so late in the evening, but explained that I could not call earlier on account of having so much to attend to on board the vessels.

"You are excusable, sir," said Mrs. ——, "and I am glad you have come, that I might thank you for the precautions you have taken to prevent marauding. My servants have not been so orderly before for a long time. They are out coon-hunting sometimes until nearly daylight in the morning, and their cries keep the family awake half the night. They are not a bad set of people though, and, if they had a master, could be easily managed, but a woman, of course, can do little to control them. Moses is seventy years old, and is not of much use now in helping govern the negroes, and he is for ever disputing with me about trifles."

At that moment a door opened, and a youth of about nineteen rushed into the room in a great state of excitement.

"Mother!" he exclaimed, "I am too late; they have surrounded the house, and I can't get back. I shall be taken prisoner."

Just then he caught sight of me, and stood at bay. He was a handsome fellow, with a strong likeness to his mother, and had on a gray suit, which was nearly concealed by a linen duster.

"What do you want here, sir," said the youth, defiantly ; "why intrude upon unprotected women ?"

"They are certainly not unprotected," I said, "with such a brave defender as you by their side. I simply called to pay my respects to the lady of the mansion, and to thank her for permission to land at her plantation."

"Which you took good care to do before asking permission," said the young man, with flashing eyes.

"George ! George !" exclaimed his mother, "this gentleman has done nothing that we can possibly find fault with, so be careful what you say. He may relieve you from your difficulty."

The boy still stood defiant, like a stag at bay, his hands clenched and his eye glittering with anger.

"Of course, dear mother," he said, "I don't intend to be discourteous to this officer, who, notwithstanding his bland manners, has surrounded the house and holds us all prisoners. If I had our battery here we'd clear the Yanks out in ten minutes."

"O George !" pleaded his mother, "you will ruin yourself and break my heart. Excuse me, sir, but he is my only son."

"Who is perfectly safe with me, madam, for I assure you I have not the least idea of molesting him."

"Then let me pass through your lines," said the young man ; "prove your expressions true by your acts. I must go or be dishonored."

Just then a young girl entered the room. She looked like a panther about to spring. "They are not going to take George, mother ! What does this mean ?" she said, and her eyes flashed fire.

There was no need to ask if these young people were brother and sister, their likeness to each other was so striking. I looked at them in admiration, and could not help wishing myself the young lady's brother, to call forth such affection from such a lovely specimen of womanhood.

"There is no occasion for alarm, young lady," I said. "I shall not trouble myself to capture unarmed persons, even although they may choose to wear a uniform which is not the most agreeable to Northern eyes."

"It is the uniform of my country," said the young man, "and I am not ashamed of it."

"Then," I said, "if you wish to honor it—and belong, as possibly you may, to 'Whistler's Battery,' now some twenty miles above here—let me advise you never to sully your honor by firing at unarmed steamers ; war is a dreadful thing at best—make it as merciful as you can.   For my part, I shall endeavor while this conflict lasts not to molest persons who may be apparently following peaceful pursuits.   Vindictive warfare can only result in embittering people.   If you know of any persons who are about to engage in hostilities against my command, say to them that when I leave this landing I shall tow the schooners in line ahead.   The schooners carry thirty-eight heavy guns, and the steamers that tow them forty-two.   To attack them with field-pieces would be a piece of gasconade, for I could sweep a dozen batteries from off the earth, and our shells might set fire to distant houses whose inmates had no idea of injuring us.   And now, sir, for your mother's and sister's sake you may take your horse and go."

"Well, sir," said the youngster, "my hand will fire no shot at you or yours, and I will report what you have said."

I raised the window and signaled to the patrol.   "Let this gentleman pass with his horse.—Good-night, sir, and a pleasant journey to you."

The young man took leave of his mother and sister, bowed to me, and in a few minutes his horse's hoofs were heard as he galloped down the road.

The mother thanked me for permitting her son to depart.

"I could have done you a greater favor by sending him north as a prisoner," I replied ; "it might have saved his life ; he is too young for such adventures."

I bade the ladies good-night, hoping I had at least planted one seed toward reconciliation.

Next morning Moses and his "bucks" were at the levee to see us off.   "Keep your bucks in order, Moses," I said.   "I shall be back here soon, and, if I find they haven't behaved themselves, will set them to shoveling coal."

"Ah, Massa Capen," said the philosopher, "I kin punish 'em worse dan dat.   I stops dar bacon an' hominy an' terbacker.   If dese niggers don't behave themselves, they shan't see de sight ob a chicken, an' if dere's anyt'ing a nigger do lub, it's de sight ob a chicken on de roost."

"And don't dispute with your mistress any more, Uncle Moses."

"Well, sar," he replied, "we done had a 'spute already dis mornin'. I said you was a Unyum ossifer, an' she say you was a Unyum ossifer, an' we 'spute about it ober a hour. God bless you, Massa Capen, an' see dat dey don' gib us po' niggers any more suffrins at de poles."

We were not molested in our progress up the river, and in due time reached Vicksburg, where Farragut was awaiting us to commence operations against the forts.

I will here mention that the young fellow to whom I have alluded was killed at the battle of Mansfield, on Red River, when General Banks and myself went up that stream in the spring of 1864. On a subsequent visit to the plantation I found the mother and sister plunged in grief. This was only one of many instances where young lives were thrown away in a hopeless cause.

Uncle Moses had proved true to his trust, but all his young "bucks" had gone on the warpath, joining the army as teamsters or enlisting on board "Mr. Linkum's gun-boats."

"Massa Capen," said Moses, "the Unyum Gub'ment done make all de black folks contraban'; now, sar, what's dat?"

"Why, Moses," said I, "that's putting a high tariff on you to protect you against foreign darkies. Contraband articles are those which are almost prohibited, and the Government claims the right to take you into service as contraband of war, so that the enemy can not use you to work for them and against us."

"Bress de Laud!" exclaimed the old man, "niggers is some consequence. I hope to see de Norf yet afore I die. Ya! ya! ya! I'll make all dem bucks 'dress me now as Mister Contraban' Moses. Good-by, Massa Capen; I's mos' sorry de war so nigh ober, cos I's 'fraid de niggers won't be no more consekence. Hope to see yer in Congeress some ob dese days, do' dis ole darkey may be brushin' close and shinin' Norfern an' Suffern gemplemen's boots."

CHAPTER IX.

PLANS FOR THE CAPTURE OF VICKSBURG—UNFORTUNATE DE-
LAYS—THE MORTAR BOATS AT VICKSBURG—A SPY AND AN
ATTEMPTED SURPRISE.

AT the time I made the proposition for the capture of New Orleans, which also included the capture of Vicksburg, President Lincoln left it to General McClellan and myself to arrange the plans.
The general considered that ten thousand troops were sufficient to
hold the city after the navy had captured it, and that an additional
ten thousand could be landed at Vicksburg under the guns of the
navy, and hold that place against any force the Confederates could
bring against it.

Had this plan been carried out, the result would have been the
grandest achievement of the war, and we would have accomplished,
with comparatively little loss of life, what eventually cost a great
deal of bloodshed and a vast outlay of money.

When New Orleans fell, the people all along the Mississippi were
astounded, for such a contingency had never entered into their calculations. They considered the forts, Jackson and St. Philip, impregnable, and the rams and ironclads quite sufficient to destroy the
entire Union navy.

In consequence of this feeling of security the large towns above
New Orleans were unfortified and Vicksburg had very few guns
mounted. If, then, the victory at New Orleans had been followed
up rapidly by ships and soldiers sent to Vicksburg, the latter place
would have fallen easily into our possession.

It is not my intention here to give a history of the war. I have
written a full account of all the events that came under my cognizance during the conflict, which may or may not be published at
some future time, but I can not help recalling President Lincoln's
words as we were planning this expedition.

"See," said Mr. Lincoln, pointing to the map, "what a lot of
land these fellows hold, of which Vicksburg is the key. Here is
Red River, which will supply the Confederates with cattle and corn
to feed their armies. There are the Arkansas and White Rivers,
which can supply cattle and hogs by the thousand. From Vicksburg these supplies can be distributed by rail all over the Confed-

cracy. Then there is that great depot of supplies on the Yazoo. Let us get Vicksburg and all that country is ours. The war can never be brought to a close until that key is in our pocket. I am acquainted with that region and know what I am talking about, and, valuable as New Orleans will be to us, Vicksburg will be more so. We may take all the northern ports of the Confederacy, and they can still defy us from Vicksburg. It means hog and hominy without limit, fresh troops from all the States of the far South, and a cotton country where they can raise the staple without interference."

Mr. Lincoln's capacious mind took in the whole subject, and he made it plain to the dullest comprehension. A military expert could not have more clearly defined the advantages of the proposed campaign.

Mr. Lincoln was, in fact, the one who, after the thing had been proposed to him, was most active in urging it on. Everybody who knew anything about the strength of the forts was called in, including General Barnard. The President would come in while McClellan and myself were discussing the matter and have his say, and there was wisdom in all his suggestions.

Carefully as the project of capturing Vicksburg was planned, it was not executed. Why, I do not know. I presume Farragut delayed his advance from New Orleans until he could secure the necessary troops to hold Vicksburg. I urged pushing on to Vicksburg, instead of which I was pushed on to Ship Island, a delightful retreat where General Butler used to send rebellious women who hooted at the Union flag.

It was at least a month after my arrival at Ship Island when I received a letter from General Butler, informing me that Farragut had gone to Vicksburg with his fleet and wanted the mortar flotilla there to bombard the forts. So it appears that in the short interval between our taking New Orleans and getting to Vicksburg the Confederates had erected heavy batteries at the latter point, sending all the way to Richmond and Norfolk for guns and munitions of war.

I presume that when Farragut found he could not get the troops he required to hold Vicksburg, he sent a detachment of vessels up to demand its surrender. The officer in command opened negotiations with the Mayor, who was courtesy itself, while devising ways and means by which to protract the conference.

The officer sent to confer with him was no match for the Mayor

in diplomacy, and, after a week's negotiation and exchange of cour-
tesies, the latter gentleman informed the officer that if he wanted
Vicksburg he must come and take it, and, as the Union flag was
offensive to the citizens, he (the Mayor) must insist on its being
withdrawn, otherwise it would be fired upon.

While this "pow-wow" was going on, the whole power of the
Confederacy was put in operation to save Vicksburg. Guns were
brought from Jackson and masked batteries erected during the
night, and the heaviest ordnance the Confederates had was hurried
from Richmond by rail. Not an hour was lost, and by the time
the officer had returned to Farragut with the Mayor's defiant
speech, Vicksburg was transformed into a small Gibraltar.

President Lincoln must have been vexed when he found that he
had lost the key to the situation, and that "the backbone of the rebellion" would not be broken for some time.

When Farragut heard how matters stood he started at once with
his whole force to try and carry out the designs of the Government
on Vicksburg, but he found a difficult task before him. The summit of the heights at Vicksburg, two hundred and eighty feet
above the river, had been strongly fortified with heavy rifled guns,
which his old-fashioned smooth-bores could not reach, and should
he attempt to pass the batteries or bombard them, the chances were
his ships would be destroyed. He had no force to land and take the
place, for the Confederate army at Vicksburg was estimated at ten
thousand men, who had been hurried thither from every quarter
where they could be spared.

Every day the rebels would mount additional heavy guns on the
heights, and they built a water-battery of twelve heavy guns about
half a mile from the levee, called by our sailors "The Twelve
Apostles." The heaviest gun they called "St. Paul the great
X-pounder," i. e., X-inch rifle.

Farragut could not bombard the forts on the heights with his
ships, nor could he land, and he was too humane to shell the city,
so he sent all the way to Ship Island for the mortar flotilla.

When the flotilla arrived it could reach the forts on the hill-
tops and silence their fire, but the enemy's gunners would run to
their bomb-proofs when they saw a shell coming, and, as soon as it
burst, would fly to their guns again. This kind of warfare was
kept up for several days, no one being hurt so far as I know on the
Confederate side, but a great deal of ammunition was expended on
both sides. The "key" that President Lincoln desired so much

remained in the rebel pocket, and it cost millions of dollars and many lives to get it out.

After a heavy day's hammering of the forts by the mortars, Farragut passed the batteries with his ships and carried out his orders to make a junction with Flag-Officer Davis above Vicksburg; but, although he could pass and repass the batteries, he saw that it was useless to sacrifice the lives of his officers and men merely for sentiment's sake, so he notified the Navy Department that he could do no more.

I found a great difference between bombarding a fort of masonry and a chain of earthworks that could have defied ten times our force, and I soon made up my mind that the "key" would not be forthcoming this time.

The mortar vessels were anchored close to the levee, ten of them only twenty-two hundred yards from the enemy's works, but concealed behind a thick wood. The other eight vessels were on the opposite side of the river, twenty-seven hundred yards from the forts, and were fair targets for the enemy, yet none of their hulls were touched, though hundreds of shot and shell whistled over them.

Finding that they could do the mortar vessels no harm, and that they were injuring their guns and wasting their ammunition, the enemy determined to try and capture the flotilla with a land force, but, as I had calculated on this, I was duly prepared for it.

On the Vicksburg side of the river were ten mortar vessels tied to the bank, with a space of ten feet between them and the levee. Six steamers were anchored on the port quarter of the schooners, and two others were in line ahead, all with broadsides bearing on the thick wood which covered the flotilla. In the middle of this wood were almost impassable swamps, which formed a perfect protection against an advance of troops from that direction. On the edge of the swamps pits had been dug five feet deep, and from these pits lines were extended to a bell mounted on shore, which was to be struck by men stationed in the pits once or twice, according to circumstances.

I was one day on shore looking at the defenses against a land attack, when a negro emerged from the woods, saw me, and appeared to hesitate whether he should advance, but, while thus undecided, two patrolmen slipped up behind him and marched him in.

He was a sleek-looking darkey, clad in a good suit of clothes of a scholastic cut—an entirely different style of negro from old Uncle

Moses, the patriarch of "———'s Landing." In fact, this person's appearance was not prepossessing.

When I asked him what he was doing, he answered, "I'm a contraban', sar, makin' my escape to the lan' ob freedom. My name is Brutus Munroe. I'm a pastor, sar."

"And, pray, to what denomination do you belong?" I inquired.

"Sar," he replied, "I'm a anarkist an' orthodox up to de hub."

"An anarkist? And, pray, what is that?" said I.

"Well, sar," said the preacher, "I believes all about de ark an' de animiles wot went in, an' I preaches dat doctrine to my people. I preaches de millanium to my people, sar, an' tells dem de time am comin' when de lion an' de lam' will lie down togedder."

"I suppose, Mr. Munroe," said I, "that when that happy day arrives the lion will lie down with the lamb inside of him."

"Mebbe so, sar," answered the sleek preacher; "an' if de lam' fines a comfortable bed dar I don' see why he should objec'. We is all ob us lam's or lions; human natur' is eberywhar de same, an' de big critters eats up de little ones."

"Well, now, tell me," said I to the preacher, "how many troops have the Confederates in Vicksburg."

"'Bout a hunder tousand, sar," he answered, promptly.

"And how many guns mounted?"

"'Bout a hunder fifty, sar, an' trains comin' in wid 'em all de time."

"Then there is no chance for us to take the place, is there?" said I.

"Oh, no, sar!" exclaimed the preacher; "a milyon men couldn't took it, it's so strong, sar."

I saw that I had got hold of a first-class romancer, and that it wouldn't do to depend on Brutus's statements.

"Well," said I, "you say you are a Union man?"

"Yes, sar, I prays fo' de President an' all oders in autority ebery Sunday befo' my people."

"But which President do you pray for?"

"I prays for 'em bof, sar—Massa Linkum an' Massa Davis—for dey bof stans in need ob prayer."

"But, Brutus," said I, "what side are you on?"

"Well, sar," he answered, "I am just now on de Lawd's side; but, Massa Captin, I see you done makin' prep'rations to go 'way. You ain't out ob powder, is you?"

"No, Brutus," said I, "we are going to stay here till the mellenium and blow all these hills down. We won't leave a mouse in Vicksburg."

"Den dat's wy you is trowin' up dem intrenchmen's. You is guardin' 'gainst precautions."

All the time Mr. Munroe was talking his eyes were wandering in every direction. At length I said to him, "How do you like the looks of things? Do you think you can remember it all?"

The preacher started; doubtless he would have turned pale if he had not been so very black.

"Ise got a werry bad mem'ry, sar. I see you is busy, an' I mought as well be goin'," and he started off.

"Stop!" said I; "you must stay and dine with me."

"No, tank you, sar," said Brutus. "I mus' go to Warrenton, whar I hole a convention wid a pastor of anodder diocese. I'll call anodder time, an'll see you offen if you stops here till de millanium."

I beckoned the two patrolmen who had brought Mr. Brutus to the levee. They immediately took charge of that worthy and prepared to march him away.

"In God's name, sar," exclaimed Brutus, who trembled like a leaf, "wha' yer gwine ter do ter me?"

"Nothing except shoot you as a spy, Mr. Brutus."

I directed that the preacher should be carefully searched and then confined on the berth-deck of one of the schooners, with a sentry over him. I was satisfied that the negro was a spy, since the Confederate lines were drawn so close that no contraband could pass them without their connivance. It was not often that the colored men acted as spies, but this was evidently an instance of it.

One of the officers devised a scheme to draw the rascal out. He selected the most intelligent negro from among our "contrabands," and, after instructing him in the part he was to play, had him conveyed on board the schooner where Brutus was, and tumbled down by his side.

The new-comer began to weep and throw himself about, as if in great agony of mind, until the preacher sternly remarked to him, "Don't yer make fool ob youse'f! Whar is yer from, anyhow?"

"Jist fo' mile below Warrenton, sah," said the pretended prisoner. "Wy, I'm one ob yer flock; I hears yer preach offen."

"Dat's nat'ral," said the preacher. "De big magnet draw all de little bits ob iron to it."

"But, mister, dey done gwine ter shoot me to-morrow, an' den wot good'll de magnet do me?"

"Hush!" said Brutus; "shut yer mud-hole, an' don't boo-hoo so." And he whispered to his companion, "Ef dey don't shoot us befo' fo' 'clock dis arternoon, dey'll nebber hab anodder chance!"

"Wot yer mean?" said the other, drying his eyes; but Brutus sat silent, not deigning to be more explicit.

At length the colored detective was taken violently ill, and, upon being carried on deck, related all that had passed between him and the preacher. It was not much, but I gathered that we were to be attacked about four o'clock, which was about the time we ceased firing the mortars each day, to let the men go to supper.

Preparations were made to receive any number that might assail us, for, in spite of Brutus, I knew there could not be more than fifteen thousand Confederates in and around Vicksburg.

By two o'clock all was ready; one watch at the guns, the other ready to join in, every man with a musket at hand, and the mortars loaded with but half a pound of powder, so as to land the shells just inside the woods. Then we waited.

About three o'clock there was a tap on the bell, then another, showing that the enemy was advancing through the woods, and in a few moments about twenty men rushed from their cover toward the bank, and were received by a volley of musketry.

Four of the enemy, including their leader, a sergeant, fell, and the rest took to their heels when they found we were ready for them.

At the same moment our steamers opened fire on the woods with shell and shrapnel, and kept it up for twenty minutes with twenty-four large broadside guns, which mowed down the trees as the reaper mows down grain!

All we saw of the enemy was the four men who were killed, and about a dozen others who retreated. I could only conjecture what force of the enemy was approaching under cover of the woods; but the precautions taken had evidently prevented the loss of some of our men, although no serious disaster was likely to befall us.

As soon as possible I sent a reconnoitring party into the woods, and found the two men stationed in the pits. Both were safe in their holes; our shells had exploded well away from them, and they had been in no danger. But beyond them it looked as if a select assortment of thunderbolts had swept over the landscape.

Great trees were shattered; the ground was furrowed in every direction, and covered with splinters of all shapes and sizes.

There was no enemy in sight, but every evidence that one had been there in the castaway knapsacks, caps, shoes, and muskets; and in the swamp was found a pair of officer's long boots, with the toes pointing toward Vicksburg. I don't blame the officer for abandoning his boots, for, under the circumstances, there was no other course to pursue.

The two men in the pits reported that some twenty men came in around the swamp to the left, and headed for the mortar schooners. They were followed by a column of soldiers, the end of which they did not see. At about the same time another column came around the other side of the swamp, and when within two hundred yards of the edge of the woods the firing commenced with musketry, and then the shells came crashing through the forest.

There was a sudden halt, and then a rapid retreat across the swamp, many of the soldiers up to their middle in the mud and water.

When I looked at the place I wondered how any man in his senses could get up such an expedition. No army could have stood ten minutes before the fire we opened on these evidently raw recruits, and no doubt their experience on this occasion increased their respect for "Lincoln's gun-boats."

The Confederates troubled us no more, and I had no idea of wasting shells on those solid hill-sides; it was different from battering a fort and shattering casemates of masonry.

From the time I arrived before Vicksburg I had wondered what had become of the ubiquitous iron-clad ram which always made its appearance from some unexpected quarter at some unexpected time.

After I left Vicksburg the ram did come out of the Yazoo River, at the time when Flag-Officer Davis had joined Farragut with his squadron from the upper Mississippi.

The ram had been generally considered a myth, for how was it possible for the Confederates to build such a vessel in so short a time on these inland waters?

However, down she came one fine morning, and passed unscathed through the whole line of our vessels, dealing death and destruction as she passed. The ships poured broadsides of solid shot into her, but they rolled from her sides like water from a duck's back. That time the Confederates had the laugh on us, and, when I heard of the adventure, I thought of Mr. Brutus Munroe's sage remark about "guardin' agin all precautions."

Previous to this episode of the ram I was ordered by the Navy Department to proceed north with ten of the mortar vessels to bombard Fort Darling, on the James River, and, much to my regret, I was compelled to leave my comrades before Vicksburg, which place I was sure would never be taken by the means that were then being used.

Farragut did all that was possible under the circumstances, and did not leave until he had demonstrated the impossibility of reducing the place without the aid of a large army.

Before I left Vicksburg I sought a final interview with Pastor Brutus Munroe, of the Anarkist Church.

A week's close confinement had told on Mr. Munroe, and he did not look so sleek by a good deal.

"Well, sir," said I, "what have you to say for yourself? Don't you think you deserve hanging as the biggest rascal in the country?"

"Well, sar," said Brutus, "'a soff answer turneff 'way raff.' De Lawd temper de water to de scalded hog. 'Pearances is agin me, sar, but I is innocent, 'deed I is."

"What do you say, then," I inquired, "about going north in this vessel and serving under the Union flag?"

Brutus scratched his head. "But who's gwine to took care ob my flock wen dar pastor done gone to de Norf? Dey'll all go straight to de debbel, sar; dey forgits in a week all dat I'm a month a teachin' 'em."

"Well, then, Brutus," said I, "go and sin no more, and try and keep your neck out of the halter." So I dismissed the preacher, who disappeared in the direction of Warrenton, and I never saw him again.

After the fall of Vicksburg, Colonel Higgins, who had been the commandant of Fort Jackson, again fell into our hands. He gave me an account of the unfortunate expedition against the mortar vessels. The Confederates supposed that Brutus had betrayed them, and if he had returned to Vicksburg he would most likely have been shot. Receiving, no doubt, some intimation of what was in store for him, the worthy preacher disappeared to parts unknown.

———

CHAPTER X.

PASSAGE OF THE MORTAR FLEET DOWN THE MISSISSIPPI RIVER— A REVIEW AT NATCHEZ—A ROSE IN THE DESERT—HONORS TO FARRAGUT AFTER HIS DEATH.

MY return down the Mississippi with the ten mortar schooners in tow was monotonous, although we were occasionally enlivened on passing a town by seeing people flocking to the river-bank to look at us.

When we passed up everything was in mourning ; very few people showed themselves, except negroes ; it was as if the white population had run away and hidden themselves. They had been taught that we were a set of buccaneers who were liable to commit any atrocities, and that a policy of non-intercourse with us was most advisable. When the people, however, saw so many war vessels pass up the river without doing any injury to private property or to unarmed citizens, they began to think we had been libeled, and even to suspect we were more to be trusted than those who were marking all the products of their industry "C. S. A.," and paying for the same in worthless Confederate currency.

There were some persons, no doubt, who saw plainly enough that the United States Government would never again allow the control of the Mississippi River to slip out of their hands, since it was so comparatively easy to hold it, with the numerous gun-boats at their disposal, in spite of rebel rams and other appliances of the enemy.

One after another the people saw the heavy works deemed impregnable by the Confederates fall into our hands, there to remain until the authority of the Government should be firmly established throughout the land. After the capture of New Orleans it was apparent that the power of the South was broken, and the people along the river were soon of the same opinion.

Vicksburg alone blocked the way, but our army and navy were gradually encircling it in their coils, and its capture was only a matter of time.

When we passed Natchez, on our way up the river, every one had retired to their houses, not a straggler was in sight, and, not knowing exactly what kind of a reception we would encounter, we stood to our guns.

Coming down, we gave ourselves no concern about hostile acts from the towns below Vicksburg, knowing the people were too wise to interfere with us.

As we approached Natchez I had the officers dress in uniform and the crews in white, while the mast-heads were decorated with our best flags.   Our decks were polished as white as possible, and everything about the vessels bore that appearance of order and neatness which characterizes well-disciplined vessels of war.

As we rounded the point and came in sight of Natchez, the hills were covered with men, women, and children, apparently dressed in their best clothes.   The white dresses and gay parasols of the ladies against the green background made a charming picture.   It looked as if all Natchez had assembled to welcome victors from a battle-field.

As we passed close in to the shore many spy-glasses were leveled on us, and we were so near that we could even see the expression on people's faces.   It was rather of surprise than hostility as they scanned the forms of more than a hundred well-dressed officers, who would have given a month's pay to have had a chance to dance the lancers with these pretty rebels.

From appearances, we judged that, should we land, we would receive a friendly welcome, although, perhaps, they were all in such good humor because of a telegram just received from Vicksburg announcing the fact that many of the mortar vessels had been destroyed and the rest had sought safety in flight.

This precious piece of news we heard from an "intelligent contraband," who boarded us in a canoe soon after we passed Natchez, and he informed us that the people had assembled to witness our discomfiture.

If, however, they expected to see shot-riddled hulls, they were disappointed, for not a scratch was visible ; and the jolly sailors, standing in picturesque groups, gave the lie to the bombastic dispatch sent from Vicksburg.

At the same time, as we had learned by experience not to put implicit faith in the statements of the negroes, we thought it likely that this one had exaggerated the matter.

Whatever the people of Natchez may have heard, their bearing toward us was not unfriendly.   Curiosity seemed their leading motive, and it was justified by the procession of well-armed vessels passing their town.

One lively gentleman, who rode down to the bank on horseback, appeared to be an oracle, as he was surrounded by a crowd of persons to whom he seemed to be answering questions. He examined us critically through a large lorgnette, perhaps in search of the mythical shot-holes.

We passed and made no sign, gliding quietly along with the current like specter vessels, leaving the great crowd behind us and approaching the lower part of the city, when I saw standing in the doorway of an arbor covered with clematis a young girl of about fourteen, dressed in white, with a chip hat, holding in one hand a white handkerchief and in the other a blue parasol.

We were so close to her that I could note the expression of her countenance without the aid of a glass as she vigorously waved her handkerchief, while I waved mine in return.

Then she opened her parasol and displayed a small Union flag, which she kissed and pressed to her heart; and so she stood until we passed, concealed from the crowd above by the small arbor.

Many in our flotilla noticed the act and removed their caps; then the flag disappeared within the folds of the parasol, and the maiden stood looking after us until we were out of sight, as if loath to lose sight of the stars and stripes.

Whether or not she suffered for her temerity we never knew, but let us hope her noble act was only seen by those for whom it was intended.

I shall never forget that little maiden, and, should she chance to read these pages, she will know that her courage was appreciated.

THE ROSE IN THE DESERT.

Farewell, little maid, may the rose and the vine
Thy beautiful arbor forever entwine,
Thy heroic act has made it divine;
Thou'rt a rose in the desert, where the flowers' perfume
Don't often linger, and where flowers don't bloom.
Yet one dewdrop may reach the heart of a rose
Which, refreshing its life, in the desert it grows.
'Twas the flash of a dream, a vision of light,
A sweet emblem of faith, when you burst on my sight.
Like the maid of the mist, in the soft vapor spray
Your young face with its halo soon melted away.
But that form in its glory will ever remain
Impressed on my soul though we ne'er meet again.

> There's many a slip 'twixt the cup and the lip,
> But whenever the rich flowing beaker I sip
> I'll drink a good health in a bumper of wine
> Wherever I am, and that toast shall be thine.

As we passed on down the Mississippi all seemed peaceful and quiet, and whatever may have been the heart-burnings and hostility to the Union, they were not exhibited.

They assumed a virtue if they had it not. Steamers were plying on the river bearing the Union flag, and the same flag floated over the barracks at Baton Rouge, where troops were stationed to preserve order in that neighborhood. It may not have been altogether agreeable to the residents, but it was beneficial to the community at large.

As we slipped past New Orleans I noticed that the shipping had greatly increased since I had last seen the place. Many Union and foreign flags were flying from the mast-heads, and the levee had quite a lively appearance.

General Butler was still in the ascendant, putting on all the style of a viceroy and slowly bringing order out of chaos.

There were many complaints against his administration, but it must be said that as long as people conformed to the regulations he established they got along well enough.

People in a conquered city can not dictate terms to the conquerors, and municipal laws must give way to military regulations.

From New Orleans to the mouth of the Mississippi Union authority prevailed, and one would hardly have supposed that a different state of affairs had so lately existed. This condition was assured for the future, for no power in the Southern Confederacy could change it.

All this was the result of the navy's work in beating down the defenses of New Orleans. The people of the United States have never realized the importance of the capture of New Orleans—the most brilliant affair of the war. That the entire plan of the campaign was not carried out does not detract from the gallantry and importance of this achievement.

Had a British naval officer performed such a service as Farragut for his country, he would have received the highest honors and the most splendid pecuniary rewards. But only when the war was over was Farragut given the rank of admiral with a salary quite inadequate to maintain his position, and seven thousand dollars less than the pay of the corresponding rank in the army, or only about equal to the emoluments of a major-general.

When Farragut died the Government indeed paid his memory the highest honors that it could, and Congress, with what seemed to them unbounded liberality, bestowed upon his widow an annual pension of two thousand dollars—about one fifteenth of one per cent interest on what Farragut's captures added to the Naval Pension Fund.

These things show plainly enough that those who employed Admiral Farragut and appropriated a great deal of credit for what he accomplished were remiss in not making greater efforts to see him amply rewarded.

Honors are very grateful things, but they become onerous unless accompanied with the means of maintaining properly the position of the recipient, and thus enabling him to keep the wolf from the door.

CHAPTER XI.

GETTING TO SEA IN THE STEAMER HARRIET LANE — PASSING COCKPIT POINT BATTERIES—A SOUTHERN-BORN OFFICER LOYAL TO THE STARS AND STRIPES—HIS DEATH AT GALVESTON.

As this is not a continuous narrative, I can not well maintain strict order in my reminiscences. I jot down the recollections as they come up in my memory.

At the time the mortar flotilla was fitted out I had no vessel assigned for myself among all the curious craft the Navy Department was buying up. It was natural to suppose that, with twenty-eight vessels under my command, I should need a place where I could perform the duties of commanding officer of the flotilla, and I was told that the "double-ender" Octorora was intended for me, although she had only recently been launched, and was not near ready for service.

In the mean while I was informed that I could go out in the Harriet Lane with Lieutenant-Commanding Wainwright, and in due course of time the Octorora would reach me.

The Harriet Lane was a very small steamer, built for a revenue-cutter, and was caught up by the Navy Department and turned into a vessel of war—a system, I suppose, we shall adhere to in case of a difficulty with a European power: fall back on the revenue marine, Coast Survey, and Fish Commission for vessels, and have a navy register filled with a formidable array of names appertaining to a lot of "rattletraps."

The cabin of the Harriet Lane was very small, and there was one little state-room which the captain naturally wanted for himself. It never struck him to offer it to me, although I was his commanding officer; but if he had, I certainly should have declined it.

In those days I was a hardy fellow, despising luxury—always traveled with as little luggage as possible, and could sleep anywhere. No doubt the department took into account my peculiarities, and said, "He doesn't mind; he's tough; send him in anything."

I went down to the Washington navy-yard with my orders, "Proceed without delay to Key West in the Harriet Lane, and take command of the mortar flotilla," etc.

Lieutenant Wainwright received me at the gangway with a smiling face, and my trunk was passed on board. Although Wainwright knew that he was to have a passenger, he seemed surprised at the trunk. He perhaps thought a little hand-bag would be all I should require, and he looked doubtfully at the *impedimenta* and said,

"I don't see how we shall be able to stow that trunk in the cabin, but I must contrive some way."

"Put it in the maintop," I said, "and get under way at once."

Wainwright looked surprised. "I am not ready for sea, sir, yet; the coal is not all on board."

"As to that," I replied, "I never saw a naval vessel that was ready for sea; nevertheless, we will get under way, and procure coal in Norfolk or Port Royal."

"But I haven't laid in the cabin-stores."

"All right," I said; "the ship-stores are good enough for me."

"Two of the officers and the cabin steward are away."

"We'll leave them then," I said.

"But," said Wainwright, "our chronometer has not come on board."

"Of course," I said, "chronometers are always slow. We will go without one, trusting to the three *l*'s—lead, log, and lookout."

Wainwright was in despair, and no doubt thought the navy was going to the d—l sure enough; but he gave the order to the first lieutenant to light the fires.

"The fires are already lighted, sir," said the young officer, Lieutenant Lee, "and steam will be up in twenty minutes."

I took to the young man at once, for I liked his prompt way of doing duty.

Next morning, by daylight, we arrived at Cockpit Point, and found there five small steamers called "vessels of war!" each mounting several rifle-guns, and forming part of a river flotilla of some fourteen vessels under Lieutenant Wyman. It had formerly been under the command of Commander James H. Ward, who never permitted a rebel battery to be erected on the Potomac.

But now the rebels had blocked our game, and we were informed that we must wait eight days so as to have a dark night for passing what was supposed to be a powerful battery at Cockpit Point.

Just then a thick snow-storm came on, and you could hardly see a ship's length.

"We will pass the batteries now," I said; "this is better than a dark night. You can follow us, Captain" (to the officer in command), "and enfilade the rebel batteries in case they open on us."

It was about 7 A.M. when we got abreast of Cockpit Point, the snow-storm held up, and everything became clear as noonday.

I stood on the wheel-house with Captain Wainwright and the first lieutenant. A puff of smoke came from the bushes on shore.

"Why, they have dared to fire on the flag!" exclaimed the first lieutenant, excitedly. He was a full-blooded Southerner, born in the very heart of Secessia.

Just then a large rifle-shell struck the rim of our port wheel, cutting it in two, and the fragments of the wheel were knocking the wheel-house to pieces.

"That was a slap in the face," said the youngster; "can't we return the fire, sir?"

"No, my young friend," I replied; "never fire at a battery when you are running it, and throw away your shot. You will have firing enough before the war is over."

Presently a shell passed through the smoke-stack and exploded just beyond.

"They have hit us again!" exclaimed the young officer. "The dastardly villains, to fire on the flag!"

Three shells followed in quick succession, cutting away an iron stack-stay, chipping off a piece of the rail, and knocking a hammock out.

"There, Mr. Lee," I said, "they will trouble us no more, as we have passed their line of fire. It would have been useless to fire at scattered guns in bushes and behind sand-hills, not knowing their distance. From what I can learn of Cockpit Battery, out of the many vessels that have run past its fire it has never yet succeeded in sinking one of them."

"Excuse me, sir, for my warmth," said the young officer. "I am a Southern man, and my family have disowned me because I would not join what they call the Confederate cause. My father says if he should ever meet me in battle he would shoot me like a dog. How can I help hating a cause that has taken all the love of my family from me?"

"Yet you don't regret your action in sticking to your flag?" I inquired.

"No, indeed," he answered; "I would die before I would desert it, and do not desire the love of my family if I can only possess it by turning traitor to my country."

"I admire your sentiments," sir; "don't let them depart from you."

Four miles below the Cockpit Battery we stopped to mend our wheel as best we could.

I took a great deal of notice of the youngster on our way to Key West, being much attracted by his patriotic sentiments and manly bearing. I knew many Southern officers who had not the moral courage to stand by their flag, and from this young man's story I could see how much he had to contend with in the step he had taken.

He had never before seen a shot fired in anger, and could not restrain his indignation at the idea of Southern men so soon forswearing allegiance to the flag under which they were born, and even firing upon it when passing along the public highway for vessels.

"I can understand," said he, "how men in an excited condition can be urged on to violence by demagogues, but I can not understand how men in cold blood can fire at a vessel belonging to the navy that has conferred so much honor on the North and on the South. I think that the river flotilla could have enfiladed Cockpit Point while we were passing, and it might have diverted the enemy's aim and saved our wheel."

"Yes," I said, "people can do anything when they want to, but perhaps they did not want to. It doesn't make a great deal of difference anyhow, and it is best not to make that battery of too much importance."

We spent three days in Hampton Roads repairing damages, and sailed thence for Key West.

The young officer served with me all the time I commanded the mortar flotilla, and his friends may well be proud of him for his chivalric courage and loyalty to his flag.

When taking leave of the officers of the flotilla at the mouth of the Mississippi, I bade good-by to young Lee, who was still first lieutenant of the Harriet Lane.

"I shall never see you again," he said, "for I feel that I have but a short time to stay here. I am not sorry, for it is dreadful to live with the hatred of those whom you love and who once loved you. I hope to die in defense of the flag, and I want my friends to know that I did my duty faithfully to my country. In case of my death, sir, will you see this done for me?"

I promised that I would do what he wished, but told him it was foolish to indulge in such morbid feelings ; that when the war was over his family would welcome him home again and would be proud of his record.

"No, no, sir," he replied, "you don't know my people. I do not wish to live to hear my parents curse me for doing what they taught me from childhood : 'Be true to the Government and the flag.'"

I never saw him again, for he was killed soon after on the deck of the Harriet Lane at Galveston, defending the flag to the last.

Galveston had been captured, and Flag-Officer Farragut sent a small detachment of vessels, among them the Harriet Lane, there to hold the place, under Commander Renshaw.

The harbor of Galveston is a peculiar one, with several channels leading to it from the bar, and a number of large mud-flats where the water is very shallow.

The vessels under Renshaw lay in the various channels out of supporting distance of each other, and the Confederate general, Magruder, determined on a bold attempt for their capture.

He fitted out three or four river-steamers packed with cotton-bales and filled with riflemen. The Harriet Lane lay nearest the town, and the sudden attack found her not properly prepared for resistance. One of the rebel steamers jammed under her guards and could not get away, nor could those on board the Harriet Lane bring a gun to bear on the enemy.

In ten minutes the numerous marksmen on board the Confederate steamer cleared the decks of the Harriet Lane; every officer and man on deck was shot down—it was a slaughter-house affair. Captain Wainwright was killed at the first volley, and directly afterward young Lee was mortally wounded.

There being nothing left to oppose them, the Confederates rushed on board and took possession of the steamer. They were led by a stalwart officer with a drawn sword.

Lieutenant Lee was lying on deck apparently dead, his head supported by the cabin steward. The Confederate officer demanded of the steward, "Who is that officer?"

"This is Mr. Lee, our first lieutenant," replied the steward, "and I think he is dead."

The Confederate leader staggered back. "God in heaven!" he exclaimed, "poor boy! is there no hope at all?" Then he cried in agony, "Speak to me! Say that you forgive us!"

The young man opened his eyes at the sound of his uncle's voice.

"I have nothing to forgive," he said, "but you saw that I did my duty to the last and died fighting for my country. Tell them all at home I ever loved them." And he expired.

I received the account of this heart-rending scene from the steward of the Harriet Lane, in whose arms the young officer died. His last request to the steward was, that he would tell me how he had died at his post in defense of the flag. The steward related the events of the massacre with such emotion that I could hardly refrain from tears, although not given to the melting mood.

Lieutenant Lee was buried among his people in his Southern home; his shadow was no longer cast between them and the sun, and it is to be hoped that the rancor which once dwelt in their hearts was buried in the grave they made him under the moss-covered oaks of his birthplace.

This sad occurrence was only one of many similar scenes which occurred during the civil war; but it was one in which I was immediately interested, and, although I have missed many a brave young fellow from my side, yet I think oftener of that young officer, with his lofty aspirations and high sense of duty, shot down like a dog by his own people without a chance to defend himself.

8

When I recall those days I can not help thinking that his Satanic majesty must have got loose upon earth to set men at work to destroy each other.

I will merely add to this a statement which shows the changes made by war and time on the lives of men. They may escape the bullet and the steel, but the excitement of such a revolution as that through which our country passed leaves an indelible mark. Of the commanding naval officers in the mortar flotilla who stood by me all through the expedition—Guest, Woodworth, Harrel, Wainwright, Breese, Watson Smith, and Renshaw—all are dead, though then in the vigor of manhood. All were gallant men, and deserving of the highest honors.

Baldwin alone lived to reach the top of the ladder, and now represents his country honorably in command of the Mediterranean squadron.

All the first lieutenants of the different steamers are dead or have left the service.

It seems but yesterday that I saw all these officers, full of life and manly aspirations, devoting their lives to their country which has forgotten them.

CHAPTER XII.

A VISIT TO THE NAVY DEPARTMENT—NEWPORT CLUB—BETS ON FAVORITE GENERALS—A SNOB—ACCUSED OF TALKING TREASON —ORDERED TO WASHINGTON—THREATENED TO RESIGN—ORDERED TO COMMAND THE MISSISSIPPI SQUADRON—A GREAT GENERAL—MORAL.

WHEN I arrived in Washington after the termination of my New Orleans expedition I called upon the Secretary of the Navy, who received me with that placidity for which he was remarkable.

Mr. Welles was never enthusiastic about anything, and never cast down, whatever misfortunes might happen.

When he was informed that the Merrimac had sunk the Congress and the Cumberland, he simply said, "Let Mr. Fox know it." If Mr. Welles did not welcome an officer warmly, it was because it was not his nature to do so; he always received one courteously.

"Good-morning!" said the secretary, as I entered the room;

"I sent for you to come north and bombard Fort Darling, on the James River; can you do it?"

"Yes, sir," I replied, "I can put fifty tons of shells on top of it; but what good will that do if there are no soldiers to hold it when we drive the enemy out? As soon as we are done bombarding, the enemy will go back and make the place stronger by piling up our broken shells."

"Well, as there are no troops available, we must give up the idea," said Mr. Welles. "Tell Mr. Faxon to have a two weeks' leave of absence made out for you, so that you can see your family. Good-morning."

So I departed for Newport, R. I., where I put myself under the care of a physician, having brought with me a case of "breakbone fever" as a souvenir of the Mississippi.

One evening I was at the Newport Club, where were assembled some thirty or forty persons, many of them vociferating loudly, so that I feared from their excitement it would soon be necessary to call in the services of the police.

An old *habitué* sat on the sofa, looking at the game of billiards I was playing. "Pray, Mr. Pell," I said, "what is all the excitement about?"

"Why," he answered, "this is our usual evening's entertainment. It is a meeting of the copperheads and radical republicans; they have just come in from dinner parties and want to see how much money they can bet without any one taking them up. Each is now bragging of his own general, and seems determined to bet him into the Presidency."

At that instant a voice cried out, "I'll bet five hundred dollars General ———— will be the next President!"

"Done," said another; "I take it up and go five hundred better," whereupon there was much shouting and some profanity, with indications of a general row.

I could not help laughing at this absurd spectacle. "What fools these mortals be," I said to my companion.

"Do you know anything of the generals they are quarreling about?" inquired Mr. Pell.

"Yes," I replied, "I know some of them."

By this time the crowd of clubmen had become so uproarious that Mr. Pell thought it time to make a diversion, and, going among the disputants, said:

"Pooh! pooh! don't quarrel about people you don't know.

Here is Captain Porter, who knows these generals, and can tell you all about them."

The crowd surged toward me, and one little fellow, with more money than brains, and whose principal recommendation was a fine set of teeth, blurted out, frantically, "Captain Porter, I bet General ———— is the greatest general the world ever saw, and will be our next President. Do you say, sir, that he is not the greatest general that ever lived ?"

"Certainly," I replied ; "I consider him no greater than Cæsar, Hannibal, Marlborough, Napoleon, not to mention others who have accomplished a great deal in the military way."

"Damn Cæsar and Napoleon and all the rest of them," said the little man. "They'd be nowhere fighting against such troops as our army have had to oppose, and in such a country as our men have to fight. What do you know of Cæsar and Hannibal that you make such an assertion ?"

"Why, sir," I replied, "I was intimate with both these generals, and took breakfast with them in the Alps, which they passed with very little trouble."

"You are making a jest of this thing, sir," said the little man, fiercely. "I can't stand jesting."

"You can't stand drinking either," I said, "for it has evidently been too much for your weak head."

Just then a copperhead sang out, "I'll bet a thousand dollars Beauregard could whip Napoleon out of his boots any time."

"What do you say to that proposition ?" turning to me.

"Let me settle this little fellow here," I replied, "before entering upon a controversy with you."

"Well, sir," said the little fellow, "I wouldn't be surprised to hear you say that Stonewall Jackson is superior to our generals."

"Well," I answered, "as you mention the subject, I will say that I have heard some people assert that Stonewall Jackson is the hardest man alive to whip."

"Hurrah for Stonewall Jackson !" shouted a copperhead. "Put up your pocket-book, little man, you're a snob !"

This made the little man very angry, and, as I seemed the least ruffled of the party and did not look as if I would get angry, he turned upon me.

"Sir, you are talking treason—yes, sir, treason. I'll bet you two thousand dollars General ———— will be the next President."

"Look here, little man," I said, "you have a good set of teeth,

and my advice to you is to try and keep them in your mouth."
Then his friends took him away.   In two minutes all was apparent-
ly good humor again, the subject of conversation was changed, and
I finished my game of billiards.

Next morning, while taking a walk, I was accosted by Dr. P.,
of the navy, who was attending me professionally.

"There are some ugly reports about you going the rounds in
Newport," said the doctor, "and I thought it my duty to tell you
of them."

"Reports about me ? Why, I hardly know anybody in the place.
Pray what are the reports ?"

"One of the stories is that you have used treasonable language,"
said the doctor.

"And who has circulated such a libel as that ?"

"Oh, I can't tell you," said the doctor, "as it was told to me
in confidence."

"But what good will this information do me unless I know the
person who has made the accusation ?"   Then I remembered the
occurrence of the previous evening at the club.

"It will put you on your guard," he said.

"But that won't satisfy me, doctor.   I insist on knowing who
the person is who has slandered me.   You are not sufficiently intimate
with me to bring such a report without telling me who is responsible
for it.   I want the man's name, so that I can call him to account,
and, unless you give it, I shall hold you personally responsible."

The doctor saw that I was thoroughly in earnest, and, after
hesitating a moment, he said : "I shall be guilty of a breach of confidence if I tell you ; besides, it is not a man—it is a lady, and you
can not hold *her* responsible."

"If she has a husband," I replied, "perhaps he can be made to
teach his wife to confine herself to the truth."

Seeing that I was determined to find out all about the matter,
the doctor said : "Well, if you insist on knowing, it is old Mrs. B.
She told me in confidence, and will never forgive me if she knows I
have told you."

"Ah !" I said, "that old spy who goes around spotting people
and giving information to the Government.   I have not even seen
the woman, and as to holding her husband responsible for what
she may say, that would be absurd ; he is a harmless old gentleman,
and I should not think of making war on him.   But pray, doctor,
what else did she say of me ?"

"She said a good many things," replied the doctor. "I think you must have offended her in some way. She says you are a brother-in-law of Semmes, and connived at his escape from the Mississippi River in the Sumter."

"Well, as I was at Southwest Pass, and Semmes got out of Pass à l'Outre, where the Brooklyn was stationed, and as that vessel chased him off the coast, there's no use in talking about it. What next?"

"Mrs. B. says you are a Southern man and a hot rebel."

"Born in Pennsylvania," I replied. "And you took all that in, did you, and you a naval officer?"

The doctor looked confused and said nothing. As I turned toward the house a dispatch was handed me from the telegraph-office :

"Proceed to Washington without delay and report to the Navy Department.   GIDEON WELLES."

"Thank you," I exclaimed ; "I will get out of this den of scandal and have some active service."

At 6 P.M. the following day I arrived in Washington and went straight to the Navy Department. Mr. Welles had gone home, but I saw the assistant secretary, Mr. Fox.

"Here I am," I said. "What is wanted?"

"We just wanted to look at you," said Fox.

"I am not much to look at after an attack of break-bone fever ; but, like the lean horse, I'm good enough to go if there's anything for me to do."

"Can you get your things out of the Octorora in two hours?" inquired Fox. "We are going to give the vessel to Lieutenant George Brown, to proceed at once to Charleston."

As the Octorora was then in Baltimore, I had not much time allowed me.

"Lieutenant Brown can have all my things," I replied. "He will need them, and I can sleep on a camp-stool, if necessary—but what is to become of my mortar vessels?" I inquired.

"They are to be turned over to Wilkes," replied Fox, "and the organization broken up."

I saw at once that something was wrong, but had no idea at the time that people were sending reports to the department, under plea of zeal for the cause of the Union, to prejudice the Secretary of the Navy against his most faithful subordinates.

The case of General Stone is one which is an eternal disgrace to the United States Government. He suffered every indignity, and, when his innocence was clearly shown, he was discharged without an apology or explanation.

Fortunately, I had strong friends in the President, Secretary Seward, and Secretary Chase, and I felt myself secure from serious assault.

Next day I saw Fox at the department and he informed me that I was to be sent to St. Louis to superintend the construction of ironclads under Commodore Hull.

I made no secret of my indignation at this information.

"This is ostracizing me," I said. "Certainly my services deserve something better. You can't send me there."

"Do you mean to say," said Fox, "that you will refuse to obey the order?"

"Not exactly that," I replied; "but I look upon such orders as an indignity. I will cheerfully obey any order where I can be of service against the enemies of my country, but treat me in that way, and I will resign, and get the merchants of New York to give me a suitable vessel, and then I will go out and show you how to catch the Alabama."

I walked away, Fox staring after me in astonishment. This was one of the few times when he got off his balance. The woman with a "B" to her name, and the little fellow of the Newport Club, Fox's intimate friend, had imposed upon him. What they really told him I never knew or cared.

I could not see the Secretary of the Navy, as he was engaged, but I wrote to him that I was ready for active duty at a moment's notice, and, until my services were required, I would like to rejoin my family in Newport.

Permission was at once given me, and I do not believe Mr. Welles ever knew I had been sent for.

I was not in the best of humor when I departed from the office, as I thought my chances for distinction were at an end. I felt sure the Navy Department was hostile to me, and that I could never get along because too stiff-necked to be a courtier. I forgot, for the moment,

"There's a divinity that shapes our ends, rough-hew them how we will."

The very wind that I supposed was blowing me to destruction was, in fact, wafting me to fortune.

I thought I would call, before leaving Washington, and pay my respects to the President. I found him in company with Mr. Seward, and both gentlemen seemed glad to see me.

"What can I do for you, Captain," said the President.

"Sir," I said, "I think of resigning from the navy and getting the merchants of New York to give me a suitable steamer, so that I may show the Navy Department how to catch the Alabama. That would suit my disposition better than superintending ironclads at St. Louis under Commodore Hull. I should fret my heart out there in a week suffering such an indignity; yet that's what the Navy Department proposes doing with me."

"They shall not do it," said Mr. Seward, jumping up. "I have not forgotten how you helped me to save Fort Pickens to the Union."

"Yes," said the President, "and got me into hot water with Mr. Welles, for which I think he has never forgiven me. I believe he would forget it, but, Seward, you won't let him. You are always flaunting your claimed success in his face, and deprecating the Fort Sumter expedition; it's like shaking a red rag at a bull. If it hadn't been for Seward, Captain, Mr. Welles would have tried you by court-martial for disobeying Seward's telegram, although you were simply carrying out my written orders—a fact which none of us remembered until you were beyond our reach."

"You were right," said Mr. Seward, "in disobeying my orders, as it saved us Fort Pickens."

"Well," said Mr. Lincoln, "if the navy hasn't broken the back-bone of the Rebellion I think it has come pretty near doing it, though, after all, Vicksburg slipped through our fingers, which was a great disappointment to me, realizing, as I do, its great importance as a depot of supplies to the Confederates; however, if I live, you shall be at the taking of the place."

The President then made me describe the battle at the passage of Forts Jackson and St. Philip, making his usual shrewd comments on the matter.

"I read all about it," he said; "how the ships went up in line, firing their broadsides; how the mortars pitched into the forts; how the forts pitched into the ships, and the ships into the rams, and the rams into the gun-boats, and the gun-boats into the fire-rafts, and the fire-rafts into the ships. Of course I couldn't understand it all, but enough to know that it was a great victory. It reminds me," continued the President, "of a fight in a bar-room at Natchez, but I won't tell that now.

"It struck me," continued the President, "that the fight at the forts was something like the Natchez scrimmage, only a little more so."

"Mr. President," I said, "that achievement of Farragut's is the most important event of the war, and all that he has received for it is a vote of thanks of Congress. The British Government would have loaded him with honors and emoluments."

"How is that, Seward?" said the President.

"I don't know anything about it," said the Secretary of State. "I am not the head of the Navy Department."

"No," replied the President, "but you don't mind running off with a navy-ship when it suits your purposes."

"Yes, sir," said Mr. Seward, "when I know it is the only way to save the honor of the nation; but Farragut will not be forgotten."

The President then summoned a messenger and said, "Go tell the Assistant Secretary of the Navy that I wish to see him at once."

I took my leave on the plea that I had to catch the train for Newport.

"Good-by," said the President; "you sha'n't go to St. Louis, you sha'n't resign, and you shall be at Vicksburg when it falls."

When I reached my lodgings in Newport I found a telegram awaiting me—

"Proceed to Washington without delay and report in person to the department.   GIDEON WELLES."

"Well," I exclaimed, "here we go this time to Fort Lafayette!" But I immediately returned to Washington in obedience to my orders.

When I was ushered into the presence of the Secretary of the Navy that high functionary smiled on me benignly, gave me his two fingers to squeeze, and asked me to be seated. My heart expanded so at my cordial reception that I felt like embracing the venerable statesman, for I thought at least I would be allowed a cell to myself at Fort Lafayette; but he didn't give me time to think much, as he handed me a sealed document.

I opened it with the air of a philosopher, determined to show the hard-hearted old gentleman that I was indifferent to my fate, and read—

"You have been appointed to command the Mississippi squadron, and you will proceed at once to Mound City, Illinois, and relieve Flag-Officer Davis, etc.   GIDEON WELLES."

I did not give way to any visible emotion, merely repeating aloud, "There's a divinity that shapes our ends," etc. After congratulating me, the secretary invited me to call and see him at his house.

As I came out of the secretary's office I met the bureau officers, and they shook me warmly by the hand. Fox was delighted to see me. Faxon, the chief clerk, smiled the first time for weeks. I had been "selected by the President!" I had friends at court! Human nature is everywhere the same, even in the little semblance of a court which we try to maintain. Every one notices when the President nods, and what it means, and the man who receives his approval is patronized at once.

What a difference there was between this reception and the one I experienced two days previous! Then I was almost driven to resign. Now I was a flag officer, with the title of Acting Rear-Admiral. Let those laugh who win. I won in spite of many obstacles, and enjoyed my victory amazingly.

I called with Mr. Fox on the President, and found him, as usual, in excellent humor.

"I promised you," he said to me, "that you should see Vicksburg fall, and now you shall do it. I want to ask you something about your plans, for, knowing all about the place, I suppose your measures for capturing it must be matured by this time.

I assured the President that my plans were very simple. A large naval force, a strong body of troops, and patience, were the only means of capturing Vicksburg.

"There was a time not long ago," I said, "when Vicksburg could have been easily captured, but it is now a second Gibraltar, and the navy *alone* could do nothing toward capturing it."

"Well," said the President, "whom do you think is the general for such an occasion?"

"General Grant, sir. Vicksburg is within his department; but I presume he will send Sherman there, who is equal to any occasion."

"Well, Admiral," said the President, "I have in my mind a better general than either of them; that is McClernand, an old and intimate friend of mine."

"I don't know him, Mr. President," I said.

"What!" exclaimed Mr. Lincoln, "don't know McClernand? Why, he saved the battle of Shiloh, when the case seemed hopeless!" (I suppose McClernand told him so.)

"Why, Mr. President," I replied, "the general impression is

that Grant won the battle of Shiloh; as he commanded the army, he would seem entitled to the credit."

"No," said the President, "McClernand did it; he is a natural-born general."

"Well, Mr. President, with all due deference to you, I don't believe in natural-born generals except where they have had proper military training, and it seems to me the siege of Vicksburg is too important a matter to trust to anybody except a scientific military man; besides, if you take troops from Grant and Sherman to give them to McClernand, you will weaken the army."

"Oh, no," said the President, "I don't mean to do that. McClernand is to go to Springfield, Illinois, and raise troops there for the capture of Vicksburg. In the mean time you can prepare to co-operate with him."

These last words of the President were a great relief to me, for I knew it would take some time to raise an army in the way proposed.

"Now," said the President, "I will give you a note of introduction to McClernand. I want you to talk the matter over with him before you leave Washington." He wrote the note, gave it to me, and I left with Mr. Fox.

"What do you think of that plan?" I said to Fox, when we were outside.

"Well, I don't know," he replied; "but, after you have talked with McClernand, suppose you stop in and tell me what you think of him."

I found the general at his hotel, and he talked in the most sanguine manner of taking Vicksburg in a week!

I listened to him attentively, but, as I did not exactly take in all the military points, I left him after he had informed me he had already received orders to enlist an army at Springfield, Illinois, and command it at the siege of Vicksburg.

I stopped in to see Fox, who said, "Well, what do you think of General McClernand?"

"I could form no opinion of him," I said. "Good-by."

"Are you not going to see the President again before you leave Washington?" he inquired.

"No," I replied, "I leave for Cairo, Illinois, in two hours, to see Grant. McClernand is going to Springfield to raise troops. He is shortly to be married, and if he proposes to recruit an army in that way, I think it will be hardly worth while to wait for him."

> Now all you old fellows who have studied the laws,
> And who make a good living by quibbles and flaws,
> Who ne'er had a gun or a sword in your paws,
>> Deceiving whose trade is,
>> Old men and old ladies,
> Don't mount heavy boots and a long "yaller" sash,
> Or expose your rich coat, or bright *sabretache*,
> In battle or skirmish, or where there's a chance
> Of a shot from a pistol or a poke from a lance.
> Be wise, stay at home, read Blackstone and Wheaton,
> And study Coke's tactics, where you can not be beaten.

CHAPTER XIII.

INTERVIEW WITH GENERAL GRANT AT CAIRO—FIRST MEETING
WITH GENERAL SHERMAN—OUR FLAG HOISTED OVER ARKANSAS
POST—GENERAL GRANT AND THE SIEGE OF VICKSBURG—HOAX
ON THE VICKSBURGERS.

I ASSUMED command of the Mississippi Squadron at Cairo, Illinois, in October, 1862. There were the sturdy ironclads that had fought their way from Fort Henry to Donaldson, to Island No. 10, and White River, and destroyed the enemy's navy at Memphis. All had done good service under their gallant commanders, Foote and Davis.

The Benton, Carondelet, Cairo, Baron de Kalb, Mound City, and Cincinnati were designed and constructed by that universal genius, James B. Eads, in less than three months, and became famous in the annals of the navy. Besides these were the Tyler, Conestoga, and Lexington.

> See the old warriors out in the stream,
> Open in many a wood-end and seam!

As soon as I arrived, the ironclads were put in the hands of five hundred loyal mechanics, and in a week were ready for any service.

The rest of the vessels under my command were not very formidable, consisting of some side-wheel river steamboats and three or

four " tin-clads," and this was the force with which the navy was
expected to batter down Vicksburg.

Soon after my arrival at Cairo I sent a messenger to General
Grant informing him that I had taken command of the naval
forces, and should be happy to co-operate with him in any enterprise he might think proper to undertake. I also informed him
that General McClernand had orders to raise troops at Springfield,
Illinois, prior to undertaking the capture of Vicksburg. I thought
it my duty to tell him this, as it was not information given to me
in confidence.

Several weeks later Captain McAllister, quartermaster at Cairo,
gave a supper party to me and the officers on the station on board
the quartermaster's steamer, a large, comfortable river boat.

Supper had been served when I saw Captain McAllister usher
in a travel-worn person dressed in citizen's clothes. McAllister
was a very tall man, and his companion was dwarfed by his superior size. McAllister introduced the gentleman to me as General
Grant, and placed us at a table by ourselves and left us to talk
matters over.

Grant, though evidently tired and hungry, commenced business
at once. "Admiral," he inquired, "what is all this you have
been writing me ?"

I gave the general an account of my interviews with the President and with General McClernand, and he inquired, "When can
you move with your gun-boats, and what force have you ?"

"I can move to-morrow with all the old gun-boats and five or
six other vessels ; also the Tyler, Conestoga, and Lexington."

"Well, then," said Grant, "I will leave you now and write at
once to Sherman to have thirty thousand infantry and artillery
embarked in transports ready to start for Vicksburg the moment
you get to Memphis. I will return to Holly Springs to-night, and
will start with a large force for Grenada as soon as I can get off.

"General Joe Johnston is near Vicksburg with forty thousand
men, besides the garrison of the place under General Pemberton.
When Johnston hears I am marching on Grenada, he will come
from Vicksburg to meet me and check my advance. I will hold
him at Grenada while you and Sherman push on down the Mississippi and make a landing somewhere on the Yazoo. The garrison
at Vicksburg will be small, and Sherman will have no difficulty in
getting inside the works. When that is done I will force Johnston
out of Grenada, and, as he falls back on Vicksburg, will follow

him up with a superior force. When he finds Vicksburg is occupied, he will retreat via Jackson."

I thought this plan an admirable one. Grant and myself never indulged in long talks together ; it was only necessary for him to tell me what he desired, and I carried out his wishes to the best of my ability.

General Grant started that night for Holly Springs, Mississippi, and, I believe, rode on horseback nearly all the way, while I broke up the supper party by ordering every officer to his post of duty, to be ready to start down the river next day at noon.

And this was the preliminary step to the capture of Vicksburg.

Grant, in his plain, dusty coat, was, in my eyes, a greater general than the man who rides around,

All feathers and fuss.

Here in twenty minutes Grant unfolded his plan of campaign, involving the transportation of over one hundred thousand men, and, with a good supper staring him in the face, proposed to ride back again over a road he had just traveled without tasting a mouthful, his cigar serving, doubtless, for food and drink.

Three days after, with all the naval forces, I started down the Mississippi, and at Memphis found General Sherman embarking his troops on a long line of river steamers, and sent word to the general that I would call upon him at his headquarters.

Thinking it probable that Sherman would be dressed in full feather, I put on my uniform coat, the splendor of which rivaled that of a drum-major. Sherman, hearing that I was indifferent to appearances and generally dressed in working-clothes, thought he would not annoy me by fixing up, and so kept on his blue flannel suit ; and we met, both a little surprised at the appearance of the other.

"Halloo, Porter," said the general, "I am glad to see you ; you got here sooner than I expected, but we'll get off to-night. Devilish cold, isn't it ? Sit down and warm up." And he stirred up the coal in the grate. "Here, captain "—to one of his aids—"tell General Blair to get his men on board at once. Tell the quartermaster to report as soon as he has six hundred thousand rations embarked. Here, Dick "—to his servant—"put me up some shirts and under-clothes in a bag, and don't bother me with a trunk and traps enough for a regiment. Here, Captain "—another aid—"tell the steamboat captains to have steam up at six o'clock, and to lay in plenty of fuel, for I'm not going to stop every few hours to cut wood. Tell the officer in charge of embarkation to allow no picking and choosing of boats; the generals in command must take what is given them—there, that will do. Glad to see you, Porter; how's Grant?"

This was the first time I had ever met General Sherman, and my impressions of him were very favorable. I thought myself lucky to have two such generals as Grant and Sherman to co-operate with.

I soon returned to my flag-ship, the Black Hawk, and gave Captain Walke orders to proceed with several vessels to the Yazoo River, take possession of the landings in order to prevent the erection of batteries, and drag the river above Chickasaw Bayou for torpedoes. Captain Walke was directed to use all possible expedition, so as to reach the Yazoo at least a day in advance of us.

We departed from Memphis as arranged, and reached the Yazoo in good time. The Cairo, one of my best ironclads, had been blown up while grappling for torpedoes; but the landing of Sherman's army had been secured.

The rest is a matter of history, and is registered in the chronicles of the times with many variations and not a few misrepresentations. The reporters who followed the army did not all confine themselves to the truth, and when I asked one of them, on a certain occasion, why he did not state facts as they occurred, he replied:

"If I stated facts I would lose my place, for nothing but sensational articles will satisfy the public."

We reached Chickasaw Bayou in safety, but the army did not get much farther.

Grant's plans were well laid—"man proposes but God disposes"—and the plans were unsuccessful after all.

When Grant started from Holly Springs he left behind him a large depot of stores on which his army depended for supplies, and marched on Grenada with a force (I think) of sixty thousand men.

General Pemberton, as soon as he learned of this movement, saw that he would be locked up in Vicksburg if he let Grant get to the rear of that place, and his plan, therefore, was to check Grant's advance until other troops could be sent by rail to re-enforce Vicksburg.

Grant and Pemberton were marching toward each other as fast as possible, when the ubiquitous General Van Dorn got in Grant's rear and destroyed his supplies at Holly Springs.

I believe, however, that Grant had partly accomplished his object by drawing Pemberton a long way from Vicksburg, with the idea that, in the latter's absence, General Sherman would have comparatively little trouble in getting into the city.

No one, at that time, had any idea of the magnitude of the defenses that had been erected in every quarter to keep a foe out of Vicksburg, as if the Titans had come to the rescue of the rebel stronghold.

Sherman at every point encountered obstacles of which he had never dreamed. Forests had been cut down in the line of Chickasaw Bayou, and through the *chevaux-de-frise* the soldiers, standing up to their waists in water, had to cut their way with axes across the dismal swamps. All this, of course, took time ; there seemed to be no other route to Vicksburg. Haines's Bluff had been fortified so that no troops could pass in that direction without it was first reduced by the gun-boats. Every available soldier in Vicksburg had been brought to the point where Sherman was making his approaches, and they worked like devils.

> Old Clootie was there in his vigor and might ;
> He held the bottle and urged on the fight,
> As he dashed with his imps o'er the blood-sprinkled plain,
> His horses' hoofs trampling the wounded and slain.
> What cared he who died in their vigor and sin,
> As long as the devil and imps could but win ?

On the first sight of the gun-boats clearing out the Yazoo, the officer in command at Vicksburg saw through the whole plan, and telegraphed at once to General Pemberton, who immediately hurried back to Vicksburg, while Grant returned to Holly Springs.

Had not General Sherman been stopped by unforeseen obstacles, he would have captured the Southern Gibraltar ; but the impediments which an energetic adversary threw in the way disconcerted all his plans.

To add to Sherman's difficulties, the rain came on—and such a rain ! The heavens seemed trying to drown our army ; the naval vessels and transports were the only arks of safety. The level lands were inundated, and there were three feet of water in the swamps where our army was operating.

Notwithstanding this dismal situation of affairs, Sherman ordered an assault on the enemy's works. Part of General Blair's and part of another division reached the interior of the works and held them for a time.

The tables were soon turned, for, just as victory seemed to crown our arms, General Pemberton appeared on the scene with his army, just returned from Grenada, and drove our small body of men out of the works back to the place from which they started.

That ended the second campaign against Vicksburg, and our disheartened troops returned to the transports, where they were free from attack, as the enemy could not follow them through the waste of waters between their fortifications and the gun-boats. We picked up all that we had landed, including an old, worthless horse, determined that the enemy should have no more than we could help.

It was still raining, and the current ran so strong in the river that the vessels had to be fastened securely to the trees. The wind howled like a legion of devils, though which side it was howling for I have no idea.

That night General Sherman came on board my flag-ship, drenched to the skin. He looked as if he had been grappling with the mud, and got the worst of it.

He sat down and remained silent for some minutes.

"You are out of sorts," I said, at length. "What is the matter?"

"I have lost seventeen hundred men, and those infernal reporters will publish all over the country their ridiculous stories about Sherman being whipped, etc."

"Only seventeen hundred men!" I said. "Pshaw! that is nothing; simply an episode in the war. You'll lose seventeen thousand before the war is over, and will think nothing of it. We'll have Vicksburg yet before we die.—Steward, bring some punch for the general and myself."

"That's good sense, Porter!" exclaimed the general, "and I am glad to see you are not disheartened; but what shall we do now? I must take my boys somewhere and wipe this out."

I informed the general that I was ready to go anywhere.

"Then," said he, "let's go and thrash out Arkansas Post." And it was arranged that we should start next morning for that place. This attempt on Vicksburg gave occasion for some fine strategy on both sides.

Had General Grant determined in the first instance to advance on Vicksburg, leaving a sufficient force of men at Holly Springs to protect the place, no doubt Vicksburg would have fallen; but he had every reason to believe that, with the plans he had made, Sherman would get in. The appointed time had evidently not arrived, and it was necessary that a final demonstration of the power and determination of the Federal Government should be made, to satisfy the Southern people that none of their strongholds could finally prevail against the Union forces, and that no earthly power could dismember the Union,

> For God in his wisdom had devised the best plan
> For the union of States and the freedom of man.

Next morning a colonel, dressed in a new suit of uniform, sought an interview with me. I knew he could not belong to Sherman's army, for all his officers had long ago worn the brightness from their accoutrements.

"I come," said he, "from General McClernand, who is at the mouth of the Yazoo River, and wants you to call and see him as soon as possible."

"Well," thinks I to myself, "that's cool!" "You can tell the general," I said, "that my duties at present are so engrossing that I am making no calls, and that it is his place to come and see me. What is the general doing, and how did he get here?"

"He has come," said the officer, "to take command of the army; he took passage down in one of your ram gun-boats."

Here was a pretty kettle of fish! I bade the officer good-morning and he took his departure.

Just then I saw General Sherman in a small boat pulled by two soldiers. I hailed him, and when he was near enough I said, "Sherman, McClernand is at the mouth of the Yazoo, waiting to take command of your army!"

Sherman looked serious as he inquired, "Are you going to call on him?"

"No," I replied, "I am not making calls just now."

"But I must," said Sherman, "for he ranks me."

In two hours General Sherman returned with General McClernand, and I received the latter on board the flag-ship with all due courtesy, and inquired if he had brought an army with him and siege-tools to insure the fall of Vicksburg.

"No," replied McClernand, "but I find this army in a most demoralized state, and I must do something to raise their spirits."

"Then, sir," I said, " you take command of this army?"

"Certainly," he replied; "and if you will let me have some of your gun-boats, I propose to proceed immediately and capture Arkansas Post."

Sherman made a remark the purport of which I have forgotten, but McClernand made a discourteous reply, whereupon Sherman walked off into the after-cabin. I was angry that any one should dare treat General Sherman with discourtesy in my cabin.

I informed General McClernand that the proposition to capture Arkansas Post had been broached by General Sherman the previous evening, and that I never let my gun-boats go on such an important expedition without me. "If," I said, "General Sherman goes in command of this army, I will go along with my whole force and make a sure thing of it; otherwise I will have nothing to do with the affair."

Just then Sherman beckoned to me, and I went in to him. "My God, Porter!" he exclaimed, "you will ruin yourself if you talk that way to McClernand; he is very intimate with the President, and has powerful influence."

"I don't care who or what he is, he shall not be rude to you in my cabin," I replied.

"Did you understand my proposition, General McClernand?" I inquired, on my return to the forward cabin—he was at that moment consulting a map which lay on the table.

"Yes," said McClernand, "I understand it, and agree to it. There is no objection, I suppose, to my going along?"

"None in the world," I answered, "only be it understood that General Sherman is to command this army."

We started as soon as possible and arrived at "the Post," a fort, mounting eleven heavy guns, on the Arkansas River. I attacked it with three ironclads and several smaller vessels, and in three hours disabled all the guns. General Sherman surrounded the place with his troops, and, after heavy losses, it surrendered—the fort, in charge of naval officers, to me, and the Confederate army of six thousand men, under General Churchill, to General Sherman.

Our flag was no sooner hoisted over Arkansas Post—January 11, 1863—than General McClernand assumed command of the army and wrote the report of the capture—a most ungenerous thing for him to do under the circumstances.

The moment the prisoners were secured and the fort rendered untenable General McClernand ordered the army to proceed to Vicksburg, and I went in company, sending a message in advance to General Grant that I anticipated no good results from McClernand's commanding the army, that it was unjust to Sherman, that I was certain McClernand and myself could never co-operate harmoniously, and I hoped he would come and take command himself. I do not know that General Grant ever received my message, but we had hardly landed the troops on the bend opposite Vicksburg when he appeared and assumed command of the army, and the third attack on the rebel stronghold immediately commenced.

The siege was conducted with great perseverance on our side and with great bravery and endurance on the other, and when Pemberton surrendered—July 4, 1863—there was nothing left for the subsistence of the soldiers or the inhabitants.

An elaborate history of the siege of Vicksburg would be a most interesting military work, but to write it would require much time and research, and a consultation not only of official documents but of the experience of the principal officers on both sides who were engaged in this memorable struggle.

General Grant has gained a world-wide reputation for his military achievements, but I think no event conferred more credit on him than the siege of Vicksburg against the most formidable series of earthworks ever erected on this continent.

I saw the celebrated Malakoff and the Redan two days after they fell into the hands of the allied English and French army, and they were nothing in comparison with the defenses of Vicksburg.

Grant's action in turning the flank at Vicksburg with but fifty-six thousand men, and defeating two armies aggregating eighty thousand strong, forms one of the most remarkable chapters in the history of the civil war.

I do not believe that any of the accounts that were written of the events transpiring around Vicksburg during the siege did justice to the subject, and I am sorry that the limit of these pages will prevent my giving even an outline of this remarkable siege.

Having encamped directly opposite to Vicksburg, our army had a good opportunity of contemplating the task before it.

It was evident that the place could not be taken from the front; the rebel army and the inhabitants were receiving all the supplies they wanted, not only *via* Jackson but by steamers from Red River. It was desirable to stop this communication.

I had under my command a semi-naval organization called the "Marine Brigade," which had done good service at Memphis and elsewhere. Several of the vessels in this organization were commanded by members of the Ellet family, the senior member of which, Brigadier-General A. W. Ellet, commanded the brigade.

Colonel Charles Ellet, Jr., a young man of twenty-two, commanded the Queen of the West, a ram improvised from a river steamboat.

I ordered young Ellet to pass the batteries of Vicksburg at night, proceed to the mouth of Red River, intercept the supplies for Vicksburg and Port Hudson, and capture everything he could overtake.

I don't know whether it was from love of glory or from want of judgment, but, instead of taking advantage of the darkness to run the batteries, Ellet chose early daylight, got well hammered as he passed the forts, and nearly defeated the object of the expedition. Not being accustomed to strict discipline, Ellet did not realize the necessity of carrying out his orders to the letter.

After Colonel Ellet reached Red River he captured several steamers loaded with provisions for Port Hudson, and having on board a number of Confederate officers; and hearing that other steamers were on their way down Red River, his youthful ardor led him to go on up that stream.

He arrived at Fort De Russy, and there, by the treachery of his pilot, was run on shore near the batteries. The enemy opened fire on the Queen of the West, killing and wounding numbers of the crew and cutting the steam-pipe. The vessel was now helpless, and Ellet and all his officers and men who were able jumped overboard and drifted down the river to a point where one of their prizes lay, got on board of her, and made their escape.

In the mean time I had prepared the ironclad Indianola and sent her down to assist the Queen of the West. The Indianola passed the batteries at night with little damage, and met Colonel Ellet and his men coming up in their prize steamer New Era.

The Indianola, with two coal-barges in tow, continued down until she reached the mouth of Red River, then turned back and proceeded up river again until near the plantation of Mr. Joseph Davis, the brother of the Confederate President.

At daylight next morning, after the Queen of the West had been abandoned, the Confederates took possession and soon repaired damages.

The Confederate ram Webb joined the Queen of the West from Alexandria, and the two vessels, well manned and armed, proceeded in search of the Indianola, came up with her at Davis's plantation, rammed her, and she ran into shoal water and sank, February 24, 1863.

We heard of the disaster a few hours after, and all my calculations for stopping the enemy's supplies were for the time frustrated ; but I took a philosophical view of the matter as one of the episodes of the war. However, it was necessary to try and prevent the rebels from raising the Indianola, and, as I was not ready to go down the river myself, as it would interfere with an important military movement, I hit upon a cheap expedient, which worked very well.

I set the whole squadron at work and made a raft of logs, three hundred feet long, with sides to it, two huge wheel-houses and a formidable log casemate, from the port-holes of which appeared sundry wooden guns. Two old boats hung from davits fitted to the "ironclad," and two smoke-stacks made of hogsheads completed the illusion ; and on her wheel-houses was painted the following : "Deluded Rebels, Cave In !" An American flag was hoisted aft, and a banner emblazoned with skull and cross-bones ornamented the bow.

When this craft was completed, she resembled at a little distance the ram Lafayette, which had just arrived from St. Louis.

The mock ram was furnished with a big iron pot inside each smoke-stack, in which was tar and oakum to raise a black smoke, and at midnight she was towed down close to the water-batteries of Vicksburg and sent adrift.

It did not take the Vicksburg sentinels long to discover the formidable monster that was making its way down the river. The batteries opened on her with vigor, and continued the fire until she had passed beyond the range of their guns.

The Vicksburgers had greatly exulted over the capture of the Queen of the West and the Indianola ; the local press teemed with accounts of the daring of the captors, and flattered themselves that, with the Indianola and Queen of the West in their possession, they would be able to drive the Union navy out of the Mississippi. What was their astonishment to see this huge ironclad pass the batteries, apparently unharmed, and not even taking the trouble to fire a gun !

Some of our soldiers had gone down to the point below Vicksburg to see the fun, and just before reaching Warrenton the mock monitor caught the eddy and turned toward the bank where these men were gathered.

The soldiers spent several hours in trying to shove the dummy off into the stream, when daylight overtook them in the midst of their work, and the Queen of the West, with the Confederate flag flying, was seen coming up the river and stopping at Warrenton.

As we afterward learned, she came up for pumps, etc., to raise the Indianola.

In the mean while the military authorities in Vicksburg had sent couriers down to Joe Davis's plantation to inform the people on board the Webb that a monster ironclad had passed the batteries and would soon be upon them. The crew of the Webb were busy in trying to remove the guns from their prize, and, when they heard the news, determined to blow her up.

Just after the Queen of the West made the Warrenton landing the soldiers succeeded in towing the mock ironclad into the stream, and she drifted rapidly down upon the rebel prize, whose crew never stopped to deliberate, but cut their fasts and proceeded down the river. Their steam was low, and for a time the mock ironclad drifted almost as fast as the Queen of the West; but at length the latter left her formidable pursuer far behind.

The Queen of the West arrived at the point where the Indianola was sunk just as the people on board the Webb were preparing to blow her up, bringing the news that the "great ironclad" was close behind. So the Webb cast off and, with her consort, made all speed down the river.

The Webb had been so greatly injured in ramming the Indianola that she had to go to Shreveport for repairs, and the Queen of the West was shortly after recaptured and destroyed.

The results of the capture of the Indianola were, however, deplorable. It is wonderful how rapidly news was transmitted along the river, and the Indianola had scarcely sunk before Farragut heard of it on board the Hartford. He was also informed that the Confederates had raised the vessel and were about to use her against his fleet at Port Hudson.

Farragut had obtained the false impression that the Indianola was a very powerful vessel, and so he thought it necessary to pass the batteries at Port Hudson and encounter her before she could get under the protection of the Confederate works at that place.

This induced him to attempt to run past Port Hudson with a portion of his fleet, when he met with considerable loss.

Owing to the smoke from the guns which hung over the river, the pilots could not see their way. The frigate Mississippi grounded opposite the forts, and there remained, while the enemy poured shot and shell into her to their hearts' content.

Her commanding officer did everything that was possible to get his vessel off; but, finding all his efforts useless, and that his officers and men were being sacrificed, he set fire to the ship and abandoned her.

As the frigate's upper works were consumed the ship became lightened; she slid off the mud-bank and, drifting down the river, blew up with an awful sound that carried joy to the hearts of the Confederates.

A thousand memories clustered around the dear old ship, and she will be handed down in history with the Hartford, whose fortunes up to this time she had shared.

Only two of Farragut's vessels passed Port Hudson—the Hartford, his flag-ship, and another which was lashed to her; so he arrived at the mouth of Red River with but a small portion of his fleet.

So much for the loss of one ironclad of which much was expected and by which little was accomplished. The Indianola lay imbedded in the mud until after the fall of Vicksburg, when we raised her.

The Vicksburg people were furious at the trick we played them, and the newspapers reviled their military authorities for not being able to distinguish an old raft from a monster ironclad! They were consoled, however, in a day or two when the news of the destruction of the Mississippi reached Vicksburg.

Notwithstanding their gallant defense, the garrison of Vicksburg were daily growing weaker while our strength was all the time increasing. They began to realize that we had come to stay until we could plant the Union flag over their stronghold.

CHAPTER XIV.

GENERAL GRANT'S PLANS FOR TAKING VICKSBURG—THE YAZOO PASS EXPEDITION—NAVAL EVOLUTIONS IN THE WOODS—PILES OF COTTON BURNED BY THE CONFEDERATES—MR. TUB, THE TELEGRAM-WIRE MAN—THE PASS AT ROLLING FORK—END OF THE STEELE BAYOU EXPEDITION.

I INTENDED by this time to have departed from before Vicksburg, and to leave it to future scribblers to write about, as no doubt they will do, just as tourists visit the plains of Waterloo to pick up relics and write an oft-told tale; but there is a fascination about the place (Vicksburg) that prevents me from tearing myself away.

Everything about that siege is an anecdote or a reminiscence worthy of being treasured up.

One of the liveliest reminiscences I have of the siege is what is called the Yazoo Pass expedition—one of three attempts we made to get behind Vicksburg with a fleet of ironclads and a detachment of the army—in which I have to say that we failed most egregiously.

At one period of the siege the rains had swollen the Mississippi River so much that it had backed its waters up into its tributaries, which had risen seventeen feet, and, overflowing, had inundated the country for many miles.

Great forests had become channels admitting the passage of large steamers between the trees, and now and then wide lanes were met with where a frigate might have passed.

The ironclads drew only seven feet of water and had no masts or yards to encumber them, and but little about their decks that could be swept away by the bushes or lower branches of the trees. I had thoughts of trying the experiment of getting the vessels back of Vicksburg in that way, and sent Lieutenant Murphy in a tug to examine the woods as far as he could go, and to let me know the results of his cruise as soon as possible.

Murphy soon returned with the most cheering news, and induced me to go with him and take a look for myself. General Grant accompanied me, and, prepared with lead-lines to measure the depth, we started off.

A few miles up the Yazoo, before reaching Haines's Bluff, we came to an opening in the woods. Under the pilotage of Murphy, the tug Jessie Benton darted into the bushes, and the man at the lead took the soundings—nothing less than fifteen feet. Presently we reached an opening between the trees sufficiently wide to admit two ironclads abreast. I suppose it was an ancient road in the forest by which to haul cotton to the river.

We followed this for five miles until we reached a forest of large trees without any undergrowth, but with width enough between them to admit the passage of our heaviest ironclad. This forest permitted us to steam along about five miles farther, when we came to a wide opening where there were but few trees. Here we found a bayou leading to the westward with from ten to twelve feet of water—more than enough for our purposes.

We knew this bayou led into the Rolling Fork, Yallabusha, and Sunflower Rivers, though there was not generally enough water in it to float a canoe. We could not ascend it then for fear of alarming the inhabitants, or letting them know the news of our arrival in these woods and having it conveyed to Vicksburg.

We saw all we wanted, and General Grant approved of the plan I proposed of going up with some ironclads, tugs, etc., and trying to get into the Sunflower; that would lead us into the Yazoo again, and we could come down and take Haines's Bluff in the rear.

General Grant also determined to send General Sherman on the expedition with ten thousand troops, and said we could make a reconnoissance if we could do no more, for he saw from the first that there was no use in sitting down before Vicksburg and simply looking at it, or bombarding it to bring about a surrender; we would have lost time, and deposited our shell in the hills, increasing their weight in iron, without getting nearer to our object. General Grant had from the first an idea of turning Vicksburg, but *how* to do it was the question. He was obliged to have transports if he went below the city and desired to cross the river to land on the Vicksburg side, and enough of these transports to carry troops and provisions. How was he to get these frail vessels below Vicksburg without passing the batteries? One shot would disable them. He could depend upon the gun-boats to pass the batteries, but there were not enough of them to convey the necessary number of troops, and they had no accommodations for carrying provisions.

Besides, it would not do to take too many of the gun-boats below Vicksburg, for it would leave the upper Mississippi unguarded, and the enemy would commence at once to erect batteries along the river and stop the transportation of troops and stores. During all Grant's operations before Vicksburg, while I had command of the river force, he never had a transport molested. I so guarded the Mississippi—from Cairo down—with gun-boats (which I was building or altering incessantly) that flying batteries and guerrillas —so called—were never able to make any headway.

General Grant had to think of all these things before he could make a move for below.

He talked with me about it, and I assured him I was ready to go the moment he desired it. He thought he might do something that would enable him to get by Vicksburg without bringing his transports under fire. He tried cutting a ditch across the peninsula, in hopes that the river would burst through there and leave Vicksburg out in the cold. This occurred finally (after the war), but too late for our operations, for, notwithstanding the high stage of the water, it refused to run through the ditch ; heavy eddies extended from the shore far out into the river and kept the current away from the bank ; there was no cutting power in the eddies.

Grant tried to make a channel through what was called Lake Providence, but some of the vessels that tried this passage got entangled in the woods, and came near remaining there.

Every known expedient had been tried without success, and now it remained to attempt the route through the woods to the west of the Yazoo River.

Sixty or seventy miles above Vicksburg there was, many years ago, an old pass into the Yallabusha and the Sunflower called the Yazoo Pass. This had long since been closed up by a deep levee, and the land, once overflowed through this pass, had become flourishing plantations.

It was proposed by some one to open the pass once more and let the water flow in, making a deep channel by which we could send in an expedition of gun-boats. These might reach the Yazoo River that way back of Vicksburg and clear the way for the troops.

This plan met with approval, and General Grant and myself determined, at the same time we were trying to get up through the woods and the bayou into the Sunflower, that we would send a naval and military expedition through the old Yazoo Pass.

This expedition consisted of two heavy ironclads, three or four light-armed vessels, and about four thousand troops in transports. The force arrived at the point selected, a few men dug a small trench with spades, and in an hour the water was rushing in with the force of a cataract, carrying away a hundred yards of the levee and inundating hundreds of acres of land. It took twenty-four hours for the water to reach a level, and then the gun-boats, without more ado, pitched in regardless of consequences, followed by the transports. Then came the tug of war. The vessels were swept along with great velocity until they got beyond the great pressure of the water, or were stopped by the trees with their overhanging branches, which brought them up all standing, bringing their smoke-stacks on deck and knocking off some of the upper cabins.

The ironclads stood the thumping better than the lighter vessels, for they had no cabins above, and all they had to fear was the loss of their smoke-stacks and boats, some of which were crushed to pieces.

All the vessels were at the mercy of the strong current. If one of them for a moment grappled a tree to hold on by, she would find another one sweeping down on her from astern, and, for fear of being crushed, she had to let go, and then all floated on together.

During the years in which the old Yazoo Pass had been closed the heavy trees had mingled their branches across the stream, and now often stopped the progress of the fleet. Then a thousand hands would be set to work with axes and saws to clear away overhead for a mile or two in advance.

Sometimes the vessels would come bump against a small " Red River raft," held securely by running vines or wedged in so strongly with a key-log that it would require hours of labor before they could get the raft loose and let it go drifting down with the current; then the fleet would push on again, and this lasted three or four days, while the expedition only progressed forty miles.

Most of the light vessels were perfect wrecks in their upper works. Their machinery and boilers held out, and that was all that was required of them. It was a painful and ever-to-be-remembered expedition to those who took part in it.

To make matters worse, the naval officer commanding the expedition showed symptoms of aberration of mind, and the other officers with him had great difficulty in getting him to pursue proper measures. The officer in charge of the troops got discontented with the hard work his men had to perform in cutting down trees and other obstructions. Still they kept pushing on, and no such word as fail was heard. All wondered how they would get out of that, or back again through that cataract; but then their orders were to push on and to come out behind Vicksburg! Day and night they moved along, taking no rest, though they would not make more than two miles in twelve hours. It was work that tried men's souls, and there are few naval officers left of all that party who can sit down and tell of that adventure. Death's avaricious hand has snatched most of them away, and it shows the effect the toil and excitement of war will have on men of iron, with nerves of steel, who, if they had been left to pursue the peaceful avocations of life, would probably have been here now.

There is an end to all hard work, privation, and exposure.

Every one is either killed or used up, or gets to some place where he can lie down and rest.

There is a certain amount of endurance sailors and soldiers possess which is kept up as long as the nerve-power holds out, and it was with a relieved feeling that the people of this expedition could finally lie down and sleep without the disturbing noise of crushing bulwarks, or the fall on the decks of decaying limbs. They did not shun death nor danger, and at last they earned their reward : "they slept."

The expedition reached an opening at last that entered another stream almost wide enough for two vessels abreast, and without overhanging trees, "Red River rafts," or sand-bars—a pleasant, swift-running stream that seemed willing to carry them whithersoever they wished to go, and they thought how their companions who had stayed behind would envy them when they heard their guns booming back of Haines's Bluff, startling the Confederates out of their secure and comfortable sleep.

They were anxious to get on, and the command, owing to the unfortunate condition of the senior officer, fell upon the next in rank, as brave a fellow as ever stepped on a ship's deck. He had the whistles blown for getting under way, and sang out, "On to Vicksburg, boys, and no more trees to saw !" The flotilla moved on about a mile, and, on turning a bend, ran almost into a fort in the middle of the river, with the channel each side blocked by sunken steamers. Heavy rifled guns were mounted in the works, and there was a large body of troops in the fort who jumped to their pieces the moment our vessels appeared in sight.

These works were all new, and the guns just mounted ; the sunken steamers had scarcely blown off their steam. They had but a few hours ago brought the guns and carriages, and thrown up breastworks on the sudden bend in the river (or half island), and seeing our forces close at hand, they had sunk the steamers to prevent our gun-boats from running past the battery. All this took our people by surprise. They knew from the truthful contrabands that there was no such work on this stream until they should reach Haines's Bluff.

Here was a check with a vengeance. Had the fort been altogether ready it would have given the lighter vessels of the expedition a warm reception as they came so confidingly down the river, and were so mixed up. As to the transports and troops, they would have fared badly. There was no way of turning the steamers around and going up stream again, for the river was too narrow.

The vessels had to get hold of each other and back up against the stream until they could reach a bend where they could not be seen. While they were doing all this they would have been exposed to a raking fire had the enemy had his powder ready. *Laus Deo!* he had not loaded his guns, and was in quite as much excitement over the apparition of two large ironclads and a dozen transports and light gun-boats with the pipes all knocked over, and their cabins and light work all gone, as was our party.

They no doubt wondered where they all came from, and how they got there.

The Yazoo Pass expedition was supposed to have been prepared without any one knowing anything about its destination except General Grant and myself and the commanding naval and military officers, and, even until a spade was stuck into the earth to open the pass, it was thought that the destination of the expedition was a profound secret. Yes, pretty much such a secret as a dozen women would keep.

Secret or not, here the expedition was met—almost at its first entrance to those inland waters—by heavy earthworks, three or four rifled cannon, and a body of troops. The question was, What was to be done ?

The ironclads, after going backward for a time, tied up to the bank, and, overlapping each other, opened fire on the enemy's work, which turned out to be named Fort Pemberton, after the wily old soldier in command at Vicksburg.

Ours was a pretty piece of strategy for getting into the rear of Vicksburg, but Pemberton's was better, as it checkmated us completely, and this often happened in the siege.

The Confederates were a wide-awake set of adversaries, full of energy and courage, and not lacking in resources. They were working with all their souls to attain an object which they considered conducive to their happiness, and they did not care whom they hurt, so long as they could succeed.

Our people, though quite as energetic as the Southerners, fought with a different sentiment. There was still some kindly feeling left in them for their foes, whose courage and endurance under great privation often called forth applause. We were not fighting with the courage of despair. A man of ordinary intellect could see the end which would be the downfall of the Southern

Confederacy. It was as plain as the writing on the wall at the feast of Belshazzar.

The Southerners were fighting with the energy of despair, hoping that some untoward event might spring up to help them. At all events, they were determined to command their enemy's respect for their courage and ability, and I don't think any brave sailor or soldier ever withheld it.

Our troops were flocking to the fields of battle by the hundred thousands at a time, when the Confederate troops began to give out in numbers. We were certain of means, suffered very little of the discomforts by sieges and bombardments experienced by the Confederates, had no rancorous feeling to urge us on, and simply desired to see the laws vindicated and the authority of the Government established over revolting States. There were occasions when we did not seem to count the value of time, and our energies, though well put forth, did not equal those of our enemies.

On our side there was not a sufficient *unity* in command ; there was a kind of "stand-off" between the army and the navy when acting together, which prevented them from working in harmony and with one purpose. There should always have been one man in an expedition in command of the whole, and his authority should have been so manifest that there would have been no appeal from his orders.

This was not the case in the Yazoo Pass expedition. Each corps commanded its men independent of the other, and there seemed no disposition to act in concert.

The course of General Grant and myself in all such matters corresponded entirely with what I have suggested. Though he had no control over me whatever, and I was never tied down by any orders from the Navy Department, but left to my own discretion, I always deferred to his wishes in all matters, and went so far as to give orders to those under my command that they should obey the orders of Generals Grant and Sherman the same as if they came from myself. Hence we always acted with the most perfect accord.

In this case the officer commanding the troops should have been subject to the orders of the naval officer. Then, I think, we would have discomfited General Pemberton's strategy by taking possession of his fort.

When the ironclads, the Chilicothe, Captain Foster, and the Baron de Kalb, under Captain Walker, opened their bow guns (the only ones they could use), the fort responded promptly, and in a short time jammed the port shutters of the Chilicothe so that they could not be opened. It was certain death for a man to go out on the bow to work with chisel and hammer, and Captain Foster had to withdraw from action until he could remedy the difficulty. In the mean time the Baron de Kalb remained and sustained the action alone, and so well was the fire directed that half an hour after the Chilicothe returned to her station the fort stopped firing, though the Confederate flag was kept flying.

Now was the time for the troops to operate; they should have been sent out as sharpshooters, should have crawled within fifty yards of the works, and kept up such a fusillade that nothing could have stood it.

The vessels could not get near to the fort without being blown up by torpedoes. One torpedo did explode right in front of the Chilicothe when she took her position the second time, and no doubt they were planted all around the works, and for some distance from them.

There were not sailors enough to undertake to carry the works in boats, and everything was at a stand-still. The army officer in command took no suggestion from any one, and declined to assault the fort (which was a low one) and have his men sacrificed. Pemberton's strategy succeeded, and our party left the place, struggling back again wearily through the Yazoo Pass, which we had taken so much trouble to clean out, having inundated many thousands of acres to no purpose at all.

Great complaints were made by both sides as to whose fault it was that there was a failure, but I told the navy I didn't want to hear anything about it; they did not get through, and didn't get the fort, and the less said about it the better. "It was just one of the episodes of the war" (my consolation when I met with a failure), and I never wanted to hear of the Yazoo Pass expedition again.

I had gone through the mill myself and knew exactly how it was, and didn't feel much like blaming any one. These expeditions don't sound badly on paper, but they were enough to try men's souls.

About the time the Yazoo Pass expedition got off I proposed an expedition to go through the woods by the same route explored by General Grant and myself.

I determined to go myself, and, to make it a success, I omitted nothing that might possibly be wanted on such an expedition. I selected the ironclads Louisville, Lieutenant-Commanding Owen ; Cincinnati, Lieutenant-Commanding Bache ; Carondelet, Lieutenant-Commanding Murphy ; Mound City, Lieutenant-Commanding Wilson ; Pittsburgh, Lieutenant-Commanding Hoel, and four tugs ; also two light mortar-boats built for the occasion, to carry each a thirteen-inch mortar and shells enough to bombard a city.

I really do believe I thought I was sure of getting in the rear of Vicksburg, and could send some more shells into the hills that would keep them fastened down to eternity.

At the same time General Sherman prepared his contingent to accompany the expedition.

General Grant was so much interested in this work that he went up to the end of the woods on one of the transports to see Sherman start on his march alongside of the gun-boats, and gave his personal attention toward pushing ahead those of Sherman's troops that had not reached us in the transports. These now and then got lost in the thick woods, and sometimes got their pipes knocked down.

This was one of the most remarkable military and naval expeditions that ever set out in any country, and will be so ranked by those who read of it in future times.

Here was a dense forest, deeply inundated, so that large steamers could ply about among the trees with perfect impunity. They were as much at home there as the wild denizens of the forest would be in dry times.

The animals of all kinds had taken to the trees as the only arks of safety. Coons, rats, mice, and wild cats were in the branches, and if they were not a happy family, it was because when they lay down together the smaller animals reposed within the larger ones.

It was a curious sight to see a line of ironclads and mortar-boats, tugs and transports, pushing their way through the long, wide lane in the woods without touching on either side, though sometimes a rude tree would throw Briarean arms around the smoke-stack of the tin-clad Forest Rose, or the transport Molly Miller, and knock their bonnets sideways.

It all looked as though the world had suddenly got topsy-turvy, or that there was a great camp-meeting in the woods on board ironclads and transports.

The difficulty was to preserve quiet, so that our presence might not be detected by the enemy's scouts. It could not be possible, I

10

thought, that the besieged in Vicksburg would not have sought an opportunity to reconnoitre our lines by means of canoes, or even communicate with some of those who were always to be found faithless to their trust.   Indeed, I would not have been much surprised to see a rebel iron-clad ram lurking somewhere in the bushes, ready to spring out on us.   They were building two of them in Yazoo City, where the ram Arkansas came from.   Why should we not meet them here ?

If one had suddenly slid down a tree and attacked us I should not have been much surprised.   The only reason why that was not likely to happen was that the Confederates were not lucky "in *Aries*," and generally managed to lose their rams and ironclads soon after they were built.   They would perform some creditable feat with these vessels, and then blow them up, or set fire to them, to keep them from falling into our hands.

Besides, I had little fear of the rams at Yazoo City, as I knew their condition, through a truthful contraband, who informed me, "Dey has no bottom in, no sides to 'em, an' no top on to 'em, sah, an' deir injines is in Richmon'."

We ran on, in line of battle, eight or ten miles through the open way in the trees, carrying fifteen feet of water by the lead-line.   Let the nautical reader imagine an old quartermaster in the "chains" of an ironclad steaming through the woods and singing out, "Quarter less three !"   Truth is stranger than fiction.

At last we came to a point where the forest was close and composed of very large trees—old monarchs of the woods which had spread their arms for centuries over those silent solitudes : Titans, like those in the old fables, that dominate over all around them.

In the distance, between the trees, would spring into sight gray, sunless glens in which the dim, soft ripple of day seemed to glimmer for a second so fancifully, indeed, that it required but a slight stretch of imagination to see the wood-nymphs disporting in their baths.

The sun seldom reached these woody glades, and, if it did, it was but to linger for a moment and disappear, like the bright star of eve, behind a silver cloud.

It all looked like some infinite world in which we were adrift, where the sky, soft and serene (which we had been accustomed to see), had been furled in anticipation of a squall.

Every turn of the wheels sent an echo through the woods that would frighten the birds of prey from their perches, whence they were looking down upon the waste of waters, wondering (no doubt) what it all might mean, and whom these mighty buzzards, skimming over the waters and carrying everything before them, could possibly be.

Our line of battle was broken on approaching the large trees; then we had to go more cautiously. What, thought I, if the trees should become so dense that we could not pass between them; what would we do then? I solved the difficulty at once. "Ram that large tree there," I said to the captain of the Cincinnati; "let us see what effect the old turtle will have on it." It was an unnecessary act of vandalism to injure the old Titan, but it would shorten our road, and we would not be obliged to go meandering about to find a channel. We struck the tree while going at the rate of three knots an hour, and bounded off, but started it about twenty degrees from the perpendicular. The light soil about its roots had become softened by the water, and the tree had not much staying power. I backed again and gave it another ram, and the weight of eight hundred tons, with a three-knot velocity, sent it out of all propriety. I hailed the ironclad astern of me, and ordered her to bend a heavy chain to it and pull it down, which was accomplished in half an hour.

I wanted to see what we could do at ramming and pulling at big trees, and our experience so gained came into play before we got through the expedition.

It was all very pleasant at first, skimming along over summer seas, under the shade of stalwart oaks, but we had no conception of what we had before us.

We had to knock down six or eight of these large trees before we could reach the point where Sherman was disembarking part of his troops. When I came up he was on a piece of high ground, on an old white horse some of his "boys" had captured.

"Halloo, old fellow," he sang out, "what do you call this? This must be traverse sailing. You think it's all very fine just now, don't you; but, before you fellows get through, you won't have a smoke-stack or a boat among you."

"So much the better," I said; "it will look like business, and we will get new ones. All I want is an engine, guns, and a hull to float them. As to boats, they are very much in the way."

At this point we ran up alongside higher land which looked like a levee.

"Is this the last of it?" I asked Sherman.

"No," he said; "steam on about twenty yards to the west, and you will find a hole through a kind of levee wide enough, I think, for your widest vessel. That is Cypress Bayou; it leads into the Sunflower about seventy-five miles distant, and a devil of a time you'll have of it. Look out those fellows don't catch you. I'll be after you."

Sherman knew every bayou and stream in that part of the country better than the oldest inhabitants knew them.

I pushed on, my fleet following, and soon found myself inside the bayou. It was exactly forty-six feet wide. My vessel was forty-two feet wide, and that was the average width of the others. This place seemed to have been a bayou with high levees bordering, reaching, indeed, above the vessel's guns.

It had been made, I suppose, into a kind of canal to connect the waters of the Sunflower by a short cut with those of the Yazoo, near Haines's Bluff. All on the left of the levee was deep water in the woods. On the other side were cornfields. The levee had stopped the further encroachment of the flood. This bayou had not been used for many years for the purposes of navigation. It had almost closed up, and the middle of it was filled with little willows which promised to be great impediments to us, but, as there was nine feet of water in the ditch, I pushed on.

Sherman told me he would follow me along the left bank of the ditch with his troops, and be up with me before I knew it, as he would make two miles to my one.

It was intended from the first that we should travel along together for mutual support. We to transport him across rivers and marshes, he to keep off sharp-shooters, whom we could not reach with our guns on account of the high banks. We left Sherman at the point where we found him arranging his men, and I pushed into the bayou with my whole force, keeping one tug in the advance with one mortar-boat, the ironclads in the middle, and the other tugs and mortar-boat with the coal-barge bringing up the rear.

We supposed we were doing all this very secretly, and were going to surprise the natives. No doubt we did surprise those who dwelt on and along the Cypress Bayou, but our movement was probably no surprise to the Confederates in Vicksburg. I am quite satisfied in my own mind that, while we were steaming along and performing naval evolutions in the woods, the President of the Southern Confederacy was reading something like the following dispatch to his Cabinet:

"Sherman and Porter pirouetting through the woods in steamers and ironclads. Are keeping a lookout on them. Hope to bag them all before to-morrow."

We had not entered the bayou more than half a mile before we saw the greatest excitement prevailing. Men on horseback were flying in all directions. Cattle, instead of being driven in, were driven off to parts unknown. Pigs were driven by droves to the far woods, and five hundred negroes were engaged in driving into the fields all the chickens, turkeys, ducks, and geese, and what were a few moments before smiling barn-yards, were now as bare of poultry as your hand. I had issued an order against capturing anything on shore, but the difficulty was to find out where the shore was, as apparently the Cypress Bayou ran right through the middle of a stable-yard.

I informed the sailors that loot naturally belonged to the army, but that prize in the shape of cotton marked "C. S. A." belonged to them. A mile from the entrance to the bayou there were two piles of cotton containing six thousand bales, and placed opposite each other on the banks of the stream in which we were then just holding our way against its two-knot current.

Suddenly I saw two men rush up from each side of the bayou and apply a lighted pine-knot to each pile. "What fools these mortals be !" I said to an officer, "but I suppose those men have a right to burn their own cotton, especially as we have no way of preventing them."

"I can send a howitzer-shell at them, sir," he said, "and drive them away."

"No," I replied, "that might kill them, and we don't want to do that except in battle."

So the two men went on with their work of destruction. They applied the torches to every part of the two piles, and in twenty minutes there was a column of smoke ascending to the skies, and the passage between the piles became very much obscured.

"How long will it take that cotton to burn up ?" I inquired of a darkey who was asking permission to come on board.

"Two day, Massa," the negro answered ; "sometime t'ree."

By this time all the outside of the cotton was blazing. "Ring the bell to go ahead fast," I ordered, "and tell those astern to follow after me." I was on board the Cincinnati. "Go ahead fast the tug and mortar-boat," and away we all went, darting through between the burning bales.

All the ports were shut in and the crews called to fire quarters, standing ready with fire-buckets to meet the enemy's *fire*.

It reminded me a little of the fire-raft at Fort Jackson, but we soon got used to them.

The fellows on the tug wet themselves and boat all over very thoroughly, and as they darted through, being below the bank, they did not suffer much ; but the paint was blistered on the boat, and the fire scorched the men.

Myself, captain, and wheelman were the only ones on deck when the Cincinnati passed through, but the heat was so intense that I had to jump inside a small house on deck covered with iron, the captain following me. The helmsman covered himself up with an old flag that lay in the wheel-house. The hose was pointed up the hatch to the upper deck and everything drenched with water, but it did not render the heat less intolerable.

The boats escaped with some blistering. The smoke was even worse than the heat, and I have often since imagined how a brave fireman feels when he is looking through a burning house in search of helpless people.

Just after we passed through the fire there was a dreadful crash, which some thought was an earthquake. We had run into and quite through a span of bridge about fifty feet long, and demolished the whole fabric, having failed to see it in the smoke.

There was a yell among the negroes on the bank, who looked on with amazement at the doings of "Mas' Linkum's gun-boats."

"What dey gwine ter do nex' ?" said an old patriarch.

The next we did was to stop and breathe after getting through that smoke, and look back and regret the loss of the cotton. The worst thing to be done with cotton is to burn it, especially when it is not your own.

Here was the Confederate Government complaining of Northern oppression, and yet their own agents were riding around on horseback, setting fire to the people's cotton to keep it from falling into our hands, while, if they had let it alone, it would not have been troubled by us, except by giving a receipt for it, and, when the war was over, the owners would have netted more than the full value of their property.

This was one of the worst cases of vandalism I had yet seen.

When all the vessels had passed through the flame and smoke we hauled up at a small collection of houses, where the negro women were running around screaming and driving in the pigs and poultry.

A burly overseer, weighing over two hundred pounds, sat at the door of a log-hut with a pipe in his mouth. He was a white man, half bull-dog, half blood-hound, and his face expressed everything that was bad in human nature, but he smoked away as if nothing was the matter—as Nero fiddled while Rome was burning.

He looked on us with perfect indifference; our presence didn't seem to disturb him at all. Doubtless he felt quite secure; that we didn't want anything so bad as he was.

I called to him, and he came down in his shirt-sleeves, bare-headed, and looked stolidly at me as if to say, "Well, what do you want?"

"Why did those fools set fire to that cotton?" I inquired.

"Because they didn't want you fools to have it," he replied. "It's ourn, and I guess things ain't come to such a pass that we can't do as we please with our own."

"Tell them we won't trouble it," I said; "it is wicked to see such material going off like smoke."

In five minutes he had a dozen negroes at his side, and they were all sent up the bayou on a full run to stop the burning of cotton. He believed our word, and we did not disappoint him.

"And who are you?" I inquired of the man.

"I am in charge of this plantation," he replied; "this is the mother of my children"—pointing to a fat, thick-lipped negress who stood, with her bosom all bare and arms a-kimbo, about ten yards away—"and these fine fellows are my children," he continued, pointing to some light-colored boys who had followed him down.

"I suppose you are Union, of course? You all are so when it suits you," I said.

"No, by G——, I'm not, and never will be; and as to the others, I know nothing about them. Find out for yourself. I'm for Joff Davis first, last, and all the time. Do you want any more of me?" he inquired, "for I am not a loquacious man at any time."

"No, I want nothing more with you," I replied; "but I am going to steam into that bridge of yours across the stream and knock it down. Is it strongly built?"

"You may knock it down and be d—d," he said. "It don't belong to me; and, if you want to find out how strong it is, pitch into it. You'll find a hard nut to crack; it ain't made of candy."

"You are a Yankee by birth, are you not?" I asked.

"Yes, d—n it, I am," he replied; "that's no reason I should like the institution. I cut it long ago," and he turned on his heel and walked off.

"Ring 'Go ahead fast,'" I said to the captain; "we will let that fellow see what bridge-smashers we are."

In three minutes we were going four knots through the water, and in one more we went smashing through the bridge as if it was paper. I looked toward the overseer to see how he would take it, but he did not even turn his head as he sat at his door smoking.

This man was but one remove from a brute, but there were hundreds more like him.

We came to one more bridge; down it went like nine-pins, and we steamed slowly on, forcing our way through small, lithe willows that seemed to hold us in a grip of iron. This lasted for an hour, during which we made but half a mile.

But that was the last of the willows for a time. Had they continued, we would have been obliged to give it up. The small sprouts, no larger than my little finger, caught in the rough plates of the overhang and held us as the threads of the Lilliputians held Gulliver.

Now we came to extensive woods again on either side, the large trees towering in the air, while underneath they looked as if their lower branches had been trimmed to give them a uniform appearance; but they had only been trimmed by the hand of Nature, whose fair impression fell on all about us. Man only marred the prospect there.

The *banks* of the bayou were high with large, overhanging trees upon them, and the long branches of the latter stretched out into the stream, endangering our pipes and boats. The channel was here exactly the width of the ironclads—forty-two feet—and we had to cut our way with the overhang through the soft soil and the twining roots. It was hard and slow work. The brutal overseer felt quite sure that we would be bagged before night. He didn't know that Sherman was right behind us with an army, and an army, too, that was no respecter of ducks, chickens, pigs, or turkeys, for they used to say of one particular regiment in Sherman's corps that it could catch, scrape, and skin a hog without a soldier leaving the ranks. I was in hopes they would pay the apostate Yankee a visit, if only to teach him good manners.

The gun-boats, at this stage of the cruise, were following each other about a quarter of a mile apart.   The only idea I can give of Cypress Bayou is to *fake* a string up and down a paper two hundred or more times.   We did nothing but turn upon our course about every twenty minutes.   At one time the vessels would all be steaming on different courses.   One would be standing north, another south, another east, and yet another west through the woods.   One minute an ironclad would apparently be leading ahead, and the next minute would as apparently be steering the other way.   The tugs and mortar-boats seemed to be mixed up in the most marvelous manner.

There was a fair road on the right of the bayou, along which Sherman's troops would have to march, and all that was required to make the situation look confusing and confounding was to have the soldiers marching beside the gun-boats.

I was in the leading vessel, and necessarily had to clear the way for the others.   The bayou was full of logs that had been there for years.   They had grown soggy and heavy, and sometimes one end, being heavier than the other, would sink to the bottom, while the other end would remain pointing upward, presenting the appearance of *chevaux-de-frise*, over which we could no more pass than we could fly.   We had to have working parties in the road with tackles and hook-ropes to haul these logs out on the banks before we could pass on.

Again, we would come to a "Red River raft" that had been imbedded in the mud for ages.   All these had to be torn asunder and hauled out with a labor that no one who had not tried it could conceive of.

Then, again, we would get jammed between two large, overhanging trees.   We could not ram them down as we did in the woods, with plenty of "sea room" around us.   We had to chop away the sides of the trees with axes.

A great many of these large trees had decayed branches, and when the heavy ironclad would touch the trunk of one (though going only at the rate of half a mile an hour, which was the most we could make at any time in the ditch), the shock would be so great, and the resultant vibration of the tree so violent, that the branches would come crashing on deck, smashing the boats and sky-lights and all the frame-work that they reached.

An hour after entering the very narrow part of the ditch, where we really had not a foot to spare, we had parted with everything like a boat, and cut them away as useless appendages. Indeed, they were of no use to us, and only in the way. When we got rid of them we got along better.

The vessels behind learned a good deal from our experience, and lowered their boats and towed them astern, though that did not relieve them entirely.

Sometimes we would have to pass a dead tree, with its weird-looking branches threatening us with destruction in case we should handle it too roughly. We received quantities of dead branches, and we never knocked a dead *tree* without suffering terrible damages.

No wonder the overseer took our going on so coolly. He expected that we would get jammed before we went a mile.

That day, by sunset, we had made eight miles, which was a large day's work, considering all the impediments, but when night came—which it did early in the deep wood—we had to tie up to the bank, set watches, and wait until daylight, until which time we hoped to give our men to rest.

But, the reader will ask, what was the Confederacy doing all this while? They may imagine that Pemberton didn't know anything about this romantic pirouetting through the woods of "Mas' Linkum's gun-boats."

Not a bit of it; he knew all about it. He had sent telegrams, no doubt, to Richmond, announcing the fact that the Union navy was making a cruise through the woods and over the farms in the Yazoo country, and would likely, in course of time, reach Richmond itself in that way. He was not afraid of Vicksburg—that never struck him—and he didn't know (or I thought he didn't) that I had two mortar-boats with which I expected to bombard Vicksburg in the rear!

No doubt the Confederate Cabinet chuckled when they were informed that the authorities at Vicksburg would, in the course of a day or two, bag the whole American navy in the western waters, though, strange to say, that idea never entered my head.

We stopped that evening about seven o'clock, and about an hour later we heard the chopping of wood in the forest. We had seen no one along the stream since we had left that burly overseer. The truthful and intelligent contrabands, in whom I was wont to repose confidence, were nowhere to be seen, whereat I marveled much, knowing their sociable disposition and the lofty aspirations they felt with regard to the liberty of their race.

They were so faithful in adherence to their protectors that they would come in in crowds with wild inventions of moves on the part of the enemy if they could not find something real to tell.

I missed these ingenious creatures, and wondered what had become of them. It was true we were hard to get at in this swamp, though there was a road on one side and a levee on the other; the southern side was an interminable waste of water and wood.

I was always of an inquiring mind, and determined to find out what the wood-chopping meant. It seemed to me that there were a dozen axes at work.

I put a twelve-pound boat-howitzer on the tug, and sent her ahead to see what was going on. In twenty minutes I heard the report of the howitzer, and then another, and another. Then a steam whistle was blown from the tug, and all was silent. No more axes heard cutting wood.

In a very short time the tug was heard returning, snorting as if carrying a heavy pressure of steam, and every now and then giving some playful screams with the whistle. The forest fairly reverberated with the sound.

The officer in charge reported that he had suddenly come upon a large body of negroes, under the charge of some white men carrying lanterns, cutting trees on the banks of the stream we were in; that they had felled a tree three feet in diameter, and this had fallen right across the bayou, closing the stream completely against our advance.

There was the secret of our not meeting the truthful contraband. He was employed in hemming us in. He was too accustomed to implicit obedience to his master to refuse to do anything imposed upon him. He was too ignorant to have formed any opinions on the subject of doing something to deserve liberty. Oppression was second nature to him, obedience one of Heaven's first laws, and he helped to chop down those trees with as much glee as children would feel at setting fire to a hay-stack.

There was but one thing to do : Move ahead and clear the channel of a tree across it, three feet in diameter, spreading its branches over an area of seventy by one hundred and fifty feet.

We worked ahead slowly with men in advance on the bank, with lanterns to show what dangers there were. We arrived at the fallen tree in less than an hour, and made arrangements while under way for removing it.

It was not a matter of great labor. Two large snatch-blocks were strapped to standing trees as leaders. The largest hawser was passed through the snatch-blocks, one end made fast to the fallen tree, and the other end taken to a steamer. "Back the ironclad hard," and the obstruction began to move slowly over the water. In less than ten minutes it was landed clear across the road, so that Sherman's soldiers wouldn't have to march around it.

A second application of this improvised "power gear," and the route was again free.

The Confederates didn't think of all that when they tried to bag us in that way. They forgot the ingenuity of American seamen.

"Now," I said to the officer in charge of the tug, "go ahead with all the speed you have, and see that no more trees are cut down to-night; and, though I shall be sorry to harm that faithful friend and brother, the contraband, if he continues to chop at any one's dictation you must give him shrapnel," and off the tug started.

We could already hear the faint strokes of the axes in advance of us, and no doubt the managers, having cut one tree down and supposing that they had blocked the game on us for the night, and not knowing our facilities for removing trees, had, as soon as they imagined themselves out of reach of the howitzer, set to work at cutting other trees, with the intention that we should never see the Sunflower, nor get in the rear of Vicksburg. The Confederates were energetic, and it was wonderful how soon they got their machinery to work.

Some twenty minutes after the tug left us we heard the howitzer firing rapidly, and then all was quiet, excepting three steam whistles, which meant *all well*.

At one o'clock that night the tug's small boat returned to us with the report that the choppers had commenced cutting about twenty of the largest trees, but that none had been completely felled; that they had captured two truthful contrabands, who informed them that the parties directing the cutting of trees were officers from Vicksburg; that they had pressed three hundred negroes into the work and made them use their axes with pistols to their heads, and gave them plenty of whisky.

"The officers are from Vicksburg!" I said; "and we thought ourselves so smart! No doubt they started before we did, and got their instructions from Richmond. What next?"

"The officer" (Lieutenant Murphy) "says, sir, he will continue on all night, and thinks no more trees will be cut down at present."

I didn't care about the trees. I was just then thinking how I would feel if they should block up the head of the pass with cotton bales and earth, and leave me and mine sticking in the mud at the bottom of the bayou.

What a time, I thought, Sherman would have digging us out—but I was sure he wouldn't mind doing it.

Nevertheless, we put out guards along the road, and slept as comfortably as if we had been at the Fifth Avenue Hotel. Somehow or other I didn't think the Confederacy could bag me as long as I had Sherman in company with his stalwart fellows—half sailor, half soldier, with a touch of the snapping turtle.

At daylight next morning we moved ahead, and all that day toiled as men never toiled before. Our vessels looked like wrecks, and there was scarcely a whole boat left in the fleet. Evening found us fourteen miles ahead, but where was Sherman ? There was only one road, so he couldn't have taken the wrong one.

I had been rather precipitate in rushing ahead with the fleet, though I could not have been of any help to Sherman, but I would have had the services of the army to stop the tree-cutting, which I now had to do myself by sending out a detachment of two hundred men from the vessels. These men were ordered to march all night along the road while the tug covered them with her howitzer.

It were vain to tell all the hardships of the third day. The plot seemed to thicken as we advanced, and old logs, small Red River rafts, and rotten trees overhanging the banks, seemed to accumulate.

The dead trees were full of vermin of all sorts. Insects of every kind and shape, such as are seen only in Southern climes, infested these trees. Rats and mice, driven from the fields by the high water, had taken up their abode in the hollow trunks and rotten branches. Snakes of every kind and description had followed the rats and mice to these old arks of safety. These innocent creatures knew nothing of the insecurity of their adopted homes in presence of the butting ironclads. Small wonder. Who would have dreamed of such things in these regions ?

A canoe might have been seen, perhaps, of late years winding its way down these tortuous channels of a moonlight night, manned by a couple of dissipated darkies out on a coon-hunt, but navigation by anything larger in these waters was unknown.

Sometimes, when we would strike against one of these trees, a multitude of vermin would be shaken out on the deck—among them rats, mice, cockroaches, snakes, and lizards, which would be swept overboard by the sailors standing ready with their brooms.

Once an old coon landed on deck, with the life half knocked out of him, but he came to in a short time and fought his way on shore. Even the coons were prejudiced against us, and refused to be comforted on board, though I am sorry to say we found more Union feeling among the bugs of all kinds, which took kindly to the iron-clads, and would have remained with us indefinitely had they been permitted to do so.

Three days' hard work and no hope of seeing the Sunflower River ! We had made one capture. Lieutenant Murphy had gone ahead and taken possession of an Indian mound as old as the deluge ; no one remembered its age.

Why had not the Confederates taken possession of the place and fortified it ? It must have been because they thought it worthless. They showed themselves to be poor judges in such matters. But Lieutenant Murphy, who had been following engineering for some years before the war, saw some strong point in this mound (which I did not), and urged me to fortify it. At length he persuaded me to let him have four boat guns to place on the top of it. "It would be," he said, "a *point d'appui* for Sherman's troops to assemble about in case they were attacked !"

"Where are the attacking forces to come from ?" I inquired.

"Can't tell, sir," said Murphy, "but I think it a strong point."

"Go ahead, then, and fortify it," I replied ; "it will keep you employed."

We had arrived nearly at the head of the pass, or bayou, to what was called the Rolling Fork, and, after all our toil and trouble, did hope to see the road clear to Vicksburg in the rear.

There was a small collection of houses at the point where we had stopped, and all the contrabands in the country were assembled there. The tree-cutters had disappeared and liberated from duty all those who had been pressed into service, but took all the axes away with them. The negroes were jubilant over being able to join "Mass' Linkum's gun-boats."

We could readily have dispensed with their services. They were only an encumbrance to us. They could give us no information. They had never been taught to think or know anything but to hoe and pick cotton. That's all they were wanted for.

We had steamed, or rather bumped, seventy-five miles, and had only six hundred yards to go before getting into the Rolling Fork, where all would be plain sailing ; but I waited for all the vessels to come up to repair damages, and start together.

I noticed right at the head of the pass a large green patch extending all the way across. It looked like the green scum on ponds.

"What is that ?" I asked of one of the truthful contrabands.

"It's nuffin but willers, sah," he replied. "When de water's out ob de bayou—which it mos' allers is—den we cuts de willers to make baskits wid. You kin go troo dat like a eel."

I thought I would try it while the vessels were "coming into port." I sent the tug on ahead with the mortar-boat, and followed on after.

The tug went into it about thirty yards, began to go slower and slower, and finally stuck so fast that she could move neither ahead nor astern. I hailed her and told them that I would come along and push them through. We started with a full head of steam, and did not even reach the tug. The little withes caught in the rough iron ends of the overhang and held us as if in a vise. I tried to back out, but 'twas no use. We could not move an inch, no matter how much steam we put on. Ah, I thought, this is only a temporary delay.

We got large hooks out and led the hook-ropes aft, and tried to break off the lithe twigs, but it was no use ; we could not move. We got saws, knives, cutlasses, and chisels over the side, with the men handling them sitting on planks, and cut them off, steamed ahead, and only moved three feet. Other withes sprang up from under the water and took a fresher grip on us, so we were worse off than ever.

Just as well, I thought, that Murphy seized upon that mound. It will be three or four days before we can get through here. He can hold it as a look-out, and if any sharp-shooters should appear he can fire on them.

Just then a rebel steamer was reported coming up the Rolling Fork and landing about four miles below. We will catch that fellow after dark, I thought. He has come up here after stores.

This was the Vicksburg granary—full of everything in the way of grain, cattle, and poultry. "Hog and hominy" was abundant.

I went at it again, and worked hard for over four hours, but not one foot did I gain with that ironclad. I wished ironclads were in Jericho.

While I was pondering what to do, and the negroes were looking on in admiration upon the ingenious devices we put into play to get rid of those willow fastenings, wondering to myself if the

Confederacy had planted these willows on purpose to keep me out of the Sunflower River, I heard the faint reports of two guns, and directly after the shrill shriek of rifle-shot, which came from directions at right angles to each other. The shells burst over the Indian mound where Lieutenant Murphy was studying the strategy of war. They were Whitworth shells. I knew the sound too well to be mistaken. I had heard them before. There were two six-gun batteries with a cross-fire upon us.

"Now's your chance, Murphy," said I to myself, "to show some good practice. You did well in selecting that mound."

I forgot for a moment that we had only four twelve-pounder smooth-bores there, with a range of about twelve hundred yards.

The two field batteries were keeping up a rapid fire, and fifteen shells a minute were coming from the enemy's spitfires and bursting in all directions, throwing the pieces of iron and the bullets of the shrapnel down on the decks of the ironclads, where they rattled like hail.

Here was a dilemma. We could not use our large guns; they were away below the banks, and lying so close to it that we could not get elevation enough to fire over.

Suddenly I saw the sides of the mound crowded with officers and men. They were tumbling down as best they could; the guns were tumbled down ahead of them; there was a regular stampede. Murphy hadn't found the top of the mound a fine strategic point, and that was the reason why the Confederates had not adopted it.

The fire from the enemy's Whitworths was incessant, and every one was running to cover.

As the retreaters passed me I shouted to them to stop. The majority obeyed, but a number kept on. They had left their guns on the road.

I made those who stopped bring the guns alongside my vessel. "You shall have them no more," I said; "you don't know how to take care of them."

The shells from the enemy came so rapidly that it became annoying, so I ordered the mortars manned, measured the distance by the sound—2,800 yards on one range, and 2,600 on the other— and opened fire.

The shells seemed to be well timed; they fell in the midst of the artillerists, and the two batteries ceased by mutual consent, while we not only kept up the fire there, but all through the woods where these parties were located.

This little diversion being over, I set to work again to overcome the willows.

"What a dodge this was of the Confederacy," I said to the captain, "to plant these willows instead of a fort! We can take their forts, but we can't, I fear, take their willows."

I stepped out to the bank (where the negroes had assembled again as soon as the shooting was over) to see if I could learn anything about willows from these innocent people.

All I could find out from them was that "dey was mo' tougher'n ropes."

"Why don't Sherman come on?" I said aloud to myself. "I'd give ten dollars to get a telegram to him."

"I'm a telegram-wire, Massa," said a stubby-looking negro, coming up to me. "I'll take him for half a dollar, sah; I'm de county telegraph, sah. I does all dat bizness."

"Where's your office, Sambo?" I inquired.

"My name ain't Sambo, sah. My name's Tub, an' I run yer line fer yer for half a dollar."

"Do you know where to find General Sherman?" I said.

"No, sah, I don' know him. Ef he's in Vicksburg, I kin find him."

"Can you carry a note for me without betraying it to the Confederates?"

"I don't understan' one of dem words, sah, but I'll take a note to Kingdom Kum if yer pay me half a dollar."

Then I told him who General Sherman was and where to find him. "Go along the road," I said, "and you can't miss him."

"I know nuff better 'an dat manner when I carry telegraph, sah. I don't go de road; I takes de ditches. It's nuff shorter an' mo' safer. On de lef' han' comin' up dars all marsh an' wata, an' a kenoe kin allers git 'long dar. I'll go de way we nigs takes when we go chicken huntin'."

"Where will you carry the dispatch?" I inquired.

"In my calabash-kiver, Massa," he answered, pointing to his thick, woolly head.

I wrote the dispatch and handed it to him. He stowed it away in a pocket in his hair, where it was as safe as a telegram traveling on a wire. I wrote:

"DEAR SHERMAN: Hurry up, for Heaven's sake. I never knew how helpless an ironclad could be steaming around through the woods without an army to back her."

I had no sooner got off the telegraph (as he called himself) than another steamer was reported as landing at the same place as the one which brought up the artillery.

Upon examining her with the glass, it could be seen that she was full of troops. Those fellows would not have landed there if they had not known that we were blockaded.

The stream, for some reason, began to run rapidly, and large logs began to come in from the Rolling Fork and pile up on the outside of the willows, making an effectual barricade. It was the water rushing down through the cut-off and creeks from the opening into the "Old Yazoo Pass" of the Mississippi River. What was doing good to those fellows was bad for us. I wondered if they had found the Confederacy as smart as we had. I had no doubt of it.

Just then the two rifle batteries of the enemy opened again viciously from other positions, and it was reported to me that two thousand men had landed and were marching to get into our rear. Pleasant, that!

I had sent the rear tug back to see if anything could be heard of General Sherman coming on. It returned with the information that ten miles in our rear the enemy were cutting down the largest trees across the pass, that eight had been felled within a short distance of each other, and the channel behind us was effectually blocked. I did not mind this so much, as I knew that Sherman was not far off.

I found another telegraph man among the negroes, and sent him off to Sherman. He pursued the same method as his predecessor, but was captured by the enemy.

We kept our mortars hard at work, but the artillery shifted position every three minutes, and were sending among us about twenty shells a minute. The men had to keep between decks.

We were in the narrowest part of the pass; it was the same width as the ironclads. We fitted in nicely—too nicely!

The Confederates had completely checkmated us. Every knight and pawn and castle was in check, and my vessel, the Cincinnati, was checkmated by the willows!

There was nothing easier than for two thousand men to charge on us from the bank and carry us by boarding. Only the enemy didn't know the fix we were in. They didn't know how it was that we could fire those thirteen-inch shell, that would burst now and then at the root of a great tree and throw it into the air. They didn't know that we had only four smooth-bore howitzers free to work, that our heavy guns were useless, below the bank. So much for their not being properly posted. But I was quite satisfied that they would know all this before Sherman came up.

We drove the artillery away about four o'clock in the afternoon. Then I sent a hawser to the tug, and another to the ironclad astern of me, while the latter made fast to another ironclad. Then we all backed together and, after an hour's hard pull, we slipped off the willows into soft water. *Laus Deo!*

Then went forth the orders to unship the rudders and let the vessels drift down stern foremost, and away we all went together with a four-knot current taking us—bumping badly—down at the rate of two miles an hour—which was twice as fast as we came up. The enemy did not discover our retreat for some minutes, but when they did they made a rush for the Indian mound and took possession of it.

After all, Murphy was right; it was a strategic point! But only with the Whitworth rifles, not with smooth-bores.

I suppose we passed that fort twenty times in following the crooked pass, and the enemy were pouring it into us all the time, but they didn't do much harm.

They were evidently greenhorns, and failed to understand that we were iron-clad and didn't mind *bursting* shell. If they had fired solid shot, they might have hurt us.

I cared very much more about that infantry than I did about the artillery. As our bow guns were bearing astern now and *up* the bayou, we could each of us give the enemy now and then, at the turns, a dose of nine-inch shrapnel, giving the same attention to their infantry, which we could see were marching in the direction we were pursuing. But our broadside guns were useless.

The artillery kept up their fire for about two hours, and then I think they began to find out that our bow guns were bearing and doing them some injury.

At dark we tied up at a point where we had about four feet of water between us and the bank, greased the ironsides, and, elevating the lower-deck guns after loading them with grape, we made the best of our position. I landed five hundred men with howitzers after dark, and placed them in position to enfilade any attacking party. Scouts were also thrown out to see if some of the enemy could be picked up, and the remainder of the crews slept on their arms at quarters. So passed the night; but Sherman's whereabouts were a continual source of conjecture to me. I was quite sure the Confederates had not captured *him.*

About ten o'clock my scouts brought in four prisoners—two officers and two sergeants—and conducted them, at my direction, into the cabin.

The commanding officer was quite a youngster, and when brought in was as stiff as a poker.

He walked up to me and, presenting his sword, said, "There, sir, you will likely recognize that; it is the sword of one of your officers who skedaddled off that Indian mound. We picked up two of them, and captured caps and shoes enough to fit out a regiment. Why, your fellows left a lot of ammunition behind them."

"Yes," I said, "but you look tired; won't you sit down and take some supper with me? I have a cold supper and wine on the table."

"I don't care if I do," he answered, "and I have the less compunction in taking it as it belongs to us anyhow. In two hours you will be surrounded and bagged. You can't escape. How in the devil's name you ever got here is a wonder to me."

"I should like nothing better," I said, "than for your friends to try that kind of business; they would learn something. But sit down, gentlemen, and eat."

They did sit down, and ate with an appetite I never saw equaled.

"We have had nothing to eat or drink since noon," said the youngster; "we could eat our grandmothers and drink up Niagara Falls."

"Drink some wine," I said, and I shoved over the sherry to them. Their throats were dry as powder-horns. "Help yourselves," I said; "don't stand on ceremony. You know it will all be yours when you surround us, and you had better get your share before the other fellows arrive."

"Won't you drink with us?" asked the youngster.

"Yes," I said, "with pleasure. Tell me how Colonel Higgins is."

"He's here," replied the youngster, "and came along on purpose to catch you. He says he'd give ten thousand dollars to do that."

"Here's his health," I said, and they all drank bumpers to Higgins.

"I can't drink with you any more now. I have to look out

for these vessels; but, as you are prisoners, and have no responsibility, you may empty the bottle if you like, and there are the cigars."

"You're a trump, and no mistake!" said the youngster; "I would like to capture you myself."

"Well, I promise you that if I surrender to any one it will be to you."

The quartette drank until they became very lively and loquacious, and boastful of what they were going to do.

"How far off are your troops?" I inquired.

"About four miles," the leader answered. "They will bag you at daylight."

"That," said I, "is about a good distance. Sherman will be on them about three o'clock, and capture the whole of them."

"Sherman!" he exclaimed; "what has he to do with it?"

"Only," said I, "that he is at this moment surrounding your troops with ten thousand men."

"Holy Moses!" he cried, "we're sold. We didn't know anything about any troops. We thought it was something like that Yazoo River affair—a gun-boat excursion, and we liked to have bagged *them*. They're wandering around in the ditches yet."

Having obtained all the information I desired, I went on deck, put a sentry over the cabin-door, had the stern-ports closed, and gave orders to call me at two o'clock.

Then the shore parties were called on board, and we went on the *back track* for three miles. We either threw the enemy off the scent, or the captured officer deceived me about the contemplated attack. We heard nothing of them, and determined to go on down again.

At the first start the leading vessel sunk the coal-barge, and there we were blocked and unable to move. It took hours to remove the coal and spread it out on the bottom.

In the midst of the work we were attacked by the enemy's artillery in the rear.

I was in the rear ironclad—bows up stream; we steamed up after the artillery, got within range, and with the bow guns scattered them like chaff. One of their guns was knocked over, and some of their men and cattle were hurt, but they were getting less timid and were gradually closing around the ironclads.

The stream cleared of the coal, we bumped along, stern foremost, down stream, knocking down dead branches from the trees upon our decks, with the usual accompaniment of vermin, until we thought the limit of ill-luck had been reached by the vessels; but we looked worse before we got through.

Sharp-shooters made their appearance in the morning. About sixty of them surrounded us. First it was like an occasional drop of rain. Then it was *pat, pat* against the iron hull all the time. The smoke-stacks seemed to be favorite marks to fire at. They no doubt took it for the captain, or the great motive power which kept us a-going.

The sharp-shooters were not, as a rule, the brightest I have seen, but then they had bomb-shells falling among them, and now and then a tree, behind which they were, would suddenly be lifted out of the ground or canted sideways. The bomb-shells were demoralizing.

I adopted a new plan. I turned *all* the guns into mortars by firing them at the greatest elevation (to clear the banks), and with very low charges. With short time-fuses and a range of about six hundred yards this had a good effect, and the sharp-shooters kept a long way off.

The smoke-stacks still attracted considerable attention from them, though it was true they had wounded some of our people.

Suddenly the Louisville, Captain Owen, brought up all standing. There were eight large trees cut down ahead of us—four from either bank, and they seemed to be so interlaced that it was apparently impossible to remove them.

I sent out two hundred riflemen, and found that they were quite equal to the enemy. They drove them to a safe distance with the aid of the mortar fire. We had been firing heavily, great guns and mortars, for two days and nights, and thought Sherman must have heard us and been worried about us, but he had his troubles in getting along as well as others. He was doing his best to come to our assistance. It may seem ridiculous for ironclads to be wanting assistance from an army, but without that army they would likely have been in an ugly scrape. Its proximity alone, without its immediate aid, made us perfectly at ease.

Under fire from the sharp-shooters we removed the eight trees in three hours, and started to push on, when we found those devils had sunk two large trees across the bayou under water, and *pinned* them down.

Another hour was spent in getting them up, and under renewed sharp-shooting. Every one was kept under cover except those it was absolutely necessary to expose. The captains and myself had to be on deck.

We had no sooner got rid of these obstructions than we saw a large column of gray-uniformed soldiers swooping down on us from the woods.

We opened mortar fire on them. They didn't mind it. On they came. They were no doubt determined to overwhelm us by numbers, and close us in. Their artillery was coming on with them. Now would come the tug of war. We were jammed up against the bank, and the stream was so narrow where we were we could not increase our distance from it. Their sharp-shooters had now taken up positions behind trees about one hundred yards from us, and our men were firing rapidly at them as they opened on us.

We had picked up a few cotton-bales along the road to make defenses, and good ones they were.

The sharp-shooters were becoming very troublesome about this time, when suddenly I saw the advancing column begin to fall into confusion; then they jumped behind trees, or fell into groups, and kept up a rapid fire of musketry. It looked as if they were fighting among themselves. But no! they were retreating before some one. They had run foul of Sherman's army, which was steadily driving them back.

The enemy were much surprised at encountering such a force. They never dreamed of meeting an army of five or six thousand men. I believe there were more.

I made signal to beat the retreat. We would have no more trouble now. But, just as I had given the order, half a dozen rifle bullets came on board, and one of them struck the first lieutenant, Mr. Wells, in the head while I was talking to him and giving him an order.

He fell, apparently dead, at my feet. I called an officer to remove him, and *he* fell dead, as I supposed, on the other's body.

Then an old quartermaster came, dragging a large quarter-inch iron plate along the deck, and stuck it up against a hog post. "There, sir," he said, "stand behind that; they've fired at you long enough," and I was wise enough to take the old fellow's advice. Poor old man! he was shot in the hand as he turned to get behind his cotton-bale.

But that was about the last of it. In the course of half an hour Colonel Smith, of the 8th Missouri, rode up and told me his troops were in pursuit of the enemy, who were in full retreat, and that we should hear no more of them. Again, *Laus Deo!*

They were a perplexing set of fellows, these rebels, and showed a great amount of courage, considering the prestige of "Mas' Linkum's gun-boats"; but then, it must be remembered, they had caught the ironclads in a ditch in the woods. They could hardly be said to be afloat.

The Confederates never dreamed of finding us where they did, or they would have come provided with torpedoes, and left us all imbedded in the mud of Black Bayou, where in future ages mementos of us would be found, and as much be known of us as was known of the Indian mound which we *did not* find such a fine strategic point.

But the rebs missed their opportunity, though they rather had the laugh on us. We had the satisfaction of knowing, however, that none of us had lost our heads, though at one time matters looked rather embarrassing.

I didn't notice a single officer on that expedition who, though exposed almost at all times to an unpleasant fire from sharp-shooters, showed the least desire to avoid being shot, except when they hurried down so rapidly from the top of the Indian mound !

I am happy to say that the two officers, who fell at my feet apparently dead, both recovered. Theirs were only scalp wounds, owing to the enemy's bad powder. They were both volunteers, and did good service all through the Rebellion.

"Old Tecumseh" came riding up, about half an hour after the last mishaps, on the old horse he had captured. He had received my county telegraph man, who explained to him pretty well how we were situated, and he had pushed on at night, by the aid of pine torches, through swamps and canebrakes, having undertaken a short cut recommended by the telegraph "operator," Mr. Tub, and found the traveling almost as bad as that experienced by the gun-boats.

"Halloo, Porter," said the general when he saw me, "what did you get into such an ugly scrape for ? So much for you navy fellows getting out of your element ; better send for the soldiers always. My boys will put you through. Here's your little nigger ; he came through all right, and I started at once. I had a hard time getting my troops over ; some of them marched over from the Mississippi.

"This is the most infernal expedition I was ever on ; who in thunder proposed such a mad scheme ? But I'm all ready to go on with you again. Your gun-boats are enough to scare the crows; they look as if you had got a terrible hammering. However, I'll start at once, and go back with you ; my boys will clean those fellows out."

"Thank you, no," I said, "I have had enough of this adventure. It is too late now ; the enemy are forewarned, and all the energies of the Confederacy will be put forth to stop us ; they will fill all the rivers with torpedoes, and every hill will be turned into a heavy fort. They have the laugh on us this time, but we must put this down in the log-book as 'One of the Episodes of the War.' We will take Vicksburg yet, when it is more worth taking."

"You are satisfied, then," said Sherman, "with what my boys have done for you and can do ?"

"Yes, perfectly so," I answered, "and I never knew what helpless things ironclads could become when they got in a ditch and had no soldiers about. Won't you come aboard ?"

"No," said he, "I must call in my men ; they could not catch those fellows if they chased them a week. Good-morning," and "Old Tecumseh" rode off on his ancient horse, with a rope bridle, accompanied only by one or two aids.

After Sherman had departed I went down into the cabin to see my prisoners. The cabin was dark, and they were sitting there very quiet.

"Well," I said to the young officer, "they have got us at last ; we are surrounded."

"I knew they would bag you in the end," he replied ; "I felt that I was not going to be a prisoner yet. Well, sir, I will see that you are treated handsomely when you surrender."

"Surrender to whom ?" I said. "What are you talking about ?"

"Didn't you say you were surrounded ?" asked the perplexed youth.

"Yes, I did," I replied, "but by Sherman's boys, and your fellows are skedaddling off as fast as they can go."

"But not faster," he retorted, "than your fellows did down that Indian mound ! But I'm sorry not to be able to take you to Vicksburg ; they'd treat you kindly there." With that he lay down and went to sleep.

The game was up, and we bumped on homeward. The current was running very rapidly now, and the vessels were so helpless, dropping down stern foremost, that we could not protect them in any way. There was no knowing what part of them would strike the trees, or when huge dead branches would fall upon the decks. Every one remained between decks except those who were absolutely required above. There was still a chance of the enemy playing us a bad trick by blocking the head of the pass at Rolling Fork; there was plenty of cotton along the road to do it with, if they only should think of it. Twelve hundred bales of cotton would turn the water off from our bayou, and in an hour after we would be on the bottom. With these unpleasant possibilities before me, I continued on homeward, and protracted my run until eight o'clock that night, when I came up with the main body of Sherman's army, which was encamped along on the road near the edge of the pass.

Encamped! I say. They had no tents, but a plentiful supply of fence-rails and bonfires of pine-knots. The whole route for miles was all in a blaze.

It was great fun for the soldiers to see our dilapidated condition. "Halloo, Jack," one fellow would sing out, "how do you like playing mud-turtle? Better stick to the briny."

Another would say, "You've been into dry dock, ain't you, and left your boats behind?"

"Don't go bushwhacking again, Jack," said another, "unless you have Sherman's boys close aboard of you; you look as if your mothers didn't know you were out."

"Where's all your sails and masts, Jack?" said a tough-looking fellow who was sailor all over, though he had a soldier's uniform bent.

"By the Widow Perkins," cried another, "if Johnny Reb hasn't taken their rudders away and sent them adrift!"

"Dry up," sang out an old forecastleman, "we wa'n't half as much used up as you was at Chickasaw Bayou!" for which the old tar got three cheers. And so we ran the gauntlet until we reached the middle of the line.

"Where's General Sherman?" I inquired of some of the men.

"He's in his tent, sir, waiting supper for you," answered one of them.

Sherman's tent! As if he would have a tent when his soldiers were lying about on fence-rails.

But I came to his tent at last; and, reader, I wish you could have seen it: it was three fence-rails set up in a triangle, but with only a small fly over the apex. It was raining hard at the time, and

Sherman was standing leaning against one of the rails, while a large bonfire was blazing brightly before his "tent"! "You go on," he said ; "I'll follow you to-morrow." We passed the compliments, and I ran on down past the lines and tied up, having run the gauntlet of jokes that were showered on us by the soldiers.

As we were getting made fast to the bank a canoe with two soldiers in it tried to squeeze past us, but got stuck between us and the bank. They had a large pile of something in the bottom of the canoe covered over with a tarpaulin.

"What have you got in those bags ?" I asked.

"General Sherman's baggage, sir," said one ; "we've just brought it up from a transport."

"General Sherman's baggage !" I said ; "how long has it been since he took to carrying baggage ? Let me see what you've got there."

"Only baggage, Admiral, I assure you," said the speaker, "except some turkeys we picked up for you on the road up here," and he uncovered and displayed a pile of picked turkeys, geese, chickens, and sucking pigs.

"Where's the baggage ?" I asked.

"Why, sir," said the man, "there was so much of it, it's coming up on a tug—a large carpet-bag of it, sir," and he handed up one of each.

The steward came, and took a turkey. "Pass General Sherman's baggage," I said to the captain, and the sailors, taking hold of the painter, pulled the canoe through.

Sherman had a hard set of boys on foraging, and they enjoyed this trip up the bayou, where they were in the very midst of the enemy's granary, and the people of Vicksburg no doubt sighed when the Yankees had found their way to the flesh-pots of the South. Most of them went without turkey, chicken, goose, or pig for many a day thereafter.

There is not much more to be said about the Steele Bayou expedition ; it didn't amount to much in effecting changes in the condition of Vicksburg, but we gained a lot of experience which would serve us in the future. We might, perhaps, have passed the willows if we had waited for the army, and got the soldiers to pull us through with ropes stretched along the bank ; but to have delayed pushing astern would have insured the cutting down of five hundred trees by the enemy, and given them time to send to Vicksburg for torpedoes and have them planted all along that ditch.

I never saw a copy of the telegram Pemberton sent to Richmond, but I imagine it was as follows :

"The enemy made an excursion into our overflowed country and pirouetted around exceedingly. 'They buttered no parsnips.' Nature fought for us, as it always does for the Confederacy. The elements even helped us. The trees fought for us against the invaders of our soil, and the huge limbs fell down upon the enemy's decks and demolished them. The vermin swarmed over them, and they returned looking like picked chickens.

"They will never try it again. Vicksburg is safer than ever, and can never fall while hog and hominy last.

"We spit on their grandfathers' graves."

I am quite satisfied that no one who went on that party desired to try it again. It was the hardest cruise that any Jack Tar ever made, and we all determined to cultivate the army more than we had done, in case we should go on a horse-marine excursion.

It was with the greatest delight that we got out of that ditch and into the open woods again, with plenty of " sea room " and no lee shores. We took our time, went squirrel-hunting in the few boats we had left, and got a fine mess of turkey-buzzards out of the old oaks which surrounded us.

In ten days more we anchored again in the mouth of the Yazoo River and commenced to repair damages.

I always carried a large steamer along with the squadron fitted as a carpenter's shop. She had a good supply of mechanics on board, with all that was necessary to repair a vessel after an action.

In a week we were all built up again, were supplied with new boats from the store-ship, and, with our new coats of paint, no one would have supposed we had ever been away from a dock-yard.

Some of the officers were talking of going again, and of the pleasure of the trip, as people who have gone in search of the North Pole, and have fared dreadfully, wish to try it once more.

This was one of the many expedients adopted to bring about the reduction of Vicksburg, and, of all of them, never one more hazardous or more laborious. The whole siege was a series of patient labors, more wearing than active excitement in the field ; and while the enemy, on the one hand, displayed the greatest endurance and determination, we, on the other, exhibited the greatest patience under many disappointments.

As President Lincoln truly remarked, " Vicksburg was the backbone of the Rebellion and the key to the situation." And, as I said, to bring about what we wanted was the best general, a large army and naval force, and—patience.

Yet on no occasion during the war did the Government and people of the North display so much *impatience* as they did about this siege. While General Grant was working with that imperturbable determination which distinguished him to try and get into the rear of the place, and his trusted generals were always ready to forward his views (as were myself and all my officers), some implacable foe, with a corps of reporters "at his beck and call," was inundating the country with false accounts of Grant's actions, which had no foundation whatever. They were the creation of a malignant brain, and were circulated from personal motives.

The worst of it was, the Government was partly influenced by the same spirit, and, had it not been that President Lincoln was governed by feelings of justice, disaster might have befallen the Union.

No ordinary general could have taken Vicksburg at all; it required a man full of military ability and knowledge, and one who knew whom to select from all the able men of the army—those who were best qualified to undertake the many vexatious problems that would arise during so important and difficult a siege.

Some men would have given it up and said that it was not worth the loss of time and the waste of human life which would ensue; some would have demanded half the resources of the Union; but Grant never wavered in his determination, or in his hopes of success.

He had a smaller force than the enemy, who, knowing the importance of the place, kept a garrison of forty thousand or more men inside the walls and forty thousand more just outside, under those they considered their ablest generals.

When General Grant had tried every rational expedient, he resorted to the last and only true one, which not one general in a thousand would have approved, and which he followed in opposition to the opinions of a majority of his commanders.

When I look back, after the lapse of nearly a quarter of a century, and remember the libels I used to read in Republican papers against the men who were doing all they could to take Vicksburg, I lose all patience with them. Fortunately, newspaper writers are not always exponents of public opinion, and the sensational articles, written on the scene of action to please the morbid taste of the public, did not have the anticipated effect, any more than the im-

placable misrepresentations made by a vindictive foe of all prominent officers had upon the President, when made to him personally.

Nearly all the clever young officers who went on that expedition
with me are dead and gone. One I know of is broken down and
on the retired list. Such is the insatiable greed of the great mael-
strom—war.

All are swallowed up who are not made of iron and steel.

Old Tecumseh and myself hold on, two tough old knots, with a
good deal of the steel in us yet, and quite enough vitality to lay
out any number of those who pride themselves upon what they
can do.

We can sit down and write out our reminiscences for the benefit
of the young men who are coming along, and perhaps they may
learn something from our experience.

CHAPTER XV.

A COUNCIL OF WAR—PASSAGE OF THE FLEET BY THE BATTERIES OF VICKSBURG—GENERAL SHERMAN VISITS THE FLEET IN ITS PASSAGE—WOODEN GUNS ON CART-WHEELS—A HANDFUL OF CORN AND A DEAD CONFEDERATE SOLDIER.

I GAVE General Grant a faithful account of our reconnoissance,
and he was satisfied that he could not carry on military operations
against Vicksburg in the way we had attempted.

"I will go below Vicksburg," he said, "and cross over if I can
depend on you for a sufficient naval force. I will prepare some
transports by packing them well with cotton-bales, and we'll start
as soon as you are ready."

"I will be ready to-morrow night," I replied, "and in the
mean time will lay in a full supply of provisions and ammunition,
and prepare coal-barges to take along."

General Grant called a council of war that afternoon on board
my flag-ship—the Black Hawk—and, after informing the generals
what he proposed to do, asked their opinions.

General McClernand did not attend the council, but wrote to
Grant approving the plan. I think General Sherman was present,
but did not favor the plan, as it would take the army a long dis-

tance from its base of supplies, and for other good reasons which Grant considered it necessary to set aside on the present occasion.

All the other generals present at the council strongly objected to Grant's plan. He listened patiently and, when they had finished, remarked, "I have considered your arguments, but continue in the same opinion. You will be ready to move at ten o'clock to-morrow morning. General McClernand will take the advance; General Sherman will remain here with his division and, if possible, make an attack on Haines's Bluff in conjunction with such of the gun-boats as the admiral may not want with him below." So ended the council.

Everything connected with this movement of General Grant's had been conducted with as much secrecy as possible, yet I believe the intended change of base was known in Vicksburg almost as soon as it was in the Union army. The Confederates had unknown means of finding out what was going on, though we certainly supposed they would know nothing of the intended movement of the *gun-boats*.

As night approached, all on board the gun-boats were in a state of pleasurable excitement at the prospect of getting away from the Yazoo River.

At the appointed hour we started down the Mississippi as quietly as possible, drifting with the current. Dogs and crowing hens were left behind, and every precaution taken to prevent the enemy from becoming aware of our design.

We knew they were to have a grand ball that night in Vicksburg, and thought the "sounds of revelry" would favor us in getting the transports past the batteries. All of these vessels had been protected with cotton-bales, and, under the management of their brave and experienced pilots, followed along in line.

I was in advance, in the Benton, and as I looked back at the long line I could compare them only to so many phantom vessels. Not a light was to be seen nor a sound heard throughout the fleet.

We approached the bend in the river where the frowning heights were covered with heavy batteries.

"We will, no doubt, slip by unnoticed," I remarked to the captain of the Benton; "the rebels seem to keep a very poor watch."

Just then a bright light along the levee illuminated everything, showing the city and forts as plainly as if it were daylight.

"The town is on fire!" exclaimed the captain. On the opposite side of the river was a large railroad station with outbuildings, and as soon as the first fire broke out, these also burst into flames. The upper fort opened its heavy guns upon the Benton, the shot rattling against her sides like hail, but she had four inches of iron plating over forty inches of oak, so that not much impression was made upon her hull. There being no longer any concealment possible, we stood to our guns and returned the enemy's fire.

Every fort and hill-top vomited forth shot and shell, many of the latter bursting in the air and doing no damage, but adding to the grandeur of the scene. As fast as our vessels came within range of the forts they opened their broadsides, and soon put a stop to any revelry that might be going on in Vicksburg.

The enemy's shells set fire to the transport Henry Clay, and she was soon in a blaze, adding her light to that of the tar-barrels kept by the enemy in readiness for the occasion, for we had not surprised them in the least by our movement to run the gauntlet.

The courageous pilot of the Henry Clay stood at his post and, with his vessel all ablaze, attempted to run past the fleet.

When a man is in trouble the world is generally down on him, and so it was with the Henry Clay; the enemy found her a good target, and showered all their attention on her.

The blazing cotton-bales were knocked overboard by the rebel shot, and the river was covered with bits of burning cotton, looking like a thousand lamps.

The men of the Henry Clay finally had to jump into the water to save their lives, while the vessel floated until she burned up.

Another transport was sunk by the rebels, but the rest of them passed the batteries, though not without suffering considerable damage.

As to the naval vessels, they had to go slowly and take the enemy's fire. The logs on their sides and the bales of hay with which they were packed saved them in many cases. We had few people killed, and the enemy's artillery fire was not much to boast of, considering that they had over a hundred guns firing at us as we drifted down stream in such close order that it would seem to have been impossible to miss us.

The sight was a grand one, and I stood on deck admiring it, while the captain fought his vessel and the pilot steered her through fire and smoke as coolly as if he was performing an everyday duty.

The Vicksburgers must have been disappointed when they saw us get by their batteries with so little damage. We suffered most from the musketry fire.   The soldiers lined the levee and fired into our port-holes, wounding our men, for we were not more than twenty yards from the shore.

Once only the fleet got into a little disorder, owing to the thick smoke which hung over the river, but the commanding officers, adhering to their orders "to *drift* only," got safely out of the difficulty.

I had just passed the last battery in the Benton, and the vessels behind were crowding rather closer than I liked, so I gave the order to "Go ahead slow," to let the line straighten up.   This soon put us a hundred yards ahead, when I was hailed by some one in a boat, "Benton ahoy!"

"Halloo!" I replied, and presently I recognized the voice of General Sherman.

"Are you all right, old fellow?"

"Come on board and see," I replied, and Sherman came over the side to hear about our fortunes.

"One man's leg cut off by a round-shot, half a dozen shell and musket-ball wounds," I said.

"You are more at home here than you were in the ditches grounding on willow-trees," said Sherman.   "Stick to this, old fellow; it suits Jack better.   There are a lot of my boys on the point ready to help you if you want anything.   They hauled this boat over for me.   Good-night! I must go and find out how the other fellows fared," and I believe he visited every vessel in turn.   He would have liked to have been in the storm of shot could he have done so with propriety.

When the Benton had passed all danger we still continued to drift on.   The cannon were yet booming, and fire was apparently issuing from a dozen burning vessels.

It might have answered for a picture of the infernal regions.

We were an hour and a half in passing the batteries, which extended along the river for about four miles.   I could not stop to ascertain what damage had been done to the other vessels, as I had to keep moving to make way for those behind me.

The sound of guns gradually decreased as the vessels passed the batteries, and then all was silent.   The fires had burned out, and the river had returned to its former obscurity.

I came to anchor around a point, and in ten minutes the gunboats began to come in sight one after another in the same order in which they had started, anchoring in line under the stern of the

12

Benton. Bunches of cotton still ablaze, and burning fragments of the wreck of the Henry Clay, continued to come down with the current, giving an old rebel, who stood on the shore abreast of our anchorage, an opportunity to call out, "Whar are yer gun-boats now? I tole yer dam' soldiers thar wouldn't be mor'n one on 'em left by ther time Vicksburg war done with 'em!"

And this worthy went to sleep, happy in the thought that the floating bits of cotton were the remains of the unfortunate gun-boats, only to wake on the morrow to disappointment.

General Grant had turned the enemy's flank with his army, I had turned it with the gun-boats; now Grant had to cross the river and trust to his brave soldiers, who were glad to do anything rather than sit down day after day with nothing to do but carry on the ordinary routine of an army. Yet such must be the fate of those who enter upon a siege like that of Vicksburg, where Nature has thrown almost insurmountable obstructions in the way of a hostile army.

Grant ought to have felt happy that night when it was reported to him that the gun-boats and transports had arrived at Carthage ready for work, for he knew that he had now a prospect of getting in the rear of the rebel stronghold. As for myself, I felt sure of success, and was certain that Vicksburg would soon be ours.

General Sherman seemed to take much interest in the passage of the fleet by Vicksburg. Not long ago he employed Mr. Taylor, an artist of New York, to paint a picture of the affair, I furnishing photographs of the vessels and other material in my possession. The picture, which is a very correct representation of the scene, is now in the War Department, while the original study hangs in my library.

When daylight broke, after the passage of the fleet, I was besieged by the commanding officers of the gun-boats, who came to tell me of their mishaps; but when I intimated that I intended to leave at Carthage any vessel that could not stand the hammering they would be subject to at Grand Gulf, everybody suddenly discovered that no damage had been done their vessels, which, if anything, were better prepared for action than when they started out!

Opposite where I lay was a body of Union troops, and, supposing it was McClernand's corps, which had the advance, I steamed up to the levee to greet them.

I found they had thrown up intrenchments, and had a log on a pair of cart-wheels to represent a field-piece.

General McClernand had pushed ahead with three or four hundred men of Osterhaus's brigade, and, upon arriving at the point where I found them, they discovered themselves confronted by a couple of Confederate regiments, who had thrown up earth-works and armed them with four guns supposed to be thirty-pounder rifles.

Generals McClernand and Osterhaus came on board the Benton as soon as she was made fast to the bank. The former seemed pleased to see us, but Osterhaus was beaming all over.

"Now," said he, "dose dampt fellers, dey'll catch it; give dem gun-boat soup!"

One of Osterhaus's staff ran up to an ensign—an old friend of his—and, giving him a fraternal hug, exclaimed, "Ah, Pill, mein Gott! how glad I am to see you! De sight of you ish petter ash goot. Effery soldier in der army ought to carry a gun-pote mit his pocket!"

"Ya! ya!" said another, "I knosh someding petter as dot. Effery man shoult pe a gun-pote; dot's what I calls de ticket for soups!"

In the works which the Confederates had thrown up opposite McClernand were two or three flags which I thought we might as well capture. McClernand requested that I would let the gun-boats get under way and settle that work.

I signaled for Captain Shirk, of the Tuscumbia, and directed him to go down and drive the Confederates out of the fort, keeping up such a rapid fire of grape and shrapnel that the enemy could not carry off a single gun.

The Confederate earth-works were distant about eight hundred yards from us on the bank of the river, and in twenty minutes' time the Tuscumbia had opened her batteries at a distance of about three hundred yards, and the enemy soon evacuated their fortifications, carrying their flags with them.

Captain Shirk returned almost immediately, having failed to carry out my orders and bring the guns with him. But when he came on board the Benton he held in his hand a canvas knapsack.

"What is that, sir?" I inquired, a little severely; "and where are those guns?"

The guns, he said, were four logs mounted on cart-wheels, and the knapsack contained all the enemy's commissary stores, which he dropped as he was running away.

In the knapsack was an old shoe and an ear of corn. Heavens!

what a commentary on the war was this! A soldier fighting for an idea he did not comprehend and against the only form of government which could insure the freedom of the poor white man of the South, and willing to live on an ear of corn a day in order that an oligarchy might be formed to bring him down to the level of a brute.

Just think of the Spartan courage, though combined with ignorance, on the part of those who bore arms for the South! Who could help admiring such men, even though fighting against them?

I witnessed many similar cases when visiting battle-fields, and, led by curiosity, examined the knapsacks of the dead soldiers.

On one occasion I found but a handful of corn; on another, a few ounces of corn-bread; and in both cases the dead men were so emaciated by hard labor and the want of proper food that they were reduced to skin and bones.

In point of endurance they set us an example it would have been hard to follow. I do not know whether we could have endured the hardships as well as they, as we were never called upon to try it. Our Commissary Department was the best in the world, and the waste of our provisions would have supplied a European army.

The presence of the gun-boats enabled General McClernand to take a more comfortable position, and he established his headquarters close by the advance of his corps, being about five miles from Grand Gulf, where it was at that time supposed General Grant would cross over if the gun-boats could drive the enemy from their batteries at that place.

CHAPTER XVI.

NAVAL BATTLE AT GRAND GULF—THREE COMMISSIONERS FROM WASHINGTON TO EXAMINE INTO THE CONDUCT OF AFFAIRS— ONE OF THE COMMISSIONERS IN A "LONG SHIRT"—TAR AND FEATHERS—LANDING OF THE ARMY AT BRUENSBURG—AMUSING STORY OF AN IOWA REGIMENT—FIRST MEETING WITH GENERAL A. J. SMITH—A CONFEDERATE RAM.

THE battle of Grand Gulf was fought April 29, 1863, and won by the navy, and it was as hard a fight as any that occurred during the war.

For more than five hours the gun-boats engaged the enemy's batteries at close quarters, the latter having thirteen heavy guns placed on commanding heights from eighty to one hundred and twenty feet above the river. We lost seventy-five men in killed and wounded, and silenced all the enemy's guns. We passed all the transports by the batteries without damage, and General Grant was at liberty to cross the Mississippi and commence operations on the Vicksburg side as soon as he thought proper.

He had marched some thirty-two thousand men to the point opposite Grand Gulf, and gun-boats and transports were all assembled there, waiting to go whithersoever they were wanted.

General Grant witnessed the action at Grand Gulf from a tug in the middle of the river.

There had come to visit the army three persons who were reported to be commissioners sent from Washington to examine into the conduct of affairs—Mr. E. B. Washburn, Governor Yates, and Adjutant-General Thomas. These gentlemen were on board the tug with General Grant during the engagement between the forts and the gun-boats, and I think were favorably impressed with the result of the conflict. For the official report of the fight I must refer my readers to the Secretary of the Navy's Annual Report for 1863.

When night came I made General Grant and the commissioners very comfortable on board my flag-ship, the Benton, for the army, by Grant's order, had brought no tents, and to old General Thomas I gave up my state-room. On such occasions people will be jolly if the company is at all congenial, and that night formed no exception to the rule.

The commissioners expressed their satisfaction that the army had moved from before Vicksburg, and that we could keep open communications with our base of supplies.

Sherman, with a large army and a considerable naval force, was left near Milliken's Bend to act as might be advisable, and Grant could either get in the rear of Vicksburg *via* Bruensburg or try some other point.

I was particularly interested that night in making General Thomas comfortable, helping him unpack his carpet-bag and get out his "*long shirt*," in which attire he looked every inch an adjutant-general! To supplement his "long shirt," I furnished him with a "night-cap," under the influence of which the old gentleman grew confidential and told me the whole story of the commission.

"Great complaints," said the general, "have come to the President from some one in the army before Vicksburg in regard to Grant's manner of conducting operations, and Mr. Lincoln therefore determined to find out for himself the true state of affairs ; so he sent the present commissioners to examine with full powers." Here the general stopped and swore me to secrecy. Mr. Washburn was sent as the fast friend of General Grant, Governor Yates as a man in whose conscientious opinions the President could depend, and General Thomas "as a military expert, who could explain to his colleagues the exact situation of affairs and the defects in Grant's plans if any existed !"

"We stopped first," said the general, "at McClernand's camp, to ascertain his style of doing things. He gave us a grand review and a good lunch, but had no ice for his champagne ; then we called on Grant, and, Admiral, I'll give you a piece of information."

"Wait a moment," I interrupted ; "your throat sounds dry ; try this glass of toddy ; it will make you sleep like a top, and you won't feel the mosquitoes."

The general drank it down without winking. "You would have made a fortune, Admiral, as a barkeeper," he said ; "you have such a talent for mixing drinks ; but don't mention what I'm going to tell you. I carry in my bag full authority to remove General Grant and place whomsoever I please in command of the army ;" and the old general drew himself up and looked at me as much as to say, "What do you think of that ?"

I reflected for a moment, and then asked whom it was proposed to put in Grant's place.

"Well," replied General Thomas, "that depends ; McClernand is prominent."

"General," I said, "no doubt your plans are well considered, but let an old salt give you a piece of advice. Don't let your plans get out, for if the army and navy should find out what you three gentlemen came for, they would tar and feather you, and neither General Grant nor myself could prevent it."

"Is it possible ?" exclaimed the general. "But I don't intend to do anything. We are delighted with all we have seen, so there will be no change. I should have pursued the same course as General Grant had I been in command myself !"

"Stick to that, General," I said, "and don't forget that I am in earnest about the tar and feathers ; now go to sleep and dream of being made major-general for the good service you will perform by telling the President that everything has been done that could be done, that the army and the navy are all right, and that Vicksburg will be ours in thirty days, if not sooner."

I never mentioned General Thomas's conversation until some years after the close of the war, when I gave General Badeau, who was then writing the "Military History of General Grant," my journal to look over.

I have read several accounts of the siege of Vicksburg, but none of them convey a good idea of the operations which led to the fall of that stronghold. The true history of the siege of Vicksburg must not be the sensational work of a penny-a-liner. It will be a chronicle of patient labor. There were no "dashing moves" while our army was sitting down before the place or before the city was turned. There was no place to dash into except the Mississippi River.

At daylight, on the morning after the Grand Gulf fight, the troops began to throng on board the gun-boats and transports, and, when all were embarked, we headed down stream instead of crossing over, and in an hour and a half hauled up at Bruensburg, on the Vicksburg side.

There some thirty-two thousand men with rations for four days were landed, and then commenced that remarkable series of movements which placed our army in the rear of Vicksburg, our troops forcing their way between two formidable armies of forty thousand men each, posted in commanding positions.

Our troops had to assail the enemy after long and tortuous marches, with a deep river on one side and almost inaccessible hills bristling with bayonets to oppose them.

It was in my opinion the most remarkable and most successful military operation of the civil war, and was the crowning move toward placing the Father of Waters once more under the absolute control of its legitimate rulers.

If any one had heretofore doubted General Grant's ability, it would seem that the latter's arrival on the heights in the rear of Vicksburg, driving Pemberton with forty thousand men into the intrenched city, and causing General Joe Johnston with an equal force to retire beyond Jackson, must have removed his doubts.

I at once opened communication with Grant's army by way of the Yazoo, and the city of Vicksburg was in a day or two sealed up so tight that even the "intelligent contraband" found it impossible to get in or out.

There we will leave the army, for we can not tell the story of the hardships and trials they underwent, the disappointments they suffered, and the fortitude they exhibited.

The entire operations were marked by a happy co-operation on the part of the army and the navy, on which success so much depends on such occasions.

It could not be expected that an army which started out with but four days' rations and cut themselves off from their base of supplies could do otherwise than live upon the country. There were certain regiments in that army which had a reputation as pot-hunters as well as fighters, and one of these was the 13th Iowa, in General A. J. Smith's brigade.

Bruensburg and the surrounding country was the great depot for live-stock, grain, etc., and, in twenty-four hours after the arrival of our army, fresh meat abounded in camp, and the soldiers' lines seemed to have fallen in pleasant places. Foraging was not prohibited; in fact, the soldiers were cautioned to save the Government rations for an emergency; so that the squealing of pigs, and the bleating of calves and sheep, and the cackling of poultry were common sounds in camp, and many a fence-rail was burned to cook provisions for some veteran who had proved himself a good forager.

The day after General Grant's arrival at Bruensburg, so goes the story, as he was sitting in his tent, the flap was pushed aside and an old rebel, who had long passed the time to bear arms, thrust his head through the opening. In his hand he held a rope, which was attached to a large, raw-boned mule with swelled knees and minus an eye. At least twenty summers must have passed over the head of this interesting animal.

The old fellow gazed curiously at the general, as if he had expected to see one of the huge ogres such as figure in the chronicles of Jack the Giant-Killer. "Be you the gin'ral of this here army?" he inquired; "ef so, I got a complaint agin one of your rigiments, an' I want you to 'tend to it to onst. I don't come here to ask favors, but to deman' my rights, for, if these ain't granted, dem my picter if yer don't see some tall talkin' w'en this here war's over an' the Confed'rit Gov'ment makes claim for damages to her loyal citizens. I'm Abel Doolittle, that's who I am, an' ef I hadn't the alfiredest nicest farm in all these parts afore your bummers come along, I'll swell up an' sneeze. An' ef you don't see me righted, w'en this blasted war is ended, you'll hear on this, I tell you! Fust comes them Confed'rit fellers an' takes two tenths uv all we got, an' gin

us a bar'l uv Confed'rit shin-plasters; then comes along *yer* blasted
pot-hunters an' takes the tother eight tenths, and never even said
Thank ye! What you think uv that?"

"Didn't they give you a receipt?" inquired the general.

"Receipt! thunder!" said the old man. "Yes, they giv' us
receipts enough, but them things ain't wuth nothin'; an', I tell you,
I'm goin' ter be paid, or you'll hear on it."

"What is your complaint?" inquired the general.

"Well," replied the old man, "I ain't got no complaint, as I
knows on just now, ceptin' the rheumatiz an' fever an' ager, same's
all ov us has at this season."

"I mean," said the general, "what charges have you to make
against any one? Speak out, and don't take up my time. Here,
Rawlins, attend to this man," and the general walked away.

"Now," said General Rawlins, "say quickly what you have to
say, and then get out of this."

"Ah, yes!" exclaimed the old man, "that's demed pretty talk.
You fellers come along and eat us out of house and home, an', when
a man wants his money, you turn up yer nose as if yer owned the
Guano Islands."

"What happened to you?" said Rawlins.

"Why," said the old fellow, "I had the finest lot ov chickens,
turkeys, pigs, an' sheep as ever you seen, but dam' my buttons ef
you fellers ain't gone an' tuk everything except this ole muel an'
an ole goose. There was two ov them geese, an' they tried one uv
'em; but ef a hull rigimint didn't break their teeth out after tearin'
away at that ole goose, well, I don't know what loosin' teeth is.
Why, Gin'ral, ef I hadn't brought the muel away they'd a eatin
him."

"But what do you expect me to do?" inquired General Rawlins. "How are you going to find out who did all that you complain of?"

"Well, I know who did it," said the old fellow; "it's one of
Gin'ral A. J. Smith's rigiments. I know the sargint what led them
men on. He belongs to the 13th Iowy, an' he kin skin a hog quicker'n grease lightnin'."

Just then General A. J. Smith walked into the tent. "Here,
General," said Rawlins, "this man has a complaint to make against
some of your boys."

"What is it?" said General Smith.

"Just what I tole this here gin'ral," replied the old man;

"your men come on ter my place an' they stole everythin' they could lay han's on, an' only lef' me an' ole goose an' this ole mucl."

The general looked at him with contempt. "Pray what regiment did all this damage?"

"The 13th Iowy," said the man.

"They weren't my men, thir," said General Smith. "Ith's a damned lie; they never were on your farm. I know my boys too well. If it had been the 13th Iowa they'd have taken everything on the place, and wouldn't have left a goose or a mule or anything else. No, thir! my boys don't do things in that way. If you don't keep your eye on that mule they'll get him away from you before sundown."

The old man turned around to gaze upon his beloved mule, then shouted, "By the great Jehosophat, ef they ain't gone an' tuk him an' leff a darned sojer at the end of the rope!"

General Smith glanced proudly around. "Ah, Rawlins!" he said, "those must have been my boys after all; if I could only hear that they had eaten the old man's goose I should be certain of it."

"They're a hard set, General," said Rawlins.

"Yes," said General Smith, "but they don't cost the Government anything for transportation, and, no matter where they camp, they find a store of provisions half an hour afterward."

General A. J. Smith was one of those glorious old veterans who shared with his men all the dangers and hardships of the campaign. He never permitted any of his command to indulge in luxuries if he could help it; and once, in trying to express his contempt for a certain person, said, "He is one of those fellows who carry a shelter-tent!"

General Smith and myself served together a good deal, and I never knew him to falter. He was as brave a man as Grant had in his army, and, although he allowed his men a great deal of latitude, he was a rigid disciplinarian.

My first meeting with General A. J. Smith was an amusing one. It took place at Fort Hindman, Arkansas. Fort Hindman, formerly called "Arkansas Post," was captured by the navy. About an hour after the surrender, when the prisoners had all been secured, a large number of Union officers on horseback were seen approaching the fort. The marines had been posted as sentinels, and the sailors were taking the prisoners off to the gun-boats. An adjutant galloped up, and, jumping from his horse, sang out, "Get out of this; everybody clear the fort. General Smith is coming to take possession. Clear out at once!" The naval officers were watching the approaching cavalcade from the summit of a mound. I was dressed in a blue blouse with nothing but a pair of small shoulder-straps to indicate my rank, and, stepping down, I said to the new-comer, "Who are you, pray, that undertakes to give such orders here? We've whipped the rebels out of this place, and if you don't take care we will clear you out also!" At that moment General Smith rode in with the cavalcade. "Here, General," said the officer, "is a man who says he isn't going out of this for you or anybody else, and that he'll whip us out if we don't take care!" "Will he, be God?" said General Smith; "will he, be God? Let me see him; bring the fellow here!" I stepped forward and said, "Here I am, sir, the admiral commanding this squadron." At this announcement Smith laid his right hand on the holster of his pistol. I thought, of course, that he was about to shoot me, but, instead of that, the general hauled out a bottle and said, "Be God! Admiral, I'm glad to see you; let's take a drink!"

This was the origin of my acquaintance with General A. J. Smith, resulting in a friendship which lasted through the war.

After landing the army at Bruensburg I steamed down the Mississippi to the mouth of Red River, where Farragut was in the Hartford, relieved him of the blockade of that stream, and he rejoined his squadron. Fort Hudson had not yet surrendered.

Then I started up Red River, took possession of Fort de Russy, and partly destroyed that work.

Farragut had cautioned me against a ram said to be building up Red River. After finishing with Fort de Russy I began to inquire about the ram, for I did not desire to suddenly encounter such an enemy while turning a bend in the river, and perhaps lose one or more of my vessels.

I entered into conversation with a man whom we met near Fort de Russy, and said to him, "Well, stranger, I hear you have a Confederate ram up here somewhere. Whereabouts is she?"

"Lemme think," said the native, scratching his head while going through the thinking process. "Yes, thar is a ram 'bout eight miles above hyar."

"Is it a powerful one?" I inquired.

"Wall, I reckon you'd think so ef you seen it; it's the allfiredest strong thing ever I seen, an' I guess at buttin' it ud knock them ar bows of yourn into smithereens."

"How large is it?" I asked.

"Wall, it's 'bout the biggest thing I ever seen."

"Tell me all about it," I said, for I was beginning to get interested.

"Wall, Gin'ral," said the man, "that's easier said than done. It's an allfired buster, an' kin beat all creation at buttin'. That's all I knows about it. I seen it on Mr. Whitler's place, as I tole yer, eight miles above hyar; an' one day, w'en I was up thar, whar thar war a bull weighin' twenty-eight hunder, an' as soon as the bull seen the ram he 'gan to paw the airth an' throwed up his tail, an' the ram put down his head an' the bull bellered, an' they went slap dash at each other, an' ef that ram didn't knock daylights out o' that bull, and knock his tail out by the roots, and his horns off, and lay him out as flat as a pancake, I'm a liar!"

"But," said I, "I am asking you about a Confederate ram—a vessel covered with iron."

"Wall, Gin'ral," said the man, "I don't know nothin' 'bout any Confed'rit ram, but I'm sure the one I seen could knock the bows off them ar turtles ov yourn afore you could wink, an' I reckon he mus' be a Confed'rit ram, seein' he war born in these parts."

Any apprehensions I might have had in regard to a Confederate ram were put at rest, and I made no more inquiries.

I was afterward informed that this simple native whom I had questioned was a Confederate officer in disguise, who regaled his friends with the story of how he had beguiled the Yankees. However, he was entirely welcome to his little joke.

CHAPTER XVII.

SIEGE OF VICKSBURG.

See those hills, with their heads so defiant and bold,
Standing up as if reared by the Titans of old;
The deep rolling river just laving their feet,
And the cool glens and valleys defying the heat.
There are caves in those hills where a ripple of light
Scarce enters within—where the darkness of night
Reigns supreme, like some great and imperial king,
Where the sun not even a shadow can fling;

For darkness is sovereign, the light of the day,
When peeping in there, flies frightened away.
The thick fog in the noon-time almost baffles the sight,
And, obscuring the sun, turns day into night.
On the rugged hill-tops great forests abound,
And the day throws no light in *that* stillness profound ;
In the foreground are gorges, rifted and torn
By fire and wind, and by swift torrents worn,
Where brambles and scrub-oaks, all twisted in one,
Bar the way to invaders or the light of the sun.
High on the plateau, higher than all,
Stands the labor of man—a marvelous wall—
Its guns and its mortars protecting the rear,
Half-moons and counterscarps, where defenders need fear
No assailants who'll come in the gloom of the night.
The ramparts are manned with men who will fight.
Each house is a castle throughout the old town,
And the front with strong works is environed around ;
The right wing is protected by a frightful abyss,
On the other side faced by a steep precipice ;
Here would be scattered assailants and all,
And they long would remember that o'erhanging wall.
On the left runs a line, showing bright in the sun,
Of earth-works in numbers, mounting many a gun,
With rough-looking rocks crowding round them in piles,
And intrenchments bewildering extending for miles.
This is Vicksburg—the heart of this terrible strife—
Prepared at all points to contend for its life.
Ah ! those beautiful valleys, so bright and serene,
The red blood will deluge their grass-plots so green ;
The hill-sides and rocks will be soon red and gory,
And in ages to come they'll be famous in story.

We surround the doomed city, the pressure's begun,
And we're throwing in missiles from mortar and gun.
Months pass, and a gloom, like the mantle of death,
Hangs over the scene, where not even a breath
Of hope could be felt. While the brave foemen fell
By the hundreds beneath our merciless shell,
We bombarded in front, we assaulted the rear,
And every attack only cost us more dear.

There's an end to endurance ; the long-gnawing fast
Could not be withstood ; the fall came at last.

In the trenches, in battle, ah ! the days of the past
Rose before the poor soldier breathing his last ;
He would turn his dimmed eyes to the light in the west,
And waft a fond sigh to those he loved best.
But how many were wrapped in the garments of Death
Who welcomed Life's ending !   War's withering breath
Had wrested from many every joy in this life,
For what joy could one find in this murderous strife ?
Many breathed their last sigh on that wide gory plain,
And welcomed the bullet that ended their pain. '
And the angels rejoice o'er the soldier's repose,
And drop tears o'er the life just brought to a close ;
For no longer he'll battle on the chill, dreary plain
With hunger and thirst, in the cold sleety rain,
Where day's turned to night, and night into day,
And where shrapnel and shell sweep hundreds away.
Thank God ! the sweet angel of mercy is by
The brave soldier who dies, and will catch his last sigh ;
Soars aloft with his soul, while never again
In hardship or battle will it grapple with pain.

The cold, bitter blasts of winter have come,
And bring back the thoughts of a once-cherished home ;
The snow, which is red with the blood of the brave,
Piles up in rifts o'er the poor soldier's grave ;
And the cold, piercing wind, in its merciless wrath,
Is howling a requiem of death in its path,
As if searching for something still further to blast,
And dealing destruction all round to the last.
The angel of mercy sits out in the storm,
A halo of light flashes round her pure form,
And she drives off in anger that demon of sin
Who is watching his chance in the storm to get in,
And now flies in dismay, back, back to his shades,
Down, down to the bottomless pit of dark Hades,
For God in his mercy claims as his own
Those fallen in war who great honors have won.

There's that broken-down soldier sitting out in the storm;
Pinched is his face and bent is his form;
His uniform's ragged, his whole look is forlorn,
His breakfast is simply a handful of corn.
Shivering he sits, most sad is his look,
He has no *commissariat*, no victuals to cook.
Torn from his home—what a terrible fate!—
To fight 'gainst his will and nourish a hate
For the flag he once loved, and that beautiful plan
The Creator designed for the freedom of man.
What can console him? what can repay
For privations he's suffered, his life thrown away?
Who sits by his side in the withering cold,
Looking so sickly, so wretchedly old?
'Tis a comrade he cares for.   He can scarce draw a breath;
He is leaving last words, he is fighting with Death.
So passes the night, so passes the day,
Hundreds by Death are oft snatched away.
Shot and shell do their work, but privations do more,
And fill up the grave-yard along the lone shore.

See that bright youth of eighteen, looking afar
At the western horizon, on the bright evening star.
Another is looking at that star in the west,
And, knowing *he* sees it, thinks herself blest.
They promised, at parting, when the rays of the sun
Were melting in twilight and the day's work was done,
They'd go out in the evening and look at that star,
And their souls be united, though parted so far.
He hears the sweet chimes of the soft vesper bell—
And quickly he knelt as it soothingly fell—
And he sends up a prayer to the Ruler on high,
And falls dead as he kneels, and wafts her a sigh,
For a ball strikes his heart.   He will see her no more;
She will watch now *alone*, *his* watching is o'er.
A cloud, dark and threatening, obscures all the west,
And that poor maiden feels she no longer is blest.
Her soldier is dead, his marching is done,
An angel stoops o'er him, a triumph is won;
A soul flies to heaven, there's joy in the skies,
There's a whisper of mercy as upward it flies.

Look at those soldiers, how they hobble away !
There's no work for them now, they can no longer stay ;
They've been wounded and starved, they go out on parole,
Their limbs are all shattered, naught is left but a soul.
At night, on the road, they'll have no place to lie,
Yet they'll struggle along, for they go home to die.
Already they see the home-fire's bright glare,
And father, and mother, and sister are there.
Though they've suffered with cold and have no place to sleep,
And live on mild charity as onward they creep,
They keep their eyes fixed on that star in the west ;
Just beneath it they hope to find welcome and rest.
Yet who pities the pains of the soldiers so poor ?
They crawl with crushed limbs past the rich man's closed door ;
Still they keep their eyes fixed on that star in the sky,
Which points out the road to their homes where they'll die.
The poor ones would help them, but they barely can live ;
They are starving themselves—they have nothing to give.
Move on ! they can't help you, they nothing can do ;
Go to some richer mansion—they are poorer than you.
And they move on.   At night on the wet soil they lie,
And they reach home at last, but to lie down and die.
And the bright star of eve still shines in the west,
And sheds its light on the graves of the soldiers at rest.
Tears are shed on the sod, a wife's last fond claim,
And the poor soldier sleeps—his last sleep—without fame.

Just observe those sweet villas, once with beauty bedecked,
They are shattered and torn, without tenahts, and wrecked.
The rose, which in clusters sheds its perfume around,
Is lying all trampled and crushed on the ground.
Gaunt desolation now dwells in those halls,
And the bomb-shells' rude blows have destroyed all the walls ;
The owls and the foxes in these rooms make their home.
Those who lived there, and loved there, now have to roam,
Seeking for shelter in damp holes in the hills,
Breathing foulest of air, and air that soon kills.
In vain they seek safety ; the deep, piercing shell
Makes their homes in the caves little better than hell ;
But, though suffering all evils, and without light of day,
They kneel down at eve and in hopelessness pray.

And the loose, yielding earth only gives them a grave,
For they die, when fast sleeping, with no hand to save.
No one can hear that loud, piercing cry
That ascends to their God (for mercy) on high.
In ages to come, men in digging below
Will find their poor bones, but they never will know
Of the anguish and pain of the inmates who fell
(In the close, pent-up cave) by the deep, piercing shell.

There are the dead in their graves — in long, mournful
    rows—
What anguish they suffered in dying ! Who knows ?
Who kept a record ? Who is there can tell
Who died of starvation, or whom by the shell ?
All we know is, they lie by the deep river shore,
A board at their heads with a *number*—no more.
Friends may ask for their bones, when the war's at an end ;
Who can tell, midst that crowd, who's relation or friend ?
What havoc those bomb-shells have made in that ground—
Heads, legs, and arms all scattered around !
No peace for the living, no peace for the dead,
What cared the gunners, so Death could be fed ?
Uprooted are coffins, and the grave-yard *débris*
Is scattered about in confusion, you see.
It were useless to try and regather the dead ;
That can not be done till the day when the dread
Trumpet calls us before God's awful throne ;
Then the dead will all rise and bone spring to bone.

That street is much torn by the thirteen-inch shell,
Cobble-stone, curb-stone are mixed up pell-mell
With remains of strong horses and dead mules in the roads—
They were all blown to pieces while drawing their loads.

See those stone-houses crushed, those church-steeples knocked
    down,
And disaster and ruin all over the town ;
No pen can describe, no language can tell,
The terrible blow of a thirteen-inch shell.
It bursts in the air, it bursts in the ground,
And scatters its death-dealing fragments around ;

13

It brings sleepless nights when it bursts in the air,
And warns the besieged that the foe is still there.

Mark that company coming from church.   A fair bride
Has an officer by her—how she clings to his side !
They have plighted their vows and are now man and wife,
And have promised to cling to each other through life.
Life's uncertain at best, and how little we know
By day or by night when will come the death-blow !
They at least hope to gather some flowers in spring,
And sit hand in hand where the mocking-birds sing,
Or list to the lark as it soars in the sky,
While the swift mountain stream goes murmuring by.
But who, in their wildest conjectures, could tell
These two were to die by a murderous shell ?
But grim Death spares neither the young nor the old.
It did not spare *them ;* the story's soon told.
Hand in hand they walked on.   A terrible shell
Burst in their midst, and both of them fell.
A Peri from paradise, lingering near by,
Flew quick to the spot and caught their last sigh,
And, springing aloft quicker than thought,
To the closed gates of heaven the welcome gift brought.
Here's a trophy for angels ; it is free from all sin ;
Wide open the gates, let me bring the gift in.
Harps of seraphs resound through the portals on high,
While God's hosts rejoice o'er the lovers' last sigh.

Hark ! hark to the sound of the evening gun !
The night-watch is set and the day's work is done.
The sentry on post walks along on his beat,
And all that is heard is the sound of his feet ;
He is thinking of mother and sisters at home,
And the bright joys of life hereafter to come.
He stops on his beat.   Say, what does he hear ?
'Tis the hoot of the night-owl which strikes on his ear.
He continues his walk with monotonous tramp,
Wraps his thin coat about him, the night-air is damp ;
He strides on while he looks at the stars in the west,
Going down, one by one, to seek their night's rest.

They would rise in the morning, and again they would set,
And, like him, make their rounds o'er their pathway—but
    yet
They were there for eternity : that he plainly could see ;
But, by mid-day to-morrow, where would *he* be ?
A breeze blows, a bough breaks, a leaf falls to the ground ;
Again he now stops to list to that sound.
Comes a shriek through the air, and a small glittering light ;
It descends through a curve and dazzles his sight.
He watches it keenly ; it comes from afar ;
'Tis a fire-fly surely, or a small falling star.
He has no time to think ; it drops at his feet
And explodes, tears up rocks.   He falls dead on his beat.
All around know the sound of that bursting too well,
And turn pale o'er the work of that merciless shell.
By starlight they bear him to the deep river's side,
And inter him in silence, where hundreds have died.

Lo ! there's an old shattered church, all ready to fall.
See how the green ivy still clings to the wall,
As a woman will cling, from the days of her youth,
To the man whom she's loved, who's lost honor and truth.
But the ivy and tendrils will fall to the ground,
And the wall, unsupported, very soon will come down.
Though holy the church, and so sacred the shrine,
Shells have no respect for walls so divine.
In war, men ne'er think of the ruin they bring
On the sweet, loving homes, or the most sacred thing.
In war, man's a demon.   His nature set free,
His soul is a desert, parched as deserts can be.
From its throne Human Reason steps down so debased,
Truth, love, pity, friendship—all soon run to waste.
Man, urged by his passions, without due restraints,
Will desecrate altars and martyrize saints.
There's glory and fame left.   Each passion a snare,
War is ruin in all shapes ; it brings but despair.
But enough of this subject.   Let us close up the theme.—
Of the great horrors there, no one would dream.—
Gaunt famine killed hundreds, and sickness as well,
But worse came from the fall of the merciless shell.

There's a *fête* in old Vicksburg.   The great and the small
Are preparing to go to the officers' ball,
Just to throw off their *ennui*, gloom, and despair,
Which, with famine and death, pervade the foul air.
The soldiers, in perfect *abandon*, no doubt,
Determine to have all their friends at a rout,
Where the music would cheer, and sweet converse would
    flow,
And sound like the echo of joys long ago.
Little dress wants the soldier : he has made his toilet,
He is booted and spurred, has skin gloves on, and yet
He needs to look in the glass to adjust his cravat,
Or admire his curls, ere he sits down to chat.
Pray, why this grand ball ?   We can only surmise.
Is 't that lovers may bask in beauty's bright eyes ?
Or that viands so rare would enliven the sight,
And that scents of sweet flowers would perfume the night ?
No, it *is* none of these.   There'll be no viands there,
No sherry nor champagne selected with care ;
No tables with ices, fruits, or salads are set,
Where the gay and the witty in laughter are met,
Where lights so resplendent reflect on the wall,
And make each one remember the officers' ball.
Yet they'll bask in the looks of the dark and the fair,
"And bring back the smiles which joy used to wear."
There *is* nothing there but music full sweet,
Which gives pulse to the heart and life to the feet.
The men come to woo the lovely and fair,
And they all come this eve to beguile away care,
As the moths, that are lost in the gloom of the night,
Will fly on, confiding, to the hot, glaring light,
Heedless, forgetting, the poor foolish things !
That in wooing the light they are burning their wings.
It is but a change in their terrible life—
To get rid, for an hour, of gloom and of strife,
Though they only could hope to go back in the morn
To their caves where they'd cherished their hatred and scorn.
The fair ones wear neither bracelet nor ring ;
They've sold all for their cause—Rebellion is king.
They are neither adorned with pearls nor rich laces ;
The attractions they have are their forms and their faces,

Which, though marked with strong lines of sorrow and care,
Possess all the grace of their class—which is rare.
They dim with their brightness each planet and star
Which beams on those beautiful dames from afar ;
No diamonds can vie with their sparkling black eyes,
Which are brighter by far than those lights in the skies,
And their faces but look more lovely and fair,
Rich framed in full coils of bright golden hair.
Dressed in plain fashion, they came one and all,
Each worthy to be the belle of the ball.
Their rich dresses have gone to the hospital store,
To be used for the wounded ; and, such as they wore,
Are the simplest and cheapest *chenille* to be found,
And their shoes are so worn their feet touch the ground.
This gay night many dance, forgetting their ills,
While others sit leaning on the cool window-sills.
Some round the ball-room gracefully walk
With their lovers, while others sit, flirt, and talk.
The ball-room's a barrack, where the murderous shell,
In the worst of the siege, never yet fell ;
And none there ever thought that shrapnel or ball
Could invade this retreat—so thick was the wall.

Silently, slowly the fleet moves away
From the mouth of the Yazoo, where in safety it lay,
And it drifts along quietly, moved on by the stream,
Not turning the wheels or using the steam,
All looking like phantom-ships groping their way
Through the darkness of night to the confines of day.
They move o'er the river with the silence of death ;
None whisper a word, or draw a long breath.
The moon has gone down, there's no sound in the camp,
Not even is heard the sentry's loud tramp.
That sentry's neglectful ; he must be asleep ;
No good soldier in war such poor vigil would keep.
Not so in this instance. The soldier's keen sight
Catches phantom-ships drifting along in the night,
And the fire leaps forth along the broad shore,
And is answered at once by the cannon's loud roar.
The ball is deserted, not a moment is lost,
Each officer rushes at once to his post.

The husband stops not to speak one fond adieu
To the wife of his soul, and the lover so true
Tears away from his idol, with sorrow and pain,
To marshal his men.   They ne'er meet again.
From fortress and valleys, from casemates on high,
Rifle-shell, shrapnel, and grape-shot now fly ;
And the fleet lends its cannon to add to the din,
And each soul is now nerved this battle to win.
But the shell from the ships sweep o'er the broad plain,
And, bursting in air, is re-echoed again
O'er the hill-tops, in caves, or wherever they fall.
They e'en burst on the scene of the officers' ball.
There is grief in the camp, and loud wailing this night,
For the wounded and dead who fell in that fight.
But the fires burned down, leaving Vicksburg in gloom,
And the phantom-ships floated on—sealing her doom.
The besieged fight boldly 'mid the fire and blaze,
But their efforts are vain ; they look on in amaze
At the phantom-ships floating along on the stream,
And passing so swiftly, without using steam.
Who can tell what despair envelops them all
As they fly to the place where the officers' ball
Had been held ?   It had been swept by the shell,
And dying and dead are now mingled pell-mell.
The eyes that once sparkled, and were wont to beguile,
Are now closed in death.   Lips no longer smile.
Their reward is in heaven for the good they have done ;
Their misfortunes are over, their battle is won.

Once more are united the blue and the gray—
Rancor and hatred have both passed away.
No longer war's ogres, the defense, and the siege,
Keep up hostile feeling—the Union is liege.
The atmosphere, filled with thick smoke and gloom,
No longer resounds with the cannon's loud boom.
Peace reigns triumphant all over the land,
And the North and the South move on hand in hand.
Death in his avarice has glutted the grave,
War has bathed its foul hands in the blood of the brave ;
But the sun shines again, as bright as of yore,
And the gay stars of heaven all twinkle once more,

While the moon, going down in its daily decline,
Sheds a soft mellow light on our tents all in line,
Where our soldiers are resting in honor and glory,
And are eulogized now in ballad and story.
The spirits of good in high heaven all smile
On the brave boys in blue—the rank and the file—
And sailors, God bless them ! who in days that are past,
In misfortune or glory, fought on to the last,
And were always so faithful, and pressed on the more,
When memory brought back the hard fighting of yore.
Dear reminiscences : they mellow with time,
And those dread scenes of war seem almost sublime,
Like old wine that's been binned and bottled for years,
Is more tasteful with age, and more precious appears.
Now we look back again on those terrible days,
And would give to each one his due meed of praise.
For those who were killed, tears of sorrow will fall,
And warm hearts in remembrance still beat for them all.

Now our flag waves serene, and its stars brightly shine,
And the sun gilds its stripes with a halo divine,
I will drink to the past in a bumper of wine.
That past which to many seemed doubtful at first
Was hopeful to me e'en when looking its worst.

In the history of the world's sieges nothing will be found where
more patience was developed, more endurance under privations, or
more courage shown, than by the Union forces at the siege of
Vicksburg, while on the part of the besieged it was marked by
their great fertility of resource in checking almost every movement
of ours, and for the long months of suffering and hardship they
underwent.

It belongs of right to General Grant to tell the story of that
event, for in no case during the war did he more clearly show his
title to be called a great general, nor did he elsewhere more fully
exhibit all the qualities which proved him to be a great soldier.

If General Grant had never performed any other military act
during the war, the capture of Vicksburg alone, with all the circumstances attending the siege, would have entitled him to the
highest renown. He had an enemy to deal with of greater force,
and protected by defenses never surpassed in the art of war.

I saw, myself (at Sevastopol), the great strongholds of the Malakoff tower and the Redan the day after they were taken by a combined army of one hundred thousand men ; and these strongholds, which have become famous in ballad and story, never in any way compared with the defenses of Vicksburg, which looked as if a thousand Titans had been put to work to make these heights unassailable. I am told that there were fifty miles of intrenchments thrown up one within the other. I don't know how true it is.

The hills above, with their frowning tops standing in defiance, were enough to deter a foe without having intrenchments bristling with cannon and manned by the hardiest troops in the Confederacy.

After it was all over, and General Grant could see the conquered city lying at his feet, he could well afford to laugh at his traducers, who were doing all they could to hamper him by sending telegrams to the seat of Government questioning his fitness for so important a command.

If those who lent themselves to such things could be followed through the war, it would be found that they never made a mark, put them where you would ; nor did they achieve any good for the Government.

That was a happy Fourth of July when the Confederate flag came down at Vicksburg and the stars and stripes went up in its place, while Meade's force at Gettysburg was driving Lee's army back to Richmond tattered and torn.

That day, so glorious in the annals of our history, lost nothing by the two brilliant events which were added to our fame, and made it still more dear to the heart of every true American.

When the American flag was hoisted on the ramparts of Vicksburg, my flag-ship and every vessel of the fleet steamed up or down to the levee before the city. We discerned a dust in the distance, and in a few moments General Grant, at the head of nearly all his generals with their staffs, rode up to the gangway, and, dismounting, came on board. That was a happy meeting—a great handshaking and general congratulation.

I opened all my wine-lockers—which contained only Catawba—on this occasion. It disappeared down the parched throats which had tasted nothing for some time but bad water. Yet it exhilarated that crowd as weak wine never did before.

There was one man there who preserved the same quiet demeanor he always bore, whether in adversity or in victory, and that was General Grant. No one, to see him sitting there with that calm exterior amid all the jollity, and without any staff, would ever have taken him for the great general who had accomplished one of the most stupendous military feats on record.

There was a quiet satisfaction in his face that could not be concealed, but he behaved on that occasion as if nothing of importance had occurred.

General Grant was the only one in that assemblage who did not touch the simple wine offered him ; he contented himself with a cigar ; and let me say here that this was his habit during all the time he commanded before Vicksburg, though the same detractors who made false representations of him in military matters, misrepresented him also in the matter above alluded to.

For my part, I was more than pleased to see Vicksburg fall, for I realized my proudest hopes in beholding the great Father of Waters opened to the sea, and lived to see all my predictions fulfilled. I was one of the first who urged that all the power of the Government should be exerted to get possession of this stronghold, and I gave my whole attention during the siege to bring about this most desirable event.

CHAPTER XVIII.

A CHIEF OF STAFF AND A CHIEF COOK—DEMOCRATIC MEETING IN THE BACKWOODS OF "EGYPT"—A JOHN GILPIN RACE.

AFTER the fall of Vicksburg I proceeded to Mound City, Illinois, to superintend affairs on the Tennessee and Cumberland Rivers, and to increase the size of the Mississippi squadron, which had diminished in numbers since the commencement of the siege.

It would be as difficult to do full justice to the navy for its persistent efforts to put an end to the siege of Vicksburg as it would be to the army for its fortitude amid privations and dangers and its discipline maintained during so peculiar a condition of affairs.

I am sure that General Grant will with pleasure testify to the zeal with which the naval forces before Vicksburg at all times cooperated with the army.

On my arrival at Mound City, I found the place under water, owing to a rise in the Mississippi and its tributaries, and we might truly be said to live among the trees.

Quite a controversy was prevailing with regard to rank between the officers of the line and staff, and Captain Pennock, chief of staff, had his hands full in trying to reconcile the numerous diffi-culties and misunderstandings. In fact, I found that I had arrived just in time to prevent a regular row at the station.

The surgeon of the fleet, Dr. P., was one of the cleverest of men personally and professionally, and afforded a fresh illustra-tion of the old saying that the most valuable goods are generally put up in the smallest packages. The fleet-surgeon was of a social disposition, and a favorite with everybody, but woe to any one who ran counter to him on the subject of rank, or invaded what he con-sidered his rights. He would get out his brace of Derringers, and whoever had affronted him must make the *amende honorable* or fight.

I had fitted up a large steamboat, captured from the enemy, as a hospital-ship to follow the squadron on the eve of a battle and take on board the wounded. The Red Rover was fitted with every comfort, and poor Jack, when sick and wounded, was cared for in a style never before dreamed of in the navy. All these arrangements were made under the supervision of the fleet-surgeon, who had full charge of the vessel when completed, but at the same time she had a commanding officer, an old steamboat man who maintained discipline among the crew.

I had been intimate with Dr. P. from the time when I was a youngster, and he took advantage of this intimacy to come to me at all hours with complaints, and if I did not succeed in pacify-ing him in one way, I usually did in another.

One day the doctor came to me. "Admiral," said he, "these fellows around here whom I rank all to pieces are running their rigs on me about my command, and laughing at me because I can't wear a pennant. Now, sir, I want you to give me a *flag* to wear. I am next in rank to you, and I think it hard I should be ridiculed by these youngsters."

"Why, Doctor," I replied, "that would be an unheard-of thing to give the fleet-surgeon a flag ; as it is, you are enjoying unusual authority, being actually in command of a vessel of war, for the captain of the Red Rover is directed to obey all your commands, notwithstanding the Regulations of the Navy provide that medical officers shall exercise no military authority. If I give you a flag, the line officers will think I have gone crazy."

"Oh, no, Admiral," said the doctor; "if *you* grant my request no one will think anything of it. It will increase my prestige. You know this is a peculiar kind of a service; give me a flag, and my happiness will be complete."

"Well, Doctor," I said, "I will think about it."

"Now there's another matter, Admiral," said the doctor; "I think the Red Rover ought to have a gun to protect herself in case of attack."

"But," I rejoined, "hospital vessels are held sacred in all civilized countries, and no one will trouble you; besides, the Mississippi is open its whole length, and there are no guerrillas along the banks."

"Yes, sir," replied the doctor, "but I might want to fire a signal-gun, and I might as well carry a thirty-pounder so that I can be ready to fight and make signals too."

"Well, I will consider the matter," I said, and the little doctor went off delighted.

In three days I had a flag of yellow bunting with an anchor in the center for the hospital ship, to be carried at the middle pole, and a thirty-pounder rifle for the bow.

The doctor was delighted when he went on deck one morning and found his flag streaming from the pole, while the stars and stripes floated at the stern and the jack ornamented the bow. He immediately put on his full-dress coat and called upon me to thank me, little dreaming that his thirty-pounder rifle was made of wood.

The doctor commenced immediately to claim increased rank, and for the next two weeks there was a constant controversy between him and the commanding officers of the gun-boats.

Although these difficulties were not brought officially before me, yet I heard of them, and was thinking of some way to remedy them, when an amusing circumstance occurred which brought the fleet-surgeon down from his high horse.

One day the doctor dined with me, and, as he loved his glass of wine, he was feeling very dignified when he got up to go on board his vessel, for the regulations required that no one should be absent from his command after sunset.

As the fleet-surgeon passed over the side the sentry presented arms, the officer of the deck touched his hat, and the doctor straightened up with the consciousness that he was now a person of increased importance.

As he walked up the levee he met a sailor who had evidently been indulging in the flowing bowl, for he pitched about like a ship in a gale of wind and took up the whole of the roadway, finally running afoul of the little doctor, which brought them both up "all standing," as the nautical phrase is.

"Whaz the mazzer with you?" said the sailor; "ain't you got nary pilot aboard?"

"What's the matter with you?" roared the doctor; "can't you see where you are going?"

"Yes," replied the man, "see well 'nuff, an', d—n it, you get out of my way or I'll knock hole 'tween wind and wasser."

"Why don't you touch your hat to me, you scoundrel?" said the doctor.

"Touch my hat to you?" he said; "wha' for?"

"Don't you see my uniform? don't you know who I am?"

"No, my little man," said the sailor; "who the devil are you anyhow?"

"I am the fleet-surgeon of the Mississippi squadron!"

"O thunder!" exclaimed the other; "well, little fellow, you've got a good berth an' you'd better hole on to it; but I'm a huckleberry above that persimmon, 'cause I'm the chief cook of the Mississippi Squadron, an' you can't come any of yer chief surgeon over me," and with that he staggered off, grumbling, "Chief surgeon, indeed, expectin' chief cook touch hat to him—whas the world comin' to?"

The doctor gazed on the fellow as he tumbled on board the flag-ship, and if he had had one of his Derringers handy I fear it would have been all up with the chief cook; but, as he hadn't, he returned to his own vessel a wiser man. He had eaten too many of the chief cook's dinners not to know the importance of that functionary, so he didn't mention the occurrence.

But there is always some one around to pick up a good joke and tell it, so I was soon informed of what had happened.

Next day, when several officers were dining with me, among them Dr. P——, I told the story of the chief surgeon and the chief cook, and no one laughed heartier than the doctor. From that time forth he was less exacting on the subject of rank, though occasionally he would talk of using his Derringers.

The doctor was a strong Democrat and a great politician, though there was not a more loyal officer in the service. He claimed that there were as many Democrats as Republicans in both the army and the navy, in which I believe he was not far out of the way.   In fact, many persons stigmatized as "Copperheads" during the war were really opposed to the Rebellion, yet such was the morbid condition of the public mind that neither party could see any virtue in the other, and the wonder is that the civil war was ever terminated until, like the Kilkenny cats, both parties had been devoured.

I never encouraged officers to discuss politics at all, and, as a rule, officers of the navy were exempt from political bias, and considered that it was their duty to heartily support the Government in any measures which might be taken to preserve the Union.   This was my view of the subject, and I tried to impress it upon others, and succeeded in excluding politics from the mess-table.

But I could not control the fleet-surgeon, who would ride ten miles on horseback to attend a political meeting, in which he would denounce the Administration and maintain that without the Democratic soldiers and Democratic money the Union cause would be hopeless.

With such views, expressed in a very forcible manner, the little doctor was likely to get into trouble, and I received one or two communications from Washington about him which made me fear that I might lose his services unless he became more guarded in his utterances.

Mound City, where the naval station was situated, is in that part of Illinois known as "Egypt," and the condition of the rural population in that quarter was rather primitive.

"A great Democratic meeting" was to be held on a certain day a few miles from Mound City, and the little doctor resolved to be present.   He therefore provided himself with a speech, borrowed a racing mare from me, and, clothed in his uniform, set out for the scene of action.

There was a large assemblage of persons of the genuine peanut-and-molasses-candy stripe, and, when the fleet-surgeon hove in sight on his racing mare, he was received with loud applause.

Speaking was fairly under way at the time, and a blood-and-thunder orator was laying down what he affirmed to be the true principles of Democracy, when the doctor interrupted him, calling out, "You don't know what Democracy means as laid down by Thomas Jefferson!"

"Who in thunder are you?" said the orator.   "You're too small a man to be a Democrat; we want fellows big enough to vote."

The doctor felt for his pistol, but, fortunately, he had left it on shipboard, so, shaking his fist at the orator, he sang out, "Wait till I get the floor, and I will strip off all your borrowed plumes and show you up in your true colors!"

"Let the little fellow speak!" cried out a dozen voices; "let's hear what true Democratic principles are," and a large man picked the doctor up and dumped him upon the platform.

"There, now, my little man," said his bearer, "let's hear a true exposition of Democratic principles. You ain't much to look at, but I'll bet you know more about Democracy than any one in this crowd."

The doctor did not require any urging; such an opportunity did not occur every day, and he at once commenced his speech:

"Fellow-citizens! you see before you a man who has never failed to maintain the true principles of Democracy under all circumstances—"

"Louder! louder!" shouted the crowd; "let's see the little man. He's got a heap of wisdom inside that brass-bound coat of his! Who is he, anyhow? Tom Thumb! Daniel Lambert!" and so on, until the doctor grew quite bewildered.

An empty hogshead was brought forward and the doctor placed thereon, in order that he might be visible to his audience.

"Now go ahead!" they shouted; "don't be bashful; don't be afraid; nobody will hurt you!"

"If I had my pistols here I'd show you who's afraid," said the surgeon, whose dander was now up. At which the crowd gave him three cheers that made the welkin ring.

The doctor soon regained his composure, and commenced again, "Fellow-citizens! you see before you—" and suddenly the head of the hogshead gave way and the orator disappeared from view.

He was fished out mad as a hornet, while the crowd shouted: "Get another hogshead! lift him on your shoulders! let's hear all about the true Democratic principles," etc. But the doctor had seen enough of these wild cats, as he called them, and would not say another word. He mounted his mare and started for home, a sadder and wiser man than when he left it.

Just after he was fairly under way a large man on horseback, in the uniform of a colonel, overtook him and entered into conversation, and they jogged along quite pleasantly.

Pretty soon there was a clattering of horses' hoofs behind them, and they beheld the blood-and-thunder orator, mounted on a big roan horse, coming at a dead run and shouting like mad.

Both the mare and the colonel's horse pricked up their ears and became so restless that it required the utmost exertions of their riders to hold them.   The orator, as he came up, gave the doctor's mare a sharp cut with his whip, singing out, "Come on, little man, let's see if you can ride as well as you can talk!"

The mare started as if shot from a gun, the colonel's horse started after the mare, and all three dashed off at a rate of speed that would have distanced John Gilpin.

Crowds of people were met along the road, all going to the Democratic meeting, and all drew out of the way to let the racers go by.

The doctor's trousers had worked up above his knees, displaying his red flannel drawers in all their beauty, and the wayfarers shouted lustily, "Go it, little red-legs!"   "Go it, Colonel!"   "Go it, Bully Bludger!"

Suddenly a bridge hove in sight which the soldiers were repairing.   They had removed the planks from one side, leaving a narrow passage for travelers.   The mare took the lead, never deviating from a straight course, and with a flying leap cleared the opening ; but, alas ! for the little doctor ; he lost his seat and fell plump into the swamp !   The other riders, more fortunate or more expert in the management of their steeds, kept the side road and went flying on after the mare, which, relieved of the weight of her rider, ran faster than ever, and reached the gangway of the Black Hawk covered with foam.

The doctor had eight miles to walk, his uniform was covered with mud, and altogether he was so battered that his friends would hardly have recognized him.

Next day I sent for him to come and dine with me, and he appeared, looking as neat as usual.

In the course of conversation I remarked, "How are politics getting along nowadays ?"

The doctor looked at me suspiciously.   "Well, sir," he replied, "I have come to the conclusion that politics in Egypt are a farce ; they are whisky politics altogether.   I haven't seen a man in this county who understands Democratic principles as laid down by Jefferson ; in fact, I don't think they are understood anywhere outside of Maryland ; but, sir, if you'll sell me that mare of yours I'll promise to give up politics altogether."   Then the doctor told me the whole story of his escapade, for he couldn't keep anything from me to save his life.

The reader may wonder what I was doing with a racing mare. I had quite a stud of horses on board the flag-ship, and they were almost indispensable at times for sending messages to army headquarters, etc.

We generally tied up to the bank instead of anchoring in the stream, and made little use of boats.

The fleet-surgeon kept to his resolution and attended no more political meetings while in the West, but after the war, when he had returned to Maryland, he became again an ardent politician, and at one time attempted to run for Congress, which he insisted was his legitimate sphere. The doctor was a credit to his corps, and by his death I lost an inestimable friend.

There are other amusing incidents in the doctor's career with which he was wont to delight his friends, for no one told a story better than he did, but my limits forbid their insertion here.

CHAPTER XIX.

SHERMAN STARTS FROM MEMPHIS TO GO TO CHATTANOOGA—FINDS A THIRTY-POUND SHOT IN HIS STOMACH—THE NAVY RELIEVE HIM—BRIDGES AND FERRY-BOATS IN ABUNDANCE—REACHES CHATTANOOGA IN TIME.

ABOUT the last of November, 1863, I was standing on the upper deck of the Black Hawk, at Mound City, when I saw a large steamer coming up the river. She stopped abreast of the flag-ship, and the captain hailed to inquire if I was on board.

When satisfied on that point the captain informed me that he was just from Memphis, and that General Sherman had left there to join General Grant at Chattanooga, Tenn., with thirty-six thousand men.

I was surprised at this intelligence, as I had not heard that such a move was contemplated, as Grant and Sherman were accustomed to inform me of any movement they were about to make where the services of the navy would be required, and in this case the navy might be of great use.

I questioned the captain of the steamer closely, and was satisfied that his statement was correct. I immediately issued orders for a certain number of vessels to be ready to move at daylight next morning; and I suggested to the army quartermaster the advisability of sending some transports loaded with stores along with the gun-boats, in case General Sherman should require them.

Colonel McAllister, who was an energetic man, went immediately to work, and by daylight his vessels were ready, loaded with everything an army could require.

When General Fremont commanded in the West he had built a number of flat-bottomed barges for the transportation of troops, one hundred and fifty feet in length and twenty-five in width. The value of these flat-boats did not seem to be appreciated, and they appear to have been little used. They would break adrift from their fastenings at Louisville, or Cincinnati, or wherever they were kept, and come floating down the Ohio, and, as I had tugs patrolling the river night and day, they picked up this flotsam and jetsam and brought it into port, where it was appropriated to naval uses. In this way we acquired six or eight barges admirably suited for flying bridges, by which an army could cross a river, and three or four of them were now prepared to go up in tow of the gun-boats.

I also sent along a large ferry-boat that we happened to have on hand, and omitted nothing that I thought would be wanted in crossing an army over a river.

The whole expedition was placed under command of Captain Phelps, and he was directed to lose no time in reaching Iuka, or "Muscle Shoals," where it was likely Sherman would attempt to cross the Tennessee River, expecting to find low water and an easy fording place.

I selected the lightest-draught gun-boats I had, some of them not drawing over twelve inches of water—in popular language, "they could run on a heavy dew."

Captain Phelps worked manfully to force his steamers over the numerous shoals he encountered. The vessels were fitted with long spars on their bows, and when they came to a shoal the spars would be fixed firmly in the ground, the vessel forced ahead, her bow lifted, and she would spring ten or twelve feet in advance, and this manœuvre would be repeated until the shoal was passed.

On the third day, however, there was no further necessity for "jumping," for the water began to rise, indicating a freshet above.

I had received due notice, by certain signs, that the river was

14

rising, and I felt sure that Sherman would have difficulty in getting his army across. The general made forced marches, but, when his advance arrived at the banks of the Tennessee, they found the shoals covered with water and the river rising rapidly.

Sherman made several attempts to cross his wagons, but the water was too deep and the current too strong. Then he tried bridge-building, but without success—the river was now "booming" and rising at the rate of twenty inches an hour.

General Sherman's experience told him that there was no hope of getting across that river for many days to come, and the situation was getting rather embarrassing.

He had started under the impression that he would reach the river at a time when the water would be at its lowest point, and he would be able to cross it dry-shod. But who can tell the vagaries of the Tennessee and Cumberland Rivers? They may be dry one day, with the prospect of so continuing for weeks, and in two hours the water may be carrying everything before it.

General Sherman thus found himself checkmated. To use his own words, he was very much disgusted with everything, and, as nothing could be done, he rode back to his headquarters, which had been established two or three miles from the river, threw himself upon his camp-cot, and "felt as if he had a thirty-two-pound shot in his stomach."

I can imagine what his feelings must have been on the eve of a great battle where his presence was expected and he unable to move. A certain combination could not be made, owing to circumstances over which he had no control, and yet the combination might have been made perfect if I had been given a week's notice of the intended move by General Grant.

I presume that Grant thought Sherman would notify me, but it all turned out right in the end, although the expedition came near ending in disappointment.

As Sherman lay on his camp-cot, trying to digest the thirty-two-pound shot which he felt in the pit of his stomach, he heard the clatter of horses' hoofs, and, looking from his tent, saw half a dozen cavalrymen coming toward him at full speed waving their caps.

The general didn't know whether the river had suddenly fallen or whether the fairies had built a bridge across the stream, but he felt that something good had happened, and was no longer troubled with the thirty-two-pound shot when the soldiers informed him that the admiral, with *all* the gun-boats, was coming up the river.

The general forthwith mounted his horse, and arrived at the river-bank in time to see Captain Phelps's squadron of fourteen vessels coming around a bend.

The soldiers had mistaken Phelps's divisional commander's flag for that of the admiral. However, it made no difference, for I was there in spirit, and no doubt there was many a man in Sherman's camp who would have appreciated the sentiment of General Osterhaus's aide-de-camp—"Effery soltier ought ter garry a gun-poat mit his bocket !"

There was great rejoicing in Sherman's army at the arrival of the gun-boats, the ferry-boat, and the barges, and Sherman was so glad to see Phelps that he almost shook his arm off. No time was lost in utilizing the material sent for the use of the army, and a bridge was thrown across the stream which defied the swift current. The ferry-boat and the smaller gun-boats lent their aid to transport the soldiers across the river, and in thirty-six hours Sherman and his men were on the other side, marching to join Grant, and rejoicing that there were such things as gun - boats, although the army did once have to march after them in the Yazoo country to keep the rebels from filling up the ditches with their *débris*.

Thus it was that the army and the navy in the West were a compensation to each other, and though at one time the soldiers might think "Effery soltier ought to garry a gun-poat mit his bocket," at another the sailors would have an opportunity of believing that every gun-boat should carry a regiment of soldiers in the foretop. In fighting on inland waters each was a necessity to the other.

Sherman reached Chattanooga in time to take a prominent part in the victory, and, when it is recollected how desperately the Confederates contested the ground on that day, we may properly inquire, What would have been the result if Sherman's splendid army had been delayed longer in crossing that river ?

"Old Tecumseh" did not mention this little circumstance in his "Memoirs," and no doubt forgot it amid the multiplicity of events that were occurring, for there was no one who more thoroughly appreciated the alertness of the navy in giving effective assistance to the army at all times, or who was more prompt to give it credit for its services.

Yet it was too much the custom in the West to ignore the services of the gun-boats, which, at the beginning of the civil war, had been attached to the army, and were at that period under the im-

mediate direction of the commanding general.   And while such an
arrangement is a proper one, where, under the circumstances, the
navy must be an adjunct to the army, yet the officers and men of
the navy should always have full credit for the service they perform.

CHAPTER XX.

WHO STARTED THE RED RIVER EXPEDITION ?—JAPHET IN SEARCH
OF A FATHER—GENERAL A. J. SMITH MAKES A FORCED MARCH
OF THIRTY-TWO MILES—CAPTURES FORT DE RUSSY—SECOND
CAPTURE OF ALEXANDRIA—GENERAL BANKS ARRIVES IN HIS
HEADQUARTERS BOAT, BLACK HAWK—CHAMPAGNE AND COT-
TON BAGGING—A DERELICT HOSPITAL STEWARD—A REVIEW OF
"RAGGED GUERRILLAS"—A. J. SMITH'S SOLDIERS CRITICISE
BANKS'S ARMY—TEARS WON'T MAKE SOUP, CHICKEN WILL—
I HOPE YOU ENJOY YOURSELF ON MY HORSE—MRS. HOLMES
GIVES THE ADMIRAL A GOOD CHARACTER—MRS. HOLMES'S
STORY ABOUT THE COTTON TRADE—THE NAVY BECOMES DEMOR-
ALIZED—BLOCKED OUT AT SHREVEPORT RIVER—GUNBOATS
TURN BACK IN THEIR TRACKS—BANKS DEFEATED—THE NAVY
DEFEATS GENERAL GREEN'S ARMY — THE GENERAL'S HEAD
SHOT OFF—A HORSE WITH A HEADLESS RIDER—SAFE ARRIVAL
AT GRAND ECORE—BANKS BORN UNDER A LUCKY STAR.

No one ever knew who started the expedition generally called
the Banks Expedition up the Red River, or what its object was.
No one cared to father it after it was over, for it was one of the
most disastrous affairs that occurred during the war.

It was like Japhet in search of a father.   It was undertaken at a
season of the year when it could not possibly succeed if it was the
intention that any number of transports should accompany it, as
well as gun-boats.

Sherman had proposed to me once or twice an excursion into
the Red River country, and I had agreed to go whenever he could
get ready; and for the purpose I went down to Natchez to meet
him, but he had to make a move upon Meridian, and that, for the
moment, put a stop to the expedition.

Sherman was well posted in all that related to the Red River—

its rises and falls, and the season of the year when it would be best to undertake an expedition up it. He had, for a long time before the war, been president of a Southern college located on this river right opposite to Alexandria, and, having the faculty of observing everything that came under his notice, did not fail to make himself acquainted with all the vagaries of the stream, which is one of the most uncertain in the South—sometimes most turbulent, and again running along so mildly that it seemed to have no life in it at all. The Red River is the most treacherous of all rivers; there is no counting upon it, according to the rules which govern other streams, and when you would bet your all that there would be a rise, ten to one the water would be lower than ever. Therefore it would require great judgment to properly enter on an expedition in that quarter if vessels of any size were to accompany it.

When I met Sherman at Natchez he said, emphatically, that it would be useless to attempt an expedition then with any hopes of success, and that we would have to defer it until late in the season; and, as I had the most implicit confidence in his judgment, I was satisfied to wait.

We did not propose simply an expedition to Alexandria; that I had already undertaken by myself, and had found no difficulty in capturing the place.

Just at the time when Sherman had given up the idea of going on an expedition to Shreveport, General Banks proposed to him and to me that we should join him in an expedition into the Red River country. Sherman went down the river to communicate with him on the subject, and informed him that he could not go himself, but would lend him ten thousand men, under General A. J. Smith, and I also consented to accompany the expedition with a large force of gun-boats. I objected at first to the arrangement on the ground that there was no chance of success, owing to the condition of the river, but Banks urged that if I did not go, and there should be a failure, the blame would be mine; so I reluctantly accompanied him.

I am not going to write an account of that expedition; a full and graphic history of it would make a large book by itself, and a very interesting one at that. Perhaps the general in his declining years may think it worth his while to use the talents he is known to possess in an eminent degree to write a history of that campaign. He has never yet made a full report on the subject to the Government, and all that I have ever seen from him in relation to the matter is his evidence before the Congressional Committee on the war, which was not characterized by that fairness to the navy which should belong to a general in the army.

I did myself spend a whole winter in collecting notes of information and in writing a strictly true and complete account of the Banks campaign, compiled from such public documents as I could obtain, from letters received from army officers connected with the expedition, and from my own observations. It will keep, however, and I don't propose to make any extracts from it here. I may attempt to show how faithfully the navy performed its part of the operations, but I don't know that I shall do much of that even. "Good wine needs no bush" is an old and good saying, and I think that the navy had very little cause to exculpate itself on any occasion when it co-operated with the army, and never entertained a difference of opinion when it came in contact with regular officers.

As soon as General A. J. Smith was ready to move, we started off together down the Mississippi for the mouth of the Red River, and ascended that stream as high as Bayou Teche, where General Smith landed and proposed to march to Fort De Russy, now rebuilding, while the gun-boats were to proceed up the river, remove the obstructions, and attack the fort. Since I was there last the Confederates had repaired the works and had made considerable additions to them, while they had also barricaded the river at the forts with a heavy timber-raft, bolted together with iron, and six feet in thickness. It was a formidable obstruction, and report said it would completely bar the way.

The river below was also full of obstructions, such as heavy piles driven down into the bed of the river. These latter covered a space two hundred yards in length, and looked as if calculated to keep out any number of vessels. The upper part of the piling had caught hundreds of logs and held them, and, if we had not arrived when we did, the river would have been blocked all the way to Alexandria. When I first saw these lower obstructions I began to think that the enemy had blocked the game on us, and how astonished General Smith would be when he arrived in front of the forts and found no gun-boats to help him! It would be mortifying to me, and might be disastrous to him; but, after looking at the obstructions carefully for a few minutes, I said, "Bosh! to think of these fellows trying to block out a party who had been on the Deer Creek expedition in the Yazoo country, who had pulled up

Titanic trees by the roots and removed giant oaks from their paths when cut down to stop their progress ; who forced their way up through seventy-five miles of logs, canebrakes, and small willows under a hot fire from sharp-shooters ! Why, this is simply silly, and shows how these Confederates waste their time to no purpose. What indefatigable energy ! What a waste of money and horse-power ! Blessed is the power of steam, by which we can undo, in a few hours, the labor of years ; and blessed is the edict of the gods, that ' whom they wish to destroy make idiots of themselves,' or words to that *effect !* "

What folly for any one to attempt to keep a naval force out of harbors and rivers by torpedoes and barricades when they have not heavy forts to protect the obstructions, or a superior naval force ! You might as well try to obstruct Niagara Falls with tooth-picks or quill pop-guns.

When I had made up my mind about these obstructions which *looked* so formidable, I simply gave the order, "Clear that away !"

Who that has not been to sea knows the devices of sailors for removing this kind of stuff ? A timber-hitch with a hawser around a pile, the hawser belayed to the bitt-heads, and half a dozen turns back with the wheels, or screw, and the whole thing is done ; and in this way a dozen gun-boats went to work, and in two hours undid the work of many months.

The piles were pulled out of the mud faster than dentists pull teeth, and with no complaints from the patient. Then came the rush of the floating logs. We had a short tussle to send them out into the middle of the stream, where they drifted on until they were emptied into the Mississippi, to be carried by that stream down to New Orleans, where they would furnish fuel enough for the poor population of that city for a whole winter.

But the delay of that work, short as it was, proved fatal to our hopes and expectations of being the captors of Fort De Russy.

We put on all the steam we could carry, but, when we got within two miles of the place, we heard the sound of heavy musketry firing, as well as of field-guns, and we knew that General Smith was there before us.

He made a forced march of thirty-two miles—one of such marches as only his men could make—and, when we turned the point with the gun-boats a mile from the heavy works, General Smith's men were hotly engaged, and ten thousand of the best soldiers I ever saw were pouring in a deadly fire upon three thousand who had sought the shelter of the earth-works.

It was wonderful to see how our men would advance from tree to tree, covering themselves as they went along, until they got within fifty yards of the enemy's works and almost surrounded them. This was the condition of affairs when the flag-ship Benton poked her nose around the point and opened on the enemy with her famous bow-battery. They waited for no more, but retreated through ways known to themselves, and they were not out of the works before Smith's men, headed by General Mower, were inside and had taken possession.

The victory, of course, belonged to the soldiers, though, no doubt, the sudden appearance of the gun-boats, when the enemy thought them completely barred out, accelerated the latter's retreat.

We might have done considerable execution among their ranks while they were retreating, but, as General Smith's troops were pursuing them and it was impossible to tell which from which in the *mêlée*, we contented ourselves with looking on. We did hope to have an old-fashioned gun-boat and fort fight, and if this place had been fully manned it would have been "worthy of our guns."

But we lost no time in regrets. Now came the question as to getting rid of the heavy floating structures about the fort. Here the power of steam was triumphant again ; three or four gun-boats put their noses against one end of it, and, opening their steam valves, pushed it right up the stream. If the projectors were looking on from some secret hiding-place, they must have been mortified. The construction of this peculiar water-gate cost the Confederates seventy thousand dollars. I gave it to the poor of the neighborhood for fuel, and in the course of a year very little of it was left.

Then we pushed on to Alexandria, General Mower accompanying us in transports with four thousand men, while General Smith remained behind to destroy Fort De Russy. He said he was determined to show these Confederates that, notwithstanding their ingenuity in building the strongest forts in the world, he wouldn't leave one stone on another. He got enough of it in three days, and, though at the end of that time he had somewhat changed the aspect of the works, their defensive power was as strong as ever ; but, finding that white soldiers could not compete with the negro labor used in their construction, he left the defaced works as a monument of the industry and energy of the Confederates, who, if they had only applied the same amount of labor on the cotton-fields as they did to their fortifications and obstructions, would have been the richest people in the world. But really, when we come to consider the herculean labors performed by the Southern people to maintain the cause which they considered so sacred, we can not withhold our admiration of their ability as soldiers.

Without doubt, they established a new era in military engineering which none have ever excelled, and on a scale only equaled by the works of the Titans of old. I am myself somewhat inclined to the belief that they secretly imported a lot of those traditional characters to assist them in their labors, but that they came in the guise of that important person generally known as the contraband.

We took quiet possession of Alexandria, established posts in and about the city, and settled down quietly to wait for General Banks and his army. The latter was marching up by way of the Opelousas road under the immediate command of General Franklin.

Three or four days after our arrival, General Banks came up in a steamer called the Black Hawk, which he used as headquarters. She was filled up pretty much with cotton bagging, rope, champagne and brandy, and cotton speculators. How the latter got on board has nothing to do with these reminiscences, and I don't care to surmise; I mention it merely as an incident.

General Banks's army had not arrived, and General Smith's troops were the only soldiers to be seen about the town.

When General Smith joined me at the mouth of the river with his division he had, I believe, just come off a long march. The clothes of his men were worn and faded, their shoes were patched, they had no tents to sleep under, though they may have had blankets. Their tents were on the transports, and the general forbade their being used without his orders. I recollect hearing him denounce some officer as a "Miss Nancy kind of a fellow" because he slept under a shelter-tent, which is a thin piece of canvas about the size of a bandana handkerchief. I could never see the use of one myself; it is like a turkey—too much for one and not enough for two; but Smith thought it a luxury that no one under his command should indulge in.

General Smith had only two wagons for his whole command. He said wagons demoralized an army more than tents did, and if he had soldiers that couldn't find a restaurant in the Desert of Sahara, and a comfortable bed in the swamps of Louisiana, he wanted to swap them off for those who could.

I recollect his coming on board my vessel, the Cricket, one morning in quite a state of excitement for him. "Admiral," he said, "I want you to give me a pair of leg-irons; I want to punish a fellow for disobedience of orders."

"Certainly," I replied, "but why don't you 'buck' him if he has done anything very bad?"

"Bucking is too good for him," said the general. "He's disgraced the whole command, so I want a pair of irons; he's worse than a felon, sir."

"Why, what has he done?" I inquired; "it must be something very bad."

"Bad, sir, did you say? Well, I call it atrocious; it's my hospital steward, and I found him sleeping out here under a tree on a camp-cot! What do you think of that?"

I laughed. "Well," I said, "it may be pretty bad, but I scarcely think it deserves so great a punishment as that; let him go this time with a warning."

"With a proviso that I shoot him the next time," he added. "But, old fellow, my conscience would feel better if I had a little of your hop-bitters, *alias* whisky; that's the only thing that can quiet me just now," and so the surgeon's steward got off.

On the day after Banks's arrival General Smith held a review of his troops for the benefit of the former. Smith's troops were not, as a rule, dandies; they often looked very shabby, but their muskets were ever ready, and their bearing was soldierly. They were a splendid set of men physically, and wouldn't have feared old Clootie himself if told to assault his breast - works in sheol. They were just such soldiers as the French had in Algiers—a kind of bashi-bazouk, or zouaves (not exactly like Billy Wilson's "lambs")—and Smith wouldn't have them other than they were; he taught them to despise danger and to scorn comfort, and did not interfere with their disposition to forage on occasion.

These were some of the boys he defended at Bruensburg when he said they would not leave a mule, an old goose, or anything else on a man's place if they once got on it.

The review came off, and General Banks and all his staff were there to see it.

General Banks was a handsome, soldierly-looking man, though rather theatrical in his style of dress, which might be accounted for through the fact that he had at one time been on the stage—so I have been told. He wore yellow gauntlets high up on his wrists, looking as clean as if they had just come from the glove-maker ; his hat was picturesque, his long boots and spurs were faultless, and his air was that of one used to command. In short, I never saw a more faultless-looking soldier. His staff were not far behind him in appearance ; they had spent the winter in the gay saloons of the St. Charles, and may have lacked a little the rough-and-ready look of the soldiers, but they were a fine-looking set of men, and exceedingly imposing in their gay uniforms.

The general and staff were all mounted—and well mounted at that—and bore themselves bravely on horseback as they rode up and down the lines, witnessed the manœuvres, then bowed with military grace and rode off.

"Those are ragged guerrillas," said Banks ; "those are not soldiers. If a general can't dress his troops better than that he should disband them."

"Walls have ears," and so have trees. This was overheard, or repeated, and reached General Smith's ears. The result was the growth of a feud which lasted through the campaign, and extended to the men of Smith's corps, who held Banks's army responsible for that remark.

The next day it was announced that Banks's army was only twenty miles distant and would make a forced march into the town, and every one was out to see the troops enter.

They came along at the appointed time, not with the long, swinging stride I had been accustomed to in Sherman's men or those of the Army of the Tennessee, but with very steady step, like veterans, shoulder to shoulder, arms at "right shoulder shift," and keeping time with martial music. Really it was a beautiful sight, and I never saw a finer-looking set of troops than those. If Banks could not get to Shreveport with that army, I thought, he never could get there at all. There were, if I remember rightly, thirty-two thousand of them, artillery and all, and they were followed by two hundred wagons! It was an imposing sight.

Among the spectators were a number of General Smith's men. They did not appear at all remarkable for their neatness alongside these wonderfully well-dressed men, who looked as if they were simply on parade, and not an army that had marched twenty miles since breakfast.

Some of Smith's men were dressed in their best ; others were in their shirt-sleeves, having stopped whatever work they were engaged in to come out for a minute and look at the "*parade*," as they called it. They were rough, brawny-looking fellows, dark as Indians and as hard as steel—such men as Cæsar led into Germany and Gaul, and with which he conquered the world. They were standing in groups or in lines, with their bare, sinewy arms across their breasts, watching keenly the marching of Banks's troops.

"Good marching that," said one.

"Yes," said another, "but them fellers 's been fed on *pâté de foie gras*, and there's too much paper shirt-collar for me."

"Twenty-six inches to the step," said another, "seventy steps to the minute; we'd beat 'em twenty steps a minute in a march, which would be more'n half a mile an hour, and them havin' such good shoes on, too."

This showed the animus which grew out of a simple remark never intended to be repeated.

From this it may be seen how careful commanding officers ought to be in drawing comparisons between different corps, for, though but temporarily attached, perhaps, soldiers, while acting together, belong all to one army, and if some of them are not quite so well clad as others, they should be given an opportunity to become equal in all respects to their comrades-in-arms without unfavorable comment. Out of those remarks grew a hostility that came near breeding trouble. These soldiers of Smith's were some of the veterans of the war; they had been through the siege of Vicksburg, and at Arkansas Post, where I had met them, and that alone would entitle them to great consideration. They couldn't get over being called "ragged guerrillas."

I was riding out a few days after the arrival of Banks's army, and saw a woman standing on a house-porch with her apron to her eyes; she was crying, and talking to a soldier who held a large hen under his arm, while listening to her very patiently. I suspected there was some wrongdoing going on, and rode up to see what was the matter. I didn't want to be considered a Don Quixote, but I thought it only right that I should protect a woman against ill-treatment. As I advanced, the woman took her apron from her eyes, which were full of tears. "O Mr. Officer!" she said, looking at me appealingly, "won't you speak to this soldier and get him to give up my hen which he has taken? She lays an egg every day, and it is all the sustenance my old mother—who is seventy years old—can get in twenty-four hours; it is all she can eat. Do talk to him," she continued, "and save our hen, and I will pray for you as long as I live."

"Well," I said, turning to the man and addressing him sternly, "you call yourself a soldier, and can stand there unmoved when a woman in tears is appealing to you about a hen which is the only means of subsistence her aged mother has; you ought to be ashamed to call yourself a Union soldier."

The man looked at me and smiled; he had evidently been talked to before.

"Do you hear my remark to you, or are you deaf?" I demanded.

"Yes, sir," he answered, "I hearn what you say, an' I'm a thinkin' on it"—he was a real live Yankee if ever I heard one talk—"but, Mr. Admiral, I jist want to put the case to you in a practical way: chickens will make soup and tears won't! Now, that ere woman's tears ain't a bit of use to me, an' this ole hen is; it'll make soup for our whole mess; and all I've got to say is this: If you can make any use of them tears, you are welcome to do so. All I's got to say agin is this: If you've got ary a dollar about you, an' 'll give it to me, you kin have this ere hen an' give it to that ere woman; and she'd better keep it locked up in her trunk, for there ain't many fellers in this army as conscientious as I am."

"There's your dollar," I said, handing him one; "give up the fowl, and promise me not to come here again."

"Well, I'll do that," he said, giving the hen back to the female, whose tears all vanished as she hugged her old friend to her breast; "but, mam, may I ask the loan of your brush to get these feathers off my coat, 'cause them messmates of mine are rather partic'lar about business matters, an' if they see feathers on me they'd suspect chicken, an' I don't want to be bucked."

The man brushed himself carefully and walked off. I knew it was not any one belonging to the 13th ————, for that regiment had certain peculiarities not to be mistaken; and, after all, I thought, Banks's men are as fond of chicken as other people; that, I think, is an inherent weakness in soldiers, be they ragged guerrillas from Iowa or propriety men from Massachusetts, and who is there would envy them so small a luxury? The hardships of a soldier are many, and he bears them with a manliness that can not be comprehended by those who stay at home and send substitutes. I am quite sure that if, in time of war, I had a substitute, and heard he was robbing the hen-roosts and cutting the throats of all the little piggies in the country, I would smile in approval. The only thing that I would require of my substitute would be that he should not trammel the movements of an army by carrying off large pier-glasses on his shoulders, which should be only capable of carrying musket and knapsack. There are worse foragers than soldiers—foragers on a larger scale, and these are frequently officers in command. I had to do something of it myself while in Alexandria, for it was a place where a man could get but little to eat except salt and canned meats. Even dogs sicken and die on that in a short time.

My weakness was for horses; I always required a horse. I was in the saddle all the spare time I could find; I did a good deal of business in the saddle, besides keeping myself in health. When I arrived in Alexandria I found myself without a horse.

My flag-ship then was a small stern-wheel boat with a crew of only forty-eight men and six six-pounder boat-guns. I had room for only one horse, and he had something the matter with him. I must have another horse, and so I told Gorringe, who was acting flag-captain *pro tem.* In less than three hours a beautiful black stallion arrived, and in the evening I took him out to try his mettle.

While riding along the river-side I met a lady on horseback— a good-natured, buxom woman—and I raised my cap as I was about to pass her, but she put herself right across the road and disputed my way.

"I hope you are enjoying yourself, sir, *on my horse,*" she said, "and I am glad I have met the gentleman who borrowed him, because I want to know the man that borrows anything from me, to be certain that he will return it. You aren't what they call a quartermaster, are you? Because, if you are, I want to get my horse back again at once. You're not, eh? Well, so much the better; you can come and see me. My name's Mrs. Holmes. You'll find my house on the right-hand side of the road down river; that horse has a trick of shying; he'll throw you off if you let him; my house is a plain yellow building with gable-ends—and he's a little spavined, but nothing to hurt—and there's a large dog-house right close to the gate, and he feeds on corn (the horse, I mean); and there, now, I haven't time to listen to you at present, but hope you will enjoy yourself riding my horse; only take care of him, and don't forget to return him before you go away. Good-evening," and off she rode.

The next morning I rode down the way indicated, and determined to call on the lady and thank her for the loan of her horse. I knew the house by her description of it. She was on the porch as I rode up, and came out to meet me.

"I am so glad to see you," she said ; "you are a good fellow to keep your promise and come to see me, though I never expected to lay eyes on you again. They do say of you Yankees that you can make use of more 'soft sodder,' and make more promises than an Indian, and keep none of them ; but I am going to trust you if I lose by it ; but I'm that mad with that thieving old admiral of yours that I can't hold my temper. What do you think the old reprobate has gone and done ? He ought to be hung on the spot, and if Kirby Smith gets hold of him he will hang him to the first tree he comes to. Here I have been all this winter curing some hams, and last year growing a little sugar-cane to make enough sugar for the family, and it's all gone ; and then the few niggers I had, they raised me twenty-two bales of the finest cotton you ever saw, and Kirby Smith was to pay me ten cents a pound for it, and it was to pass through the Union lines, and that cotton would have netted me on the ground thirteen hundred and twenty dollars, Union money, which would be just seventy-nine thousand two hundred dollars, Confederate scrip—and I would have stowed it away, and at the end of the war, when Confederate money was at par, I'd a pocketed a pot of money—when just as I was fixing it all up to be delivered to Kirby Smith, who was to deliver it to General Banks, in comes that old skinflint of an admiral, and he seizes all my cotton and hams and sugar, and has it sent on board his vessel.

"There, now, what do you think of that ? and that horse hasn't thrown you yet, has he ? And he is the worst old rascal I ever heard of in all my born days (the admiral, I mean), and if you'll just rub his legs, from the knee down, every morning, with British oil, before you use him, and every night before bedding him down (the horse, I mean), he will go along very well while you are here, which I don't think will be long, for they do say that when Kirby Smith ships all the cotton on the transports and gets an order for the money he'll give you fellows just ten days to get out of the country, and will capture every mother's son of you ; and I only hope he will capture that old admiral of yours, and I want to be at his hanging, and I'm not the only one by a long shot. And if poor dear Holmes was alive and here he'd go on board of that old rascal's boat and just cowhide that cotton out of him; but the poor, blessed creature, when he heard the war had broke out, had some business in Galveston, and I haven't heard of him since, and I am a woman and can't protect myself, and have to submit to the stealing of that old scapegoat. But he's got no conscience, the old sinner—or I might say *skinner*, for both names suit him."

"But, my dear madam," I said, taking the floor from her abruptly and not at all surprised that Mr. Holmes had permanently emigrated to Texas, "I am surprised that you have come to such conclusions without being better posted. The very day we arrived here the admiral issued a positive order that all private property should be respected, and if you have lost anything it will be restored to you."

"Bosh!" she said; "and you are fool enough to believe that kind of stuff? If he issued any order, it was that he might do all the stealing himself. Don't you trust him; I know all about the old villain. Do you know him personally?"

"Yes, madam," I replied, "I am very intimate with him, and shall take the first opportunity to let him know of this outrage and your opinion of him, and you will see how quickly he will remedy it. Do you know the name of the vessel and the captain who took your property?"

"Yes, I do," she replied; "don't you suppose I followed my property to your old admiral's stow-hole? Didn't I ask one of the sailors, and didn't he tell me the vessel was the ironclad ———, Captain L.? Yes, he did, and a big red-faced man he is (I mean the captain), and looks like a man who would not mind robbing a hen-roost; I suppose he goes 'snaks' with that cotton-stealer, the admiral."

"Well, my good madam," I said, "I will lay the whole matter before the admiral, and if he doesn't right matters I am mistaken."

"You dear, good man," she said, "I believe you will, and you can keep my horse as long as you like, only return him; and now you just come in and take some mince-pie and milk; I made it myself (the pie, I mean), and both of them make twenty pounds of butter a week (my two cows, I mean), and they are—"

"Yes, madam, I will step in and enjoy the milk and mince-pie," and I walked on the porch and regaled myself upon what I had not tasted for some years.

When I returned to the vessel, I sent at once for the captain of the ———, and inquired of him about the charge made against him by Mrs. Holmes, which he admitted, his excuse being that he thought it public property, as he was satisfied that it belonged to the Confederate Government, though it was not marked "C. S. A.," the brand with which nearly all cotton was marked.

I told him to return all the cotton, sugar, and hams at once, and that I would only give him four hours to do it in ; and, if he had not men enough to handle it, to borrow from some other vessel ; that I didn't know whether I would try him by court-martial or not, and that I would censure him in a general order, which I did that afternoon.

Suffice it to say that the goods were all returned to Mrs. Holmes intact, and in the time I specified.

I rode down to Mrs. Holmes's next day to see if the order had been properly executed.

Mrs. Holmes saw me a long way off from the porch, and ran out to the gate to meet me.

"Oh, you dear, good man !" she exclaimed, "I got all my things back ; not a thing lost, thanks to you, and no thanks to that old cotton-stealer, your admiral ; I know all about him, and they say he steals cotton by the thousand bales at a time. I've almost a mind to give you that horse of mine ; only you've been too good a friend to me, and I won't deceive you ; he's spavined in both legs, and, if you were to ride him ten miles and let him stand half an hour, he couldn't move an inch. I'll do better than that by you ; I'll give you a horse fit to carry a king."

"Sell him to me," I said ; "I don't take gifts."

"I can't sell him," said Mrs. Holmes ; "he isn't mine to sell ; he belongs to a Confederate colonel who was wounded at Fort De Russy. The colonel is up-stairs, and the horse is in my stable ; you can have him."

"Is the colonel on parole ?" I asked.

"No," she replied, "he is nearly well now, and is going down the river in a boat to-night ; he can't take his horse, and will leave him in my care, so you can have him."

"Thank you, no," I said, "I can't have anything to do with the matter ; I want to know nothing about it. It is not my place to go about and pick up wounded men who are on a sick-bed and make prisoners of them, so I won't betray your confidence ; yet don't tell me any more, or I may *have* to inform on you."

"You dear, good man !" said Mrs. Holmes, again returning to

her adjectives, "and what *can* I do for you? Let me do some kind act?"

"Only lend me your spavined horse until I leave here," I replied, "and that is all the favor I ask."

"There is one thing you must do," she said, "and that is, give me your name before you go."

"That I will do with pleasure, and, if you will give me pen, ink, and paper, I will write it down for you."

She ran off for the articles, and soon returned with them. I wrote my name in full, and under it "The great old robber of the widow and the orphan."

I handed it to her and she read it. Her face turned the color of a peony.

"It can't be," she said, in a husky voice. "Have I been such a fool as that? Oh, no, you are fooling me, and yet I might have known it if I had thought a minute," and the good woman sat down and did what all women do under difficulties—she cried. Then she went out and brought me in a glass of milk. "There," she said, "I am so ashamed of myself that I can't talk."

"Well, my good lady, I have only one piece of advice to give you: don't believe every man who tells you that a Union officer is a scoundrel because he wishes to bring you people back into the Union, even if he has to do it by force. Now you can do me one favor, and it will cost you nothing. You said it was well understood that General Kirby Smith had made an arrangement with some one by which the Union army was to march into this country and be allowed to take out all the cotton without molestation, that this cotton was to be transferred to New Orleans in our Government transports, and that the owners of the cotton are to receive ten cents a pound for it upon its arrival at New Orleans. Is that so? and, if so, who is your authority for the statement?"

"It is all true," she replied, "from beginning to end, and this very cotton you sent back to me is sold on those terms," and she gave good reasons for believing her statement.

Here was a revelation to me. A large number of transports and private steamers were daily coming into Alexandria from New Orleans, Memphis, Vicksburg, Cincinnati, and elsewhere—all prepared to take cargoes of cotton, and the majority of them carrying stores of all kinds to trade off for cotton. Here was a scheme of corruption and fraud gotten up for the ostensible purpose of getting cheap cotton to keep our looms employed, but in reality to make large fortunes for the most unscrupulous men who were ever in the employ of the Government. The whole matter was finally brought before the Investigating Committee on the War, and if that committee did not bring to light the outrageous frauds that were perpetrated on that occasion it was because when they dug down their spades would strike some skull it was not desirable to disturb, and those who had charge of the investigations got over them as soon as possible. An effort was made to connect the navy's good name with the cotton speculations going on, but it failed *in toto.*

The only thing the navy had to do with cotton was seizing Confederate cotton marked "C. S. A." and turning it over to the Treasury, which was the final result, for all the cotton seized by naval vessels in Western waters was sent before the Court of Admiralty at Springfield, Illinois, and it was disposed of without any regard to claims the navy might have on it.

This cotton business, as practiced in Alexandria, made a rather ugly chapter in the history of the war. It was not an army and navy entering a rebellious State to put down insurrection and bring people back to their duty; it was an army of cotton speculators, commanded by General Greed, General Avarice, General Speculation, and General Breach of Trust, with all their attendant staff of harpies, who were using the army and navy for the vilest purposes —those generals who hold always a high position in war, and fall in *after* an army to gather up the crumbs which it leaves behind it.

A number of these closed up the ranks of Banks's army; they were in the van as well, and on the wings; they were like the crows of Pensacola, which go to sea for a living, and are deterred by no weather.

I was a great marplot to this expedition in some respects; I was not let into the secrets, and was very much like a bull in a chinashop—constantly running foul of some piece of crockery and smashing it; I was so stupid that I could not be made to understand how an army could enter an enemy's country and make terms with him to purchase all the cotton, and let it go out of the country without making a struggle to prevent it.

I don't know how it was that I was kept in the dark. There were lots of people who seemed to have been let into the secret— fellows who came all the way from Washington with permits to "trade within the enemy's lines."

They would bring their permits to me; I would examine them,

indorse on the back "Not approved," and sign my name to it. They would then tell me indignantly that they had a steamer at the mouth of the Red River full of merchantable articles, the list of which, when examined, would be found to include military boots, slouch hats, gray cloth, quinine, bowie-knives, etc. I would tell them that the only traders we allowed were fellows with muskets in their hands.

One fellow sent me up word from the mouth of the river that "he would have me out of that in ten days." I sent a vessel in chase of him, with orders to capture him and take his vessel and cargo before the Court for Confiscation; but he was too fast; he was up at St. Louis, had transferred his cargo, and was hired out to the Government before the gun-boat found him.

I was powerless as an infant to prevent supplies from reaching the enemy.

Steamers would come up, under army protection, full of cotton speculators, among whom were included ex-governors of States, ex-senators, relatives of people in Washington, rich merchants from New Orleans—"their name was legion"—and they stalked openly about Alexandria with "lean and hungry look," like so many hungry wolves seeking food in midwinter.

I wonder if Sherman would have carried on war in that way? I would bet a thousand dollars he would have hung some of those fellows.

This army had two hundred wagons. Instead of marching on to Shreveport, they were employed in Alexandria hauling cotton, which was shipped in steamers and sent to New Orleans; or rather, I should say, it was stored ready for shipping.

We went into elections, as far as the army authority would reach, instead of marching off, while General A. J. Smith and General Mower were chafing at this kind of war and volunteering to go on ahead and capture Shreveport in a week.

If Sherman had been there we would not have stopped in Alexandria a day, but would have pushed on to the end, unless we might have stopped a short time to hang the cotton speculators and such like.

Even the navy became demoralized. We had regular instructions to seize the enemy's cotton wherever we could find it, and have it condemned before the Admiralty Court—*enemy's* cotton—including all that marked "C. S. A." An immense amount of cotton had been so marked by the Confederate Government before the capture of New Orleans, with the expectation of shipping some hundreds of millions of dollars' worth abroad for the cotton looms at Manchester and elsewhere, but that little game was spoiled by the capture of New Orleans, and now came this new scheme for getting all the cotton to New Orleans for transshipment to the looms of the North.

Naval officers complained to me that they were losing a chance of making prize-money, and they thought they were at least entitled to the cotton along the banks of the river. I unwisely consented to that, and the very next day I saw a large wagon going along followed by a gang of sailors. The wagon was drawn by four large mules, having painted on their sides in large red letters " U. S. N." The cotton-bales in the wagon were marked, in the same color, " C. S. A."

Some one with me innocently asked me what those letters meant. "They mean," I replied, "the United States Naval Cotton-Stealing Association. I don't mind taking cotton in boats, but I can't stand the mule business," and I stopped it at once. It had been going on for two or three days, but amid all the army teams I had not noticed this particular one.

Upon inquiring where the sailors got their wagon, I was informed that "*they had borrowed* it from the army about midnight," had painted it red so that it would not be known, and had *borrowed* the mules in the same way; they shaved them and daubed them with paint, so that their mothers wouldn't have known them.

Orders were then given that no cotton should be touched without an order from me.

Ah ! no man can imagine what a fascination there was in a bale of cotton, especially at a time when each was worth one thousand dollars, and, if it could be condemned by an Admiralty Court, would make a good prize-fund.

I had some people under me who could smell a bale of cotton a mile off.

After I had given that order, one of the gun-boats, coming up the river, espied a pile of cotton consisting of thirty bales; the captain hauled alongside the bank and took it on board and brought it up, reporting the fact to me upon his arrival.

"Throw it overboard," I said.

The captain looked at me with a heart-broken expression, but there was no appeal. He obeyed the order; the cotton floated on down the river. Another gun-boat, coming up, fell in with it, and the captain, with joy in his heart, stopped and picked it up, brought it on, and reported to me.

"Throw it overboard again, and read the last order about cotton," I ordered.

"But this was in the water, sir," he explained.

"Throw it overboard at once," I repeated, and overboard it went, the sad eyes of the sailors following it regretfully as it floated down stream.

Next day the dispatch-boat General Lyon arrived. The captain reported to me that he had picked up thirty bales of cotton floating down the river; it was the same that had been picked up before. There was no getting rid of it. I let it remain on the Lyon, and it went to Cairo, before the Admiralty Court at Springfield, and was condemned, sold, and the proceeds put into the Treasury, being finally paid back to the owner, who had never lost sight of his thirty bales of cotton since 1863.

He recovered his money in 1880, seventeen years after he lost the cotton.

It would take a large volume to tell the history of cotton transactions at Alexandria. In the examination before the committee on the war there was a very considerable amount of evidence and some "tall lying." I never knew myself until I read that evidence how human nature was given to castigating his Satanic majesty around the lower extremities of an arborescent vegetable, but I am quite satisfied that on the occasion alluded to Congress did not get at the truth, nor did it desire to do so. Wherever it stuck down a spade it struck a politician.

Well, it has all passed away, as have many of the actors in the scenes at Alexandria and thereabout, but I do pray sincerely that, if we ever do have another war, it won't be in a cotton country, where an army will be commanded by Generals Greed, Avarice, and Corruption—three commanders under whom, if a victory is gained, the benefits thereof will accrue only to themselves.

We must move on; we have to go to Shreveport. We started for the purpose of taking that, and here we are at Alexandria still —days after arriving here, and with nothing to detain us.

We push off at last and go to Grand Ecore, pitch our tents again, and look as if we were going to take root. I have taken up three of Fremont's large flat-boats to be used as bridges and to bring back cotton in. There is no use blinking at the cotton question. Cotton was king all the way through on that expedition.

At Grand Ecore I turned the barges, or flat-boats, over to General Banks to be used as a bridge across the river so that we could communicate on both sides. The bridge was thrown over in two days. Captain Phelps came and reported to me that Colonel Clarke was filling them up with cotton.

"Let him do it," I said; "we will capture it when the flat-boats are full," which we finally did, and it went into the Treasury. Generals Greed and Avarice did not get a bale of it, and I am sure no one in the navy did.

At Grand Ecore the army came to with the two bowers and both sheet-anchors, and finally got out anchors astern, and there it lay—well, just ten days before moving on.

All this time those army-wagons did nothing but haul in cotton. Cotton was king here, as it had been all along the road and on the river. It was a perfect Juggernaut; it crushed everything else; transports went to Alexandria with it, and stored it away for further transportation; the looms of Massachusetts were provided for for years to come, and the sinews of war in the South would be much strengthened. What a practical way to carry on war, and how the "Neros fiddled while Rome was burning"!

How A. J. Smith, Franklin, Emory, and Mower fretted under it all, no man could tell; but it was a reign of cotton; they could not appeal. They were led to believe it was by order of the Government. Who knows to this day whether it was or not?

It was certain there was some understanding between *somebody* and General Kirby Smith. The latter kindly moved back as we advanced and left the cotton to go to New Orleans, and, when we had emptied the country, we moved on as the hand-organ man and the monkey do when they have taken all the sixpences.

At last we all moved on from Grand Ecore for Shreveport. Every one smiled pleasantly, but could not help wondering why an army, requiring to make a rapid march, should encumber itself with two hundred wagons when there were twenty transports going all the way by water.

But let us skip all that. It is a page in our history that may never be written. The expedition was a series of mistakes from beginning to end. I made some myself, no doubt, but the greatest of all I ever made was in permitting myself to be deluded into going where I knew there would be a failure unless a more propitious time should be selected.

Let it all go; there is no more room for it here. This is a book of anecdotes, and most of this matter is too serious to enter upon.

On the way up to Shreveport I had two thousand five hundred of General A. J. Smith's men with me under command of General Kilby Smith. We were to land them at the mouth of the Shreveport River, and march them to meet Banks when he should arrive.

Oh, the snags and sand-bars we ran upon! We had no pilots of any account, and got along by main strength and nonsense. If one got on a bank, another would haul him off, and there was not a vessel there that did not haul the others off three or four times before we got to Loggy Bayou—the name is significant enough without saying any more in regard to it.

The people all along were kind to us as we went up, and gave us information cheerfully whenever we asked it. Only it was curious that their information led us into all kinds of difficulties. Where they told us the deep water was, we found shoals and snags, and where we were told to go through a cut-off we found it a blind. But how could these poor people know? Likely they had never been on a steamboat or on the river in their lives.

When we arrived at the mouth of the Shreveport River we found ourselves blocked out. A very large steamer was laid right across the channel, with her bow resting on one bank and her stern on the other. Human hands could not move her. If we burned her we would fill up the shoal spot just beneath her; there was just three feet of water between her keel and the bottom. Of course, her being there was an accident! But as she was put there at high water, and left there, it looked to some of us as if there was purpose in it. We would have to move her piecemeal, and it would take time. I proposed to General Smith to land his artillery, and that he and myself should reconnoitre. The artillery was landed, and we rode back a mile; everything seemed peaceful. "What nice people these are!" I said to General Smith as we rode along; "they let us go over their country and don't fire a shot at us; but at the same time let us keep our eyes open.

"Halloo! what is that I see running along there in the high grass? By all that's holy, those are scouts, General!" I exclaimed, "and they are running to tell of our coming. But they are not General Banks's scouts; they come under the head of the genus guerrilla; they carry muskets."

"I see," he said.

" Banks has had a battle and has been defeated," I continued. " We are running into a trap ; we must turn back, and get down river with those transports when it is dark, or we will be cut off. Embark your artillery and let us prepare for defense, and to move at six o'clock. We will have a victorious army on us by eight o'clock to-morrow morning."

The embarkation took place, and we moved at six o'clock quietly, and with little steam, placing the gun-boats so as to protect the transports. I found that five or six large transports, which had been added to the expedition, were continually getting aground on account of their heavy draught of water, but I stayed behind as whipper-in, and had smaller vessels made fast to them, to pull them off the sand-banks and snags, and so got along very well.

The good people who met us on the way up, at the different landings, seemed so sorry to see us going back ; they got their guns out and saluted us, but, unfortunately, the guns were shotted. They killed a number of our men, and they kept up such a continuous salute that at last we began to suspect their sincerity.

At first the balls came like single drops of rain, then more of them, then they came in showers, and we were absolutely obliged to land and take on cotton-bales for protection to the soldiers and other persons on the transports.

Of course we fired back ; but what harm could that do to people who were in deep rifle-pits, screened by trees or in a canebrake ? The affair reminded me very much of the retreat of the French from Moscow, only this wasn't *retreating ;* we were getting out of the enemy's country as fast as we could !

The people were now no longer polite to us. When we got down about sixty miles some one hailed us from the bank and said he had a dispatch for us ; it was some one who had thought of us as going confidingly on to meet General Banks at Loggy Bayou.

The dispatch read : " General Banks badly defeated ; return." Here was a dilemma to be placed in : a victorious army between us and our own forces ; a long, winding, shallow river wherein the vessels were continually grounding ; a long string of empty transports, with many doubtful captains, who were constantly making excuses to lie by or to land—in other words, who were trying to put their vessels into the power of the Confederates—and a thousand points on the river where we could be attacked with great advantage by the enemy ; and the banks lined with sharp-shooters, by whom every incautious soldier who showed himself was shot.

We could not use our artillery, as the sound would betray our position to the more distant and powerful body of the enemy's force.

As soon as I read the dispatch I gave the order "Move on," and we went ahead with increased speed ; but about one o'clock the next day we were brought to a stand by batteries erected below us. I had dropped astern to whip in the loiterers—a troublesome business. One captain got ashore and deserted his vessel with the crew in the boats. I hitched on to the steamer, pulled her out of the mud, and towed her along. She had a number of horses on board. What a prize she would have been to the enemy !

Firing commenced ahead, and I pushed on to give directions, and, as I turned a point, an attack was made on the rear by twenty-five hundred men with artillery, under General Green, a Texas man. It took me but twenty minutes to arrange about the batteries in front, and, as soon as I heard the firing in the rear, I pushed on back again and found two of the gun-boats, Captains Bache and Selfridge, and the transport on which was General Kilby Smith, engaged with this force under General Green, while a larger body of troops were advancing in the distance. The gun-boats made terrible slaughter in the enemy's ranks with their heavy guns, and General Smith, having mounted his field-pieces on the upper deck of the transport behind cotton-bales, also poured in a heavy fire from artillery as well as muskets.

We made short work of the enemy, though they fought like devils, and fell over the levee into the water when wounded or killed. General Green had his head blown off, and his horse went galloping over the field with a headless body hanging to him ; the ground was literally covered with the enemy's killed and wounded, and they left their artillery on the field. I had no time to look after it ; I had too much to do to look after all those transports. I got them all by the batteries before sunset, and was rid of the rebel army for the night.

All the next day sharp-shooters followed us along the banks and picked off our men occasionally, but we had no longer any reason for not firing the artillery, and, as we kept that going during the day, we had the advantage of them.

We arrived at a point four miles from Grand Ecore, where I supposed the army was, and, as I came up with the vessels ahead, I found every one of them stuck fast in the mud—all in a bunch and surrounded by sharp-shooters. There was a smart fight going on, but our men were getting to be adepts at this kind of business, and could hold their own. As my vessel was of light draught, I passed on through them, telling them to keep up their fire, and that I would send some troops up. Ten minutes later I met General A. J. Smith, with some fifteen cavalrymen, riding rapidly along the bank. I told him the situation of affairs, and that I would send up more troops, which I did ; and at eight o'clock that evening all my gun-boats and transports anchored safe and sound at Grand Ecore, after an exciting trip as we could desire—three hundred miles up an enemy's river.

As soon as I arrived I mounted my horse and rode to General Banks's camp, about a mile from the town ; it was dark when I arrived there, and I could only see the twinkle of the lights through the canvas tents.

There were about twenty tents pitched about the general's headquarters—beautiful white tents glimmering in the early darkness, and they were surrounded by a rope rove through posts four feet high.

A sentry and a sergeant were stationed at the entrance, and when I said I wanted to see General Banks they told me that I could not pass ; that the general would not be disturbed.

"But I must see him," I said ; "my business is imperative."

"Can't help it, sir," said the sergeant ; "so are my orders."

"Well, then," I said, "here goes," and, putting spurs to my horse, I jumped him over the rope and rode up to the general's tent, which I knew by its greater relative size. I dismounted, made my horse fast to a post, raised the general's curtain, and walked in. The general was very glad to see me, as he had not heard of our arrival and felt uneasy about us.

He was looking as placid and as handsome as ever ; he wore a handsome dressing-gown, a velvet cap on his head, and comfortable slippers on his feet. His tent was a marvel of neatness and comfort, and everything bespoke the soldier.

"Well," he began, "how did you get back here ? I felt uneasy about you. You have interrupted me in the most pleasing occupation of my life. I was just reading Scott's tactics, which I do every night before I go to bed ; but I am so glad to see you back that I shall lay my book down without regret."

"I got back," I replied, "by main strength and nonsense ; more by good luck than good management ; we floundered along night and day with only a few good pilots, and had it not been for 'a good little angel that sits up aloft and looks out for poor Jack' I should have been nowhere; I was born under a lucky star."

"And that counts in a man's life," said Banks; "I was born under a lucky star also."

"If that is so, how is it that the rebels defeated you so at Mansfield?" I inquired.

"Defeated me?" repeated the general; "why, sir, I defeated them all to pieces, though I had to retreat for the want of water, and I had to come back here."

"Why," I said, "you only had six miles to march to touch the Red River, that would have supplied you with water. The dispatch some one sent me said you were badly beaten, or I would not have returned all the way. I certainly expected to meet some one from you at the mouth of the Shreveport River; that ominous silence showed me that something had happened to you."

"Nothing has happened to me," said the general, "except that I have fallen back," and I left him under the delusion that he had won the battle of Mansfield, or Sabine Cross Roads, or whatever name that unfortunate affair was known by.

But I am not going to write a history of the battle of Mansfield; that will keep. I must, however, mention one little event that occurred there. When the enemy broke through our first lines they came in contact with that sturdy old soldier, A. J. Smith, with his corps of eight thousand men. I had twenty-five hundred of them with me on the vessels. The Confederates had been pretty roughly handled by the two corps they first fell in with, and no doubt lost many men, but when they came butt up against a solid phalanx of Spartans, and were mown down by the hundreds, they turned and fled, Smith steadily pursuing them, causing them to throw away their arms and knapsacks. There were only sixteen thousand of the enemy against some thirty thousand of our men, and these, when they had first broken our lines, captured all Banks's wagons and a large portion of his artillery. All this General A. J. Smith recovered, and remained master of the field, while Banks, with the main army, retreated on toward Grand Ecore.

The Confederates had been broken up entirely, their arms were scattered all along the road, and this news General Smith sent by an aid to General Banks, but received in return an order to retreat. He again sent word to General Banks that he was not only in possession of the field, of the wagons, and artillery, but he knew that the Confederate army was broken up, and the road was open to Shreveport.

Another order came to "retreat immediately," and Smith had to obey, leaving the wagons and guns on the field of battle.

When the enemy sent in a flag of truce next day to ask permission to bury their dead, they found no one on the battle-ground but their own surgeons attending their wounded, and our guns and wagons looking on mournfully at the melancholy scene. Of course, the Confederates did not lose much time in gathering them all in, and good use they made of them before they got through with our party.

Next day, when General Smith came up with Banks, he called on him to report, when General Banks, with that courtesy which always distinguished him, said, "General Smith, allow me to thank you for saving my army; but for you, sir, all would have been lost."

Smith took advantage of the opportunity to deliver a retort for those remarks General Banks had the credit of making about the appearance of his men. "Don't thank me, sir," he said; "it wasn't I who did it; it was those d—d ragged guerrillas of mine, and, if you will let us, we will turn around now and march into Shreveport."

It was a heavy hit if Banks remembered making the remark.

No one could ever understand—and never will—how it was that, after the Confederates had been so cut up and completely defeated by Smith's corps, our army never turned toward Shreveport again. My own opinion is, that if there was any agreement made with Kirby Smith that we might come and take the cotton out, it was done to entrap us, and, when our army was moving along in perfect security and without expectation of being molested, they were attacked at a point very favorable for the enemy, with the fatal result mentioned, though this takes no account of the subsequent inactivity.

Some good historian may take the matter up one of these days and unravel the mystery. Then the truth may come out. I am certain of one thing, and that is, if General A. J. Smith and myself had been there alone with the forces we had, we would have gone to Shreveport without any trouble.

After all, nothing was gained by this expedition, for the moment our army retreated the Confederates set fire to their cotton-bales, and, instead of being converted into greenbacks, it went off in smoke.

CHAPTER XXI.

THE ARMY PROPOSE TO MOVE AWAY FROM GRAND ECORE—SINK-
ING OF THE EASTPORT—PUMP HER UP—EASTPORT BLOWN UP
—THE CRICKET COMES TO GRIEF—GUN-BOAT FLEET CAUGHT IN
A DILEMMA—PROVIDENCE SUPPLIES THE MAN TO RELIEVE
THEM—A ROW WITH A MILITARY GOVERNOR.

> "And he swelled like a tadpole on a rather large scale,
> With a very large stuffing-pin stuck through his tail."

I FOUND the river at Grand Ecore falling fast, and, notwithstanding General Banks informed me he was going to Shreveport, I
worked the ironclads through the mud into water deep enough to
float them.

I ordered the Eastport, the heaviest of them all, down to Alexandria, but she had not proceeded more than two miles on her way
to that place when she encountered a sunken torpedo and had a
large hole knocked in her bottom.

There was no time to be lost. The Eastport was aground with
her hold full of water. I went to Alexandria, where I had left two
steamers fitted with steam pumps to fish up sunken vessels. In
three hours after I returned with them the Eastport was afloat,
the two steamers towing her down the river and pumping her out
at the same time.

The Eastport was a ram which had been brought up Red River
especially to contest the point of strength with a Confederate ram
at Shreveport, but those extravagant people, after spending many
thousands to build a formidable vessel, blew her up on our approach,
and left themselves only the formidable ram to which I have elsewhere alluded as having knocked the bull's tail out by the roots !

When I returned from Alexandria, General Franklin came on
board and said to me : "Has General Banks told you of his intention to fall back on Alexandria ? Orders have been quietly issued
for the army to move this afternoon."

" And what is to become of all these transports ?" I said ; "they
don't belong to me. I have already escorted them six hundred
miles, and they have not been a particle of use."

"I don't know," replied Franklin ; "I thought I would tell
you what was on foot, so that you wouldn't be taken by surprise."

I went straight to General Banks, and, without giving my authority, informed him of what I had heard, but the general told me he would not move for some time to come. Nevertheless, I started all the transports for Alexandria under convoy of the fleet, keeping four small vessels with me.

That night the army moved off, and at daylight not a tent was to be seen.

The Confederates, with extraordinary energy, had got all right again. They didn't stay defeated long. They rigged up the guns they had captured from us with horses taken from our wagons, and, with fresh forces, came on after the army like a swarm of hornets whose nest has been disturbed.

General Banks's army had not proceeded far before it was again attacked, but the troops were now under charge of General Franklin, and the enemy got the worst of it all the way down.

Banks, with an escort, preceded the army to Alexandria, leaving Franklin with the troops to follow at his leisure.

At Cane River the Confederates made a sharp attack, but Franklin gave them such a warm reception that they were satisfied to follow at a respectful distance ; but they did follow us until we were out of the country.

I remained at Grand Ecore until I had gathered up some provisions and guns which the army had left behind, and then started after the Eastport, which was going slowly down the river in tow of the two pump-boats.

To recount the trouble we had with this vessel would be too tedious. She would sink, and we would pump her out and get her afloat again ; but at last she stuck hard and fast in a bed of logs, and, as there was nothing more to be done, we blew her up with fifty barrels of powder, after removing from her everything of value.

So careful were the two pyrotechnists in charge of the explosion (Captain Phelps and myself) to see that the powder all exploded, that we came very near going up with the vessel. Phelps was in a boat near the bow, and I was in a boat but a very short distance off, and great pieces of the hull fell all around us.

The Confederates, who had been constantly watching our movements and waiting their chance, had now assembled near this point some twelve hundred men, and took the opportunity to pay their compliments to us.

The other small gun-boats were lying at the bank near by, not suspecting an attack, but still prepared for one, as was always the rule.

The Confederates discharged their rifles and made a rush to carry the vessels by boarding, but met with such a warm reception that they were glad to retreat. The sailors followed them into the woods and succeeded in capturing a non-commissioned officer, who gave us all the information we wanted for a good mess of pork and beans.

This information quickened our movements down the river, and we lost all appreciation of the scenery, so intent were we upon getting to Alexandria.

It seems that the Confederates, having failed to make any impression on the troops under Franklin, had determined to fall back on the river and, if possible, capture *us ;* and that a force of three thousand men with three companies of artillery was already posted at a point on the river below us, and, as our prisoner expressed it, would give us "Glory, Hallelujah !" when we got there.

The rebs in this quarter were a saucy and independent set of fellows, and the prospect of punishment didn't seem to make them a bit more respectful. I rather admired them for their independent spirit ; they were foemen worthy of our steel, and can be relied on now to defend our country, if necessary, against the world combined.

Their valor was equal to that of the Northern soldiers, and their endurance, I think, greater. Had they been the people of any other nation, our troops would have walked over them without much difficulty.

When we left Grand Ecore, about five hundred negroes of both sexes and all ages took passage with us, anxious to reach "the land of freedom." When the Eastport was blown up I put them on board the two pump-boats, thinking that would be the safest place for them in case we were attacked, for I presumed the Confederate gunners would devote themselves to sinking the "tinclads," for so our light-draught gun-boats were called, having but one eighth of an inch of iron over their thin wooden sides. I never supposed the Confederates would fire at these helpless negroes ; but one never knows.

I got the two pump-boats right astern of my vessel, with another "tinclad" astern of the pump-boats, and the other two vessels bringing up the rear. My little flag-ship, the Cricket, had six twelve-pound boat-howitzers (smooth bores), and carried forty-eight officers and men. The other "tinclads" had each about the same number, except the Juliet, which carried the Eastport's crew.

One of the Cricket's guns was mounted on the upper deck forward to command the banks, and a crew of six men were kept stationed at it, ready to fire at anything hostile.

We went along at a moderate pace to keep within supporting distance of each other. I was sitting on the upper deck reading, with one eye on the book and the other on the bushes, when I saw men's heads and sang out to the commanding officer, Gorringe, "Give those fellows in the bushes a two-second shell!" A moment after the shell burst in the midst of the people on the bank.

"Give them another dose," I said, when, to my astonishment, there came on board a shower of projectiles that fairly made the little Cricket stagger. Nineteen shells burst on board our vessel at the first volley. It was the gun battery of which our prisoner had told us. We were going along at this time about six knots an hour, and before we could fire another gun we were right under the battery and turning the point, presenting the Cricket's stern to the enemy. They gave us nine shells when we were not more than twenty yards distant from the bank, all of which burst inside of us, and as the vessel's stern was presented they poured in ten more shots, which raked us fore and aft.

Then came the roar of three thousand muskets, which seemed to strike every spot in the vessel. Fortunately, her sides were musket-proof.

The Cricket stopped. I had been expecting it. How, thought I, could all these shells go through a vessel without disabling the machinery? The rebels gave three cheers and let us drift on; they were determined to have the whole of us. They opened their guns on the two pump-boats and sunk them at the first discharge. The poor negroes that could swim tried to reach the shore, but the musketeers picked off those that were in the water or clinging to the wrecks. It was a dreadful spectacle to witness, with no power to prevent it; but it turned out to be the salvation of the Cricket. All this took place in less than five minutes.

The moment the Cricket received the first discharge of artillery I went on deck to the pilot-house, saluted by a volley of musketry as I passed along, and as I opened the pilot-house door I saw that the pilot, Mr. Drening, had his head cut open by a piece of a shell, and the blood was streaming down his cheeks. He still held on to the wheel. "I am all right, sir," he said. "I won't give up the wheel."

Gorringe was perfectly cool, and was ringing the engine-room bell to go ahead. In front of the wheel-house the bodies of the men who manned the howitzer were piled up. A shell had struck the gun and, exploding, had killed all the crew—a glorious death for them.

"What are you trying to do, Gorringe?" I inquired.

"Trying to get her broadside round to open on the enemy."

"Leave that for some other occasion," I said. "I doubt if there's anybody left to fire a gun. There are times to fight and times to get out of range. This is one of the latter. We are helpless. Let her drift, and I will go down and see what is the matter with the engine."

As I left the pilot-house and walked to the stern to go below, the enemy again opened with their musketry; but we had by this time drifted some two hundred yards away, and the fire did us no damage.

One soldier ran along the bank and fired twice at me, or at those on deck behind the cotton-bales. I seized a musket, with the intention of shooting the fellow, but suddenly bethought me that it was not my business to shoot people, but only to direct others to do it; so I handed the musket back to the owner and said, "Shoot that fellow."

The sailor fired, and the soldier fell dead, being, so far as I know, the only man we killed of the enemy during the engagement.

When I got below on what we called the fighting deck a shocking scene was presented. Twenty-four persons, half of the crew, lay on the deck killed or wounded, among the dead a poor woman (wife of the captain's steward), who had her right arm and shoulder shot away. The guns were nearly all rendered useless by the enemy's shell, the side of the vessel and her stern were riddled, and everything seemed torn to pieces.

"Fire the guns off," I ordered, "even if you can't hit anything. Don't let them think we are hurt." Three contrabands loaded and fired one of the guns, the only one fired after the first; there was no one to fire them.

In the engine-room I found the engineer dead, with his hand on the throttle-valve. He was standing ready to obey orders from the deck when killed by a shell. In his convulsions he turned off the steam, which caused the vessel to stop. His two assistants were wounded.

I opened the throttle and the engine moved, for it had not been injured. We proceeded slowly down the river, and in three minutes were around a point.

The Confederates soon finished all the contrabands that were swimming in the river or clinging to the wreck. Some of them may have got ashore, but we never saw any of them again.

As soon as the pump-boats were sunk the battery opened on the little "tinclad" Juliet, following astern of them, and raked her fore and aft, killing and wounding many of her crew and cutting her steam-pipe in two, enveloping the vessel in a cloud of vapor.

The rebels troubled themselves no more about the Juliet, and she drifted under the bluff where the battery was placed. The bluff was sixty feet high, and the Confederates could not reach the vessel with their guns or musketry. The people on board took advantage of the circumstance, quickly repaired the steam-pipe, and during a lull in the enemy's firing, owing to the vessels above having opened with some heavy guns, slipped away and joined her consorts up stream.

I wondered why the vessels above did not follow me. They waited till night, and then ran the batteries, and were pretty well cut up in doing so.

Our fight was short and one-sided, for the Confederates had it all their own way, and there was no help for it.

The rebel army which Franklin had kept at bay turned round on that poor little squadron of "tinclads." They had not forgotten how badly we had defeated General Green's division, covering the ground with killed and wounded, and determined to get even with us; but they had not the satisfaction of stopping a single gun-boat, or even one of the transports which were so unwisely tacked on to the squadron.

The Cricket had thirty-eight shells explode on her decks in less than four minutes; the Juliet almost as many. The other two "tinclads" did not fare so badly.

Most of the white men on board the pump-boats escaped.

I had a relative on board the Cricket who had gone on the expedition "*to see sheol.*" He was satisfied that what he had seen was next door to it, and he was willing to return to his post.

As I came out of the engine-room I saw a contraband holding on to Mrs. Holmes's horse. "Why, Bob," I said, "you are a bigger coward than that horse; you are frightened to death, and ought to be ashamed of yourself."

"No, Massa," answered Bob, "I ain't no coward. Dis nigger stan's by his colors to de las'. If you was half as frightened as dis chile you'd swim fo' de sho'. I've got what you call de moral courage, sar."

And so he had, and that sort of courage is better than physical bravery. I took Bob home with me after the war and made him my coachman.

In August, 1884, I received a letter from Pilot Drening, whose cool bravery on this occasion deserves remembrance, yet a grateful country has so far withheld a pension to which he is clearly entitled. He must be upward of eighty years of age.

GALENA, ILLINOIS, August 27, 1884.

ADMIRAL PORTER, Washington, D. C.

DEAR SIR: Your very kind letter is received, and with many thanks I wish you long life and happiness. Twenty years have passed since the battle, yet I remember each name of the killed, wounded, and living, and how by a miracle we were saved from such terrible firing to see the greatness of the country that our comrades died to save.   Yours respectfully,
T. G. DRENING.

As soon as possible I proceeded down the river to Alexandria to bury the dead and have the wounded properly cared for. I could do no good to those above; they had to run the batteries as we did. Four miles below I fell in with Captain Selfridge in the light ironclad Neosho. Had I had a single ironclad we could have driven off our assailants, but "tinclads" don't amount to much in a fight against artillery. I sent Selfridge up to attack the batteries. Pretty soon afterward I fell in with Lieutenant Bache in the Lexington, who had been engaged all the afternoon with flying Whitworth batteries. The Lexington was a good deal cut up, but Bache's eight-inch-shell guns were too much for the enemy, so that we had at least one success that day.

I do not mention our little incident as a battle, but simply to show the kind of experience to which the navy in the West was subjected, and the courage which the officers and men exhibited. It is one thing to be on the open ocean, able to see your enemy and know that you can give gun for gun in manly fashion, instead of being shot at from behind bushes and banks. Think of being pursued day after day by a party of bushwhackers watching from behind trees a chance to pick you off!

One can hardly realize the danger to which the pilots and engineers of the squadron were exposed. I have seen a pilot receive a ball in his brain just as his hand touched the wheel. The pilots were targets for the enemy to shoot at, and he who could boast that he had killed one was a popular man.

The pilots were mostly Western men by birth, but passing their lives on the Mississippi brought them into intimate relations with the Southern people, who looked upon all that were loyal to the Union as traitors to the Southern cause.

I never knew one of these men to quail in the presence of danger, and when I have beheld them passing a battery with balls flying all about them, I have been struck with the coolness they displayed.

I think there is a magnetism in a ship's wheel in time of action which is communicated to the helmsman. He feels that the lives of all are in his hands, and I never knew a pilot faithless to his trust.

When I reached Alexandria in the Cricket I was surprised to find the fleet above the "falls." The rocks were all bare a mile above the place where I left the vessels when we started up river.

Red River had *run out*, as it were, and left the vessels high and dry, with no chance of getting down until a rise came, of which there was not the slightest prospect.

There was a narrow channel cut by the flow of water (for ages past) through the middle of the flat rocks, and, as the Cricket drew but eighteen inches, Pilot Drening succeeded in taking her through, and we lay once more in our old berth at the levee, which was now lined with merchant-steamers. Cotton was king, and his subjects mustered strong in Alexandria.

We held the town and the surrounding country for a distance of some six miles, and the different divisions of the army were posted in the most advantageous positions.

General Banks had practically relinquished the command of the troops to General Franklin, under whose management every one felt safe. Besides, why should thirty thousand men fear an attack from sixteen thousand, which was about the largest the Confederates could muster?

The army-wagons were busily employed in hauling cotton, which was loaded on the steamers from plethoric store-houses, yet here was a whole fleet caught in a trap and no one apparently concerned about it except the officers and men whose duty it was to defend it.

Soon after I arrived at the levee Generals Banks and Hunter came on board the Cricket. I don't know what the latter was doing in that part of the country, but presume he came on a mission from the Government.

These gentlemen inquired which vessels I could best afford to blow up, as there was no likelihood of a rise in the river, and the army had to be moved out of that. The horses were getting *thin* for want of oats!

I was lying quite helpless on my bed at the time, suffering from a troublesome complaint; but this cool proposal to destroy the gun-boats that had done so much service, and had really, so far, saved the army, was too much for me.

I jumped up, forgetting my pain. "None of the gun-boats shall be destroyed," I exclaimed. "I'll take them out as I brought them in. A. J. Smith will stand by me, and we will show you that we can hold our own. I'll wait here for high water if I have to wait two years." The two generals could make nothing out of me, and soon departed.

Captain Selfridge next came to see me. "A bad fix we are in, sir," he said.

"I don't think so," I replied; "we will get out of it all right."

"What do you propose to do, sir," inquired Selfridge.

"I propose to get out by an act of Providence," I replied, and I quoted Shakespeare: "There's a divinity that shapes our ends."

"But," said Selfridge, "that won't hold water, which is what we want just now."

Just after, General Franklin called and informed me that he had in his corps a Colonel Bailey, who had formerly been a lumberman in the rivers of Maine, and that he proposed to get my whole fleet over the "falls" by building dams to raise the water some fourteen feet, which was amply sufficient.

I said to the general that I had no doubt Colonel Bailey could do it, and that I had been expecting just such a man to turn up. "There's a sweet little cherub that sits up aloft to keep watch for the life of poor Jack."—"Bring your lumberman here, General," I said; "no doubt he has more plain practical ideas about him than all of us put together."

When Colonel Bailey arrived he explained how he proposed to dam the river and get the vessels over the obstructions.

"If damning the river would do any good, we should have been out of this long ago," I said. But the colonel did not appear to understand the joke.

I wrote to General Banks, requesting him to approve of Colonel Bailey's proposition, which he did promptly, and the colonel had at his disposal eight thousand men and all the cotton and sugar machinery in the neighborhood with which to make ballast for the cribs.

I believe that few people realize what eight thousand disciplined men can do when under the direction of a master mind ; but I will here insert the letter I wrote at the time to the Secretary of the Navy :

FLAG-SHIP BLACK HAWK, MISSISSIPPI SQUADRON,
MOUTH OF RED RIVER, May 16, 1864.

SIR : I have the honor to inform you that the vessels lately caught by low water above the "falls" at Alexandria have been released from their unpleasant position. The water had fallen so low that I had no hope or expectation of getting the vessels out this season, and, as the army had made arrangements to evacuate •the country, I saw nothing before me but the destruction of the best part of the Mississippi squadron.

There seems to have been an especial Providence looking out for us in providing a man equal to the emergency. Lieutenant-Colonel Bailey, acting engineer of the 19th Army Corps, proposed a plan of building a series of dams across the rocks at the "falls" and raising the water high enough to let the vessels pass over. This proposition looked like madness, and the best engineers ridiculed it ; but Colonel Bailey was so sanguine of success that I requested General Banks to have it done, and he entered heartily into the work. Provisions were short and forage was almost out, and the dam was promised to be finished in ten days, or the army would have to leave us. I was doubtful about the time, but had no doubt about the ultimate success if time would only permit. General Banks placed at the disposal of Colonel Bailey all the force he required, consisting of some three thousand men and two or three hundred wagons. All the neighboring steam mills were torn down for material, two or three regiments of Maine men were set to work felling trees, and on the second day after my arrival in Alexandria from Grand Ecore the work had fairly begun. Trees were falling with great rapidity ; teams were moving in all directions, bringing in brick and stone ; quarries were opened ; flat-boats were built to bring stone down from above; and every man seemed to be working with a vigor I have seldom seen equaled, while perhaps not one in fifty believed in the success of the undertaking.

These "falls" are about a mile in length, filled with rugged rocks, over which, at the present stage of water, it seemed to be impossible to make a channel.

The work was commenced by running out from the left bank of the river a tree-dam, made of the bodies of very large trees, brush, brick, and stone, cross-tied with other heavy timber, and strengthened in every way which ingenuity could devise. This was run out about three hundred feet into the river; four large coal-barges were then filled with brick and sunk at the end of it. From the right bank of the river cribs filled with stone were built out to meet the barges. All of which was successfully accomplished, notwithstanding there was a current running of nine miles an hour, which threatened to sweep everything before it.

It will take too much time to enter into the details of this truly wonderful work. Suffice it to say that the dam had nearly reached completion in eight days' working time, and the water had risen sufficiently on the upper falls to allow the Fort Hindman, Osage, and Neosho to get down and be ready to pass the dam. In another day it would have been high enough to enable all the other vessels to pass the upper falls. Unfortunately, on the morning of the 9th instant the pressure of water became so great that it swept away two of the stone barges, which swung in below the dam on one side. Seeing this unfortunate accident, I jumped on a horse and rode up to where the upper vessels were anchored and ordered the Lexington to pass the upper falls if possible, and immediately attempt to go through the dam. I thought I might be able to save the four vessels below, not knowing whether the persons employed on the work would ever have the heart to renew their enterprise.

The Lexington succeeded in getting over the upper falls just in time, the water rapidly falling as she was passing over. She then steered directly for the opening in the dam, through which the water was rushing so furiously that it seemed as if nothing but destruction awaited her. Thousands of beating hearts looked on anxious for the result. The silence was so great as the Lexington approached the dam that a pin might almost be heard to fall. She entered the gap with a full head of steam on, pitched down the roaring torrent, made two or three spasmodic rolls, hung for a moment on the rocks below, was then swept into deep water by the current, and rounded-to safely into the bank. Thirty thousand voices rose in one deafening cheer, and universal joy seemed to pervade the face of every man present.

The Neosho followed next, all her hatches battened down and every precaution taken against accident. She did not fare as well as the Lexington, her pilot having become frightened as he approached the abyss and stopped her engine, when I particularly ordered a full head of steam to be carried ; the result was that for the moment her hull disappeared from sight under the water. Every one thought she was lost. She rose, however, swept along over the rocks with the current, and, fortunately, escaped with only one hole in her bottom, which was stopped in the course of an hour.

The Hindman and Osage both came through beautifully without touching a thing, and I thought if I was only fortunate enough to get my large vessels as well over the falls, my fleet once more would do good service on the Mississippi.

The accident to the dam, instead of disheartening Colonel Bailey, only induced him to renew his exertions, after he had seen the success of getting four vessels through.

The noble-hearted soldiers, seeing their labor of the last eight days swept away in a moment, cheerfully went to work to repair damages, being confident now that all the gun-boats would be finally brought over. These men had been working for eight days and nights up to their necks in water, in the broiling sun, cutting trees and wheeling bricks, and nothing but good humor prevailed among them.

On the whole, it was very fortunate the dam was carried away, as the two barges that were swept away from the center swung around against some rocks on the left and made a fine cushion for the vessels, and prevented them, as it afterward appeared, from running on certain destruction.

The force of the water and the current being too great to construct a continuous dam of six hundred feet across the river in so short a time, Colonel Bailey determined to leave a gap of fifty-five feet in the dam, and build a series of wing-dams on the upper falls. This was accomplished in three days' time, and on the 11th instant the Mound City, Carondelet, and Pittsburg came over the upper falls, a good deal of labor having been expended in hauling them through, the channel being very crooked, and scarcely wide enough for them.

Next day the Ozark, Louisville, Chillicothe, and two tugs also succeeded in crossing the upper falls. Immediately afterward the Mound City, Carondelet, and Pittsburg started in succession to pass the dam, all their hatches battened down, and every precaution taken to prevent accident.

The passage of these vessels was a most beautiful sight, only to be realized when seen. They passed over without an accident, except the unshipping of one or two rudders. This was witnessed by all the troops, and the vessels were heartily cheered when they passed over. Next morning at ten o'clock the Louisville, Chillicothe, Ozark, and two tugs passed over without any accident, except the loss of a man, who was swept off the deck of one of the tugs. By three o'clock that afternoon the vessels were all coaled, ammunition replaced, and all steamed down the river, with the convoy of transports in company.

A good deal of difficulty was anticipated in getting over the bars in lower Red River. Depth of water reported, only five feet; gun-boats were drawing six. Providentially, we had a rise from the back-water of the Mississippi, that river being very high at the time, the back-water, extending to Alexandria, one hundred and fifty miles distant, enabling us to pass all the bars and obstructions in safety.

Words are inadequate to express the admiration I feel for the abilities of Lieutenant-Colonel Bailey. This is, without doubt, the best engineering feat ever performed. Under the best circumstances a private company would not have completed this work under one year, and to an ordinary mind the whole thing would have appeared an utter impossibility. Leaving out his abilities as an engineer, the credit he has conferred upon the country, he has saved to the Union a valuable fleet worth nearly two million dollars. More: he has deprived the enemy of a triumph which would have emboldened them to carry on this war a year or two longer, for the intended departure of the army was a fixed fact, and there was nothing left for me to do, in case that event occurred, but to destroy every part of the vessels, so that the rebels could make nothing of them. The highest honors that the Government can bestow on Colonel Bailey can never repay him for the service he has rendered the country.

To General Banks personally I am much indebted for the happy manner in which he has forwarded this enterprise, giving it his whole attention night and day, scarcely sleeping while the work was going on, tending personally to see that all the requirements of Colonel Bailey were complied with on the instant.

I do not believe there ever was a case where such difficulties were overcome in such a short space of time, and without any preparation.

I beg leave to mention the names of some of the persons engaged on this work, as I think that credit should be given every man employed on it. I am unable to give the names of all, but sincerely trust that General Banks will do full justice to every officer engaged in this undertaking when he makes his report. I only regret that time did not enable me to get the names of all concerned. The following are the names of the most prominent persons :

Lieutenant-Colonel Bailey, acting military engineer, Nineteenth Army Corps, in charge of the work.

Lieutenant-Colonel Pearcall, assistant.

Colonel Dwight, acting assistant inspector-general.

Lieutenant-Colonel W. B. Kinsey, 161st New York Volunteers.

Lieutenant-Colonel Hubbard, 30th Maine Volunteers.

Major Sawtelle, provost marshal, and

Lieutenant Williamson, ordnance officer.

The following were a portion of the regiments employed : 29th Maine, commanded by Lieutenant-Colonel Emerson ; 116th New York, commanded by Colonel George M. Love ; 161st New York, commanded by Captain Prentiss ; 133d New York, commanded by Colonel Currie.

The engineer regiment and officers of the Thirteenth Army Corps were also employed.

I feel that I have done but feeble justice to the work or the persons engaged in it. Being severely indisposed, I feel myself unable to go into further details. I trust some future historian will treat this matter as it deserves to be treated, because it is a subject in which the whole country should feel an interest, and the noble men who succeeded so admirably in this arduous task should not lose one atom of credit so justly due them.

The Mississippi squadron will never forget the obligations it is under to Lieutenant-Colonel Bailey.

Previous to passing the vessels over the falls I had nearly all the guns, ammunition, provisions, chain-cables, anchors, and everything that could affect their draught, taken out of them.

The commanders were indefatigable in their exertions to accomplish the object before them, and a happier set of men were never seen than when their vessels were once more in fighting trim.

If this expedition has not been so successful as the country hoped for, it has exhibited the indomitable spirit of Eastern and Western men to overcome obstacles deemed by most people insurmountable. It has presented a new feature in the war, nothing like which has ever been accomplished before. . . .

I have the honor to be, very respectfully,
Your obedient servant,
DAVID D. PORTER, Rear-Admiral.

Hon. GIDEON WELLES,
Secretary of the Navy, Washington, D. C.

When all our vessels were over the dam the army prepared to move. The gun-boats took their batteries on board, which had been hauled around from above the falls.

For nearly two miles below where the vessels lay imprisoned a flat rock was extended, over which I walked dry-shod, and in a week Colonel Bailey had raised the water to a height sufficient to float the gun-boats.

How blank the Confederates must have looked when they found that their prey had escaped ! As for myself and officers, we never forgot the service that Colonel Bailey had rendered us, and the remembrances we gave him will be handed down to his descendants and show future ages the estimation in which he was held.

Through him we saved a valuable set of vessels, without which the Mississippi would for a time have been given over to the incursions of guerrillas—a set of cowardly scoundrels who had no claim to the title of soldiers.

When the Confederates saw that the fleet was likely to escape over the dam they assembled a force of artillery to stop the passage of the vessels below Alexandria, and attempted to force the lines of the Union army on the single road that led to the point they desired to reach.

General McClernand had command of the outposts four miles from Alexandria, and directly on the road the Confederates desired to travel. The latter made a sudden and vigorous attack, causing a stampede among our troops, after which the enemy set fire to McClernand's camp.

Everything had passed so pleasantly since our return to Alexandria that no one suspected such a mean trick (!) on the part of the Confederates, but the latter did not seem to mind the strictures which were passed upon them.

When this attack occurred I was in General Smith's camp, distant about a mile and a half from the scene of action. As soon as the general heard the firing he mounted his horse and galloped off to the front, ordering General Mower to follow with the troops of his division. It was a fine sight, those gallant fellows falling into line and going off at double quick after their gallant leader. I went along to see the fun, and, in twenty minutes after the alarm, Smith's men were on the ground and busy putting out the fire.

As soon as the Confederates saw Smith and his men coming they decamped without having time to carry off any plunder, but they gained their point in turning McClernand's position.

Smith's soldiers soon extinguished the fire, which had not done much damage, but, when they came across a lot of clothing which had been broken into by the enemy, they saw an opportunity which might not soon occur again, and proceeded to help themselves, leaving their old clothes for the quartermaster, so that he could square his accounts ; and, seeing McClernand's men reforming, they gave three cheers and marched back to camp.

General Banks rode up to General Smith on the latter's return, and, with a courtly salutation, said, " General, I have again to thank you for timely help, and I shall not fail to notice the conduct of yourself and men in general orders."

" It wasn't me, General," said Smith ; " it was my d—d ragged guerrillas !" General Smith thought himself even for the remark which he had quoted, and which, perhaps unjustly, had been ascribed to General Banks.

Smith and his men had not long returned before McClernand's quartermaster claimed his clothing, which was considered by the "ragged guerrillas" as a very good joke.

The latter said the clothing was recaptured from the enemy, and was a lawful prize of war. How the matter was settled I never learned, but I think Smith's men went back to Memphis better dressed than when they started out.

The next day, when everything was ready for the march, Captain Selfridge informed me that he had been down the river in a tug and found the water lower in many places than it had been above "the falls," and inquired what I would do about it.

I told him that Providence would take care of us ; that we would get out of the river without any more damming.

Selfridge looked very doubtful, and probably thought the hard work up the river, sitting up all night drinking strong coffee and smoking cigars, had affected my brain ; but I felt confident that we should have water enough to get out of Red River. We had had so many narrow escapes that I did not believe Providence would desert us now.

Banks's advance-guard started, and he went with it, while A. J. Smith was to bring up the rear. It would be twenty-four hours before the latter was to set out, and, if the water did not come in that time, I had determined to ask him to hold on until it did.

Next morning, when I awoke, I found the water not only rising, but running *up* river.

The explanation of this phenomenon was that, while the Red River was down to its lowest level, the Mississippi was rapidly rising, and had attained a height of fifteen feet or so above the level of Red River. The surplus water was forced up Red River, and in a few hours reached its level at Alexandria, so that we had more water than was necessary, and went on our way rejoicing.

Two or three days before we left Alexandria a circumstance occurred which seemed at one time likely to give rise to serious complications. I hardly like to mention the matter, as I have endeavored to avoid all subjects tending to reflect upon any one personally, and have in consequence been obliged to omit much that would be interesting.

When General A. J. Smith and myself reached Alexandria on our way up Red River we were the captors, if a place that offered no resistance, and whose inhabitants made us welcome, could be said to have captors.

We were there several days before General Banks and his main army arrived.

The town had many large store-houses for cotton, corrals for cattle, and stables for horses—everything, in fact, that an army would require in that line.

I needed a place where I could keep stores for the fleet, which were brought in by the semi-monthly mail-steamer belonging to the station, and so took possession of a small stable near the levee where my vessel made fast. The building contained three horse-stalls and space for two carriages, and suited me very well, though I had only one horse at the time to accommodate.

When General Banks's army appeared, the quartermasters were running about in every direction to find buildings to accommodate their stores, and one of these officers had some twenty barrels which he had no place for except a store-house in the center of the town, which did not suit his convenience. He therefore asked Lieutenant Gorringe for permission to put the barrels in our stable *temporarily.*

There they remained for more than a fortnight, when our store-vessel arrived with a quantity of supplies which it was necessary to discharge at once.

Lieutenant Gorringe therefore requested the quartermaster to remove his barrels, as there was no room in the store-house; but that high functionary said "he would see him damned first," adding, "You navy fellows have no business on shore anyway, and can keep your stores on board your vessels; I shall take that store-house for myself."

When Gorringe reported the facts to me I told him there was but one thing to be done, as the dispatch-boat could not be kept waiting, and to put the quartermaster's barrels outside the door and notify him to remove them.

Ten minutes after the quartermaster received this notice he appeared on the levee, swearing harder at Gorringe than did the army in Flanders, and declaring that our stores should not be put into the stable.

The quartermaster went at once with a complaint to General ———, the military governor of Alexandria, a very clever and usually courteous gentleman; but I presume the quartermaster had told his own story, and led the general to suppose that his authority had been interfered with; so he came at once to the levee with the quartermaster, both in a very angry frame of mind.

The general ordered Lieutenant Gorringe to stop putting stores into the stable or he would send him to the guard-house!

To this Gorringe paid no attention, and the order was repeated in terms still more emphatic.

Gorringe was not a person of angelic temper, and had a proper appreciation of the respect due him as an officer of the navy.

"If you use such an expression as that to me again," he said to the general, "I will run my sword through your body!"

The general's rage was now at white heat, and he swore that he would not only put all the stores into the street, but he would arrest Gorringe and put him in the guard-house. And forthwith he started off for a guard to put his threat into execution, while Gorringe stepped on board the Cricket and reported the case to me.

I at once directed fifty marines and two boat-howitzers, with their crews, to be landed for the protection of our stores and the officers and men of the navy who were simply attending to their duty.

I said to Lieutenant Gorringe, " I hope you have sailed long enough with me to know my views in such matters, and how to defend yourself and the Government property placed under your charge."

When the military guard of twenty men arrived at the levee to arrest Gorringe, they were much astonished to find themselves confronted by the marines.

The military governor was checkmated, and, like all men who have exceeded their authority, he did not know what to do. He was much more civil than on his first visit, and asked Lieutenant Gorringe what he was doing there with his marines.

"I am here," answered Gorringe, "by order of my commanding officer, to protect naval property, and prevent any person in the navy from being arrested while performing his duty."

" Disband your forces at once," said the military governor, "or I will proceed to extremities."

" You can do so as soon as you please," said the other.

This was a dilemma for the military officer, who, though invested with power to preserve the peace, had no authority to interfere with another branch of the service, especially as the commander-in-chief of the naval forces was equal in rank to the general in command of the army, perfectly independent of him, and co-operating with him at his own volition, for during the whole war the Navy Department left me entirely free to do as I thought proper in this respect, and gave me no orders to co-operate with anybody.

" I must see the admiral at once," said the military governor. To which Lieutenant Gorringe replied that he would inform the admiral that the general wished to see him, which he accordingly did.

" Ask him to come on board," I said ; and the general shortly entered the cabin, where I was busily writing. I arose and politely requested him to be seated until I could sign and send off a letter. This document was to Gorringe and simply said " Hold on !"

I then made some observations to the general on the beautiful weather we were having, and the satisfaction I experienced at seeing him in a position requiring so much judgment and forbearance, and that our co-operation so far had been of such a pleasant nature that I should always look back to this time with the most delightful recollections, as there could not by any possibility be any misunderstanding between the army and navy, their duties being so distinct from each other, and the only chance of their clashing would be through the stupid blunder of an irresponsible officer.

For myself I felt sure that no one under my command would take the liberty of interfering with any army officer.

The military governor could scarcely contain himself while I was calmly talking, and, as soon as possible, commenced giving me his version of the case, and how my officer had threatened him with his sword, etc.

"Ah, then you are the gentleman who damned my lieutenant; I really wonder he didn't run you through, for he is very easily excited."

The general looked astonished that I did not adopt his view of the case.

Then I told him he had not only forgotten himself in regard to Lieutenant Gorringe, but that he had been guilty of great discourtesy toward myself and the navy, and that I would support Lieutenant Gorringe to the last. The general went away a sadder and, I hope, a wiser man.

While the general was on board my vessel a large crowd had assembled at the stable, and reports flew rapidly around the town that a riot had taken place between the soldiers and sailors.

"Halloo, boys!" said some of General A. J. Smith's men, "there's a row between Banks's men and the navy; let's stand by the navy." So down came five or six hundred of Smith's corps and ranged themselves alongside the marines, showing by their looks that they meant business, while the military governor's guard evidently took little interest in the dispute. It was generally understood that the trouble was about the occupancy of an old stable that had been used by the navy ever since the capture of Alexandria, and the feeling was all in favor of the navy.

The military governor, upon consideration, withdrew his guard and left us in peaceable possession.

Shortly afterward I received a letter from General Banks informing me that the navy had taken possession of a quartermaster's store-house, and that I must deliver it up at once! If I failed to do this and any unhappy consequences should grow out of the affair, all the responsibility would rest upon my head, etc. In reply, I informed the general that my head could bear all the responsibility, and that I would hold on to that stable as long as there was a shot in the locker.

17

That ended this foolish business. General Banks had not re-covered from the effects of the battle of Mansfield or Sabine Cross-Roads, and thinking he might need the aid of the gun-boats before he got through, he did not care to exasperate the sailors. Then he may have thought his troops would be indisposed to enter upon such an enterprise.

Above all, General Banks was a good-natured man who disliked trouble, and doubtless thought the navy very ungrateful, after he had given them the opportunity of seeing the Red River country, to act in such an unfriendly manner.

Before General Banks quitted Alexandria the transports were filled up with cotton, and a large number of negroes of all ages as-sembled at the levee to take passage to New Orleans.

One steamer, heavily loaded and in convoy of a small " tin-clad " gun-boat, started down the river, and some sixty miles below the town the two vessels were attacked by the battery which had suc-ceeded in forcing its way by McClernand's division. The guns were so placed as to have a complete cross-fire on the vessels. The gun-boat was soon cut to pieces and the one with the cotton burned.

The news of this disaster reached Alexandria the night previous to our departure, and an order was thereupon issued to land all the cotton from the transports, and it was pitched on shore without any care for its safety; at the same time the town of Alexandria was set on fire in a dozen places, principally in the store-houses filled with cotton.

The conflagration was a terrible one, and as the army marched away and the transports left the levee, they were covered with cin-ders and blazing flakes of cotton from the burning buildings. At one time I thought all the transports would be consumed, and it only needed that to make the retreat the most melancholy affair of the season.

The inhabitants rushed to the levee with such household goods as they could save, in hopes of getting away in the steamers; but they were not allowed to go on board, and the last I saw of them they were sitting by their property, weeping as only those can weep who have lost their homes.

I felt for these poor people, but could not help them, for there was no room for them on board the gun-boats, which had to be in readiness to drive away the batteries that might be raised along the river to oppose our passage.

The burning of Alexandria was a fit termination of the unfortunate Red River expedition, although it was very hard on many poor people who had taken no part in the Rebellion.

The cotton speculators were properly punished for the greed which had brought them into the country, but, although great losses were entailed upon many persons who had taken part in the hostilities against the United States and thought themselves safe from our armies, yet the cause of the Union received no benefit.

The expedition was originated more for the purpose of getting cotton out of the country through an understanding with the enemy than for vindicating the laws and re-establishing the authority of the United States Government; and it was certainly conducted in violation of military principles.

I have given here a brief outline of operations in Red River, but have prepared a detailed account of the whole matter, which, for the present, I withhold from publication.

The morning after we started from Alexandria I arose at daybreak to see the army march by, General Banks taking the road along the river, where he could have the co-operation of the gun-boats. As the troops passed by next morning, their commander-in-chief was lying on the ground ("his martial cloak around him"), worn out with fatigue and responsibility. It reminded me of Napoleon sleeping in the snow while his troops were marching by to descend into the plains of Italy.

Everything progressed favorably. General Emory led the advance and General A. J. Smith brought up the rear, and the enemy, although constantly skirmishing, kept at a respectful distance. Our troops finally embarked and left the country with perfect satisfaction, the Confederates being equally pleased to get rid of them.

Behold the difference ! Grant landed at Bruensburg with thirty-two thousand men, whipped eighty thousand, and invested Vicksburg, which he finally forced to surrender.

Banks entered the Red River country with forty-two thousand men and two hundred wagons. Twenty thousand Confederates claimed that they drove our army from the country.

It was not really so bad as that, but the army ought to have stayed there.

Under Grant or Sherman, or many of the officers composing that army, it would have gone not only through the Red River country, but into Texas, without any trouble, for that army consisted of as fine material as ever went into the field. It would have been more than a match for any army the Confederates could have opposed to it.

I think General Banks had a great deal to contend against besides the enemy. Providence was manifestly against the expedition, doubtless displeased to see so fine an army used for such an unworthy purpose, and was determined it should receive mortification instead of victory.

Yet, although deprived of victory, we had no great loss of life to complain of, and much useful experience was gained. It was certainly an interesting and instructive episode of the war.

Out of all the fine fellows who served with me in the Red River expedition, but few remain in the navy. Death has claimed many of them, and some, worn out with disease, are on the retired list.

Of those who accompanied me to Loggy Bayou, I recall only Selfridge as still in active service. He has only attained the rank of captain, and had to wait long and patiently for that.

I have not eulogized my officers in this connection, but in my official reports to the Secretary of the Navy I have done them justice, and I don't think any of them ever found fault with me for not appreciating their services.

Selfridge has had a singular career. He had the fortune to serve in ships that went to the bottom. He first was sunk in the Cumberland, in Hampton Roads, by the rebel ram Merrimac; then he joined me in the Mississippi, and was blown up in the Yazoo River by a torpedo. I immediately ordered him to the command of the Conestoga, and some time afterward that vessel was run down by one of our own rams and went to the bottom.

I told Selfridge that, to cure him of his habit of sinking, I would order him to the "turtle-back" Neosho and change his luck. "You have tried all the other kinds of vessels," I said, "and they either go up or down with you; take the Neosho, and may your shadow never be less."

Selfridge started in search of fame, and did good work with the vessel while in command of her. After the Red River expedition I sent him up the Mississippi, and in a few days followed after.

One day I saw a sand-bank in the middle of the river, and the Neosho in the middle of the sand-bank. "Here," I exclaimed, " is Selfridge in a new *rôle*."

Selfridge came on board to explain the mystery. He had anchored at a point where the rebels were trying to pass some cattle across the river, and he determined to prevent them. It was the only road, and they had to turn back with their cattle. Probably the river fell faster than usual ; but one morning the Neosho was high and dry, and there was no necessity of going away from the ship for sand to holy-stone decks with.

As soon as Selfridge had made his report I said : " Come, pack your trunk and go with me. The vessel is in an excellent position, commanding that road ; no one can get at her to board her, and we'll leave her in charge of the first lieutenant."

I took Selfridge to Mound City and gave him command of the powerful ram Vindicator, after which everything went along smoothly with him.

He accompanied me on the Fort Fisher expedition, and only lost a foretopmast, and has had good luck ever since. His was a curious series of mishaps, yet in all of them he gained reputation.

CHAPTER XXII.

TAKE COMMAND OF NORTH ATLANTIC SQUADRON—RENEW AN OLD ACQUAINTANCE—A VISIT FROM GENERAL BUTLER—THE GENERAL'S FLAG-SHIP BLOWN UP—SAVE THE GENERAL FROM A DUCKING—THE GENERAL VISITS THE MALVERN WITH A PLAN OF POWDER-BOAT TO BLOW UP FORT FISHER—AN ENSIGN SETS THE PLAN TO MUSIC AND RHYME—A STEAMER AND ONE HUNDRED AND FIFTY TONS OF POWDER REQUIRED TO DO THE WORK —THE ADMIRAL, IN THE EXCITEMENT OF THE MOMENT, TELEGRAPHS FOR FIFTEEN THOUSAND TONS OF POWDER—THE CHIEF OF BUREAU OF ORDNANCE OFFERS HIM MOUNT VESUVIUS AND NIAGARA FALLS TO DO THE WORK WITH—THE POWDER-BOAT DISTURBS THE SENTINELS AT FORT FISHER—FORT FISHER DOES NOT BLOW UP WORTH A CENT—A TRAP SET FOR BLOCKADE-RUNNERS—AN IRISH TORPEDO-BOAT—FALL OF WILMINGTON.

IN October, 1864, I took command of the North Atlantic squadron, with directions to bombard Fort Fisher and the other defenses at the mouth of Cape Fear River.

From my study of the subject I was satisfied that the reduction of these works could only be accomplished by a combined military and naval force, and General Grant had promised that a body of troops should be ready at the proper time—when all the naval vessels had assembled in Hampton Roads.

General Grant was anxious to do everything he could to forward the expedition; but, as the troops would have to be taken from General Butler's command, which occupied an important position on the left bank of the James River, they could not be removed until arrangements were made for other troops to take their place.

I was walking with General Grant at City Point, on the James River, when I espied General Butler approaching, and said to Grant: "Please don't introduce me to Butler. We had a little difficulty at New Orleans, and although I attach no importance to the matter, perhaps he does."

"Oh!" said Grant, "you will find Butler quite willing to forget old feuds, and, as the troops who are to accompany you will be taken from his command, it will be necessary for you to communicate with him from time to time." So when General Butler came up the introduction took place. The general was very pleasant, and I invited him to lunch with me on board the vessel in which I had come up the river; so a good understanding was apparently established between us.

From my knowledge of General Butler's peculiarities, I thought it best we should not co-operate in so important an affair as the attack on Fort Fisher, for when men have once had an encounter of sharp words they are not likely ever again to be in complete accord with each other; and the general and myself had had a little difficulty at New Orleans at a time when he had not been long enough in military employment to understand the courtesy due from the officers of either branch of the service to the other. I presume I had my peculiarities as well as the general, one of them being a determination not to submit to rudeness from any one.

As far as I was concerned, I did not intend to let past differences stand in the way, but I feared the general had not forgotten the trouble, and that it might interfere with the important operations that were intended.

I therefore suggested to General Grant the propriety of sending some one in command of the land forces with whom I would be in entire accord, and Grant thereupon said he would send General Weitzel in command, a selection with which I was quite satisfied.

General Butler made himself very agreeable in his intercourse with me, and was apparently very busy in making preparations for embarking the troops that were to go to Fort Fisher. We visited

each other and hobnobbed together. I was pleased with his zeal
for the success of the expedition, and as General Weitzel was always
with him when he visited my flag-ship, I took it for granted that
Weitzel's going in command of the troops was a fixed fact.

Butler made many visits, but the troops were not forthcoming,
though winter was approaching, and it was necessary we should
commence operations before it became too stormy on the coast.
The fleet was all ready, and, as time passed, my patience was becoming exhausted.

In a leisure interval I went up the James River to Dutch Gap
in the flag-ship Malvern to give orders to the vessels that would be
left there in my absence. The cutting of the canal at Dutch Gap
was a very good idea, contrary to the general impression, and should
have been undertaken earlier in the war.

While I was at Dutch Gap, General Butler came up to see me
in the Greyhound, which was his headquarters when afloat. This
vessel deserved her name, for she was a long, lean-looking craft,
and the fastest steamer on the river.

The general informed me that Mr. Fox, Assistant Secretary of
the Navy, wished to see me without delay at Hampton Roads on
important business, and, as my flag-ship was rather a slow vessel,
he would take me down in the Greyhound. To this I agreed.

The Greyhound had been lying about an hour at the bank when
we started down river.

The vicinity of Dutch Gap was a kind of neutral ground between the two armies, where prisoners were exchanged, and all sorts
of people seemed to be hanging around the neighborhood. I never
saw so many hang-dog-looking rascals congregated together in one
place. The Confederates doubtless had spies there all the time
among the adventurers who always follow in the wake of a great
army.

I found General Schenck on board the Greyhound as Butler's
guest; he had suffered from his wounds, and was taking a little excursion for the benefit of his health.

There were no arms on board the Greyhound to my knowledge
except General Butler's sword, which, though a formidable-looking weapon, was of no use to any one except the owner, who seldom
laid it aside.

The general's boat's crew wore *his* uniform, but had not so much
as a pop-gun among them.

There was a captain and a pilot, an engineer, several firemen and coal-heavers, a couple of deck-hands, and a cook and steward.

I never carried a sword or pistol at any time; neither did General Schenck; so here was a vessel, totally unarmed, carrying two major-generals up and down the James River with nothing to protect them, to say nothing of an admiral who seldom traveled in such a careless fashion.

The two generals immediately sat down to a political discussion, while I thought I would take a turn through the upper saloon of the Greyhound, which was fitted like most passenger-steamers of her class, although her saloon may have been a little more gorgeous than usual. She cost the Government only about $500 a day, and carried the general with great speed from point to point where his services were required. Every general of importance had a vessel for this purpose, but the Greyhound was the gem of them all.

It was about half an hour after we started down the river that I went up to the saloon, and there I found half a dozen of those cut-throat-looking fellows, such as haunted Dutch Gap, scattered through the apartment.

I was so much struck with the appearance of these men and the confusion they exhibited that I said to one of them, "What are you doing here? Does the Greyhound carry first-class passengers?" The fellow glared impudently at me and said, "We are just lookin' round to see how you fellers live; we ain't a doin' no harm."

Not wishing to let these men see that I suspected them, I walked about quietly, as if amusing myself, while they, one after another disappeared below.

I went immediately to General Butler and said, "General, I don't particularly care to be captured just now, as I have important business on hand, and I don't suppose you do either; but you have a cargo of the worst-looking wretches on board this vessel that ever I laid eyes on; hadn't you better look after them before they do any harm?"

The general acted promptly and ordered the captain to round-to at Bermuda Hundreds, and turned our passengers over to a guard to give an account of themselves, much to their disgust. After a thorough search to see that there were no stowaways on board, we proceeded on our way, no one attaching much importance to the fellows whom we had put ashore, as it was supposed they were merely loafers trying to get to Hampton Roads free of expense.

We had left Bermuda Hundreds five or six miles behind us when suddenly an explosion forward startled us, and in a moment large volumes of smoke poured out of the engine-room. The engineer at once closed the throttle-valve, stopping the vessel, and opened the safety-valve ; the steam rushed out, and the Greyhound howled louder than her living namesake would have done.

The generals stopped their conversation, and the crew seized the planks lying about the deck and jumped overboard.

"What's that?" exclaimed General Butler.

"Torpedo!" I answered. "I know the sound."

The vessel was now in flames amidships, and the upper saloon filled with smoke like that from coal-tar. We were cut off completely from the crew, whom we did not know had jumped overboard.

I was in full vigor at that time, and possessed considerable bodily strength. The general's gig hung at the port quarter, its bow resting on a house abaft the wheel. I put my shoulder under the boat and raised it from its rest, while the steward hauled in the slack of the tackle. When the boat was clear of the wheel-house I lowered the after-tackle and left the boat hanging within two feet of the water. I then lowered a smaller boat on the starboard side, put the steward and stewardess in her, and bade them look out for themselves. In the mean time some of the gig's crew had swam around to the gangway, and we all got into the boat and shoved off, with the exception of the captain of the steamer, who worked his way aft, hauled down the colors, and seated himself on the rudder, whence we took him off.

From the moment of the explosion until the time of our leaving the Greyhound was certainly less than five minutes, yet the flames made such progress that the general's aid, who had gathered up some of his papers and was the last one to get into the boat, had his hand burned.

We picked up the rest of the men who were floating in the water, and then lay on our oars watching the conflagration. The Greyhound was now wrapped in flames from one end to the other, and, in newspaper parlance, was a "grand spectacle."

There was one melancholy event connected with the destruction of the Greyhound. General Butler had two or three fine horses on board, and their cries when the flames reached them were dreadful to hear, but their sufferings lasted only a short time, and their last groans were unheard amid the roaring of the flames, the crashing of timbers, and the noise of the steam, which continued blowing off to the last.

I think I saved General Butler a ducking on that occasion, if not his life ; but I am afraid he forgot the service, although I would have worked as hard to get him out of that vessel, even had I known beforehand he would try to injure me.

Shortly afterward an army transport, loaded with troops for Hampton Roads, came along, and General Butler proposed we should take passage in her ; but I had had enough of army steamers for one day, and, knowing that we should soon meet a navy tug, I proposed to pull on down the river. In half an hour we met the tug, went on board, and turned her back to Fortress Monroe.

The firemen were just going to dinner as we embarked, but kindly volunteered to relinquish their meal to us ; so we sat down to pork and beans served in tin plates with iron spoons, and enjoyed it as much as if it had been a dinner at Delmonico's.

I do not know that there was ever any investigation into the loss of the Greyhound. My theory was that the fellows put ashore at Bermuda Hundreds had planned to capture General Butler and destroy the Greyhound, and I believe they were provided with torpedoes to throw among the coal, which they could easily do when the firemen's backs were turned. They could also have saturated the wood-work in the vicinity of the engine and fire-rooms with tar-oil with very little chance of detection.

When the torpedo was thrown into the furnace with the coal, it soon burst, blowing the furnace-doors open and throwing the burning mass into the fire-room, where it communicated with the wood-work. Perhaps the shell may have contained some volatile matter which caught the saturated wood. We were furnished with such shells ourselves during the war, but never used them. Only a few months ago the inventor inquired of me how many had been expended by the navy during the war, probably with the idea of claiming a royalty.

In whatever manner the Greyhound was set on fire, I am sure it was not one of the ordinary accidents to which all ships are liable. In devices for blowing up vessels the Confederates were far ahead of us, putting Yankee ingenuity to shame.

When we reached Hampton Roads a large assembly of the general's friends was there to congratulate him on his escape from death, but the rest of us were unnoticed. I slipped on board one of the vessels of the squadron and invited myself to take tea with the captain, but resolved to keep clear of army steamers in future.

We waited patiently for the soldiers promised by General Grant. It was no use to attack Fort Fisher without them, for, although we might disable the guns, we could not take possession of the place. The defenders would stow themselves away in bomb-proofs, and would be safe against our fire. All I wanted of the army was to occupy the works after I had finished with them. I supposed they would have some fighting to do, but did not think they would meet with any great loss.

One day General Butler came on board the Malvern, accompanied by General Weitzel, some of his staff, and a reporter, and said that he had an important communication to make to me.

I had a faint hope that there was now a prospect of getting the fleet off to Fort Fisher. I saw plainly that I could not get away until General Butler chose to send his troops, for at that time Butler was in the zenith of his power and seemed to do pretty much as he pleased.

When we were all in the cabin, including Captain K. R. Breese, my fleet-captain, General Butler said, "The communication I have to make is so important that I deem it necessary to observe the greatest secrecy." Then he and Weitzel and the stenographic reporter whispered together. This was a common practice with these gentlemen when they visited my ship, as if they hesitated about taking me into their confidence; but I was willing to stand almost any nonsense if I could only get off, although by nature not of the most patient disposition.

"Mr. Reporter," said the general, "don't you miss one syllable that I say, and put it down exactly as I say it. Weitzel, you pay attention. Remember, this proposition is altogether mine. I have never mentioned it to anybody except you." Then he whispered for a while to Weitzel, and took his seat, evidently much excited— something like a hen that has laid an egg.

My patience was rapidly evaporating when the stenographer got down to his work, the general watching every word he wrote. General Butler seemed so intent on his project, and so earnest, that I began to be curious to hear all about it. I had not the faintest idea what he was driving at. It certainly could not be a balloon attack, for we had no balloons, and couldn't get them without an act of Congress. Perhaps, thought I, he intends to introduce rattlesnakes into Fort Fisher on the sly; but this idea I at once dismissed; there was nothing in the Constitution which would authorize such a proceeding.

I whispered to Captain Breese, "The general is going to propose his 'petroleum bath,' such as he has already proposed to use on James River. He is going to attack Fort Fisher from seaward by setting afloat tons of petroleum when the wind is on shore, and, by igniting it, knock the rebs out of their boots!" I thought the absurdity of such an idea would be a great recommendation, especially as it would cost a great deal of money, for at that time there was great competition in Washington as to which department could make the largest expenditure.

At length the reporter stood up and read what he had taken down. I never obtained a copy of the precious original, but one of my aides got hold of it and turned it into rhyme. As well as my memory serves me it ran as follows :

> "You have, no doubt, heard of the River Thames,
> A stream just about the size of the James,
> Where at Erith the magazine burst into flames:
> > 'Twas a great magazine,
> > Strong as any you've seen,
> But 'twas blown into atoms, just by a spark
> Getting into the powder. A fool in the dark
> Sat smoking a penny cigar in a barge
> Filled up with explosives which he had in charge.

> "For miles away, it is reported to me,
> There was not to be seen a house or a tree
> That was not shattered, blown up, or blown down;
> There was not a glass left in the neighboring town,
> > And the birds on their perch
> > Took an awful lee lurch;
> The cows milked water, the dogs lost their bark,
> All owing to powder and a very small spark.
> The hens stopped laying, the cats got afraid
> To enliven the night with their sweet serenade."

There was a good deal more of this, but it has been forgotten. The amount of it was that the general proposed to blow up Fort Fisher with a "powder-boat" laden with one hundred and fifty tons of powder. He argued the subject with so much eloquence, and showed such a knowledge of pyrotechnics, that no one could controvert his opinions.

When the matter of the proposed powder-boat had been submitted, I saw at once that here was something to simplify matters very much, requiring no act of Congress or interference of the Committee on the Conduct of the War!

The army and navy had plenty of bad powder and worthless vessels—in fact, material for half a dozen powder-boats if necessary.

I don't know whether the general claimed the powder-boat as an original idea, but there is nothing new under the sun, and such a means of attack has been employed before.

I arose from my seat, and in a short speech accepted the general's plan, at the same time eulogizing the head that could conceive such a brilliant idea. The navy and the powder-boat would be all-sufficient, and I rather liked the notion, as the expedition would be entirely a naval affair, and I was not anxious to repeat my Red River experience on the Atlantic coast.

I think I stood higher in General Butler's estimation at that moment than I have ever done before or since, for, on the whole, he didn't seem to fancy me, as I had an unpleasant way of speaking my mind freely and not permitting any one to interfere with my business.

I don't hesitate to say that I encouraged this scheme of a powder-boat, for in it I saw the road to success, and I was pleased to see that, notwithstanding General Butler's enthusiasm at the idea of blowing up Fort Fisher, he was not at all disinclined to have the navy go along, and *also the contingent of troops that had been originally proposed!*

Many persons have ridiculed General Butler's plan, but in war it is worth while to try everything, and some of our most scientific officers in Washington were so much impressed with the idea of the powder-boat that they carefully investigated the subject. The result of their calculations went to show that if a hundred and fifty tons of powder, confined in an inclosed space, could be *at once* exploded at a short distance from Fort Fisher, the concussion would displace so much air and so rapidly that it would kill every living thing in the vicinity, and wipe the sand fort out of existence.

At this lapse of time I have forgotten how much faith I really had in the project, but I must have been somewhat excited, as I telegraphed to Captain Wise, Chief of the Bureau of Ordnance, Navy Department, that I wanted fifteen thousand tons of powder to blow up Fort Fisher, instead of one hundred and fifty tons, the amount asked for by General Butler. I was vexed at Wise's answer : " Why don't you make a requisition for Niagara Falls and Mount Vesuvius ? they will do the job for you."

This little mistake of two ciphers would indicate that I was not so phlegmatic as usual, so I really think I must have believed in the scheme.

After General Butler and his staff had departed, Captain Breese said to me : " Admiral, you certainly don't believe in that idea of a powder-boat. It has about as much chance of blowing up the fort as I have of flying ! "

" And who knows," I said, " whether a machine may not soon be perfected to enable us all to fly, as it only requires a forty-horse power in a cubic foot of space, and a propeller that will make such a vacuum that the air will rush in and drive the thing along."

Breese looked disappointed that I should lend myself to such a project. I directed him to make signal to the powder-magazine and inquire how much powder they had on hand.

Breese sighed as he walked out of the cabin, and I thought I heard him say " All bosh ! "—but one has to be a little deaf occasionally.

In answer to a telegram, I was told by the Navy Department to take any steamer I wanted for blowing up, for both the War and Navy Departments highly approved the powder-boat scheme ; in fact, General Butler had a right to be proud of the support he received from some of the most " scientific " men in both branches of the service.

I sent a tug to Newbern, North Carolina, for the steamer Louisiana, a valuable vessel, worth at least a thousand dollars ! I calculated that by passing hawsers around her and " setting them taut," she would hold together long enough to get to Fort Fisher.

Next day the powder-boat arrived at Hampton Roads, and Captain Jeffers, of the Ordnance Bureau, came from Washington to take charge of loading her and laying the " Gomer fuse," which would ignite any quantity of powder quicker than lightning—that is, if the fuse went off, which it sometimes failed to do.

Several young army officers fresh from West Point also appeared on the scene, bringing with them a cart-load of books relating to explosives, and in the course of their researches one of them discovered that the illustrious Chi-Fung, a Chinese general, had blown up an enemy's fort with gunpowder several centuries before the discovery of America, but whether he used a powder-boat history did not say.

The day the steamer arrived I sent an officer to General Weitzel's camp to find out quietly if anything different from usual was going on. He returned shortly after and informed me that they were telling off the contingent that was to go to Fort Fisher, that transports were assembling near Dutch Gap, and everybody was talking hopefully of what the powder-boat would do. The soldiers seemed to fancy they would have an easy job, as the fort and all its contents would be blown away.

"Breese," I said to the fleet-captain, "I hope now you believe in the powder-boat. Issue an order for all the vessels to be ready to sail at noon to-morrow, and have two steamers on hand to tow the powder-boat down."

I then visited the powder-boat, and never saw greater enthusiasm. Officers were hard at work in their shirt-sleeves, and the "Gomer fuse," like a huge tape-worm, was working its way through piles of powder-bags. Every bag had a piece of fuse around it, so that there would be no mistake about its going off.

In the cabin of the powder-boat was a peculiar clock to fire the fuse at any time desired. There were candles that would burn a given number of minutes and then explode, and there were hand-grenades that would fall at a given time and set the vessel on fire.

These were fine contrivances; but I ordered half a cord of pine-knots piled up in the cabin, to be ignited by the last man who left the ship, and this was what finally did the work.

The powder-boat left that night, and next day at noon the fleet, consisting of seventy-five or eighty well-armed vessels, got under way from Hampton Roads, the flag-ship Malvern bringing up the rear.

As the flag-ship quitted the anchorage the transports were sighted with the troops on board.

We all arrived at the rendezvous near Fort Fisher, and every one was enjoined to be cautious.

The fleet lay some ten miles off shore, but the commanding officers of vessels were advised not to have too much steam up for fear of bursting their boilers when the explosion took place. One captain asked if it would not be prudent to send down top-gallant masts and yards, and brace the lower yards sharp up. I told him " No," for there might be a gun or two left in the works after the explosion, and he would need his sail to get out in case a shot should perforate his boilers.

General Butler's transports lay at New Inlet, some distance to the northward, but I supposed he would soon be on the ground to stand by and charge the ruined works after the explosion.

At ten o'clock on the night succeeding our arrival the powder-boat was towed in abreast of the fort and anchored near the shore, the clock was started, candles lighted, hand-grenades fixed, and the wood-pile ignited—not a soul in the fort aware of the terrible fate that awaited them.   In ten minutes the powder-boat blew up, and the ships stood in to the attack.   Official accounts will tell the rest.

> " But the powder-boat *didn't*, like that on the Thames,
> Set houses and barns and the towns all in flames;
> And the dogs still barked, and no cats were afraid
> To disturb the mild night with their sweet serenade."

The night the powder-boat was exploded a boat from shore came off with four deserters from the enemy.   I asked what effect the explosion had on the people in the fort.

"It was dreadful," said one of the men ; "it woke up everybody in Fort Fisher!"

But I do believe, notwithstanding, that the explosion had its effect on the enemy, for next morning, when the ships attacked, the Confederates fought as if they meant business, and the powder-boat waked them up to some purpose.

It was not General Butler's fault that the scheme was not a success.   Something was wrong in the powder, or it could not all have exploded ; for, while standing on the deck of the Malvern the morning after the surrender of Fort Fisher, the earth-works seemed to be in motion, the light was obscured by smoke and sand, amid which I could see the bodies of many people carried up in the air, and I heard a great explosion which shook the earth.   Then I learned that Fort Fisher had blown up and killed a number of our men—yet only four tons of powder exploded.

This would indicate that the conception of the powder-boat was a good one, and, if it could only have been got near enough to the fort or inside, and *all* the powder exploded, it would have demolished the works and their occupants.

I shall always feel under the greatest obligations to the powder-boat, for, although it failed to blow up Fort Fisher, it did what nothing else could have done—it started the expedition off.   Considering all things, it was a cheap experiment in pyrotechnics, for the powder cost not more than sixty thousand dollars, and the vessel was absolutely worthless.

Had she not gone up in a blaze of glory she might to-day have figured on the navy-list as an effective vessel of war, while slowly decaying at her berth in Rotten Row!

After the failure to capture Fort Fisher I wrote to General Grant, "Send me the same soldiers with another general, and we will have the fort." So the soldiers were sent under command of General Terry, and, after a fight that did credit to all concerned, we succeeded on January 15, 1865.

Then we worked our way up the Cape Fear River, all of which has been duly recorded in the official reports of the day.

After Cape Fear River was in our possession it struck me that it would be a good plan to set a trap for blockade-runners, who could not have heard of the change of affairs, and I put the indefatigable Lieutenant Cushing at work to establish decoy signals and range-lights, and this, with the assistance of the "intelligent contraband," who was always on hand, Cushing soon accomplished.

On the night of the 19th of January two long, light-colored objects were seen moving up the Cape Fear River, and in a few moments came to anchor near the flag-ship. These were the Stag and Charlotte, two blockade-running steamers, and they had hardly got their anchors down before our boats boarded them and summoned them to surrender.

The officers and passengers of the Charlotte were just sitting down to an elegant supper, in honor of their safe arrival, when the boarding officer walked into the cabin and announced to the astonished company that they were prisoners.

"The Yankees have got us, by thunder!" exclaimed one of the revelers, while consternation for the moment reigned round the board.

Among the passengers were several distinguished Englishmen, one or two of them officers of the British army, in search of adventures, and they were not particularly delighted at the turn affairs had taken.

The captain of the steamer had been captured before, and took his present mishap as a matter of course; but one of his passengers could not be made to comprehend how one of her Majesty's merchant vessels could be taken possession of in a friendly port while peaceable passengers were eating their supper.

"Look here, sir," said he to the boarding officer, "aren't you joking? You certainly wouldn't dare to interfere with one of her

18

Majesty's vessels; the Admiralty would quick send a fleet over here and dampen you fellows. This is all a joke, I know it is, and I want to go on shore at once."

"You have very singular ideas of what constitutes a joke," said the boarding officer. "I don't think you could understand one unless it was fired at you out of a thirty-two pounder."

"But," said the Englishman, "how can you fire a joke out of a thirty-two pounder?"

This remark "brought down the house," and the captain of the blockade-runner suggested that they had better eat supper first and discuss the joke afterward.

This affair turned out to be a very lucrative night's work, as the Stag and Charlotte were filled with all kinds of valuable goods, including many commissions for "ladies of the *court*."

In the cabin of one vessel was a pile of bandboxes, in which were charming little bonnets marked with the owners' names. It would have given me much pleasure to have forwarded them to their destination, but the laws forbade our giving aid and comfort to the enemy, so all the French bonnets, cloaks, shoes, and other feminine *bric-à-brac* had to go to New York for condemnation by the Admiralty Court, and were sold at public auction.

These bonnets, laces, and other vanities rather clashed with the idea I had formed of the Southern ladies, as I had heard that all they owned went to the hospitals, and that they never spent a cent on their personal adornment; but human nature is the same the world over, and the ladies will indulge in their little vanities in spite of war and desolation.

It looked queer to me to see boxes labeled "His Excellency, Jefferson Davis, President of the 'Confederate States of America.'" The packages so labeled contained Bass ale or Cognac brandy, which cost "His Excellency" less than we Yankees had to pay for it. Think of the President drinking imported liquors while his soldiers were living on pop-corn and water!

I had supposed that blockade-runners were mainly filled with arms, ammunition, and clothing for the troops; but the Charlotte, Stag, and Blenheim, captured by us at the mouth of the Cape Fear River, were not entirely laden with army supplies. The main cargo of one vessel was composed of articles for ladies' use, and all three were plentifully stocked with liquors and table luxuries.

There were many dreadful sights at Fort Fisher, and much hard work to engross our time and thoughts, yet there were ridiculous incidents as well.

After the surrender of the fort all the smaller vessels of the fleet had to cross the bar of Cape Fear River, where at most there was but eleven feet of water.   In the attempt they got fast in the mud, some twenty of them mixed up in apparently inextricable confusion, but in a few hours they were all across "the rip" and at anchor inside Cape Fear River.

Early next morning (February 18, 1865) an attack was made on Fort Anderson, a well-built star fort armed with nineteen heavy guns and situated on the right bank of the river.   Like their other works, Fort Anderson was not well protected in the rear.   The Confederates, it would seem, did not calculate their forts would be taken, thinking them proof against an enemy's fire and not anticipating that troops would ever be landed in their rear.   If such were their calculations, the enemy were grievously disappointed.

In the attack on Fort Fisher we had burst nearly all the Parrott guns in the fleet; so I had telegraphed to Captain Wise, chief of the Ordnance Bureau, to send me twenty eleven-inch smooth-bores, shot and shell, triangles for hoisting, etc., and in four days the articles arrived in a fast steamer from New York, which shows how promptly the Ordnance Bureau did business during the war. It was four days then before we could commence operations on Fort Anderson.

The night before we attacked that place I had a *mock monitor* constructed very much like the one which did such good service on the Mississippi.   I knew that the enemy had the channel planted with torpedoes, and piles were driven in such a manner that vessels would have to pass right over where the torpedoes were sunk.   At about 11 P. M. I had the monitor towed up, and let go within two hundred yards of the enemy's works.

The monitor floated with the flood-tide to within a short distance of the batteries, when the enemy opened fire with heavy guns and musketry, and exploded some of the torpedoes, all of which did the monster no harm, and she finally floated off toward Wilmington, not troubling herself to keep in the channel, but crossing flats where there were only a few inches of water !

All the next afternoon the monitor Montauk lay close in to the fort, keeping up a constant fire, while we mounted our eleven-inch guns ; and this was the monitor that the enemy thought had passed by in the previous night.

Just before dark that evening a veracious "contraband" paddled alongside the Malvern in a canoe and informed me that the enemy had a powerful ram and torpedo-vessel ready to come down upon us after dark that night.

I was surprised at not having heard of this ram before, but I prepared to receive her. Every vessel was to keep two boats ready, the boats' crews armed for boarding, and each boat was provided with a heavy net on a pole, with which to foul the torpedo-vessel's propeller.

The idea was for the boats to get alongside, cripple the enemy's propeller, and then carry the vessel by boarding. Two picket-boats were kept about six hundred yards ahead of the leading vessel, and a strict watch was kept on board the gun-boats; but the picket-boats got so far ahead that they missed what they were watching for.

The Malvern lay in the middle of the line. I had no idea that any torpedo-boat would trouble us, and was just going to bed when shouts attracted my attention, and I heard orders for the boats to shove off from several vessels. Then came pistol-shots and hurrahs enough to account for half a dozen torpedo-boats.

"Thank fortune!" I said to Captain Breese, "I have been looking out for rams and torpedo-boats for the last three years, and have never yet seen one; but I think we'll get this fellow sure if they only carry out my orders."

By this time the river was alive with boats dashing by in desperate efforts to reach the scene of conflict, and, as they came up with the enemy, they joined in with loud cheers. "There he goes!" I heard them shout. "Head him off!" "Here he comes!" "Give him a volley!" This shouting and firing continued for several minutes, and I wondered why they did not board the enemy, saying to the captain, "That thing will get a crack at some of the vessels above us, and if they sink one it will block the game on us, for there is only room for one vessel to go along at a time. The channel has but eleven feet of water, and is only sixty feet wide. Why don't they board, as I ordered them to do?"

Then the vessels above commenced firing howitzers and musketry. "That is sheer folly," I said. "They will never capture the thing in that way. That vessel is probably a turtle-back, with an inch thickness of iron. He'll sink one of those vessels as sure as a gun. Jump into the boat, pull up there, and tell them to board the thing, whatever it is, at all hazards."

The captain shoved off, and in five minutes the strange vessel seemed to be coming down on us. "Look out!" I heard them shout, "Give it to him!" "Now's your chance!" Then a volley of musketry and three cheers.

"Here he comes!" shouted the lookout in the forecastle, "and all the boats after him," and, sure enough, the boats were all pulling after the thing and making a great clatter as they laid to their oars.

All the vessels had lanterns over the side, and one vessel incautiously burned a "Coston signal," which for a moment made everything as light as day.

To my great relief a shout arose, "We've got him! Tie on to him! Double-bank him with boats!" and such shouting and cheering as only sailors can accomplish.

The struggle was ended, the enemy was ours. I heard an officer give the order to "take the enemy in tow and stop their noise."

I thought to myself, "I must issue an order to-morrow rebuking the officers and men for making so much noise," and when Captain Breese returned alongside I tried to appear indifferent.

"Well, sir, we got him," said the captain.

"And a time they had of it. Why didn't those fellows do as I told them—jam his screw with the nets?" I inquired.

"He hadn't any screw, sir," replied the captain.

"Then what had he?" I inquired.

The captain laughed. "It was something worse than a ram; it was the biggest *bull* I ever saw. He was swimming across the channel when he was first espied. I don't wonder they took him for a torpedo-boat, he got through the water at such a rate."

"A bull!" I exclaimed. "And so I am not to see a ram after all. Tell them to keep a good lookout, notwithstanding the capture of the bull," and I laughed heartily at this absurd episode—so much more ridiculous in reality than even in the narration.

That evening General Schofield, who had assumed command of the army after the capture of Fort Fisher, had landed some troops to take Fort Anderson in the rear, and at eight next morning (February 18th) I attacked Fort Anderson with all the gun-boats, which, with their newly mounted eleven-inch guns, soon silenced the enemy's guns, and the Confederates abandoned the work and fled, to avoid capture by our troops coming up in their rear.

Off we went again on our way up river till at a point where the water was shoal. Fort Strong, on the left bank, opened on us and succeeded in boring some good holes in our vessels; but, with the aid of our eleven-inch guns, in twenty minutes we had all the firing to ourselves, the enemy evacuating the fort, on which we hoisted our flag. An hour later the army marched into Wilmington, and we were masters of the situation.

I reached Wilmington on the afternoon of February 22, 1865, soon after the army had entered the city. The river-bank was covered with negroes, and, as soon as the vessels arrived, a salute was fired in honor of the day, causing the darkies to suddenly scatter in all directions, under the impression that we were bombarding the town.

While we were at Fort Strong a contraband informed us that the enemy were going to let a hundred torpedoes drift down upon us at night and blow us all to pieces! I therefore ordered a double line of fishing-nets spread across the river, so as to intercept any visitors of this sort. It was a bright moonlight night, and, although we had little faith in the negro's story, we kept a good lookout all the same.

At about eight o'clock I saw a barrel drifting down the river, and, hailing the Shawmut, directed them to send a boat and see what it was. Acting Ensign Trufant was in command of the boat, and, pulling close to the barrel, fired his pistol into it, whereupon it exploded, dangerously wounding the officer and killing two and wounding several of the crew.

The barrel was a floating torpedo which in some unaccountable manner had got past the nets, and the contraband's information was correct.

A short time afterward a torpedo caught in the Osceola's wheel and knocked the wheel-house to pieces, knocked down some of her bulkheads, and disturbed things generally.

The torpedo-nets intercepted many of the same kind of devices, which were sunk next morning by firing musketry at them from a safe distance. But for the information given by the contraband which led to the precaution of setting the nets, I might have lost several of my vessels that night.

The night after we arrived at Wilmington we had another alarm. The vessel highest up the river opened fire on something, the next one took it up, and so did all the others until it came to my vessel, when I discovered through my night-glass a large steam launch floating down stream. She was towed alongside, and it proved to be the same launch in which I had sent Cushing to blow up the Albemarle a few weeks previous.

After the destruction of the Albemarle the torpedo-vessel fell into the hands of the enemy, and was sent to Cape Fear River to operate against our vessels ; but the Confederates were not lucky with torpedo-boats, so she again fell into our hands.

The events occurring on the Cape Fear River and about Fort Fisher and Wilmington would make an interesting book, but I can spare but little space for them here.   I will, however, mention one incident which occurred the day after the capture of Fort Fisher.

I was in a steam launch on the river, directing in person how to get over the bar, when I saw a large steamer anchor near the flag-ship, while the latter fired a salute of fifteen guns, which meant that some high functionary had come into port.   I soon learned that Mr. Stanton, the Secretary of War, had arrived.   He had been to Savannah to see General Sherman, and stopped in at Fort Fisher, not knowing it had fallen.

I immediately went on board to see Mr. Stanton, whom I found seated at the head of the dinner-table with a napkin under his chin. He arose and put his arms around my neck and kissed me—imagine such a thing of Mr. Stanton !   " I love you," he said, " the President loves you, the people love you, for you have—" but I refrain from stating the reason assigned by Mr. Stanton for the deep affection with which I was universally regarded ; but it was not for my part in the capture of Fort Fisher.

" What can I do for you ? " said Mr. Stanton.   " Ask anything, and you shall have it if it's in my power to give it."

" Thank you," I said, " I want nothing for myself, but you can do me a great favor by promoting General Terry on the spot. He has done his duty like a good soldier, and his reward should not be postponed."

Mr. Stanton ordered General Terry to be sent for immediately, and, while we were awaiting his arrival, Mr. Stanton opened his heart to me on a subject which, as it was strictly confidential, I forbear to repeat.

When General Terry came on board, the Secretary of War received him with great warmth, and, after some conversation, retired with his private secretary into the after-cabin, where he remained for about twenty minutes.

General Terry had been up all the preceding night, and was worn out with fatigue ; and his brother, who accompanied him on board, went to sleep with his head leaning against the cabin-door, where he slept and snored to the amusement of the company.

When the secretary reappeared he presented the general with an official document containing an appointment of Major-General of Volunteers, and then shook the general's brother by the shoulder. "Wake up, young man," he said ; "here's something for you."

Young Terry opened his eyes and stammered an apology for falling asleep in the presence of such high functionaries, but, when he looked at the paper given him by Mr. Stanton, he rubbed his eyes as if he thought himself dreaming. "By Jove," he said, "I went to sleep a captain and woke up a major." I think General Terry and his brother were two as contented men as I had seen for some time.

Mr. Stanton was a much-abused man, yet when he did anything to reward an officer he did it gracefully and liberally—unlike the head of the Navy Department, who, so far from thanking me for my efforts at Fort Fisher, wrote me a rude letter because I had given the five oldest officers of the squadron commendatory letters when we parted after the capture of the fort.

General Terry took no horses with him to Fort Fisher. He was lame at the time, and could not sit on a horse. I accordingly sent an officer to Smithville to procure me a horse and buggy—the best he could find. The officer departed at once in a double-banked boat, and, on arriving at the little town, found a doctor's horse and gig standing in front of that gentleman's house. The officer jumped into the buggy and drove off—not a very polite thing to do, but it was a case of military necessity—and, getting horse and buggy into the boat, brought them both down to me. There chanced to be nobody around at the time, as the town was nearly deserted, so no one witnessed the abstraction of the doctor's equipage ; but when the unfortunate physician came out of the house he couldn't understand what had become of his horse and buggy. He could not suppose that the reliable animal had run away, and no one around there would have stolen him, so for some time the doctor was in a high state of excitement.

General Terry was much pleased with the horse, and could have been seen early and late traveling around in the doctor's gig, attending to military matters, for Terry had no liking for fuss and feathers, and cared little for outward appearances so long as he was comfortable.

When we were done with the horse and buggy they were sent

back one morning before daylight, and when the owner arose from his slumbers he found the faithful steed standing patiently at the door with a good supply of oats in the vehicle.

CHAPTER XXIII.

THE PRESIDENT VISITS CITY POINT—BECOMES A GUEST ON THE MALVERN—ANXIETY TO HAVE THE ARMY MOVE ON THE ENEMY'S WORKS—TWO MIRACLES—EVACUATION OF PETERSBURG—THREE LITTLE KITTENS—PRESIDENT REFUSES TO SEE VICE-PRESIDENT JOHNSON AND PRESTON KING—HOW MUCH WILL YOU TAKE FOR THAT TRICK?—VISIT TO PETERSBURG—THREE CHEERS FOR UNCLE ABE—CAN'T WE MAKE A NOISE?—FOUR CONFEDERATE IRONCLADS BLOWN UP—THE PRESIDENT VISITS RICHMOND—AN OVATION WORTHY OF AN EMPEROR—A NEGRO PATRIARCH—ENTRANCE INTO RICHMOND—A BOUQUET OF FLOWERS FROM A PRETTY GIRL—PRESIDENT LINCOLN IN PRESIDENT DAVIS'S MANSION—RETURN ON BOARD THE MALVERN—A VISIT FROM THE LATE JUSTICE CAMPBELL—A VISIT FROM DUFF GREEN—COMPLICATIONS—RETURN TO CITY POINT—A GENERAL WHO WENT OFF IN A FIZZLE.

IN the latter part of March, 1865, the President came down to City Point, with some members of his family, in a large steamer called the River Queen. He came, in the first place, for rest; he looked much worn out with his responsibilities since I had last seen him, and needed the repose he sought. He was also very much interested that the army should move upon the enemy, and, though I am quite sure that he had the most unbounded confidence in General Grant and his judgment, yet I am of opinion that he considered himself a good judge of the time when operations should commence.

The Army of the James was to have moved some days sooner than it did, but it came on to rain, and with such effect upon the ground that it was impossible for the troops to move at all.

Infantry, of course, can always move, but it would have been an impossibility to move baggage and artillery.

At this moment it was desirable that no mistakes should be

made, and that the army should not move a day sooner than was necessary. Every day was improving our condition and making that of the Confederacy worse. All the ports along the coast had been captured; blockade-running was at an end, and the Confederates could no longer depend upon the sea for supplies. What they did obtain at that time was from their own resources, and these were very small indeed. How they ever managed to maintain their armies was a mystery to me, and must have astonished the military men of our side who had splendid commissariats to draw from.

General Grant most likely knew to a day when the enemy's provisions would give out, and when they would ask to surrender; he was preparing to move when President Lincoln came down.

The President was evidently nervous; the enormous expense of the war seemed to weigh upon him like an incubus; he could not keep away from General Grant's tent, and was constantly inquiring when he was going to move; though, if he had looked at the wagons, stuck fast in the thick red mud of the surrounding country, he would have known why no army could operate.

I attached myself to the President at his own request, and did all I could to interest him by taking him up and down the river in my barge, or driving about the country in General Ingals's buggy with two fine horses. I saw that, without being aware of it, he was pushing General Grant to move more than circumstances justified, and I did all I could to withdraw his attention from the subject.

Mr. Lincoln had a wonderful faculty for understanding the topography of a country, and he was quite familiar with the one in which the army was about to operate; he carried a small chart in his pocket, on which were marked all the rivers and hills about Richmond, with the city itself, and the different points where General Lee had his forces posted, the lines of defense, and, in fact, all the information that a general of an army wanted.

During our rides—which were always within the lines—he would stop and spread out his chart on his knees and point out to me what he would do if he were the general commanding, taking good care, at the same time, never to interfere in any way with General Grant, whom, I rather think, he considered the better strategist of the two.

I had often heard of the wonderful power of the President in telling anecdotes, but no one could form an adequate idea of his ability in this line unless he had been alone with him for ten days as I was.   He had an illustration for everything, and if anything particular attracted his attention, he would say, "That reminds me of something that occurred when I was a lawyer in Illinois," or, "when I was a boatman on the Mississippi."   He was not at all ashamed of any business he had ever been engaged in, because it was honest business, and he made an honest living by it; and he told me many stories of his earlier life, which were as creditable to him as anything he was engaged in while occupying a higher sphere.

Mr. Lincoln seemed to me to be familiar with the name, character, and reputation of every officer of rank in the army and navy, and appeared to understand them better than some whose business it was to do so; he had many a good story to tell of nearly all, and if he could have lived to write the anecdotes of the war, I am sure he would have furnished the most readable book of the century.

To me he was one of the most interesting men I ever met; he had an originality about him which was peculiarly his own, and one felt, when with him, as if he could confide his dearest secret to him with absolute security against its betrayal.   There, it might be said, was "God's noblest work—an honest man," and such he was, all through.   I have not a particle of the bump of veneration on my head, but I saw more to admire in this man, more to reverence, than I had believed possible; he had a load to bear that few men could carry, yet he traveled on with it, foot-sore and weary, but without complaint; rather, on the contrary, cheering those who would faint on the roadside.   He was not a demonstrative man, so no one will ever know, amid all the trials he underwent, how much he had to contend with, and how often he was called upon to sacrifice his own opinions to those of others, who, he felt, did not know as much about matters at issue as he did himself.   When he did surrender, it was always with a pleasant manner, winding up with a characteristic story.

In the strife between the North and the South there was no bitterness in Mr. Lincoln's composition; he seemed to think only that he had an unpleasant duty to perform, and endeavored to perform it as smoothly as possible.   He would, without doubt, have yielded a good deal to the South, only that he kept his duty constantly before his eyes, and that was the compass by which he steered at all times.   The results of a battle pained him as much as if he was receiving the wounds himself, for I have often heard him express himself in pained accents while talking over some of the scenes of the war; he was not the man to assume a character for feelings he did not possess; he was as guileless in some respects as a child. How could one avoid liking such a man?

The vessel he came up in—the River Queen—went off to Norfolk a day or two after his arrival at City Point, and I invited him, or rather he invited himself, to stay with me on board the flag-ship Malvern, which was a small vessel with poor accommodations, and not at all fitted to receive high personages. She was a captured blockade-runner, and had been given to me as a flag-ship. I retained her because she was small and drew but little water, and I could run about in her night and day, enter shoal harbors and inlets, and altogether she suited me.

I had only one large state-room in the cabin, one small after cabin that would hold a sofa and four chairs, and a small forward cabin that would dine ten. I could not "sling a cat around by the tail," but then I did not want to do that, so the arrangements were to my taste. It was in this unpretentious place that I invited the President to accept my hospitality, and he accepted it with as little formality as if it was his own home he was going into. What pleased him was that he got away from the outer world; no one could get at him but those whom he desired to see; no one could intrude upon his privacy, and he slept with every guard about him—so far as his personal safety was concerned—that he could desire.

What he liked best of all was that no one could ask him for an office.

I offered the President my bed, but he positively declined it, and elected to sleep in a small state-room outside of the cabin, occupied by my secretary. It was the smallest kind of a room, six feet long by four and a half feet wide—a small room for the President of the United States to be domesticated in, but Mr. Lincoln was pleased with it. He told me, at parting, that the few days he had spent on board the Malvern were among the pleasantest in his life.

When the President retired for his first night on board, he put his shoes and socks outside the state-room door. I am sorry to say the President's socks had holes in them; but they were washed and darned, his boots cleaned, and the whole placed at his door.

When he came to breakfast he remarked:

"A miracle happened to me last night. When I went to bed I

had two large holes in my socks, and this morning there are no holes in them. That never happened to me before; it must be a miracle!"

"How did you sleep?" I inquired.

"I slept well," he answered, "but you can't put a long blade into a short scabbard. I was too long for that berth." Then I remembered he was over six feet four inches, while the berth was only six feet.

That day, while we were out of the ship, all the carpenters were put to work; the state-room was taken down and increased in size to eight feet by six and a half feet. The mattress was widened to suit a berth of four feet width, and the entire state-room remodeled.

Nothing was said to the President about the change in his quarters when he went to bed, but next morning he came out smiling, and said: "A greater miracle than ever happened last night; I shrank six inches in length and about a foot sideways. I got somebody else's big pillow, and slept in a better bed than I did on the River Queen, though not half as *lively*." He enjoyed it hugely, but I do think if I had given him two fence-rails to sleep on he would not have found fault. That was Abraham Lincoln in all things relating to his own comfort. He would never permit people to put themselves out for him under any circumstances.

That day I handed him a telegram from Mr. Seward, reading, "Shall I come down and join you?"

"No," he said, "I don't want him. Telegraph him that the berths are too small, and there's not room for another passenger."

"But," I said, "I can provide for him if you desire his presence."

"Tell him, then, I don't want him; he'd talk to me all day about Vattel and Puffendorf. The war will be over in a week, and I don't want to hear any more of that." So Mr. Seward did not come. Mr. Lincoln was determined that none of his Cabinet should come down to City Point, where he intended to propose the terms of surrender himself. He had made up his mind that this fraternal strife should cease in one way or another. I don't know what his conversations with General Grant were, but, from the tenor of his conversations with me, I know that he was determined the Confederacy should have the most liberal terms. "Get them to plowing once," he said, "and gathering in their own little crops, eating pop-corn at their own firesides, and you can't get them to shoulder a musket again for half a century."

He did not want any of his Cabinet down there to contest the views he had formed in regard to this matter, nor to try to turn him from his plans.

I think General Grant started his army off four days sooner than he would have done had not the President been so anxious to bring the war to a conclusion, for that was what moving meant. Any one who knew anything about the war knew that when our army approached Petersburg or Richmond, at that time, it meant the surrender or annihilation of the Southern army. They had nothing left to fight on, and though they might have made a desperate defense, yet the men who led them to battle would have been simply committing murder.

When our army did get some twenty miles away from City Point the artillery stuck fast in the thick red soil, and General Meade told me afterward that it sometimes took eight horses to haul a field-piece clear of the mud. It would have been a bad thing to be caught in that way.

As the army advanced, a telegraph-wire was laid out and a telegraph-office established under the direction of Colonel Bowers, who collected all the dispatches. The President used to sit there nearly all day receiving telegrams, and I sat there with him. "Here," he said once, taking out his little chart, "they are at this point, and Sheridan is just starting off up this road. That will bring about a crisis."

"Now let us go to dinner; I'd like to peck a little."

Then we came back and received the news of the evacuation of Petersburg. "We will go there to-morrow," he said.

There were three little kittens running about the hut in which the telegraph-office was situated. Mr. Lincoln picked them all up and put them on his little chart on the table. This was a step from the sublime, it is true, but it showed the feelings of the man at a moment when the fate of a nation was hanging in the scales. He could find time to look at God's creatures and be solicitous for their comfort.

"There," he said, "you poor, little, miserable creatures, what brought you into this camp of warriors? Where is your mother?"

"The mother is dead," said the colonel.

"Then she can't grieve for them as many a poor mother is grieving for the sons who have fallen in battle, and who will still grieve if this surrender does not take place without bloodshed. Ah, kitties, thank God you are cats, and can't understand this terrible strife that is going on. There, now, go, my little friends," he continued, wiping the dirt from their eyes with his handkerchief; "that is all I can do for you. Colonel, get them some milk, and don't let them starve; there is too much starvation going on in this land anyhow; mitigate it when we can."

Just then a midshipman came up to the door of the hut with a message for me from Commodore Radford. He informed me that Vice-President Johnson and Preston King were on board the Malvern, and wished to pay their respects to the President.

I never saw such a change in any one in my life as took place in Mr. Lincoln at this announcement. He jumped up from the chair where he had been playing with the kittens and rushed to the door where the young officer was delivering his message. The President was greatly excited, and the habitual benevolent expression had left his face; he was almost frantic. "Don't let those men come into my presence," he said. "I won't see either of them; send them away. They have no business here, any way; no right to come down here without my permission. I won't see them now, and never want to lay eyes on them. I don't care what you do with them, nor where you send them, but don't let them come near me!" and he sat down in his chair looking like a man it would be dangerous for any one to anger.

"Certainly, Mr. President," I said, "your wishes shall be attended to. I will see that you never meet either of these gentlemen."

I told the midshipman to go back to Commodore Radford and tell him "the President could receive no one to-day nor to-morrow"; to go on board my ship and get all the champagne and cigars and other liquors, and entertain the two gentlemen on board the Phlox (Radford's dispatch-boat), and take them where he pleased, but under no circumstances to let them come in the President's way. Mr. Lincoln heard all the message, and when I went into the hut again he was sitting there as composed as if nothing had occurred to disturb his equanimity, while the usual benevolent expression shone on his face as before.

He never referred to those two gentlemen again, and I never knew, nor could I imagine, why he was *disturbed* at the announcement of their names.

I have my own impressions on the subject, but don't care to put them on paper.

Commodore Radford did as I requested; took them off somewhere and entertained them. He made a strong friend of Mr. Johnson, who looked after his interests while he was in the White House, and I, without intending it, made a strong enemy, with whom, however, I made it a rule never to come in contact.

The day after this occurrence Mr. Lincoln received a message from General Grant informing him that a railway-car would be ready for him at City Point, that he could come out on the railroad which ran within a few miles of Petersburg, and that he would find horses at the nearest point to take him to the city.

In consequence, we prepared to start at the appointed time. The President got into the car of which I was the only other occupant, seated himself, and, as he never lost any time, proceeded to read his newspapers.

There was no assembling of crowds in those days to witness the going or coming of a President; people had too much to do. Time was money, and those found loitering had their pay docked; so we passed along unnoticed.

I wore a naval cap which had been copied from those worn by railroad conductors, and a blue flannel short sack with four small navy-buttons on it. I might easily have been mistaken for a conductor.

I was standing on the front of the car, having locked the rear door to prevent any one from intruding upon the President. We expected the locomotive every minute. Three men came up to the car; they were nicely enough dressed—had even white cravats, which would seem to indicate that they were either divines or theological students, but I could tell at a glance that they were neither of these; they had not a clerical look aside from their neck-wear, and, to save my life, I could not have placed them. They were impudent enough to be anything.

One of them spoke. "Conductor," he said to me, "is that the President?"

"Yes," I answered, "it is."

"We want to see him," said the other.

"Can't do it," I replied.

"Who will prevent us?" said the first.

"I will; the President won't see any one."

"He will see us," was the retort, "and see him we must."

"It can not be done," I said; "the President can not be intruded upon."

"We will see for ourselves," said the stranger. "You don't

know. Have you any orders to prevent persons from approaching the President ? ”

“ No,” I said, “ none. I do it on my own responsibility.”

“ Then, in that case, you have taken a responsibility quite un-authorized, and we will call.”

With that two of them came up on the platform. I merely closed the car-door, and put my hand on the door-knob.

“ Will you let us pass ? ” said one of the white neck-ties.

“ You can pass on over the platform,” I said, “ but nowhere else ; you can’t pass through this door.”

“ Who will stop us ? ” queried the white ties.

“ I will, if possible,” I answered.

At that they all laughed ; they were well-made fellows, and, being quite conscious they could master me, they became very insolent.

All this time the President was apparently reading his news-paper, but in reality looking over the top of it, very much amused at the controversy going on between me and the white ties. He said afterward that he would have come to my assistance and ordered them away, only he thought I could manage to get rid of them.

The two men on the platform, having expended all their eloquence on me, and finding me decidedly opposed to their entry, proceeded to extremities. One put his hand on mine to remove it from the knob, and the other took me by the shoulder.

Quick as thought both the white ties were sprawling in the mud—one at each side of the car—and they were invited up to try it again, with the information that the next time they ventured upon the car they would get a pistol-ball through them.

I had no pistol ; I only told them so for effect.

They were very angry at their unceremonious removal, but did not care to attack the citadel again. The engine had now arrived and hitched on, and off we went on our way. But what a careless thing it was to be going about with the President without a guard to protect him ! I never thought of any danger to him at the time. Our people were not given to assassination, and if any one had told me that the President stood in danger of his life, I would have laughed at him.

There were no guards to be obtained at City Point ; every soldier had gone with the army. I might have brought some marines, but, confident in my own ability to keep off loafers, I neglected

19

to take any cautionary measures, and I only wonder that the catastrophe which finally took place did not occur while the President was at City Point—there were so many opportunities.

Mr. Lincoln laughed heartily when he saw the two white ties lying in the mud, and wanted to know "how much I would sell that trick for. I intend," he continued, "never to travel again unless you go along."

We arrived at Petersburg Landing, and found Lieutenant Robert Lincoln—the President's son—there with horses for the President and his son "Tad," but none for me. The escort was not a very large one, consisting only of the lieutenant, a sergeant, and three or four troopers ; it was all in keeping with the President's retinue since he first started on this expedition, but it never seemed to strike him as wanting in any way.

He was much amused all the time, and particularly so when I got one of the soldiers to dismount and let me have his raw-boned white horse, a hard trotter, and a terrible stumbler. How the Government became possessed of such an animal the Lord only knows.

I won't pretend to describe my adventures on that horse, and the number of times he ran away with me—the only way by which I could keep up with the President, who was splendidly mounted —but we finally reached Petersburg in safety, and were received at headquarters.

I had no sooner arrived than I inquired of Lieutenant Dunn, one of Grant's staff, if I could buy the horse upon which I had ridden. He said he thought I could, and would see the quartermaster about it ; but the President, who heard our conversation, put in a protest.

"Why in the name of all that's good do you want that horse, Admiral ?" exclaimed the President. "Just look at him first ; his head is as big as a flour-barrel !"

"That's the case with all horses' heads," I said.

"Well, look at his knees ; they're sprung. He's fourteen years old if he's a day ; his hoofs will cover half an acre. He's spavined, and only has one eye. What do you want with him ? You sailors don't know anything about a horse. Get some of these soldier fellows to pick you out a beast and you will get a good one. Don't you let him buy that horse, Mr. Dunn ; get him a good one."

"But I want it for a particular purpose," I said ; "I want to buy it and shoot it, so that no one else will ever ride it again."

That pleased the President mightily; he said it was the best reason he had ever heard for buying a horse.

We spent a most agreeable day at Petersburg. The streets were alive with negroes, who were crazy to see their savior, as they called the President; and it was found necessary at last to eject them from the doorways *vi et armis*.

The tobacco-stores were all open, and every one seemed to be helping himself to the delicious weed. It was mostly put up in small bales of three pounds each. Some one presented me with four packages, and I tied them upon the saddle of my horse, which I had determined to ride back again by way of enjoying a better horse in case I should ever come across one.

The President took a fancy to have four little bales also; they were a genuine curiosity to him, and Tad wanted four bales because his father had them.

Thus accoutred, we started out on the return journey, my horse cutting all kinds of capers without being able to throw me. The President paid me a high compliment. "Admiral," he said, "you mistook your profession; you ought to have been a circus-rider. I don't think there's another man in the United States, besides his owner, who could ride that horse half a mile."

Several regiments passed us on route, and they all seemed to recognize the President at once. "Three cheers for Uncle Abe!" passed along among them, and the cheers were given with a vim which showed the estimation in which he was held by the soldiers —a class of men who had in their ranks as much intelligence as any in the country; more real, good common sense than many others, and who understood the situation of affairs as well, if not better, than those who pretended to more wisdom. One good-natured fellow sang out, "We'll get 'em, Abe, where the 'boy had the hen'; you go home, and sleep sound to-night; we boys will put you through!" It was not a very courtier-like speech, certainly; it was homely and honest; and so they cheered us all along the road.

In the mean time Grant continued his approaches on toward Richmond until he reached the Appomattox apple-tree where General Lee surrendered, with all the troops and appurtenances under his immediate command.

While these movements were taking place the President, myself, and Tad were making excursions up and down the James River in my barge. We would make fast to a tug with a long line, and let her tow us. If this is not the luxury of locomotion, I don't know what is, and it certainly seemed very grateful to the President then. He said he should always look upon this time as the real holiday of his administration. He seemed almost to forget that he had any public cares. He knew that the war was practically over, and he never thought of the future but as a vision of bright prosperity, wherein, with the black spot scratched from our escutcheon, we would move on as a liberty-loving people, and attain the highest position among the nations of the earth.

Poor man! he little thought then how short was the time in which he would be allowed to contemplate the new state of affairs, and how many years would elapse before the millennium he dreamed of could be established. Perhaps it was a wise dispensation of Providence which took him from after-scenes so little in accordance with his feelings, wherein he would not have been permitted to indulge in the whole-souled plans he had formed for the reconstruction of the Republic.

About this time we heard of the arrival of Sherman at Newbern after his march to the sea, and he was now confronting General Joe Johnston in a position whence the latter would have to fight his way or surrender. This was good news to the President. "If proper terms are offered," he said to me, "and with wise management, these two armies will lay down their arms in a week, and then all the Confederate armies will follow their example. It will be like those rows of bricks boys sometimes put up : knock down the first one, and the rest all follow. The Confederates are tired of it, and so are we."

The night before Richmond was evacuated by the Confederate forces we were sitting on the Malvern's upper deck, enjoying the evening air. The President, who had been some time quiet, turned to me and said, "Can't the navy do something at this particular moment to make history ?"

"Not much," I replied ; "the navy is doing its best just now holding in utter uselessness the rebel navy, consisting of four heavy ironclads. If those should get down to City Point they would commit great havoc—as they came near doing while I was away at Fort Fisher. In consequence, we filled up the river with stones so that no vessels can pass either way. It enables us to 'hold the fort' with a very small force, but quite sufficient to prevent any one from removing the obstructions. Therefore the rebels' ironclads are useless to them."

"But can't we make a noise?" asked the President; "that would be refreshing."

"Yes," I replied, "we can make a noise; and, if you desire it, I will commence."

"Well, make a noise," he said.

I sent a telegram to Captain Breese, just above Dutch Gap, to commence firing the starboard broadside guns of the vessels above, to have the guns loaded with shrapnel, and to fire in the direction of the forts without attempting any particular aim, to fire rapidly, and to keep it up until I told him to stop. The firing commenced about nine o'clock, the hour when all good soldiers and sailors turn in and take their rest.

The President admitted that the noise was a very respectable one, and listened to it attentively, while the rapid flashes of the guns lit up the whole horizon.

In about twenty minutes there was a loud explosion which shook the vessel.

The President jumped from his chair. "I hope to Heaven one of them has not blown up!" he exclaimed.

"No, sir," I replied. "My ear detects that the sound was at least two miles farther up the river; it is one of the rebel ironclads. You will hear another in a minute."

"Well," he said, "our noise has done some good; that's a cheap way of getting rid of ironclads. I am certain Richmond is being evacuated, and that Lee has surrendered, or those fellows would not blow up their ironclads."

Just then there was a second explosion, and two more followed close after.

"That is all of them," I said; "no doubt the forts are all evacuated, and to-morrow we can go up to Richmond. I will telegraph to Captain Breese to take the obstructions up to-night, or at least enough of them to let the Malvern go through."

The telegram was sent, and the work of moving the obstructions commenced at once. It was completed by eight o'clock the following morning, and several of the smaller vessels went through, got their boats out, and began sweeping the river for torpedoes.

At daylight it was discovered that all the forts had been set on fire and evacuated, and nothing was to be seen of the ironclads but their black hulls partly out of water.

General Weitzel, who commanded the army on the left of the

James, was marching into Richmond, and the whole tragedy was over.

"Thank God," said the President, fervently, "that I have lived to see this! It seems to me that I have been dreaming a horrid dream for four years, and now the nightmare is gone. I want to see Richmond."

"If there is any of it left," I added. "There is a black smoke over the city, but before we can go up we must remove all the torpedoes; the river is full of them above Hewlit's Battery." It would have been simple destruction to attempt to go up there while the Confederates were in charge, and we could not have accomplished anything without a loss of life and vessels that would have been unjustifiable; it was better as it was, and the only course was to co-operate with the general of the army according to his own desire.

When the channel was reported clear of torpedoes (a large number of which were taken up), I proceeded up to Richmond in the Malvern, with President Lincoln on board the River Queen, and a heavy feeling of responsibility on my mind, notwithstanding the great care that had been taken to clear the river.

Every vessel that got through the obstructions wished to be the first one up, and pushed ahead with all steam; but they grounded, one after another, the Malvern passing them all, until she also took the ground. Not to be delayed, I took the President in my barge, and, with a tug ahead with a file of marines on board, we continued on up to the city.

There was a large bridge across the James about a mile below the landing, and under this a party in a small steamer were caught and held by the current, with no prospect of release without assistance. These people begged me to extricate them from their perilous position, so I ordered the tug to cast off and help them, leaving us in the barge to go on alone.

Here we were in a solitary boat, after having set out with a number of vessels flying flags at every mast-head, hoping to enter the conquered capital in a manner befitting the rank of the President of the United States, with a further intention of firing a national salute in honor of the happy result.

I remember the President's remarks on the occasion. "Admiral, this brings to my mind a fellow who once came to me to ask for an appointment as minister abroad. Finding he could not get that, he came down to some more modest position. Finally he asked to be made a tide-waiter. When he saw he could not get that, he asked me for an old pair of trousers. But it is well to be humble."

The tug never caught up with us. She got jammed in the bridge, and remained there that tide.

I had never been to Richmond before by that route, and did not know where the landing was ; neither did the coxswain, nor any of the barge's crew. We pulled on, hoping to see some one of whom we could inquire, but no one was in sight.

The street along the river-front was as deserted as if this had been a city of the dead. The troops had been in possession some hours, but not a soldier was to be seen.

The current was now rushing past us over and among rocks, on one of which we finally stuck.

"Send for Colonel Bailey," said the President ; "he will get you out of this."

"No, sir, we don't want Colonel Bailey this time. I can manage it." So I backed out and pointed for the nearest landing.

There was a small house on this landing, and behind it were some twelve negroes digging with spades. The leader of them was an old man sixty years of age. He raised himself to an upright position as we landed, and put his hands up to his eyes. Then he dropped his spade and sprang forward. "Bress de Lord," he said, "dere is de great Messiah ! I knowed him as soon as I seed him. He's bin in my heart fo' long yeahs, an' he's cum at las' to free his chillun from deir bondage ! Glory, Hallelujah !" And he fell upon his knees before the President and kissed his feet. The others followed his example, and in a minute Mr. Lincoln was surrounded by these people, who had treasured up the recollection of him caught from a photograph, and had looked up to him for four years as the one who was to lead them out of captivity.

It was a touching sight—that aged negro kneeling at the feet of the tall, gaunt-looking man who seemed in himself to be bearing all the grief of the nation, and whose sad face seemed to say, "I suffer for you all, but will do all I can to help you."

Mr. Lincoln looked down on the poor creatures at his feet ; he was much embarrassed at his position. "Don't kneel to me," he said. "That is not right. You must kneel to God only, and thank him for the liberty you will hereafter enjoy. I am but God's humble instrument ; but you may rest assured that as long as I live no one shall put a shackle on your limbs, and you shall have all the rights which God has given to every other free citizen of this Republic."

His face was lit up with a divine look as he uttered these words. Though not a handsome man, and ungainly in his person, yet in his enthusiasm he seemed the personification of manly beauty, and that sad face of his looked down in kindness upon these ignorant blacks with a grace that could not be excelled. He really seemed of another world.

All this scene was of brief duration, but, though a simple and humble affair, it impressed me more than anything of the kind I ever witnessed. What a fine picture that would have made—Mr. Lincoln landing from a ship-of-war's boat, an aged negro on his knees at his feet, and a dozen more trying to reach him to kiss the hem of his garments! In the foreground should be the shackles he had broken when he issued his proclamation giving liberty to the slave.

Twenty years have passed since that event; it is almost too new in history to make a great impression, but the time will come when it will loom up as one of the greatest of man's achievements, and the name of Abraham Lincoln—who of his own will struck the shackles from the limbs of four millions of people—will be honored thousands of years from now as man's name was never honored before.

It was a minute or two before I could get the negroes to rise and leave the President. The scene was so touching I hated to disturb it, yet we could not stay there all day; we had to move on; so I requested the patriarch to withdraw from about the President with his companions and let us pass on.

"Yes, Massa," said the old man, "but after bein' so many years in de desert widout water, it's mighty pleasant to be lookin' at las' on our spring of life. 'Scuse us, sir; we means no disrespec' to Mass' Lincoln; we means all love and gratitude." And then, joining hands together in a ring, the negroes sang the following hymn with melodious and touching voices only possessed by the negroes of the South:

> "Oh, all ye people clap your hands,
>   And with triumphant voices sing;
> No force the mighty power withstands
>   Of God, the universal King."

The President and all of us listened respectfully while the hymn was being sung. Four minutes at most had passed away since we first landed at a point where, as far as the eye could reach, the streets were entirely deserted, but now what a different scene appeared as that hymn went forth from the negroes' lips ! The streets seemed to be suddenly alive with the colored race. They seemed to spring from the earth. They came, tumbling and shouting, from over the hills and from the water-side, where no one was seen as we had passed.

The crowd immediately became very oppressive. We needed our marines to keep them off.

I ordered twelve of the boat's crew to fix bayonets to their rifles and to surround the President, all of which was quickly done ; but the crowd poured in so fearfully that I thought we all stood a chance of being crushed to death.

I now realized the imprudence of landing without a large body of marines ; and yet this seemed to me, after all, the fittest way for Mr. Lincoln to come among the people he had redeemed from bondage.

What an ovation he had, to be sure, from those so-called ignorant beings ! They all had their souls in their eyes, and I don't think I ever looked upon a scene where there were so many passionately happy faces.

While some were rushing forward to try and touch the man they had talked of and dreamed of for four long years, others stood off a little way and looked on in awe and wonder. Others turned somersaults, and many yelled for joy. Half of them acted as though demented, and could find no way of testifying their delight.

They had been made to believe that they never would gain their liberty, and here they were brought face to face with it when least expected. It was as a beautiful toy unexpectedly given to a child after months of hopeless longing on its part ; it was such joy as never kills, but animates the dullest class of humanity.

But we could not stay there all day looking at this happy mass of people ; the crowds and their yells were increasing, and in a short time we would be unable to move at all. The negroes, in their ecstasy, could not be made to understand that they were detaining the President ; they looked upon him as belonging to them, and that he had come to put the crowning act to the great work he had commenced. They would not feel they were free in reality until they heard it from his own lips.

At length he spoke. He could not move for the mass of people —he had to do something.

"My poor friends," he said, "you are free—free as air. You

can cast off the name of slave and trample upon it; it will come to you no more. Liberty is your birthright. God gave it to you as he gave it to others, and it is a sin that you have been deprived of it for so many years. But you must try to deserve this priceless boon. Let the world see that you merit it, and are able to maintain it by your good works. Don't let your joy carry you into excesses. Learn the laws and obey them; obey God's commandments and thank him for giving you liberty, for to him you owe all things. There, now, let me pass on; I have but little time to spare. I want to see the capital, and must return at once to Washington to secure to you that liberty which you seem to prize so highly."

The crowd shouted and screeched as if they would split the firmament, though while the President was speaking you might have heard a pin drop. I don't think any one could do justice to that scene; it would be necessary to photograph it to understand it.

One could not help wondering where all this black mass of humanity came from, or if they were all the goods and chattels of those white people who had for four years set the armies of the Republic at defiance; who had made these people work on their defenses and carry their loads, the only reward for which was the stronger riveting of the chains which kept them in subjection.

At length we were able to move on, the crowd opening for us with shouts. I got the twelve seamen with fixed bayonets around the President to keep him from being crushed. It never struck me that there was any one in that multitude who would injure him; it seemed to me that he had an army of supporters there who could and would defend him against all the world.

But likely there were scowling eyes not far off; men were perhaps looking on, with hatred in their hearts, who were even then seeking an opportunity to slay him.

Our progress was very slow; we did not move a mile an hour, and the crowd was still increasing.

Many poor whites joined the throng, and sent up their shouts with the rest. We were nearly half an hour getting from abreast of Libby Prison to the edge of the city. The President stopped a moment to look on the horrid bastile where so many Union soldiers had dragged out a dreadful existence, and were subjected to all the cruelty the minds of brutal jailers could devise.

"We will pull it down," cried the crowd, seeing where his look fell.

"No," he said, "leave it as a monument."

He did not say a monument to what, but he meant, I am sure, to leave it as a monument to the loyalty of our soldiers, who would bear all the horrors of Libby sooner than desert their flag and cause.

We struggled on, the great crowd preceding us, and an equally dense crowd of blacks following on behind—all so packed together that some of them frequently sang out in pain.

It was not a model style for the President of the United States to enter the capital of a conquered country, yet there was a moral in it all which had more effect than if he had come surrounded with great armies and heralded by the booming of cannon.

He came, armed with the majesty of the law, to put his seal to the act which had been established by the bayonets of the Union soldiers—the establishment of peace and good-will between the North and the South, and liberty to all mankind who dwell upon our shores.

We forced our way onward slowly, and, as we reached the edge of the city, the sidewalks were lined on both sides of the streets with black and white alike—all looking with curious, eager faces at the man who held their destiny in his hand; but there was no anger in any one's face; the whole was like a gala day, and it looked as if the President was some expected guest who had come to receive great honors. Indeed, no man was ever accorded a greater ovation than was extended to him, be it from warm hearts or from simple ceremony.

It was a warm day, and the streets were dusty, owing to the immense gathering which covered every part of them, kicking up the dirt. The atmosphere was suffocating, but Mr. Lincoln could be seen plainly by every man, woman, and child, towering head and shoulders above that crowd; he overtopped every man there. He carried his hat in his hand, fanning his face, from which the perspiration was pouring. He looked as if he would have given his Presidency for a glass of water—I would have given my commission for half that.

Now came another phase in the procession. As we entered the city every window flew up, from ground to roof, and every one was filled with eager, peering faces, which turned one to another and seemed to ask, "Is this large man, with soft eyes and kind, benevolent face, the one who has been held up to us as the incarnation of wickedness, the destroyer of the South?" I think that illusion vanished, if it was ever harbored by any one there. I don't know what there was to amuse them in looking on the scene before them, but certainly I never saw a merrier crowd in my life, black or white.

We were brought to a halt by the dense jam before we had gone a square into the city, which was still on fire near the Tredegar Works and in the structures thereabout, and the smoke, setting our way, almost choked us.

I had not seen a soldier whom I could send to General Weitzel to ask for an escort, and it would have been useless to send one of the contrabands, for he would have been too much interested in seeing the sights and in looking at the President, from whom none of them took their eyes. I don't think any one noticed the rest of the party.

I think the people could not have had a gala day since the Confederates occupied Richmond as headquarters. Judging from present appearances, they certainly were not grieving over the loss of the Government which had just fled.

There was nothing like taunt or defiance in the faces of those who were gazing from the windows or craning their necks from the sidewalks to catch a view of the President. The look of every one was that of eager curiosity—nothing more.

While we were stopped for a moment by the crowd, a white man in his shirt-sleeves rushed from the sidewalk toward the President. His looks were so eager that I questioned his friendship, and prepared to receive him on the point of my sword ; but when he got within ten feet of us he suddenly stopped short, took off his hat, and cried out, "Abraham Lincoln, God bless you ! You are the poor man's friend !" Then he tried to force his way to the President to shake hands with him. He would not take "No" for an answer until I had to treat him rather roughly, when he stood off, with his arms folded, and looked intently after us. The last I saw of him he was throwing his hat into the air.

Just after this a beautiful girl came from the sidewalk, with a large bouquet of roses in her hand, and advanced, struggling through the crowd toward the President. The mass of people endeavored to open to let her pass, but she had a hard time in reaching him. Her clothes were very much disarranged in making the journey across the street.

I reached out and helped her within the circle of the sailors' bayonets, where, although nearly stifled with the dust, she gracefully presented her bouquet to the President and made a neat little speech, while he held her hand. The beauty and youth of the girl —for she was only about seventeen—made the presentation very touching.

There was a card on the bouquet with these simple words: "From Eva to the Liberator of the slaves." She remained no longer than to deliver her present; then two of the sailors were sent to escort her back to the sidewalk. There was no cheering at this, nor yet was any disapprobation shown; but it was evidently a matter of great interest, for the girl was surrounded and plied with questions.

I asked myself what all this could mean but that the people of Richmond were glad to see the end of the strife and the advent of a milder form of government than that which had just departed in such an ignoble manner. They felt that the late Government, instead of decamping with the gold of the Confederacy, should have remained at the capital, and surrendered in a dignified manner, making terms for the citizens of the place, guarding their rights, and acknowledging that they had lost the game. There was nothing to be ashamed of in such a surrender to a vastly superior force; their armies had fought as people never fought before. "They had robbed the cradle and the grave" to sustain themselves, and all that was wanted to make them glorious was the submission of the leaders, with the troops, in a dignified way, while they might have said, "We have done our best to win, but you have justice on your side, and are too strong for us; we pledge ourselves to keep the peace."

Instead of remaining to protect the citizens against ruffianism, the Confederate authorities of Richmond left that to our troops, and I will say no soldiers ever performed a trust more faithfully. At the moment of which I speak the majority of them were engaged in putting out the fires that were started as the enemy left the town, determined, it seemed, to destroy all the public works, so that we could derive no benefit from them. They would have been about as useful to us as the old "hay-ricks" which encumbered the navy list at the end of the war.

At length I got hold of a cavalryman. He was sitting his horse near the sidewalk, blocked in by the people, and looking on with the same expression of interest as the others.

He was the only soldier I had seen since we landed, showing that the general commanding the Union forces had no desire to interfere, in any case, with the comfort of the citizens. There was only guard enough posted about the streets to protect property and to prevent irregularities.

"Go to the general," I said to the trooper, "and tell him to send a military escort here to guard the President and get him through this crowd!"

"Is that old Abe?" asked the soldier, his eyes as large as saucers. The sight of the President was as strange to him as to the inhabitants; but off he went as fast as the crowd would allow him, and, some twenty minutes later, I heard the clatter of horses' hoofs over the stones as a troop of cavalry came galloping and clearing the street, which they did, however, as mildly as if for a parade.

For the first time since starting from the landing we were able to walk along uninterruptedly. In a short time we reached the mansion of Mr. Davis, President of the Confederacy, occupied after the evacuation as the headquarters of Generals Weitzel and Shepley. It was quite a small affair compared with the White House, and modest in all its appointments, showing that while President Davis was engaged heart and soul in endeavoring to effect the division of the States, he was not, at least, surrounding himself with regal style, but was living in a modest, comfortable way, like any other citizen.

Amid all his surroundings the refined taste of his wife was apparent, and marked everything about the apartments.

There was great cheering going on. Hundreds of civilians—I don't know who they were—assembled at the front of the house to welcome Mr. Lincoln.

General Shepley made a speech and gave us a lunch, after which we entered a carriage and visited the State-House—the late seat of the Confederate Congress. It was in dreadful disorder, betokening a sudden and unexpected flight; members' tables were upset, bales of Confederate scrip were lying about the floor, and many official documents of some value were scattered about. It was strange to me that they had not set fire to the building before they departed, to bury in oblivion every record that might remain relating to the events of the past four years.

After this inspection I urged the President to go on board the Malvern. I began to feel more heavily the responsibility resting upon me through the care of his person. The evening was approaching, and we were in a carriage open on all sides. He was glad to go; he was tired out, and wanted the quiet of the flag-ship.

We took leave of our hosts and departed.

I was oppressed with uneasiness until we got on board and stood on deck with the President safe; then there was not a happier man anywhere than myself.

I determined that the President should go nowhere again, while under my charge, unless I was with him and had a guard of marines. I thought of the risks we had run that day, and I was satisfied before night was over that I had good cause for apprehension.

We were all sitting on the upper deck about eight o'clock that evening, when a man came down to the landing and hailed the Malvern (the vessel had come-to off the city during the day), saying that he had dispatches for the President. I told the captain to send a boat to the shore to bring off the dispatches, but not to bring the bearer. The boat returned with neither dispatches nor man. The boat-officer said the man would not deliver the dispatches to any one but the President himself.

"Let him come on board," said the President.

"Don't you think we should be careful whom we admit after dark, sir?" I asked.

"Well, yes," he replied; "but these dispatches may be from General Grant, and the man may be only obeying his orders literally."

I ordered the boat to go back and bring the man on board, determined to stand near the President when the dispatches were delivered.

I knew that General Grant would send dispatches only by an officer, and the midshipman in the boat told me this was not one.

When the boat returned to the shore the man was gone. As I suspected, he was a bogus dispatch-bearer. The circumstance was very suspicious.

I inquired about the appearance of the person when seen by the officer of the boat.

"He was a tall man with a black moustache, wore a slouch hat and a long cloak, a regular theatrical villain—one of the stereotyped play robbers."

That man was, without doubt, Wilkes Booth, who sought the President's life. It would have suited Booth's tragical spirit to slay him on such an occasion; it would have added greatly to the scenic effect.

In the course of a half-hour another hail came from the shore, from which we lay not more than twenty yards. A person wanted a boat ; a sailor from the Saugus wanted to report himself on board. There was no such vessel in the fleet, though there was one in the navy. I sent an officer and four men in the boat to bring the man off, not to let him escape, and, when in the boat, to put hand-irons on him. Then I swept the shore with a night-glass, but could see no one. The boat landed a minute later. There was no man to be seen. The boat's crew ran up and down the river and looked over the bank, but no one could be found.

These two circumstances made me more suspicious, and every care was taken that no one should get on board without full identification.

The President himself felt a little unpleasant and nervous, and that night a marine kept guard at his state-room door.

Next morning, at ten o'clock, Mr. John A. Campbell, late Justice of the Supreme Court of the United States, sent a request to be allowed to come on board with General Weitzel. He wanted to call on the President. He came on board and spent an hour. The President and himself seemed to be enjoying themselves very much, to judge from their laughter.

I did not go down to the cabin. In about an hour General Weitzel and Mr. Campbell came on deck, asked for a boat, and were landed.

I went down below for a moment, and the President said : "Admiral, I am sorry you were not here when Mr. Campbell was on board. He has gone on shore happy. I gave him a written permission to allow the State Legislature to convene in the Capitol in the absence of all other government."

I was rather astonished at this piece of information. I felt that this course would bring about complications, and wondered how it had all come to pass. I found it had all been done by the persuasive tongue of Mr. Campbell, who had promised the President that if the Legislature of Virginia could meet in the halls of the Confederate Congress it would vote Virginia right back into the Union ; that it would be a delicate compliment paid to Virginia which would be appreciated, etc.

Weitzel backed up Mr. Campbell, and the President was won over to agree to what would have been a most humiliating thing if it had been accomplished.

When the President told me all that had been done, and that General Weitzel had gone on shore with an order in his pocket to let the Legislature meet, I merely said : "Mr. President, I suppose you remember that this city is under military jurisdiction, and that no courts, Legislature, or civil authority can exercise any power without the sanction of the general commanding the army. This order of yours should go through General Grant, who would inform you that Richmond was under martial law ; and I am sure he would protest against this arrangement of Mr. Campbell's."

The President's common sense took in the situation at once. "Why," he said, "Weitzel made no objection, and he commands here."

"That is because he is Mr. Campbell's particular friend, and wished to gratify him ; besides, I don't think he knows much about anything but soldiering. General Shepley would not have preferred such a request."

"Run and stop them," exclaimed the President, "and get my order back ! Well, I came near knocking all the fat into the fire, didn't I ?"

To make things sure, I had an order written to General Weitzel and signed by the President as follows : " Return my permission to the Legislature of Virginia to meet, and don't allow it to meet at all." There was an ambulance-wagon at the landing, and, giving the order to an officer, I said to him, " Jump into that wagon, and kill the horse if necessary, but catch the carriage which carried General Weitzel and Mr. Campbell, and deliver this order to the general."

The carriage was caught after it reached the city. The old wagon horse had been a trotter in his day, and went his three minutes. The general and Mr. Campbell were surprised. The President's order was sent back, and they never returned to try and reverse the decision.

Mr. Campbell evidently saw that his scheme of trying to put the State Legislature in session with the sanction of the President had failed, and that it was useless to try it again. It was a clever dodge to soothe the wounded feelings of the South, and no doubt was kindly meant by the late Justice Campbell, but what a howl it would have raised at the North ! .Mr. Campbell had been gone about an hour when we had another remarkable scene. A man appeared at the landing, dressed in gray homespun, of a somewhat decayed appearance, and with a staff about six feet long in his hand. It was, in fact, nothing more than a stick taken from a wood-pile. It was about two inches in diameter, and was not even smoothed at the knots. It was just such a weapon as a man would pick up to kill a mad dog with.

"Who are you, and what do you want?" asked the officer of the deck. "You can not come on board unless you have important business."

"I am Duff Green," said the man. "I want to see Abraham Lincoln, and my business concerns myself alone. You tell Abraham Lincoln Duff Green wants to see him."

The officer came down into the cabin and delivered the message. I arose and said, "I will go up and send him away," but the President interposed.

"Let him come on board," he said; "Duff is an old friend of mine, and I would like to talk to him."

I then went on deck to have a boat sent for him and to see what kind of a man this was who sent off such arrogant messages to the President of the United States. He stepped into the boat as if it belonged to him; instead of sitting down he stood up, leaning on his long staff. When he came over the side he stood on the deck defiantly, looked up at the flag and scowled, and then, turning to me, whom he knew very well, he said, "I want to see Abraham Lincoln." He paid no courtesy to me or to the quarter deck.

It had been a very long time since he had shaved or cut his hair, and he might have come under the head "unkempt and not canny."

"When you come in a respectful manner," I said, "the President will see you; but throw away that cord of wood you have in your hand before entering the President's presence."

"How long is it," he said, "since Abraham Lincoln took to aping royalty? Man, clothed in brief authority, cuts such fantastic capers before high heaven as make the angels weep. I can expect airs from a naval officer, but I don't expect them in a man with Abraham Lincoln's horse sense."

I thought the man crazy, and think so still. "I can't permit you to see the President," I said, "until I receive further instructions; but you can't see him at all until you throw that wood-pile overboard."

He turned on his heel and tried to throw the stick on shore, but it fell short, and went floating down with the current.

"Ah," he said, "has it come to that? Is he afraid of assassination? Tyrants generally get into that condition."

I went down and reported this queer customer to the President, and told him I thought the man insane; but he said, "Let him come down; he always was a little queer. I sha'n't mind him."

Mr. Duff Green was shown into the cabin.

The President got up from his chair to receive him, and, approaching, offered him his hand.

"No," said Green, with a tragic air, "it is red with blood; I can't touch it. When I knew it, it was an honest hand. It has cut the throats of thousands of my people, and their blood, which now lies soaking into the ground, cries aloud to Heaven for vengeance. I came to see you, not for old remembrance' sake, but to give you a piece of my opinion. You won't like it, but I don't care, for people don't generally like to have the truth told them. You have come here, protected by your army and navy, to gloat over the ruin and desolation you have caused. You are a second Nero, and, had you lived in his day, you would have fiddled while Rome was burning!"

When the fanatic commenced this tirade of abuse Mr. Lincoln was standing with his hand outstretched, his mouth wreathed with the pleasant smile it almost always wore, and his eyes lighted up as when anything pleased him. He was pleased because about to meet an old and esteemed friend, and better pleased that this friend had come to see him of his own accord.

The outstretched hand was gradually withdrawn as Duff Green started on his talk, the smile left the President's lips as the talker got to the middle of his harangue, and the softness of his eyes faded out. He was another man altogether.

Had any one closed his eyes after Duff Green commenced speaking, and opened them when he stopped, he would have seen a perfect transformation. The hearer's slouchy manner had disappeared, his mouth was compressed, his eyes were fixed, even his stature appeared increased.

Duff Green went on without noticing the change in the President's manner and appearance. "You came here," he continued, 'to triumph over a poor, conquered town, with only women and children in it; whose soldiers have left it, and would rather starve than see your hateful presence here; those soldiers—and only a handful at that—who have for four years defied your paid mercenaries on those glorious hills, and have taught you to respect the rights of the South. You have given your best blood to conquer them, and now you will march back to your demoralized capital and lay out your wits to win them over so that you can hold this Government in perpetuity. Shame on you! Shame on—"

Mr. Lincoln could stand it no longer; his coarse hair stood on end, and his nostrils dilated like those of an excited race-horse. He stretched out his long right arm, and extended his lean forefinger until it almost touched Duff Green's face. He made one step forward, to place himself as near as possible to this vituperator, and in a clear, cutting voice addressed him. He was really graceful while he spoke—with the grace of one expressing his honest convictions.

"Stop, you political tramp," he exclaimed, "you, the aider and abettor of those who have brought all this ruin upon your country, without the courage to risk your person in defense of the principles you profess to espouse! A fellow who stood by to gather up the loaves and fishes, if any should fall to you! A man who had no principles in the North, and took none South with him! A political hyena who robbed the graves of the dead, and adopted their language as his own! You talk of the North cutting the throats of the Southern people. You have all cut your own throats, and, unfortunately, have cut many of those of the North. Miserable impostor, vile intruder! Go, before I forget myself and the high position I hold! Go, I tell you, and don't desecrate this national vessel another minute!" And he made a step toward him.

This was something Duff Green had not calculated upon; he had never seen Abraham Lincoln in anger. His courage failed him, and he turned and fled out of the cabin and up the cabin-stairs as if the avenging angel was after him. He never stopped till he reached the gangway, and there he stood, looking at the shore, seemingly measuring the distance, to see if he could swim to the landing.

I was close behind him, and when I got on deck I said to the officer in charge, "Put that man on shore, and if he appears in sight of this vessel while we are here, have him sent away with scant ceremony."

He was as humble at that moment as a whipped dog, and hurried into the boat when ordered.

The last I saw of him he was striding rapidly over the fields, as if to reach the shelter of the woods. When I returned to the cabin, about fifteen minutes later, the President was perfectly calm—as if nothing had happened—and did not revert to the subject for some hours.

"This place seems to give you annoyance, sir," I said. "Would you prefer to get under way and go to City Point, where we are more among friends than here ?"

"Yes," he answered, "let us go. I seem to be 'putting my foot into it' here all the time. Bless my soul, how Seward would have preached, and read Puffendorf, Vattel, and Grotius to me, if he had been here when I gave Campbell permission to let the Legislature meet ! I'd never have heard the last of it. Seward is a small compendium of international law himself, and laughs at my 'horse sense,' which I pride myself on, and yet I put my foot into that thing about Campbell with my eyes wide open. If I were you, I don't think I would repeat that joke yet awhile. People might laugh at you for knowing so much, and more than the President ! I am afraid that the most of my learning lies in my heart more than in my head."

We got under way and steamed down the river. While we had been up at Richmond the gun-boat people had completed the removal of the torpedoes from the river-bed and laid them all out on the banks, where they looked like so many queer fish basking in the sun, of all sizes and shapes.

The President had originally proposed to come up on horseback, but I told him that "there was not a particle of danger from torpedoes ; that I would have them all taken up." When he saw them all on the bank he turned to me and said, "You must have been 'awful afraid' of getting on that sergeant's old horse again to risk all this." We got down safe, however ; there was not enough danger to make it interesting. The President had some quaint remarks about everything we saw, particularly about Dutch Gap, which, he said, "ought to have been commenced before the war— at least ten years. Then," he said, " you might have had a chance of getting your gun-boats up that way. By the way, your friend the general wasn't a 'boss' engineer. He was better at running cotton-mills. How many people did it cost for that jetty ?" he asked.

"One hundred and forty killed there as far as I can learn," I answered.

Then he went into a discussion of the generals of the war—what difficulties he had in making appointments, etc. He illustrated each case with a story. In speaking of one general, he said it reminded him of a friend of his—a blacksmith—he knew out in the West when he was a boatman.

This old friend was celebrated for making good work, especially axes, which were in great demand at that day. No boatman had a complete outfit unless he had a good axe.

"One day he said to me, 'Lincoln, I have the finest piece of steel you ever saw; I got it on purpose to make an axe for you, and if you will sit down and tell me a good story you shall have the axe when it is finished.' 'Go ahead,' I said, and I sat down to tell the story while he made the axe.

"My friend the blacksmith first put on a huge piece of fresh coal, and blew it up until it was at a proper heat—the coals glowing; he took up the piece of steel and looked at it affectionately, patted it all over, then, 'Lincoln,' he said, 'did you ever see a piece of steel equal to that? It'll make you a companion you will never want to part with, and when you are using it you will think of me.' Then he put it into the fire, and began to work his bellows while I commenced my story.

"He blew and blew until the steel was at a deep-red heat, when, taking it out of the fire and laying it on the anvil, he gave it a clip with a four-pound hammer. Lord bless you, how the sparks flew, and the big red scales also! The blacksmith hit it about a dozen blows and then stopped. 'Lincoln,' he said, 'here's a go, and a bad one too. This lump of steel ain't worth the powder that would blow it up. I never was so deceived in anything in all my life. It won't make an axe. But I'll tell you what it will make. It will make a clevis,' and he put it in the fire again and went through the same performance as before. Then, when it was heated, he laid it on the anvil and commenced to hammer it. The sparks flew, and so did the scales, and in a minute half of it was gone. The blacksmith stopped and scratched his head, as men often do under difficulties. 'Well,' he said, 'this certainly is an onery piece of steel, but it may get better nearer the heart of it. I can't make a clevis of it, but it will make a clevis-bolt. It may have some good in it yet. After all, a good clevis-bolt is not a bad thing.'

"He put it into the fire again, and this time got it to a white heat. 'I think I have it now, Lincoln,' and he pounded away at it until I was almost blinded with scales.

"'This won't do,' he said. 'I certainly don't know my trade to allow a thing like that to fool me so. Well, well, it won't make a clevis-bolt, but I have one resort yet; it will make a ten-penny nail. You will have to wait for your axe,' and he put the metal into the fire again.

"This time he didn't blow it; he let it get red-hot naturally, and when it was as he wanted it, he put it on the anvil again.

"'This,' he said, 'is a sure thing. I am down to the heart of the piece. There must be a ten-penny nail in this.' But he was mistaken ; there was only a small piece of wire left. He was actually dazed.

"'Durn the thing,' he said. 'I don't know what to make of it. I tried it as an axe, it failed me. Then it failed me as a clevis. It failed me as a clevis-bolt, and the cussed thing wouldn't even make a ten-penny nail !'

"'But I'll tell you, old fellow, what it *will* make,' and he put it into the fire again until it and the tongs were at white heat. Then, turning around, he rammed it into a bucket of water. 'There, durn you, you'll make a big fizzle, and that's all you will make !' and it sputtered and fizzed until it went out, and there was nothing of it left.

"Now that's the case with the person I was speaking of," continued the President. "I tried him as an axe. I tried him as a clevis. He was so full of shakes he wouldn't work into one. I tried him as a clevis-bolt. He was a dead failure, and he wouldn't make even a ten-penny nail. But he did make the biggest fizzle that has been made this war, and fizzled himself out of the army.

<blockquote>
"' With a shocking bad name,
And his credit at zero,
He was contented to stay
At home as a hero ! ' "
</blockquote>

We anchored a short time afterward, and were glad to be looking on the quiet wharves at City Point.

That evening the sailors and marines were sent out to guard and escort in some prisoners, numbering about a thousand, more or less, who were placed on board a large transport lying in the stream.

The President expressing a desire to go on shore, I ordered the barge and went with him.

We had to pass the transport with the prisoners ; they all rushed to the side with eager curiosity ; all wanted to see the Northern President.

They seemed perfectly content ; every man had a hunk of meat and a piece of bread in his hand, and was doing his best to dispose of it.

"That's old Abe," said one of them. "Give the old fellow three cheers," said another; while a third called out, "Halloo, Abe, your bread and meat's better than pop-corn."

This was all good-natured and kindly. I could see no difference between them and our own men, except that they were ragged and attenuated from want of wholesome food. They were as happy a set of men as I ever saw; they could see their homes looming up before them in the distance, and knew the war was over.

"They will never shoulder a musket again in anger," said the President, "and if Grant is wise he will leave them their guns to shoot crows with, and their horses to plow with; it would do no harm."

CHAPTER XXIV.

GENERAL SHERMAN ARRIVES AT GOLDSBORO'—SHERMAN CALLS ON THE PRESIDENT—COUNCIL ON BOARD THE RIVER QUEEN—PRESIDENT LINCOLN'S KIND INTENTIONS TOWARD THE CONFEDERATE ARMIES—LET THEM HAVE THEIR HORSES TO PLOW WITH, AND THEIR MUSKETS TO SHOOT CROWS WITH—"THERE ARE NO SOUTHERN RAILROADS; MY BUMMERS HAVE TAKEN THEM ALL UP"—WHY SUCH A HOWL AT THE NORTH—LEE SURRENDERS—THE PRESIDENT RETURNS TO WASHINGTON—SEND OFFICERS WITH HIM TO PROTECT HIS PERSON—HIS DEATH—THERE LIES THE BEST MAN I EVER KNEW.

I MUST now go back a little.

While General Grant was preparing to march and surround General Lee at Richmond, Sherman was coming rapidly with all his veterans toward Goldsboro', North Carolina, which place he reached on the 21st of March, 1865. There he effected a junction with the forces of Generals Schofield and Terry, which had come up from Wilmington. This combination gave Sherman an effective force of at least eighty thousand men.

When Sherman arrived at Goldsboro' his army was literally without clothes and very short of provisions. It was necessary that they should be supplied at once, and it was so important that he should see General Grant and ascertain the exact position that he determined to come to City Point. The President also desired to see him at that place, and I think General Grant sent him a communication to that effect.

Leaving General Schofield in command of the army, Sherman took the small steamer Russia from Morehead City and proceeded in her to City Point, arriving on March 27th. He was received on board the River Queen by the President with that warmth of feeling which always distinguished him when meeting any of the brave men who had devoted their lives to crushing out the great Rebellion.

General Sherman spent a long time with the President, explaining to him the situation in his department, which was very encouraging.

At this moment Sherman's army was holding General Joe Johnston's forces in North Carolina in a position from which he could not move without precipitating a battle with some eighty thousand of the best troops in our army. It was thought at that time that Johnston would endeavor to make a junction with General Lee at Richmond, which, in the light of subsequent events, would have been an impossibility. Again, it was thought that Lee would attempt to escape from Richmond and try to effect a junction with Johnston. Quite as impossible as the other move, for at that moment Sheridan was pushing his cavalry across the James River from North to South, and with this cavalry intended to extend his left below Petersburg so as to meet the South Shore road, and, if Lee should leave his fortified lines, Grant would fall on his rear and follow him so closely that he could not possibly fall on Sherman's army in North Carolina, besides which Sherman felt confident that with his eighty thousand men he could hold his own against Johnston and Lee combined until Grant came up with the Army of the James.

The morning after Sherman's arrival the President held a council on board the River Queen, composed of General Grant, General Sherman, and myself, and, as considerable controversy was caused by the terms of surrender granted to General Joe Johnston, I will mention here the conversation which took place during this meeting in the River Queen's cabin.

I made it a rule during the war to write down at night before retiring to rest what had occurred during each day, and I was particularly careful in doing so in this instance.

At this meeting Mr. Lincoln and General Sherman were the speakers, and the former declared his opinions at length before

Sherman answered him. The President feared that Lee—seeing our lines closing about him, the coast completely blockaded, his troops almost destitute of clothing and short of provisions—might make an attempt to break away from the fortified works at Richmond, make a junction with General Joe Johnston, and escape South or fight a last bloody battle.

Any one looking at the situation of the armies at that time will see that such an attempt would not have been possible.

Sherman had eighty thousand fine troops at Goldsboro', only one hundred and fifty miles from Richmond and one hundred and twenty miles from Greensborough, which latter place cut the Richmond and Danville Railroad, the only one by which Lee could escape.

The President's mind was made easy on this score, yet it was remarkable how many shrewd questions he asked on the subject, and how difficult some of them were to answer. He stated his views in regard to what he desired; he felt sure, as did every one at that council, that the end of the war was near at hand; and, though some thought a bloody battle was impending, all thought that Richmond would fall in less than a week.

He wanted the surrender of the Confederate armies, and desired that the most liberal terms should be granted them. "Let them once surrender," he said, "and reach their homes, they won't take up arms again. Let them all go, officers and all. I want submission, and no more bloodshed. Let them have their horses to plow with, and, if you like, their guns to shoot crows with. I want no one punished; treat them liberally all round. We want those people to return to their allegiance to the Union and submit to the laws. Again I say, give them the most liberal and honorable terms."

"But, Mr. President," said Sherman, "I can dictate my own terms to General Johnston. All I want is two weeks' time to fit out my men with shoes and clothes, and I will be ready to march upon Johnston and compel him to surrender; he is short of clothing, and in two weeks he would have no provisions at all."

"And," added the President, "two weeks is an age, and the first thing you will know General Johnston will be off South again with those hardy troops of his, and will keep the war going indefinitely. No, General, he must not get away; we must have his surrender at all hazards, so don't be hard on him about terms. Yes, he will get away if he can, and you will never catch him until after miles of travel and many bloody battles."

"Mr. President," said Sherman, "there is no possible way of General Johnston's escaping ; he is my property as he is now situated, and I can demand an unconditional surrender ; he can't escape."

"What is to prevent him from escaping with all his army by the Southern railroads while you are fitting out your men ?" asked Grant.

"Because," answered Sherman, "there are no Southern railroads to speak of ; my bummers have broken up the roads in sections all behind us—and they did it well."

"But," said Grant, "can't they relay the rails, the same as you did the other day, from Newbern and Wilmington to Goldsboro' ?"

Sherman laughed. "Why, no," he said, "my boys don't do things by halves. When they tore up the rails they put them over hot fires made from the ties, and then twisted them more crooked than a ram's horn. All the blacksmiths in the South could not straighten them out."

"Mr. President," said Sherman, turning to Mr. Lincoln, "the Confederacy has gone up, or will go up. We hold all the line between Wilmington and Goldsboro', where my troops are now fitting out from the transports. My transports can come up the Neuse River as far as Newbern. We could flood the South with troops and provisions without hindrance. We hold the situation, and General Johnston can surrender to me on my own terms."

"All very well," said the President, "but we must have no mistakes, and my way is a sure way. Offer Johnston the same terms that will be offered to Lee ; then, if he is defiant, and will not accept them, try your plan. But as long as the Confederate armies lay down their arms, I don't think it matters much how it is done. Only don't let us have any more bloodshed if it can be avoided. General Grant is for giving Lee the most favorable terms."

To this General Grant assented.

"Well, Mr. President," said Sherman, "I will carry out your wishes to the letter, and I am quite satisfied that, as soon as Richmond falls, Joe Johnston will surrender also."

Sherman, at the end of that council, supposed he was acting under instructions, which he carried out, so far as I can understand it, pretty much as the President desired.

The council over, and the President being desirous that General Sherman should return to his command as soon as possible, the latter determined to return that afternoon by sea.

I gave him the naval steamer Bat to take him back again to his post—a vessel that could make sixteen knots an hour—and he was soon at his headquarters.

I shall never forget that council which met on board the River Queen. On the determinations adopted there depended peace, or a continuation of the war with its attendant horrors. That council has been illustrated in a fine painting by Mr. Healy, the artist, who, in casting about for the subject of an historical picture, hit upon this interview, which really was an occasion upon which depended whether or not the war would be continued a year longer. A single false step might have prolonged it indefinitely.

Even at the last, when the Confederates were known to be in most straitened circumstances—without food and clothing for their troops or forage for their animals, short at the same time of ammunition, without which their armies were useless—they had powerful forces in and about Richmond, which, if once united with General Johnston's army, would have made a most formidable array. Eighty thousand men, handled by such men as General Lee and General Johnston, would have been a hard army to beat. We had had so many proofs during the war of the ability of those generals and soldiers to hold their own against superior numbers, that we knew very well what they could and would do when driven to desperation.

Though seemingly brought to the end of their tether, they were still able to fight one more bloody battle—so bloody that it would have brought sorrow to the hearthstones of very many thousands, North and South.

Mr. Lincoln saw all this; he often talked to me about it, and when he came to City Point it was with the intention to bring about a peace, even if he had to waive some point to the Confederate generals.

The kindness of his intentions was shown when he agreed to the late Justice Campbell's proposition to allow the Virginia Legislature to convene in the State-House at Richmond, as related in the last chapter.

Another proof of Mr. Lincoln's determination to bring about peace was that he would not permit any member of his Cabinet to join him at City Point.

Mr. Seward telegraphed several times to the President for an invitation to visit him at that place, with other members of the Cabinet; but Mr. Lincoln, on each and every occasion, positively declined to have them come there. He had his own views, and determined to carry them out, unhampered by the opinions of his advisers.

General Grant and the President were in perfect accord in all matters relating to the surrender of the Confederate forces ; for, while the latter had the most implicit faith in General Grant's ability as a leader of armies, he had also great confidence in his good judgment and humane feelings.

Grant's most generous treatment of the Confederate army at Vicksburg, after its surrender, satisfied the President that he would be equally generous to Generals Lee and Johnston. I am quite sure that General Grant shared the convictions of the President, that we should deal with the Confederates in the most generous manner and thereby bring about a lasting peace.

I was present almost always at the interviews between the President and General Grant, and, though the former did most of the talking, General Grant agreed with him in his views of the situation.

Thus it was that Sherman, after his interview with the President on board the River Queen, became impressed with the latter's desire to terminate hostilities without further bloodshed, and that the most liberal terms should be conceded to his opponents.

Why it was that such a howl was sent up at the North when General Sherman entered into an agreement with General Johnston I don't know, especially as that agreement was to be submitted to the Government for confirmation.

There are points in those terms of capitulation which, it seems to me, should only have been decided upon by the Government itself, which, it will be perceived, is what General Sherman intended in the agreement drawn up between him and General Johnston. He had been so impressed with the President's views of concluding a peace that he desired only to carry out—after his death—what he supposed to be his policy, and which, if living, he felt certain Mr. Lincoln would have approved.

At least he would have considered it, and would not have "rejected it with the disdain" exhibited by the new President, Andrew Johnson, through his Secretary of War, Edwin M. Stanton.

It seemed to be the policy of the Secretary of War to lose no opportunity to throw a stone at those who had made themselves prominent in the Rebellion. Even if Sherman had made a mistake, his great services entitled him to better treatment than he received at the hands of Mr. Stanton.

How deeply he felt this treatment was shown when he arrived in Washington with his troops, and was invited upon the platform whence the President and his Cabinet were reviewing them. He deliberately refused to take Stanton's hand when the secretary stepped forward to greet him.

It is now twenty years since the interesting events referred to took place ; most of the actors in those scenes have gone to their final resting places. The passions which animated men in high places have died out, but Grant and Sherman still live, and are gratefully remembered by their countrymen for the invaluable services they rendered during the most trying times of the Republic's existence.

After the surrender of General Lee, the President, being satisfied that everything would be settled according to his wishes, determined to go to Washington, and I was only too glad to have him go. I had a strong feeling that something would happen to him if he remained longer at City Point. I was so anxious about him that I obtained his permission to send an officer up with him, who was never to leave his side. For this purpose I detailed Lieutenant-Commander John Barnes (the commander of the Bat) to go on board the River Queen, and never to leave the President's side, even at meals. If I remember rightly, I also sent two ensigns, who were to keep watch over his state-room at night. Directions were given to have the River Queen thoroughly searched before she started, to see if there were any strange men on board, and to arrest and confine any strangers who might be found on the vessel during the passage up. In fact, no precaution was omitted that would insure the President against violence.

The Bat, as already stated, was a very fast vessel. I directed Lieutenant-Commander Barnes to have her run close alongside the River Queen all the way up to Washington, and to have her ready to render assistance in case of necessity. I had not forgotten how the Greyhound had burned up, and how near we had all come to being badly burned, or having to swim for it.

Barnes was further ordered to be armed at all times, night and day, and to hold his position of guard to the President until he landed him safe in the White House.

This duty was performed most effectually and agreeably to the President, who felt very much pleased to have Barnes about him, and made him sit near him at all his meals.

As soon as the President had arrived safely at the White House,

Barnes returned to me. I still felt uneasy, and determined to go to Washington myself and see that Mr. Lincoln did not expose himself to the attacks of assassins.

I jumped on board the Tristram Shandy, and directed her commander to put on all steam and land me in Baltimore, thinking I could get to Washington sooner by that route. We arrived early in the morning, and I sent a mate on shore at once to get me a conveyance to the depot. The mate returned in about twenty minutes. His ghastly face told an awful tale ; he could not speak when he came into the cabin, but fell upon the sofa and shook like an aspen-leaf.

"What is the matter with you ?" I asked. "Be a man and tell me ; is the President dead ?" My prophetic soul told me that must be so. It was some time before the man could speak. At length he stammered out, "Assassinated !" and then I knew I had come too late. I might, perhaps, have saved his life with my persistent precautions, which he did not at all object to. I should have been about him until all excitement was over, and would have impressed the Cabinet with the necessity of guarding his person. I am not now, and never have been, given to great emotions ; but when I heard of Mr. Lincoln's cruel death I was completely unmanned. I went immediately to Washington and saw him as he lay in his grave-clothes ; the same benevolent face was there, but the kindly smile had departed from his lips, and the soft, gentle eyes were closed for ever.

"There," I said to a friend, "lies the best man I ever knew or ever expect to know ; he was just to all men, and his heart was full to overflowing with kindness toward those who accomplished his death." I have been satisfied that the persons who called at the Malvern were some of the assassins who would have killed him there if they could have got on board, and they could easily have escaped in the confusion by jumping overboard and swimming to the shore, which was not more than twenty yards distant. Moreover, I do not think that the prime instigator of the deed was ever suspected, though I have my own opinion on the subject, as also had Senator Nye, that stanch old patriot who held, in the latter part of the war, a position somewhat analogous to that of a minister of police, or was in consultation, by the wish of President Lincoln, with the police authorities of our great cities. He picked up many interesting incidents in relation to the President's assassination which he talked about freely to me ; but he was a prudent man, and a politician, and did not desire to raise questions which might affect his personal interests in the future.

Perhaps it was better for Mr. Lincoln's happiness that he died when he did. Had he lived, he would likely have been involved in bitter political feuds, owing to his liberal opinions in regard to the reconstruction of the States. He was of too sensitive a nature not to feel the shafts that would have been hurled at him by those whom he thought to be his friends, and he would not likely have been permitted to carry out his ideas. As it was, he died a martyr to a great cause, and venerated by all those who loved the Union; and while the names of many who held high places in the State will be forgotten, the memory of Abraham Lincoln will live in the hearts of his countrymen while the art of printing exists—by which his name can be handed down to posterity.

CHAPTER XXV.

THE following story is supposed to have been written by the admiral's coxswain, and is founded on facts. It is somewhat embellished, as a tale of this kind would naturally be when related by a coxswain, since persons in that rating are apt to be afflicted with lively imaginations:

CORPORAL FOSTER AND HIS DOG.

I was serving on the Lakes during the war when a call came from the Mississippi squadron for some blue-jackets. Me and some other sailors determined to ship, so we met together and took a few schooners all round.

At the rendezvous we found an old retired sailing master in the navy, Mr. Handspike, sitting under a tree with his coat off, trying to keep cool, and an old civilian doctor following his example.

We were the first chaps that had offered, and old Handspike's eyes glistened as he looked at the chance of hooking three likely-looking chaps, although I rather shook in my shoes when he eyed my short leg.

"Never mind my leg, sir," I said. "I am good at beating to windward in making a long and short leg of it, though I can't sail fast off the wind."

"Well," said old Handspike, "what can *you* do, Jack, on board a man-o'-war?"

"Sir," says I, "I can hand, reef, and steer, box the compass, heave the lead, and make all the hitches and bends in creation."

"Ah," says he, "we don't want none of those things in the Mississippi navy. Can you catch sheet lightning as it goes by you?"

"Yes, sir," I said, "and give it a start of one hundred yards."

"Can you slide down a water-spout, Jack?" said the old man. "Dive deeper and come up drier than a mermaid? Can you timber-hitch two catamounts together, can you swim across Niagara River heading up stream, can you clove-hitch a stern-wheel boat's shaft to a cotton-wood tree, and can you skin a live alligator with your teeth? for them's the kind of boys we want in the Mississippi squadron, and we wants lots of 'em."

"Yes, sir," says I, "I can do all that, and more too; but my name ain't Jack; it's Jim Blazes, from Ocrakoke Inlet, at your service, and I'm just the fellow you want in the navy to set a torpedo under the bottom of an enemy's vessel."

"How will you prove all that, Jim Blazes?" said old Handspike; "it strikes me you're pulling rather a long bowline."

"Well, sir," said I, "here's Jack Tiller and Joe Easty; they'll swear to it on 'Bowditch's Navigator,' and if you'll write to Ned Blinker, on board the ironclad My-Aunt-don't-know-Me, he'll tell you he's seen me do all I brag of often's the time. Ned and me sailed together three voyages; he knows all about me; but so does Jack Tiller here; he's truth itself."

"Looks like it wastly," said old Handspike. "Well, Jack Tiller, what can *you* vouch for?"

"I don't exactly know, sir, what pint of the compass that is," said Jack; "but this I do know: Jim Blazes is as good a fellow as ever robbed an apple-orchard, and he ain't a chap as would prewaricate about such a small matter as you've been talkin' about. I never knowed him to slip up on his word mor'n five times in my life; once was when he promised Captain Spanker that he wouldn't drink but fifteen 'tots' and would come on board in twenty-four hours, 'stead of which he drank about five hundred 'tots' and stayed ashore a week; and when the captain asked Jim how he come for to do it, he said he made a little mistake in his figures; and the captain had such confidence in Jim, and knew that he'd sooner die than prewaricate, so he said it was all right and made him a present of a bran new sou'wester."

"Well," said old Handspike, "I see you three fellows are all of a kidney, and I suppose either one of you can do as much as Jim Blazes claims to be able to do."

"Not quite, sir," said Jack Tiller. "I can beat Jim on the chain-lightning dodge, and Joe can beat him divin', but we're a hull team, Mr. Ossifer, and you'd better ship us."

"Well," said the jolly sailor, "you've passed your professional examination, and I'll turn you over to Dr. Lollipop. Put 'em through, Doctor, mentally and physically. You diagnose them as well as I did in seamanship, and we'll have three of the best fellows shipped this season."

"Well, my man," said the doctor to me, "how old are you ?"

"My name is Jim Blazes," says I, "sir, but I don't know how old I am."

"What countryman are you ?"

"Don't know, sir. My father was Irish, and he married a Scotchwoman. Then my mother died and my father married a Frenchwoman ; then my father died and my mother married a Frenchman ; then my mother died and father married an Indian squaw ; and then my father died and mother married a member of Congress."

"Stop there !" roared old Handspike ; " you're lying now sure."

"No he ain't," said Jack Tiller ; "it's all true, as I could prove to you if I had some papers now on board the My-Aunt-don't-know-Me, in charge of that friend I spoke of."

"Well, Mr. Blazes, did you ever have the measles ?"

"Yes, sir," said I, "three times."

"And the chicken-pox ?"

"Yes, sir ; and I've had the small-pox six times."

"I never heard of such a case before," said the doctor in astonishment.

"Oh, yes, sir," said I ; "it's a different disease in different parts of the world. In Africa they vaccinates from the rhinoceros, and up in the Artic they vaccinates from the polar bear."

"Well, Mr. Blazes, did you ever have the whooping-cough ?"

"Frequently," said I ; "and I always cure myself by taking a little of Mrs. Winslow's Soothing Syrup. I always carries a bottle with me wherever I goes."

"Let me see it," said the doctor, "if you have any, for I believe you're stuffing me."

I handed out my bottle and the doctor tasted the medicine ; then

he took a good swig, and, winking his eye at the sailing master,
"I'll be hanged," says he, "if this here ain't prime whisky."

Old Handspike took a nip, and, looking at me sternly, said :
"Jim Blazes, it's against the law to take whisky into the navy ;
you'll have to leave this bottle with me."

"No you don't, sir," says I.　"I know the law as well as anybody, and to guard against all precautions I have labeled that medicine 'Hop Bitters'; that's what all the officers do, and they know
the ropes."

The doctor stared at me.　" One more question," said he, "and
I am done with you.　Have you cut your eye-teeth yet, Mr.
Blazes ?"

We all passed our examination and got our certificates, also a
passage ticket to Cincinnati, where a Government steamer was to
take us to Mound City, near Cairo, Illinois.

To make a long story short, we arrived safe in Cincinnati, not a
man of us deserting—we were not that kind of rot ; but I mustn't
forget to mention that old Handspike gave us some ham sandwiches
and a bottle of soothing syrup to take along with us in the cars,
so we hadn't the slightest desire to leave our seats.

When we reached Cincinnati we marched to the United States
steamer Champion at the levee, and found ourselves, with over a
hundred other sailors, booked for Uncle Sam's Western navy.

The captain sang out, "Stand by to cast off !　All aboard !" and
told the first officer to sit on the safety-valve, and away we went
down the river to the tune of "Yankee Doodle," played by a steam
calliope stuck up abaft the wheel-house.

I now considered myself enlisted for the war and liable to be
fired on at any moment by the numerous guerrillas who infested
the river-banks, and I was ready to fire back as soon as I could find
out where the muskets were kept.

Besides the officers of the Champion, we had on board as passengers Captain Foster, known as "Corporal Foster," and an aid
to the admiral, both of whom were going down to join the squadron.

Corporal Foster had with him no less than six setter dogs, for
what purpose no one could imagine.　They were the rummest set I
ever saw—up to all kinds of tricks ; and one brown dog, which the
corporal called Ned, was a wonderful animal, and could beat the best
acrobat I most ever saw.　Ned would take a nip from the corporal's
flask whenever he was invited, but he would never take a drink

from any bottle unless it was marked " Hop Bitters " or " Soothing Syrup."

Such was the discipline of the navy at that time, and such the anxiety to conform to the law of Congress against spirituous liquors, that no officer or man in the service would take a drink out of a bottle unless it was marked " Medicine."

The admiral's aid was a jimmy-looking youngster, up to his knees in a pair of long boots, with the seat of his trousers " re-enforced " like a cavalry man. This led me to believe that his business was to go about on horseback ; but when I got to learn how things were done in the Mississippi fleet, I ceased to wonder. I did not know how soon I might be called upon to grapple with chain lightning or go to the weather-earring of a smoke-stack.

Corporal Foster soon got acquainted with everybody in the steamer, and there wasn't a sailor there who didn't want to serve under his command in case the corporal got one. He said he was only a privateer, and was going down without orders to see if he could get the admiral to let him have one of the India-rubber iron-clads building in Louisville.

Says the corporal to the aid, " How is the admiral on dogs ? Is he weak ?"

" Well, rather," said the aid ; " he's fond of shooting."

" If that's the case," said the corporal, " I'm all right. I'll get the best ironclad on the river. There's only one man I'll give my dog Ned to, and that's the admiral, and he'll kill more birds in a day with Ned than he could with twenty other dogs."

On the 10th of May, 1863, the Champion hove in sight of Mound City, and everybody rushed on deck to see the navy-yard. I could see nothing but water and trees, with occasionally a chimney appearing through the woods ; but at last the navy-yard was pointed out to me with a large wharf-boat lying alongside of it.

But, my eyes, what a navy-yard ! It was all among the trees that lined the bank of the river. There was ten fathoms of water where Mound City once reared its imposing head of fifteen houses. The Mayor's house was out of the water, occupying an Indian mound, which gives the place its name.

Everything that was above water was in full activity. All kinds of shops for building and equipping a navy were on rafts and in steamboats ready for transportation to any part of the Mississippi ; indeed, it was not uncommon to see the whole navy-yard get under way from Mound City and proceed where it was most needed.

As soon as we arrived a signal went up from the wharf-boat—
"Vessels send to Champion for detachments of men"—and in less
than half an hour I was on board the Forest Rose bound up the
Tennessee River. Before I left I made Jack Tiller promise to
write and let me know everything that went on, and a short time
after my arrival I received the following letter :

"DEAR JIM : Here I am all ship shape and Bristol fashion
A, No. 1, copper fastened, and sound in timber-heads, dead-eyes,
and chain-plates, and app'inted coxswain to the admiral on board
his flag-ship when he gits one, until which times he and his coxswain hists their flag on board the U. S. wharf-boat supposed to be
lyin' alongside the levee at Mound City.

"Well, Jim, perhaps you'll wonder how all this came about,
and I can only say my good looks done it for me. After we was
put in line on the quarter-deck of the wharf-boat, the admiral says
to me, 'What can *you* do, Jack ?' 'Anything you please, yer
honor,' says I. With that the admiral picks up a fifty-six-pound
weight, slings it three or four times round his head, and then let it
fly at me, saying, 'Catch that, Jack !' and catch it I did all over,
for before I knowed it I was all in a lump on the quarter-deck, and
didn't know which was me and which was the fifty-six-pounder.

" 'That's lesson fust, Jack Tiller,' says the admiral. ' I wants
my coxswain allers to be ready for emergenses and never to lie when
the truth will answer better. You'll be all right after bein' with
me a week,' says the admiral ; 'now pick out a crew for my barge.'

" 'Yes, sir,' says I, ' yer honor, but there ain't no barge, least-
wise above water. I'm tole there's an old one down in the mud as
belonged to Admiral Foote when he fust come out here.'

" 'Never you mind about the barge, Jack Tiller ; that'll come
afore you know it. Go look after the barge's crew ; no man less
than six feet wanted, and they must be able to do everything.'

" Just then Corporal Foster came on board and introduced hisself to the admiral, all his dogs sittin' in a row on their stern-sheets
with their right paw to their forelock, same as if they was a touchin'
of their hats.

" The admiral looked at him very stiff, and says he, 'Sir, it's
customary for officers to call on me in uniform. See Navy Reggerlations.'

" 'Why, Lord bless me, Admiral !' says the corporal, ' if you'd
only knowed how I've been fixed, you'd give me credit for gittin'

here any fashion. I started from Injianner on a mule to jine you, and strapped my chist on the critter's back in such a way as I never supposed he'd git it loose ; but the fust day out and twenty miles from home, blest if he didn't unlash that chist and kick it all to pieces. My clothes was so wallered in the mud that you couldn't tell a full-dress coat from a ditty-bag. And here I am all stannin' in the best I got with my sword on.'

" ' Sir,' says the admiral, ' the reggerlations forbid any officer to wear any part of his uniform in citizens' dress.'

" With that Corporal Foster unbuckles a rusty-lookin' sword which looked as if it had been lyin' six years at the bottom of the river, and, turnin' to the dogs, says, ' Here, Ned, take charge of this here sword,' and with that the dog got on his hind legs and wobbled to his master, tucked the sword under his arm, and tuk his station among his shipmates.

" Says the admiral, ' That beats blanegan. I think that dog knows mor'n you do, Capting.'

" ' Jist so, Admiral, and he kin command a squadron as well as any officer in your fleet. There's no knowin' what he can't do ; try him, sir.'

" ' Ned,' said the admiral, ' tell my steward to bring me and Capting Foster a glass of hop bitters.'

" Ned laid down the sword and scampered off, and in less than two minutes he returned draggin' in the steward by the leg with the two glasses of hop bitters, which was drunk in no time, and bizness perceded.

" ' Now, Admiral,' says the corporal, ' I brought them six dorgs all the way from Injianny jist for you to pick and choose from, an' for that matter you can have the hull kit an' biler of 'em.'

" I tell you, Jim, the Foster stock went up quicker than I ever seed it in Wall Street. If there was any pint the admiral was weak on, it was huntin' dorgs, an' I berlieve if he was engaged in attackin' a battery an' a flock ov quail flew over, he'd take his dorg an' go in persute ov 'em.

" ' Well, Capting Foster,' says the admiral, ' I'd like 'em all, but I h'aint got no flag-ship gist yet, and I'm only boardin' for the present on to this here wharf-boat. When I get a flag-ship I'll fit 'em all up comfortable ; they'll help while away many a weary hour.'

" ' What kind of a flag-ship do you want, Admiral ? ' says the corporal.

"'Well,' says the admiral, 'I want a big double-engine steme-bote as can accommydate twenty sekkertaries and clerks, have lots of state-rooms, a place for twelve horses, two cows, a lot of hens, et cetrur, et cetrur.'

"'Good-mornin',' says Corporal Foster, an' off he went with the dorgs to borry a tug of the fleet capting, an' very soon he was a steamin' down to Cairo. As he came in toward the levee there was a big steamer a comin' up, with her name in big letters between the smoke-stacks, Uncle Sam.

"Corporal Foster hailed her, and says he, 'Lay to; I want to examine your papers,' says he. The corporal went aboard, slapped the capting on the back and shuck his hand till he nearly wrung his arm out. Says he, 'Where's your papers, Capting?'

"'Why,' says the capting, 'I h'aint got no papers, and wot's more, I never heerd of sich a thing!'

"'Then,' said Corporal Foster, 'I seize you as a prize and der-ilick.'

"'A what?' says the capting.

"'A derilick,' says the corporal, 'and you must prepare to go along with me.'

"'Well,' says the capting, 'I never heerd of no sich perceed-in's; this war has turned everything topsy turvy, and there's no more virtue in the land,' says he.

"'Wot's your old craft wuth?' says the corporal.

"'She's wuth so much to me,' says the capting, 'that I won't sell her.'

"'I didn't ask you to sell her,' says Foster; 'I only intend to buy her.'

"'It takes two to make a bargain,' says the capting, 'and you can't buy her without my permission.'

"'Well, wot is she wuth anyhow, Capting?'

"'Thirty-five thousand dollars,' said the capting, 'and I guess it'll bother you to raise the money, for you don't look as if you could raise five dollars.'

"'Fust and foremost,' says Foster, 'I seizes you as a bony fidy prize, a derilick without papers on the high seas, for if these aint the high seas I don't know what is. Second, I go your thirty-five thousand dollars and five thousand better, and close the bargain. Third, I seizes you for pub. ser., which takes away all ownership from you and rests it in Uncle Sam. Fourth—'

"'Hold on there, Mister,' yelled the capting, 'that's enuff. I see plain that sum of them there clauses is goin' to fotch me. I cave in; gimme forty thousand dollars and take the old critter, an' my heart's broke.'

" 'All right,' says the corporal; 'steam up to the wharf-bote an' we'll settle the bizness. Here, Jack Tiller, take the helm.' Jim, you bet I was there, and the way I steered that ole Uncle Sam into the wharf-bote was a caution. I only mashed one carpenter-shop, sunk the iron-plating department, and broke the paddles off the port wheel.

" 'She's yourn now,' says the capting; 'you kin do as you please with her—let her rip. But on the hole, Coxsin,' says he to me, 'you done as well as I ever see the navy do in these waters, if not a little better.'

" The Uncle Sam was soon tied up, and the mechanics was all so busy in swimmin' that they didn't notice any irregularities in the performance of the everlootion.

" Corporal Foster walked into the front parlor of the wharf-bote with his dorgs, took off his hat, while all the dorgs sat on their stern-sheets in the most respectful manner.

" 'Admiral,' says the corporal, 'your flag-ship is alongside, an' ready to perceed to sea at a moment's notice.'

" 'What flag-ship do you mean, Foster?' says the admiral, and jumped up, lookin' out the winder at the big steamer loomin' up above the wharf-bote, with a wooden Indjun representin' Black Hawk standing up fifteen feet high between the smoke-stacks.

" 'Jist what I wanted, Foster,' says the admiral; 'how'd you git her?'

" 'She hadn't no papers,' says the corporal, 'an' I seized her as a prize. She was a derilick, and I have no doubt she comes under the head of flotsam and jetsam. Then I bought her out for forty thousand dollars and seized her for pub. ser. the way the army does.'

" 'That's the strongest claws of all,' says Foster, 'and when I tole the captin you was that kind of a man who, if he wanted his great uncle's bones for the pub. ser., he'd take 'em, he caved in. The vessel's yourn, with everything a man can want—crew, cooks, stewards, incloodin' bed and table linen,' says the corporal.

" The paymaster was called in and the hull matter was soon arranged. The Uncle Sam was ourn and the owner had his forty thousand dollars. The captin sat there very melancholy. 'Admiral,' says he, 'there aint no more virtue in the land since this war bruk out. You've done bruk my heart; me an' my old gal as has stuck together for thirty years must part. You'll get a flag-ship as is a flag-ship; her upper works is from fair to middlin', but she wants an entire new hull; her bilers were condemned eight years ago, and she can't carry only ten pounds of steam. Her shaft is broke in three places, but you can't see it for the putty. We keeps six siphon-pumps agoin' and the steam pipes all the time. Her steam-chist has busted thirty-six times in the last two years, and killed four men, and she's bin on fire twenty-two times. She's full of rats, cockroaches, and bedbugs, but if her cook can't make the best lobscouse and slapjacks in this country I'll eat him. I couldn't get no charter,' says the captin, 'for the army wouldn't tech me. I tried to get seized for the pub. scr. No, sirree, no one wanted the likes of the Uncle Sam. I offered to sell her for twelve thousand dollars, but they said she wasn't good for anything but fire-wood. An' here in the nick of time comes this navy feller and relieves me from all my difficulties. Wall, arter all, there's more vartue in the country than I thought there was, and I wishes you all a good-mornin',' says he; 'and don't forgit Jim Longeye in case you wants to buy another bote.'

"The admiral looked at Foster and Foster looked at the admiral. 'Admiral,' says Foster, 'I don't believe a word of it, sir, an' I'll find out quicker than you can skin an eel,' and he started on his inspection.

"On his way round the steamer he diskivered a big bote twelve feet long an' eight feet wide; so he sends for the carpenter an' orders her to be cut in two in the middle and lengthened fifteen feet, ordered a new bow and stern put into her, new sides, new bottom, thwarts, and stern sheets, so that, when she was finished, the admiral had as nice a barge as ever you see.

"Corporal Foster was perfectly satisfied with the inspection of the Uncle Sam, an' went to work to onst to move the admiral an' all his baggage right on board. A bottle of Mrs. Winslow's syrup was broke over her bows an' the Uncle Sam was transmogrified into Black Hawk, an' the admiral's flag hoisted at the mizzen, an' there she was all ship shape an' Bristol fashion.

"Foster painted her with three rows of sham port holes, an' if she warn't the most dangerous lookin' ship of the line I ever see, my name ain't Jack Tiller.

"When Corporal Foster had fixed the admiral to his satersfaction he put a brass collar on the dog Ned, with 'Admiral Porter' engraved on to it, an' wen the other dogs seen it, bless me if they didn't set on to their stern sheets, with their tongues lollin' out, and duck their heads to him, an' they allers arterwards showed him the respeck due to their superior officer.

"The next day arter all this was done the admiral says to Foster, says he, 'Foster, I owe you one ; I'm a goin' to order you to command the Indier rubber iron clad Larfyett. She's a double back-action, copper fastened, invulnerable A number 1 ship of war now buildin' in Loocyville. Here's your orders, so git up an' git without delay.'

"The corporal grinned all over, an' says he, 'Admiral, you'll find I'll handle her without gloves,' an' so, makin' his *salam*, he started for Loocyville.

"You must know, Jim Blazes, that I'm allers about the admiral, an' he can't do nothin' without me ; that's the how and whyfore I sees all and hears everything that's goin' on.

"I can't tell you all the doin's of this here fleet, but I will tell you some of the doin's of that remarkable dorg Ned, what I never seen the likes on afore. He takes his seat regular right by the admiral's desk waitin' for orders. He'll empty the waste basket, call the steward when hop bitters is wanted, wich keeps him tolerable busy, bring the admiral's slippers, and walk in to dinner when it's ready.

"He's learned to read the steme indykater hisself, an' wen there ain't enuff steme on he'll carry a log of wood in his mouth to the furniss and make a fireman chuck it in. He'll bark like blazes if the night lamps ain't lit in time, an' wen he sees a rebel skulkin' on the banks he'll seize a musket from the rack an' pass it to a marine to fire. I'm most afrade to tell you all the dorg can do, for you're such a allfired whopper teller yourself that you won't berleeve anybody wot's telling you a reasonable thing.

"Why, one day Ned seed a officer a takin' a five gallon demmy-john of wisky abord his ship. He seized it by the handle and run it right abord the flag, for he knowed as well as any Christian it was agin' the reggerlations. Yet he'd let fellers carry boxes and boxes of hop bitters on bord an' never sed a word, cos that warn't agin' the law.

"Another time a officer accidentally took the admiral's cap. Ned ran after him, grabbed the admiral's cap off his head, ran aboard the flag ship, and laid the trofee at his marster's feet.

"But to hurry up my story. I ain't a goin' for to tell you about the takin' of Vicksburg ; it was tuk, an' no mistake, an' the admiral ordered Corporal Foster in the Larfyett to the mouth of Red River, an' follered him down in a short time.

"Wen we got there in the Black Hawk, Foster was a lyin' in his vessel at widdow Angler's landin', an we hauled in there likewise an' staid several days.

"The second day two ladies come down to the levee to see the admiral, an' was admitted on bord; an' now, Jim, I'm goin' to tell you the funniest thing you ever heern tell on. These ladies had already pade Corporal Foster a visit, an' he prepared the admiral as to what kind of craft they was. There was all kinds o' craft along the river, but we never see nothin' as quite come up to them two.

"These ladies warn't at all put out wen they went in to the cabin to find a dozen officers all in uniform. They was both in short huntin' skirts, had on high top boots, an' carried double bar-reled guns an' fixin's, and each had a pinter dorg.

"'How air you, Admiral?' says the oldest one. 'I'm Mrs. Angler an' this is Mrs. Jenkins. We're uncommon glad you've come, coz all we Union people is sufferin' dreadful at the han's of the rebbels, an' we wants pertection,' an' she smole sich a smile as no admiral could resist.

"'Yes,' says Mrs. Jenkins, 'we've bin crazy to see you, an' we set up all night watchin' for your lights.'

"'Yes, marm,' says the admiral, bowin' low, 'it is deliteful to see so much Union feelin' all along the river. Why, they did nothin' but fire off guns all the way down, an' the only objection to it was, they forgot to take out the shot. In consikence, they bruk some of my winders an' killed my best cow.'

"'Oh, mi, how shockin'!' said the widder Angler. 'Deer Admiral, I'll give you two fresh cows to make up, for I'm Union all over, ain't I, Julia?'

"'Yes, dear,' says the widow Jenkins, 'an' I go ten better than you, for I'll give the admiral four fresh cows with calves.'

"'Thank you, marm,' says the admiral, 'I borrowed as many as I wanted from the *Union peeple* along the river, but I'm much obleeged to you.'

"'You've jist come in the nick of time,' says Mrs. Angler. 'Genral Kirby Smith, C. S. A., is goin' to make a raid on our side of the river, an' you kin help me run in my cotting to the river bank, where it'll be safe under your guns till I kin send it to New Orleens on Ginral Banks's pass.'

"'Madam,' says the admiral, 'I can't meddle with these matters. It's agin' my orders. I turns 'em all over to the Treasury agints.'

"'But, Admiral,' says the smilin' widder, 'we is so Union you'll make a diffrunce in our case. Besides, Admiral,' she wispered, "wen the six hundred bales gits under your guns you'll get a check for twenty thousand dollars for your oldest darter.'

"'Thank you, marm,' says the admiral, 'but my darters is pervided for ; their grate grand unkil died lately an' left 'em a million dollars apiece.'

"'Well, then,' says the widder, 'it'll do fer your son ; he won't turn hiz nose up at twenty thousand.'

"'No, marm,' says the admiral, 'certingly not. My son is a second lootenant of marines, an' he's already laid up sixty thousand dollars off his pay.'

"'But then yourself, Admiral,' smiled the pretty widder. 'You wouldn't mind having the money to buy a pretty cottage after this kruel war is over.'

"'Thank you kindly, marm,' says the admiral, 'but I've got six cottages aready, an' kin only occupy one at a time. I hev one at Newport, one at Cape May, two at Long Branch, a palace in Pennsylvania, an' a magnifercent mansion at Annapolis Junction. No, thank you, another cottage would be the fether as would brake the kamel's bak. Besides, marm, the U. S. Government takes most libberul care of me while livin', an' propose at my deth to give my wife a penshun of ten thousand a year, with five thousand to each ov my children. Besides, I saved over six hundred thousand dollars ov my lootenant's pay, an' what would I want more ? But,' says the admiral, 'I shall be extremely happy if you ladies will breakfast with me,' wot was eggsactly wot them two widders wanted. They had tried that game with Corporal Foster, an' if he'd a bin there a week longer by hisself, or if he'd bin admiral, he'd a caved in sure, for they'd nearly reached his price.

"Lord bless you, Jim, how them pretty widders did rattle away at that table under the effex of the shampane the admiral served out to them, while he hisself stuck to hop bitters ! They sailed all around him, and flung out their handsomest flags in way of signal.

"But the admiral was like Nelson at Copenhagen : he allus put his spy glass to his blind eye.

"Then they fired on him with every gun they kud bring to bare, at long an' short range, with grape an' shrapnel. Then they'd make all sail, in hopes he'd give 'em a chance ; an' when they seed he wouldn't, they'd double reef their topsails an' furl their courses. But it warn't no use. He sot and sipped hop bitters, an' nary a shot of theirn ever struck him below the water line ; an' wen any of his riggin' was shot away he'd splice an' knot it together agin so handy that they'd never see how it was done.

"At last the widders caved in, an' Mrs. Jenkins says, in a pout, 'Admiral, you hain't got no heart or you couldn't resist the plees of two han'som' wimmen.'

"'Thank you, marm,' says he, 'jest so ; I never have no heart after breakfast, an' if you please, marm, I'll attend now to orficial bizness.'

"'But, Admiral,' sez the widder Jenkins, 'we've come pertick-erly to ask you to come a shootin' with us. We have millions of game on the place, an' the finest dorgs in Louisianner.'

"'Now,' says Corporal Foster, 'the admiral's a goner. He can't stan' that.' An' sure enuff he couldn't. Says he, 'I don't care if I do jist try my dorg Ned, who, I'm tole, is the best dorg for huntin' in the world.'

"Lord, Jim Blazes, how them two smiled all over ! It wos like ships in stays an' the sales all beginniu' to flutter.

"The admiral went an' put on his huntin' cote an' called Corporal Foster, an' says he, 'Do you know I thinks them are widders intends to git me out in the country a huntin,' an' wen my gun is fired off to capture me an' turn me over to the rebbels ? So you come along too. Jack Tiller, you carry my bird bag, an' put a rewolver into your pocket. An' Foster,' says he, 'git us haf a doz-en bawl cattriges apeece ; we don't know what fellers these widders may have stowed away in them bushes out yander.'

"But didn't the crew stair wen they see the admiral an' his reti-new ! An didn't the widders giggle an' skip along like two young deer !

"Widder Jenkins says to the admiral, 'Parley voos frongsay ?' 'No, thank you, marm,' says he, 'not too much,' though the ole koon he knowed the French 'parley voos' like a duck. Then the widders began to jabber in French together, wile the admiral he tuk in every word they sed.

"Says widder Angler, 'I jist want you to cross this feeld an' look at my pile of cotton. I know youre hart will relent, Admi-ral, wen you see it,' an' she tole the other widder, in French, 'there was a pile of fifty bales all by theirselves, an' wen I tell him it's hisn it'll fetch him sure ; no man kin stan' that.'

"Just at that moment the dog Ned began to sniff the air, an' crawled along to a Virginny fence; then he jumped on the fence and stuk out his tale like a tug's tiller, an' then he turned his hed an' looked at the admiral.

"The admiral crawled up an' looked through the fence; then he let drive both barls, when, hevins an earth! I never heerd such a flutterin' as there was in that field. The Ad. had seen a large covey of quail sittin' with their heds together, an' he killed every one in the lot.

"The dog Ned ran off barkin' an' growlin' in a most unaccountable manner. All the hair on his back was turned the t'other way, an' he looked more like a catamount than a dorg. After barkin' hisself horse an' refusin' to be passerfied, he run away clean, only stoppin' once to sit up on his stern sheets an' put his paw to his nose, as much as to say, 'I knows you, Dicky Riker.' That was the last the admiral seed of that ere dorg for a long time to come.

"'Jack,' says the admiral, 'present them birds to the ladies.'

"'Does you suppose I'd tech your birds?' said widder Jenkins, turnin' up her lip like the clew of a mizzen royal. 'What do you take me for? Why even your dorg is disgusted with you. No, sir, I'm a sportsman, not a pot hunter, an' if that's what you Yankeys calls sport, I'd advise you not to gun much round this country, or you'll get lynched.' The admiral was cool as possible, while Missus Jenkins was a bilin' over. Then widder Angler tuk it up. Sez she, 'Ef I was in reach of a justice of the peece I'd hev you arrested, sir, for poachin' an' trespassin'. There ain't a admiral in the Confed'rit serviss as would hev done sich a thing. It maid even your dorg desert the flag, the dirty rag you sale under. An' there's Captin Foster looks as if he was a goin' to desart you too, an' sarve you right.'

"Foster didn't say a word, but he looked mighty glum.

"'What's up, Foster?' says the admiral; 'is you a sidin' with the ladies?'

"'Well, sir,' says the corporal, 'that's werry sharp practis. I an' Ned ain't use to that kind of shootin', an' ten to one he'll commit sooicide.'

"'Not a bit of it,' says the admiral; 'he's a desarter, an' if I catch him I'll try him by court martial an' shoot him. *Bong joor*, ladies,' says he; '*jer parl frongsay komme voo!*' an' off he walked back to the ship.

"The widders tried to persuade Corporal Foster to go gunnin' with them, but he saw the signal from the flag ship where the admiral had arrived for all ossifers to repare on board. So he hed to say good bye to the ladies, an' we didn't see them widders no more.

"Wen Corporal Foster got on bord the flag, the admiral says to him, 'Foster,' says he, 'that was a mighty narrer escaip we had. Did you see them fellers a movin' among the bushes? I knew wen I slottered them ere birds the two sportin' widders would rile up, an' my objec' was to pick a quarrel an' not go no further. They'd a had us in ten minutes more.'

"'Thunder!' says Foster, 'who'd a thort it? now I see it awl. Old Sam Weller was rite about widders, an' no mistake.'

"'Well, Foster,' says the admiral, 'this is a lesson to you; keep clear of them widders; don't call on 'em, an' be perticilar an' don't take tea with 'em. If you catch Ned, try him an' hang him. I'm goin' right up river, an' as you're short ov men, I'll leave Jack Tiller an' the barge's crew with you, an' mind, look out for the widders.'

"Haf a hour arter that the flag ship was a boomin' up river an' I was under command of Corporal Foster.

"The fust thing ole Foster did was to stick a long hickory pole over the bow an' rig a torpedo catcher, which was a deep net descendin' below the bottom.

"That same night there was a tremenjous flutterin' in the net, an' the lookout sings out, 'We've cotched a alligaiter!'

"The captin run forrard with a Springfeeld rifle an' sings out, 'Who's there? I'm goin' to shoot!'

"'Don't shoot,' hollers out a feller in the net. 'I'm a torpedo an' I might explode!'

"'Ah,' sez the corporal, 'you're there are you? Bring up fifteen more Springfeelds an' stan' by to fire wen I tells you. Now, Mister, answer my questions or I'll blo' you to smithereens.'

"'Anythin' you like, Mister Ossifer, but don't fire. I'm a Union man.'

"'Wot kinder torpeder you got there?' says Foster.

"'Two twenty pound dynymite, bound to explode in forty minutes.'

"'Let 'em explode then,' says Foster. 'They can't hurt us!'

"'O Lord! save me,' says the torpedo.

"'Who sent you on this expydition?' says Foster.

" 'Widder Angler an' widder Jenkins,' says he.

" 'Jump inter the gig, boys,' says the corporal, 'an' take them ere things an' put 'em right under widder Angler's stable ;' an' werry soon we planted them torpedoes accordin' to orders.

" We hauled the prisoner outer the net an' stowed him away in the cole hole.

"Then we sot an' waited, an' in a few minutes if there wasn't a commotion in them regions my name isn't Jack Tiller. The barn wos full of hay and cotting, an' wen the torpedoes busted the explosion sounded like as if a thousand guns had gone off all to once. Stones, planks, an' shingles fell around us like hale. One old mule lit rite on top of our safety-valve. Then the ruings tuk fire, an' the burnin' of Moskow wasn't a circumstance to it.

" 'I guess we're even with them widders, Tiller,' says the capting. 'Just look at 'em streakin' across the feeld,' an' sure enuff, by the lite ov the fire there was the widders goin' lickety split across the country, makin' for the woods, an' they hadn't stopped to put on their huntin' soots either—not much ! It struck me they looked as much like Wenus as anythink I ever see.

"Cows, hosses, dogs, cats, pigs, an' chickens was all runnin' for deer life, an' it was enuff to make a cat larf to see 'em jumbled together an' goin' like mad.

" 'That's the last torpeder the rebs ever sot for us, an' I rekon wen the rebbel Sekkertary of the Navy heern tell on it he larfed t'other side ov his mouth.

"Just two months arter this a ole nigger come alongside in a kanoo, an' says he, 'Massa Captin, I bring you some noos by wich you kin make your fortin'. My ole massa is a Union man, an' about a week ago the rebs done give him a beatin' with a cowhide coz he wud continer to draw his penshon from Uncle Sam. He said he'd be a Union man as long as they'd pay him, an' I bleev they'd all a done the same.'

"Then the ole darkey tuk from his wool a small roll of paper informin' Captin Foster that some of Kirby Smith's ossifers an' men had been haulin' cotton with mule teams to a place three miles below the mouth of Red River ; that there was now one hundred and twenty bales ready for shipment at that point, an' if Captin Foster would start that nighte at 12 he would bag all the cotton, the soldiers, an' the steemer that was goin' to take it to Noo Orleens. An' the ole darkey would pilot him to the pint where the capter could be maid.

"If there was anything Corporal Foster had a nose for it was cotton. I've known him, goin' down the river twelve knots a hour, sniff the air an' then give the horder to round to, an' sure enuff berhind the levee would be a bail or so of cotting wich he would littrally bag.

"Thare was grate excitement on bord the Larfyette. Fifty men was picked out an' armed with Remington rifles, five botes was got ready, an' by ten that nite we was all prepaired.

"Corporal Foster had on a ole suit of gray an' a slouch hat; his trousers were stuck in his boots, an' he looked like a reglar hoosher an' no mistaik.

"The five botes sheved off, the ole nigger goin' as gide in charge of two men, who had orders to blow the top of his hed orf in case of any trickery.

"'I shoodn't be susprized,' says the corporal, 'if I come in contact with them two widders before I git back. If I do, an' they're up to any of their tricks, I'll give 'em sich a spankin' they won't be able to set down for a week,' says the corporal.

"In an hour we arrived within harf a mild of the place, an' then went ashore, leavin' a few men in charge of the botes, an', piloted by the ole darkey, we crawled along under the levee as quiet as mice; au' arter a while the ole darkey pinted out the waggins, an', by the lite of a fire, the rebs was seen sittin' around eatin' their grub very quiet an comfortable.

"'Now, boys,' says the corporal, 'I'm goin' in to hold some conversation with them fellers. You crawl up towards 'em; wile I'm talkin' to 'em an' amoosin' 'em you creep in an' surround 'em. Wen you heer me sing out "Corporal Foster," advance on 'em with fixed bagnets, but mind don't fire onless I tell you. Now,' says he, 'guard agin all precautions.'

"The capting walked along, an', on account of the stampin' of the mules, the rebs didn't heer him, an' he was right among 'em afore they knowed it. He hadn't even a jacknife to defend hisself against the sixteen men the rebs had. The fust thing they knew, says he, 'How are you, pards, kin you give a feller some supper?'

"In a instant there was a dozen muskets pinted at the corporal.

"'Who are you?' says the leader of the gang, 'an' wot in thunder are you doin' here?'

"'Wall,' says Foster, 'I ain't afrade, anyhow; I'm too hungry, an' this havin' been made a free country by the Confed'rit Government, I guess I can peramberlate round without axin' any one's opinion. Hev you anything to say to that, Gin'ral?'

"'The kompliment of bein' called gin'ral was too much for the rebbel ossifer, an' he lowered his musket, sayin', 'Stranger, you come mitey neer gettin' a ball thro' your hed just now, an' you must be a darned fool to go wanderin' round among sodgers.'

"'I'm allers gettin' into trouble,' says the corporal, 'wanderin' round where I oughtn't to, an' I hev three or four balls in my hed now in conserkence. The fact is, I seen them cows up thar an' was a lookin' for a bucket to milk 'em in. I couldn't use my hat,' says he, 'coz it's full of holes.' An' so it was, sure enuff, for the corporal used his hat for a target wen he practiced with a rifle.

"'Look here,' says Foster, 'can't you give a feller a mouth-full?'

"'Well, yes,' says the leader, 'pervided you do your share of loadin' the steamer when she comes.'

"'Of course,' says Foster; 'I'll not only do that but I'll put more cotton on board than any three men here.'

"'Bosh!' they all sung out, 'but if you don't we'll cob you.'

"'All right,' says Foster, who sot hisself down and began to eat so voracious that the rebs thort he was goin' to breed a famin'.

"'Grashus heavings!' says the hed rebbel; 'stranger, if you don't stop you'll bust your biler!'

"'I ain't eten nothin' solider 'an milk for three days,' says the corporal, an' then he began tellin' stories an' a shoutin' an' a laffin' so that they didn't hear us closin' in around 'em. But the captin saw the ends of our bagnets as they poked over the levee, an' thort it was time to be movin'. Stretching hisself, he says, 'Gin'ral, considerin' I'm expected to put most of this cotting on board a steamer to pay for my supper, I must say this is the meanest square meal I ever sot down to. If the Confed'rit Guv'ment can't do no better'n that, it had better git up an' git. On the hull, I berleeve I'll shirk my contrack, and won't tech the cotton onless you give me a bottle of wiskey an' a boned turkey.'

"With that the leader of the gang jumps up an' sings out, 'Seize that feller an' duck him, an' make him drink a bucket of river water.'

"'As sure as my name is Corporal Foster,' says the captin in a loud voice, 'the fust man that moves dies.' An' the rebels found themselves covered with 4 dozen rifles. The rebbels subsided to wonst wen they found how things was goin'. Our master at arms slapped the darbies on to the men, an' a guard was put over the ossifers.

"'Now,' says the corporal to the prisoners, 'boys, what do you think of the damned ole hoosher, as one of you corled me just now? But don't be fritened; I won't eat you, notwithstandin' your bad supper. But it was the best you had, an' I'll give you a better one.'

"'Here, Mr. Spangler,' says he to the fust lootenant, 'take all these peeple back to the karts. I see the lites of the steemer a comin' up. Keep 'em under strick gard, an' if any man tries to signal that steemer, or hollers to put 'em on their gard, bagnet him at once.'

"Pretty soon a big fast stemebote come up to the levee and threw out her lines, wich our men made fast to the trees.

"Doorin' this time thirty ov our men was behind the cotton bales, an' the moment the gang plank was run out they rushed abord, heded by our cheef engineer and assistunts, who tuk charge of the mersheenery.

"Captin Foster walked quietly up to the stemebote captin, who had jist lit a pine torch which showed the han'some countenance ov our ole frend Captin Longeye, who sold us the Uncle Sam.

"The poor devil was took quite aback wen he saw the corporal, an' wen that ole Injannyman tuk from the bak ov his cote a Arkansaw tooth pick two feet long and hauled a revolver out of his pocket, Captin Longeye dropped his torch an' sot down on a box cov'rin' his face with his han's. 'The jig's up,' sez he, 'an' I'm a goner agin!'

"'Yes,' sez the corporal, 'you're derilick agin on the hi' seas, an' you'll be hung for violatin' the articles of war, wich forbids givin' aid an' comfort to an enemy. Put the darbys on him,' says Foster to the master at arms, 'an' tie him to a stanchion,' which was done. Then the corporal lectered him on the enormity ov his crimes, sellin' a vessel to the Gov'ment wich he admitted hisself wasn't seaworthy. Then committin' piracy on the high sees by touchin' cotton which he knew the navee was only waitin' for a chance to gobble. Then his consortin' with rebbels, the enemies of the Guv'ment, an' last, but not the leest, violatin' the Constitooshun ov the United Staits in not obtainin' the admiral's permishun to navergate these waters. 'Horrible!' says Captain Foster, 'horrible!'

"Old Longeye hadn't a word to say, but could only grone and cry, 'I'm a goner!'

"'Now, Tiller,' says Corporal Foster, 'you take the wheel, and mind you don't sink half a dozen macheen shops and run agin the bank.'

"In three hours we had all the cotton, oxen, mules, and prisoners on board the steemer, an' in harf an hour after we was alongside the Larfyett, me a steerin', an' I tell you, Jim Blazes, the way I brought that there vessel to her position would a done your heart good to see.

"I only smashed the Larfyette's port quarter bote an' knocked orf six paddle bords by runnin' into the tug wich was lyin' astern. You never seen a come too done better in the navee, tho' ole Long-eye, in his spite at bein' took prisoner, did say to me, 'You know as much about steerin' a Mississippi stemebote as a elephunt does about dancin'.' The only anser I maid was to put a rope round my neck an' hold it up very significant, wen he subsided with a grone.

"Wen we mustered the rebbels on bord the Larfyett we found we had the follerin' prisoners : Kurnel Krawfish, C. S. A., Major Grayback, Captins Dumplin, Bushhead, an' Leaky, two sargents, one korporal, an' eight privates. The ole darky, who had been our pilot an' done such good servis, went home before the rebbils could ketch site of him, informin' one of our men that he would be alongside the Larfyette some fine mornin' with his wife an' eight children with a lot of chickens an' turkeys belongin' to the Confed'rits. The last thing he sed was, 'I shall take all the spoils ov the Confeds, Massa, an' mo' besides.'

"Corporal Foster invited the kurnel an' major to mess in the cabin, an', supposin' they was tired, showed them to their stait rooms. As the kurnel was about to shet his door he says to the corporal the fust words he had spoke to him. 'Captin Foster,' says he, 'the thing I hate wust about this bizness is havin' to sleep a nite under the folds ov the blarsted Union flag ; it's enuff to maik a man sick !'

"'Well,' sez the corporal, 'don't let that trouble you, for the last time I spent the nite in that ere stait room it was run away with bed buggs and cockroaches, an' I couldn't close my eyes. There must be about a million of 'em there now. If you like, I'll lay an American flag over the bed, an' the bugs can't get through it, though the cockroaches will flop down from the cracks overhead.'

"Well, you may bet your life Kurnel Krawfish, C. S. A., sub-sided, an' we heered no more from him till next mornin'.

"'Wen the kurnel an' major was called to brekfast their faces looked as if they had had small pox. They didn't say nothin', but sot down an' et.

"'Kurnel,' says Corporal Foster, 'here's some spring chickens off widder Angler's farm an' some fresh eggs, an' here's some splendid porter house stakes off them cattle of yourn, an' some nice butter an' hominy from Captin Longeye's stores. Help yourself, an' eat as much as you want, for if all your meals is like that supper of yourn last nite you must be allfired hungry.'

"'Never mind, sir,' says the kurnel, mity dignified; 'every dorg has his day, Captin Foster. It may be your turn next, so you'd better stop pokin' fun at me; an' remember, sir, I'm a pris'ner.'

"'I sha'n't forget it,' says the corporal, 'an' have doubled the sentrys, with orders to put a bullet through the fust pris'ner what goes too near the ship's side.' Arter that, ov course the conversation warn't animated.

"The pris'ners had been aboard two days wen Captin Leaky come to Corporal Foster an' says he, 'Captin, I've somethin' very particlar an confidenshal to tell you.'

"'Well, start your mill,' says old Foster, 'an' grind out your meal,' wich was a figger of speech the ole man sometimes used for short.

"'Well, sir,' says Leaky, 'the kurnel and the major is both goin' to be married, an' the weddin' is sot for this day week, an' all the preparations is maid.'

"'Jerusalem!' says Foster. 'Well, go on.'

"'Now,' says Leaky, 'I'm come from the kurnel to ask if you'll parole us long enuff to hav' the seremony performed. Me and Captin Dumplin and Bushhead is to be groomsmen, an' the kurnel will giv' a solem' promiss to come back the day arter the weddin' and stop with you until we are reg'larly exchanged.'

"'No, sirree,' says the corporal, 'not if this Court know hisself. Why, do you suppose I want to hav' the admiral hang me for aidin' an' abettin' the enemy, which he would do easy as rollin' off a log? Not as you knows on. I'm not one ov them kind. Let the weddin' wait. Perhaps arter a time the parties will cool off.'

"Leaky begged and praid for an hour, tellin' wot a horrible condishun they was placed in, an' wot suffrins the captin mite save the two lovely hangels wot they was about to lead to the hymenial halter wen this catastrophy overtook 'em, an' wen all the money they expected to use in gettin' the bridle truesow was gobbled up by the capture ov the cottin.

" ' May I ask,' says Corporal Foster, ' wot mought be the names ov them two luvly angels as is goin' to lead them hossifers to the halter ? '

" ' Well,' says Captin Leaky, ' I will tell you in strick conferdence. Perhaps their naims an' suffrins will tech your hart. If you could only know them ladies you would wencrate 'em for their virtoos, innosense, an' beauty. They are so kind an' angel like they wouldn't hurt a mouse, an' all their time is spent in works ov chairity. Kurnel Krawfish hopes to lead to the hymenial halter the bootiful Missus Jenkins, my cousin, the widder ov the lait Kurnel Jenkins, who cut his throat six months ago in a fit of delirium tremens. Major Grayback proposes to jine hands with the luvly an' accomplished widder Angler, whose late husband didn't come forward to jine the Confed'racy wen the war broke out. As it is a case ov wife desertion, we pronounce 'em divorced.'

" ' I see,' says Foster.

" ' Now, captin,' says Leaky, ' I put the matter afore you as a hi' toned Kristian gentleman who loves his feller creeters an' who can picter to his own gen'rous sole the evils that will foller if this weddin' should be postponed, the ag'ny ov them there lovely angels whose nites pass in teers owin' to the capter of their future husban's, the dispare ov the two noble men you hold as pris'ners, the disappintment ov we three young men who have spent three barrils full of Confed'rit notes buyin clothes an' weddin' presents, an' the satisfaction it will give two other fellers who are also courtin' the widders an' rejoicin' over the misfortins ov we pore fellers this very moment.'

" ' Look a hear, Leaky,' says Foster, ' you're a young man, an' that's why you talk so much like a idiot. Don't you remember wot Sam Weller's father told him—"Don't have nothin' to do with widders." '

" ' Yes,' says Leaky, ' but these isn't the common run ov widders ; they're angels.'

" ' Jes' so,' says Foster ; ' I've heard ov 'em, an' their bein' angels may make a diffrunce. But on the hole I like the way the Hindows treat their widders ; they burn 'em up ; an' in some ov the South Pacific I'lands they like the widders so much they eat 'em. I've no doubt these officers would do the same six months after marriage ; an' by keepin' 'em here until they are exchanged, the widders will marry them other fellers, an' these two gallant officers will thank me in the end.'

" ' You are a hard harted man, Captin Foster,' says Leaky,
bustin' into teers an' cryin' like a child.   But Foster only said, ' It
can't be done, an' there's no use talkin'.   I don't want to be hung,
an' I won't be for the angelest widder in the Southern Confed'ricy.'

" Captin Foster seemed to be reel sorry coz he couldn't graterfy
the young feller ; but Leaky soon got over his disappintment, as
Foster cheered him up.   At last Leaky says, ' Captin, I'll thank
you for a chew of terbakker.'   Then the captin' knowed he was
saved.

" Then they talked ov various matters and things till Leaky forgot all about the widders an' his unhappiness, till finally he sed,
' By the way, Captin Foster, do you kno' we captured your admiral ? '

" ' Captured wot ? ' says Foster, jumpin' up, an' me an' all the
men as was near closed up to heer wot was sed.

' " Yes, sir,' says Leaky, ' your admiral is in our possession a
pris'ner ov war.'

" ' How in thunder did you hear that ? ' says Foster.

" ' Well,' says Leaky, ' I saw him captured.   I was thar.'

" ' When ? ' says Foster.   ' Speak quick, or you'll hear from me.'

" ' Well,' says Leaky, ' it was about three weeks ago we cort him
swimmin' across the river, picked him up, and hav' had him ever
since.'

" ' Bosh ! ' says Foster.   ' I heered from the admiral four days
ago ; he's in Cairo.'

" ' But,' says Leaky, ' we captured a brown setter dorg with a
brass collar marked " Admiral Porter," an' we call him the " Admiral," and if there's one person been to see him after hearin' the
admiral was captured, there's been a thousand.   He's the rummest
dog I ever seen, an' can do more tricks than a slite ov hand performer.   People tried so hard to steal the dorg that the kurnel had
to detail a gard ov ten men to watch him.'

" ' Jupiter ! ' says Foster, ' how wonderful is the ways ov Providence !   If I hadn't captured this ere party I'd never heerd of that
ere dorg agin.   There should be some compensation in orl things,
an' I think the kurnel deserves his reward an' his widder.   I'll tell
you what I'll do, Leaky.   You can say to your kurnel that I'll exchange your hole party for that dorg, pervidin' he is brought to
me safe and sound under a flag of truce along with those too booti-

ful widders, when the exchanges of the officers will be maid out an' they can go where they pleas'. Moreover, I pledge myself to have maid for the weddin' out ov old Longeye's flour, sugar, and eggs a hundred pounder cake for the weddin' feast an' will put into the middle ov it a diamant ring wuth not less than a hundred dollars.'

" 'Will you ?' says Leaky, his eyes stickin' out with astonishment, an' away he run down into the cabin to tell the kurnel wot Foster had sed.

" In about haf a minite Kurnel Krawfish bounced on deck, his face red as a biled lobster, his hare standin' on end, an' his eyes stickin' out. He walked strait up to Corporal Foster, who was busy that moment seein' how often he could squirt terbakker juice into a spit box.   He didn't see the kernel, but, when the old feller sung out, 'Captin Foster, how dare you offer me sich a insult ?' et cetery, and so forth, 'Hello,' says Foster, 'wot's up, whose killed, and what's soured the milk ?'

" ' 'Why,' says Kurnel Krawfish, 'you've offered me an' my officers the greatest insult one man could offer another, proposin' to exchange me for a setter dorg !'

" ' 'Yet,' says Foster, 'Captin Leaky jumped at the offer, an' nearly broke his neck in the hurry to get to the cabin.   Did he tell you ov my proposin' to throw in a hundred pound cake, an' to get the two pretty widders here to receeve you an' take you home ?'

" ' 'What !' says the kurnel, 'does my ears dereceive me ? Am I alive ? Does any one dare address such talk to me an' live ?'

" ' 'Yes, sir,' says Foster, 'I dare, an' there's the shore, an' you needn't consider yourself a pris'ner durin' the time you an' I are settlin' any little dispoot.'

" The kurnel looked as if he would like to jump on Foster, but the corporal was six feet four an' had a arm like a blacksmith.   So the kurnel quieted down an' walked back to the cabin, went into his stait room, where he tuck all his meals, an' couldn't be persuaded to come out.

" This lasted two days, an' it only wanted five days ov the time sot for the weddin', while, as Leaky techingly remarked, 'them two angelic widders was a bustin' their harts and weepin' pearly tears, every one ov wich was wuth a fortin.'

" Forternately, greef don't last for ever, an' wisdom comes by experience.

" In the course ov forty eight hours the kurnel wanted to see his widder, the major wanted to see hisn, and the three captins wanted to git the wuth ov the nine barls of Confed'rit munny they had spent atween 'em in weddin' presents an' outfits. Major Grayback didn't see things in the same lite as the kurnel, and the three captins thought Krawfish a darned ole fool for puttin' on sich ares.

"There was a grate pow wow goin' on all day long for three days among the pris'ners, an' they almost wore the cabin ladder out runnin' up an' down.

"The rest ov 'em went down on their knees to the kurnel, till finally Major Grayback told him he beleeved he wanted to git outer his engagement to the angelic Missus Jenkins, an' that the other feller who was a courtin' of her would carry her off, an' he hoped to dance at his weddin', for wich languidge Kurnel Krawfish said he demanded satisfaction as soon as they got on shore.

"Howsomever, that last remark ov the major was the camel as broke the feather's back, an' the kurnel said, 'Do as you dam plees, only I shall resine from the army as soon as I am married an' go au' establish myself in Timbuctoo. Don't let me,' says he, 'ever see that man Foster's face agin, even wen I am leevin' his ship; an' if ever I take him pris'ner I will put him to death on the spot.'

"'I don't see how that can happen, Kurnel,' says Grayback, 'as it isn't likely Foster will ever go to Timbuctoo; an' if he does, you will be so glad to see a white man there you'll embrace him on the spot.'

"Captin Leaky lost no time in tellin' Foster the kurnel had agreed to the exchange, and seemed reddy to bust with delite. Foster then handed him the follerin' paper for signin':

"'We, the undersigned, for the mutual benefit ov the Gov'ments ov the United Staits and the Suthern Confed'racy, do cov'nant an' agree to what is hereinafter set forth, whiz:

"'Captin Foster, better known as Corporal Foster, does agree to liberate the Confed'rit officers whose names are sined to this paper, an' permit them to return to there homes in exchange for one brown setter dorg call Ned, a desarter from the Mississippi squadron, provided the said dorg Ned is delivered into the hands of Captin Foster on bord the U. S. S. Larfyett, free ov expens to the United Staits, within three days' time from dait, wen the Confed'rit officers whose naims are sined to this paper shall be allowed to depart with their side arms an' effects.

"'Provided further, That the said dorg Ned, a desarter from

the Navy ov the United Staits, shall be handid over to the sed Foster by those two angelic widders, Mrs. Jennie Angler an' Mrs. Julia Jenkins, in person, to whom a recete in full will be given for the saim.

" 'Provided further, That the sed Foster binds hisself to have maid a weddin' cake not less than one hundred pound wate, in the highest stile ov art, for the weddin' ov the two angelic widders aforesaid ; which cake he is to present to them on the quarter dek ov the Larfyett as a piece maker.

" 'Unto wich the hi' contractin' partys do hereunto set there hans an' seels this   day ov   .'

"This dokkyment was submitted to all the parties consarned, who awl agreed to it except the kurnel.   He almost jumped out of his boots in his raige.

"He wouldn't here of his fieansay visitin' Foster's ship, an' he demanded to see Captin Foster at once.

"The corporal invited the hull party into the cabin to discuss the matter amercably, an' said he would satisfy 'em all that the terms was the best in the world for all parties consarned, an' said how easy it was for 'em all to get off for only one pris'ner in return.

" 'Do you mene to put us on a par with a dorg ?' says the kurnel.   'That's outragus !'

" 'An' then,' says Foster, 'just think ov our lib'rality in purvidin' a hundred pound cake to eat at the weddin', to say nothin' ov the bootiful present that will be in the insides ov it.'

" 'Konfound your kake an' present !' says the kurnel ; 'I want none ov it.'

" 'Jes' so,' says Captin Foster.

" 'An' let me tell you, Captin Foster,' says the kurnel, 'I objec' to any lady ov my acquaintance, especially one to be connected with me by marriage, visitin' your ship under any circumstances whatsomever.'

" 'Jes' so,' says Foster, 'but let me tell you I heered yesterday through an old darkey named Washington Buggs that "hi jinks" was bein' plaid while you was away, that Kurnel Fiddles was clean gone on your widder, an' she had promised if she didn't here from you in five days he should have a favor'ble anser.   The kurnel promises to spend nine barls ov Confed'rit scrip on the widder in case she'll hav him.'

"'Kurnel Krawfish jumped up an' rushed around the cabin, say-in', 'Woman, thi name is fralety,' ''Twas always this from chile-hood's 'our,' an' a lot ov other stuff I can't remember.

"''Jes' so,' says the corporal, 'it was allers so ever since I en-tered the navee, an' it allers will be so. An' I will furder remark that Mister Buggs, the cullud gentleman aforesed, importer ov the abov' mentioned startlin' news, did say in my presence that the angelic widder, Mrs. Jenkins, was very sweet on Kurnel Fiddles.'

"''I'll shoot Fiddles on site!' roared the kurnel, 'even if it's at the imenial halter.'

"''Jes' so,' says Foster, 'but Buggs says he thort if Kurnel Krawfish would appear on the ground soon as possible the widder would drop old Fiddles like a hot pertater. Furthermore, the kul-lerd gentleman said he bleeved the aforesed Kurnel Fiddles was a practicin' his trix upon the widder, an' magnetizin' her as sure as there are possums in ole Virginny, the State he come from.'

"''Poor deluded darlin'!' said the kurnel. 'Captain Foster, I accept the terms you offer, an' will get my fiansay here, out ov the way ov that willian's matchinations. If you'll permit me, Captin, I'll marry her on bord here, an' if you'll gimme a old kanoo, I'll drift with her all the way to Bayou Lafoorch.'

"''Jes' so,' says Foster, 'but how about your gettin' marred under the foles ov that detested flag a floatin' there?'

"''Oh, anythin' to save my widder from the matchinations ov that willian Fiddles—"the menes justifys the ends."'

"''Jes' so,' says Foster, 'but, as I wants you all to celebrate the cuttin' ov the pound cake, you must git marred to home.'

"After all matters was settled satisfactory, the kurnel held out his hand to Foster, an' the corporal shuck it so the kernel had to rub it that nite with operdeldock.

"Not a moment was lost, an' the tug bote (Jessie Benton) was to go up with a flag ov truce an' bring down the ladies and the pris-'ner Ned.

"Then Captin Leaky wrote a letter to each ov the angelic wid-ders an' to some other young ladies in the destrick.

"The tug left at two in the arternoon, an' was expected back before sunset, an' you may imagine there was joyful times on bord the Larfayett.

"About five o'clock the tug was reported comin', an' wen she got close the quartermaster said as how blue and red signals was a flyin', but he cooden't make 'em out. But wen the tug come close we see it was the enchantin' widders, an' our dorg Ned in the bow a barkin' like mad.

"As soon as the tug got alongside, Ned jumped abord an' flung hisself at Captin Foster's feet; but the captin didn't notiss the trator, but tole the master at arms to put the kriminal in dubble irons an' put a gard over him. An' away slinked pore Ned with his tale atween his legs an' teers runnin' out ov his eyes like they was pored out ov a waterin' pot.

"Corporal Foster receeved the two ladies at the gangway, who jumped abord like two fairys into the arms ov their futur' husbans. There was never such joy an' happiness on ship bord since Noer's arc grounded on Mount Aryrat. All hans tuck tea that evenin' in the captin's cabin, an' kep up the enchantment till late at nite.

"In the course ov conversation the widder Angler remarked to Captin Foster, 'Captin, if you had accepted my invitation to tea that nite I asked you, the boot'd a bin on the other leg, an' you would now have been in Shreveport.'

"'Jes' so,' says Foster; 'but how so?'

"'Well,' says she, 'I had Major Grayback stowed away in the kitchen with eight men ready to carry you orf.'

"'Jes' so,' says Foster, 'an' jus' before dusk I seen 'em in the distance, an' in case I had gone on shore I had detached twenty marines to surround the house. If the major will remember, wen he come out that nite he couldn't find his hosses. We captured 'em, an' not wishin' to cors bloodshed an' stampede your chickens, we let matters rest there.'

"The widder Angler never smiled a mite, an' Major Grayback tried to turn the conversation.

"'But,' sed the pretty widder Jenkins, 'we came neer baggin' that ole pot hunter ov an admiral, an' if he'd a gone a mile furder we'd a bagged the pare ov you, an' we'd now be showin' you off in a cage.'

"'Jes' so,' says Foster, 'only the ole pot hunter was wider awake than any ov us. Wen he left the ship he ordered twenty marines to foller him on shore as soon as he'd got four hundred yards away an' keep close to us all the time. Seein' your men in the bushes, an' not wishin' to have you ladies accerdenterly get a ball in your bussles, he took advantage ov the oppertunity to fire into them birds an' distrack your attention. As you got mad an' abused him, he pretended to be too, an' turned back; but if ever you meet the officer who commanded those Confed'rit soldiers, he'll tell you he was so hard chased he had to throw off his milingtary boots, an' his men had to throw away their guns an' 'napsacs, an' we picked 'em all up.'

"Widder Jenkins didn't smile a mite after this, an' the kurnel tried to change the conversation also.

"Then they all sed they was tired, an' went to bed, the ladies sleepin' in the captin's cabin.

"Next mornin' at eight o'clock the tug was reddy to take all the Confed'rits to their homes, an' all sed they was sorry to leeve. As they was gettin' into the tug, Foster says, 'Ladies, there's one pusson you never asked about, an' that is your torpedo you sent down on me one nite, an' who got hooked into our torpedo net. We've got him yit, but you kin have him if you want him.'

"'Good Heavings!' sed the widders, 'we thort you killed him; you're a deer good man; do give him to us.'

"'Jest so,' sed the corporal. 'Master at Arms, bring up the Confed'rit torpedo,' an' up come the most remarkable objec' you ever see.

"It was a human bein' stripped to his waste, with the American flag painted all round his body an' the Union jack in the middle ov his chest. His legs from the 'nees down wos painted with red and wite stripes. One side ov his face was blue, t'other side red. Oh, but he was a booty! The women shreeked wen they see him, an' the crew give three chairs.

"But the torpedo was too glad to git away on any terms. He dove hed foremost into the tug an' hid hisself among the kole. It took him a mouth to get that ere paint off, for it was dried on an' covered with two cotes ov varnish.

"Well, the ladies waved their handkerchefs an' the men their hats, an' the tug was soon lost site ov in the mouth ov Red River. The last thing we see was the big weddin' cake on top ov the pilot house, but we never agin sot eyes onto them angel widders an' their fyansays, but we heered on 'em once more on their weddin' nite.

"Now, that job bein' off Corporal Foster's hands, he sent for the fust lootenant, an' says he, 'I'm a goin' to try Captin Longeye an' condem the steemer Lively Peggy for bein' derilick an' for her captin affordin' aid an' comfort to the enemy an' for gen'ral depravity.'

"'But, captin,' says the fust lootenant, 'a Cort of Admiralty can't be established without a act ov Congris.'

"'Congris be whittled,' says the corporal. 'I'll show you that

I'm a law unto myself an' can establish any kind ov court I plees. Sims the pirate did it, why shouldn't I ?   Bring up the pris'ner, Captin Jim Longeye.'

"The corporal went to his cabin, sot out pen, ink, an' paper on his table, and sot down in full uniform to wait for old Longeye.

"Pretty soon the ole raskle appeered in charge of a orderly an' the fust lootenant an' sot hisself down in a chare.   'Stan' up, pris-'ner, in the presence ov the Cort,' said the corporal, 'an' hold up your right hand.'

"Captin Longeye was quite pail an' looked chopfallen.   His eyes wos red, an' he hed evidently been dosin' hisself with hop bit-ters, ov which the corporal had sent him a full allowance.

"'I don't know as I'm a pris'ner,' says Longeye, 'an' I don't reckernize enny Cort of Admiralty this side ov Springfeeld, Illinoy.'

"'Jes' so,' says the corporal, 'an' I'm a branch ov that Cort. Now, Captain Longeye, you had best be quiet.'

"'Well, sir,' says Longeye, 'I spose I must go when the devil drives.'

"'Jes so,' says Foster.   'Now,' says he to his clerk, 'take down the pris'ner's ansers.'

"'I would like to know, Captin Longeye, what you are doin' up here consortin' with rebbils an' runnin' off C. S. A. cottin wich ov rites all belongs to the U. S. Gov'ment ?'

"'You may ask the question,' says Longeye, 'but it don't foller that I'll anser it.'

"'Write down,' says Foster, 'derilick on the hi' sees, givin' ade an' comfort to the enemy an' violatin' the articles for the better gov'ment ov the navee.'

"'I objec' to that,' says Longeye.

"'Jes' so,' says Foster ; 'rite down "disrespect to Cort—fine fifty-eight dollars."'

"'Lord help me !' says Longeye, 'I'm in the hans of the Fillis-tines an' must cave in.'

"'Jest so,' says Foster ; 'I'm glad you have come to realize your precarious condition, for if you don't swing it won't be becors you don't deserve to.'

"'Now, Captin,' says Foster, 'plees inform me, so help you Bob, how much you cleered wen you palmed the Unkel Sam off on to the Admiral as a A No. 1 copper fastened ship insured Lloyds.   You told us you offered her for twelve thousand an' couldn't get that.'

"'That was all gas,' says Longeye. 'I was only braggin'.'

"'Jes' so,' says Foster; 'rite down "lyin' an' cheetin' the Gov'-ment out ov twenty-eight thousand dollars."'

"'No, sir,' says Longeye, 'I only cleered eighteen thousand dollars as I'm a Christian.'

"'Write down "lyin'" agin,' says Foster; 'he ain't no Christian; also "takin' advantage ov the Guv'ment in the hour ov need, wen evry man an' cittyzen (except navy ossifers) should come forward an' offer all they have for their country's use." One more question, Captin Longeye, an' I'm done.

"'Wot was you loaded with wen you landid an' communicated with the Confed'rit gov'ment?'

"'Well,' says Longeye, 'you may ask as many questions as you like, but it don't foller that I'll anser.'

"'Jess so,' says Foster. 'Mr. Jedge Advocit, rite down "10 hogsheads ov hams, 60 barls ov flower, 40 pare milingtery boots, 10 sets waggin harness, 30 revolvers, 7 hogsheads of sugar, 200 yards caliker, 200 pares yarn stockens, 2 baby cradles, 1,000 gallons rifle wiskey, et cetrer."'

"'Heavins and arth!' ses old Longeye; 'why that was all stowed under the cole. I hope the informer will be struck dum.'

"'Jess so,' says Foster. 'Now, pris'ner, stand up an' hear the sentens ov this Cort:

"'You will forfet the 160 bails ov cotton you stole from the U. S. Guv'ment. You will forfet all them stores with wich you intended givin' aid an' comfort to the rebbels, an' you will pay down ten thousand dollars, the amount you swindled the Guv'ment out ov wen you sold us the Unkel Sam. You can pocket the eight thousand extry, but you don't get outer mi hans till you pay up the balance.'

"'Where in blazes am I goin' to git ten thousand dollars from wen I ain't got ten sents?' says old Longeye, in a rage.

"'Jess so,' says Foster, 'but we found gist eighteen thousand dollars stowed away in that caliope ov yourn wich wouldn't play no how. So our engineer he tuk it to peeces an' found the munny. We'll just take ten thousand out an' you kin return the rest to the feller what it belongs to; no doubt you'll very soon have him en-quirin' for it.'

"Longeye fell on the deck as if he was shot, an' Foster says, 'Gentlemen, the case is closed agin' the pris'ner, an' the Cort stands ajourned siney dye.'

"All the officers an' men who had assembled at the cabbin doar to witness the proceedins applorded the just desision of Corporal Foster, an' wen we got on the forecastle we drew up ressolushuns votin' Corporal Foster a regular bric', an' recommendin', without a dissentin' voice, that five thousand dollars shoold be divided at once among the crew ov the Larfyett, under the hed ov salvage, an' the rest be pade to them wen they was discharged, under the hed ov prize money.

"In the meen time Captin Longeye lay like a ded man, altho the corporal pored near a gallon ov hop bitters down his throte, sayin', 'Let him injoy awl he can wile he lives.'

"Arter awhile he begin to sigh, repeetin' the immortal Webster's last words—'I ain't ded yit'—wen the corporal gave him a big tumbler ov the bitters, an' Longeye sot up on his elbo' an' looked all round.

"Wen his eyes rested on the corporal, says he, 'You'll ketch it for this, I tell you; you'll shake in your butes wen you hear I come up on a pars from Gin'ral Banks. An' here it is'—pullin' a paper outer his pocket an' readin' as follers:

"'Kno awl pussons that Captin Jim Longeye is authorized to proseed up river to sich points as he may seleck in the steemer Lively Peggy, an' open traid along the river, an' all ossifers ov the U. S. Gov'ment are cawled on to give him ade an' encouragement an' not to throw any hobstacles in his way wen hopening traid an' follerin' his legitimate bizness.

"'Given under mi hand an' sele this 26 day ov June, 1863.

"'BANKS,
"'Major Gin'ral, &c., &c.'

"'Jess so,' says Foster, 'an' wen you git back thar, if ever you do git back, you jist say to Gin'ral Banks or enny other gin'ral that I'm the commandin' gin'ral in this ere diocese, an' I reckernize no passes that don't come from the Admiral who is kommander in cheef on these hi' sees.

"'Now, Captin, I'll let you go with the Lively Peggy, coz I'm sartin to ketch you agin at derilick matters in less than a month. You hed better keep along with you a bag ov ten thousand dollars, as that'll be the amount I shall ginrally assess you. I shall divide your stores among me an' mi ossifers an' men. An' now'—spekin to the fust lootenant—'let him go an' compleat his kargo.'

"Captin Longeye went off a wiser if not a better man, an' after transferrin' all his cottin to our dispatch bote, the Gin'ral Lion, wich had just arrived, he steemed down the river fritenin' all the birds from their roosts with the horrible music from his darned ole calliope.

"Ten days arterward we see a bote pullin' up the other side ov the river with two men in her, an' wen she got hi' enuff up to allow fur the currant, she struck across fur the Larfyette.

"Wen the bote come alongside, who should appere but Marcus Aurelius Washington Buggs, the kullered gentleman who piloted us to the plaice where we captured the rebs an' cottin.

"Mister Buggs was accompanied by his father, who helped him pull the bote, his wife, eight children, his mother, granfather an' granmother (who was parrylized), six dorgs, four piggs, an' chickens too numrous to menshun.

"Besides awl this, in the stern sheats ov the bote was a quantity ov fine furniture, beddin', lookin' glasses, et cetrer, et cetrer, an' as Marcus Aurelius rose up in the bote an' wiped his forhed, he sings out, 'Here I is, Massa Corp'ral Foster; I tole you you see this ole darkey agin soon.'

"'Why, where did you come from, Marcus Aurelius, an' where are you bound?' says the corp'ral.

"'Well, Massa,' says the ole nig, 'I'm jist come from spilin' the Egyptians, an' escaped from 'em troo de Red See, an' I comes to recebe de pertecshun ov de Union flag.'

"'But,' says Corporal Foster, 'how did you come by that nice furniture?'

"'Well, I'll tell you, Massa, an' wen I done tell you you'll say, "Well done, good an' faithful serpent."

"'You must know, Massa Foster, dat dat ar weddin' took place six days ago wid de two ossifers an' de two widders, an' since dat time dars bin a cooin' like turkle doves.

"'Yesterday they kinder waked up an' maid up a gran' pick nick, an' all the village jined in. Yesterday mornin' dey all startin' intendin' not to come back till ten o'clock at nite.

"'Dere wasn't a wite pusson lef in de village, so wen dey was all out ob site I went to wuk spilin' the Egyptians rite an' lef, an' wen I had as much as my bote would hole I put out wid my famly an' here I is, tank de Lord, 'longside Massa Abe Linkum's gumbotes.'

"'Why,' says Foster, 'you ole raskle, I call that stealin' or robbin', praps both. You'll be hung if they catch you.'

23

"'Well, Massa Foster, it's a hard ting to tell wot's the diffruns 'tween steelin' an' robbin' or takin' in time ov war. You takes a bale ov cottin' wen you sees it lyin' on the levee, an' you rides orf on a hoss widout askin' who ones him, an' you walks inter a house an' takes wot prize you likes, an' you takes steembotes an' sugar an' cotton from people wot don't owe you nuffin. I only tuck my *wages*, Massa. Me an' mine hev wucked fur dem people goin' on morn a hundred yeers, an' they ain't pade us a cent. So we just help ourselves to *part* payments until we get a chance for de rest.

"'I'me tired ob libin' souf, an' me an' my fambly feel de want ov a more northern climate, specially arter spilin' de Egyptians. I kalkerlates our massa owes dis fambly 'bout eighteen thousand dollars fur de wuck we don fur dem, an' we pade ourselves in part— dat's all dere is to it.'

"'You are a suttle kasuist, Mr. Buggs,' says Corporal Foster, 'an' know how to draw nice distinctions.'

"'No, Massa,' says Marcus Aurelius, 'I ain't as bad as dat, no how, leest wise I don't know wat kind ov a animal dat is, as all I know ov drawin' is drawin' water an' totin' wood.'

"'Well, Granny,' says the corporal to the ole woman, 'how is you gettin' on?'

"'Me, Massa?' says the ole woman; 'my name ain't Granny; it's Rebecker; my ole man he's name's Isack. We's ole colored pussons ov de olden time; we done live togedder sixty yeers like Isack an' Rebecker wat de Skripter tell about, an' in all dat time we nebber hab a diffrunce ob opinion.'

"'Ceptin',' says Isack, 'dat time wen you cut my hed open wid de meat ax, an' dat odder time wen you done knock dese front teef out wid a flat iron.'

"'Yes, honey,' says de ole woman, 'we did disagree once a little about Mirandy Bobtale, but dat warn't noffin, nohow.'

"'An' Rebecker,' says Isack, 'you remembers de time you trow hot bilin' water on my foot an' laid me up fur two week?'

"'Yes, chile, but I only intended fur to scall your big toe wat you was a warmin' by de fire, an' was a tryin' to stick it inter de hoe cake. Dat was accident.'

"'Dat's so,' says Isack, 'an' I muss say youse bin a blessin' to me dese long years.'

"'Massa,' says Rebecker, 'I just wants some information. As Marcus Aurelius says, dis climate don't agree wid us nohow, an' we tinks ov movin' to Sarrytoga or Nooport, whar I'm told de climate is werry salubrious, an' I'm tole de quality is gwine away ebry summer to Yewrip, an' we kood git a cottage dar on resonable terms. I got in dis yer bag a hull pile ov Cornfed'rit greenbacks, nuff to live on all my life. I'se atey (84) foor now, an' Isack is ninety two, an' I gess dis'll las us till our time come.'

"'I only know ov two houses to let in Newport just now,' says Corporal Foster; 'one is Mr. Belmont's an' the other Mr. Lorillard's, but I guess you kin git ether on 'em at resonable raits. Now go alongside the Gin'ral Lion an' deposit your spiles, an', Marcus Aurelius, come back an' tell us about the weddin'.'

"So the boat shoved off an' shipped all the darkeys on board the Lion.

"Then Marcus Aurelius Washington Buggs returned an' reportid that he had deposited his passengers accordin' to orders.

"'Now, Mister Buggs,' says Foster, 'tell us about the weddin'.'

"'Well, Massa Captin,' says Buggs, 'it was thuswise:

"'Lots ov peepil was invited to see de ceremony at de house ob Gin'ral Blazes, de unkel ob de widder Jenkins, an' de performance ob de nupshall cerrymony was done by ole Bishop Crabtree, who tie de parties togedder so fass nuffin can ebber loose 'em.

"'Ebry ting was splendid—de brides was dress in der wite sattins an' lace wails an' gole slippers, an' all de jewelry dey could poke on em, an' dus dey was 'scorted inter supper. Dar was a table full ob grub fit fur a prince to set down to, an' all dat was wantin' to make it purfexin was a rale ole Virginny possum stuffed with inyons.

"'Dar was de big poun cake loomin' up like a eight tousan bail team bote, an' ebry eye was upon it. Dar was two cross mark on it whar de nife was to be stuck wen dey went fur de rings wot you sed was dar.

"'Each widder tuck a nife, an' wen de wurd was give dey socked 'em in up to de handle. Den come a eggsplosion like a pistil, wen de widders drapped de nives an' hollered like a hous on fire.

"'Den evry one sing out "Torpedo!" an' sich a gittin' outer doors you neber did see. Dey all run like so many rats, an' some ob em run tree mile.

"'Dis ole darkey crawl under de table an' lay dere waitin'. Fus I heerd suthin goin' like a 'larm clock, then somethin' struck up a chune, den some little bells rung, den de music go on onst mo', an' finin' dat dis ting go on adfernitum, an' no more exploshun tuck plaice, dis ole nig poke out he hed an' look at de cake, an' dar I see de most bootiful ting dis ole nigger neber saw befo. I open my eyes wid amazement, an' so cumfustered was I dat I thunk I was in parradise. I saw dat dar was no harm dar, an' I shouted to 'em all to come back an' see a 'mazin' site.

"'It warn't no use tellin' 'em de trufe for half a hour, an' den I succeeded in gettin' 'em all to come back too de weddin' feest. An' wot you think I see, Massa?

"'Dar was de poun' cake wid de top blowed orf, an' dere was a bootiful figger ob liberty wid de Union flag in her han' a leanin' ober a kullerd gemman in chanes, an' a motter in her odder han'— "Freedom to de slabe." An' she was a 'knockin' orf de shakles (as was on de kollered gemman's legs) wid a hammer. An' wat you tink dem shackles was? Wy two bootiful gole rings sot with diamants marked with eech widder's name, an' as they teched dem the musikle box plaid "Hale, Kolumby" an' den "Yankey Doodle," an' den dey all listened kind o' tranced until it woodn't play no mo', an' den you mought a heerd a pin drap.

"'Den de grooms went up an' tuck de shackles offer de cullud gemman's legs an' put 'em on de ladies' fingers, an' dey embraced each odder an' shed teers.

"'"Deer Captin Foster," says the widder Jenkins, "I'd kiss him six times ef he was here!" "And I," says Mrs. Angler, "would guv him twenty! Wy dese yere rings mus' a coss foor barls ov greenbax. If de kurnel an' de major had a known what dey was about, they'd a presented us with suthin' ov this kine for 'gagement rings, an' den dar wouldn't been any fuss about Kurnel Fiddles."

"'An' then ebry one gib three chairs for Captin Foster, an' dis ole nigger an' his posterity gib twenty—an' dat's all dere is ob it, Massa Captin.

"'De weddin' was kep' up till nex mornin' an' "Yankee Doodle" an' "Hale Columby" was plaid all nite long, an' dat's de fust spark o' Union feelin' I eber see.'

"'I am much oblceged to you, Mr. Buggs,' says the corporal, 'fur your interestin' narrytive,' says he, 'an' here's five U. S. one dollar greenbax for you, bran new ones at that, an' they're wuth morun ten barls ov Confed'rit notes.'

"Mr. Buggs's eyes opened wide as sorcers; he had never seen anythin' like it before. 'Wy,' says he, 'de Confed'rit greenback bears no mo' comparison to dis dan a skunk does to a elephunt.'

"'Now,' says the corporal, 'get along on bord the Lion; thar's the last bell ringin',' an' Mr. Buggs, bein' anxious not to lose his passage, shuck hans with everybody an' started, an' we never saw the Buggs fambly agin.

"Well, Jim Blazes, my tail drors to a klose. I hev only to say that Captin Foster reported the general fax ov the case to the admiral an' wrote a official letter about Ned the desarter, ov wich this here is a troo coppy :

" ' U. S. S. LARFYETT, MOUTH OV RED RIVER,
" ' —— 6th, 1863.

" ' ADMIRAL : I beg leeve to inform you that the desarter dorg Ned is now in my persession an' in dubble iruns under gard ov a sentry. I cannot, as you directed, try him an' hang him without a fully orthorized cort, an' I hev not officers enuff to form a cort. The cort should consist ov 13 to impress the squadron with the importince ov the occashun an' show 'em that dissipline mus' be manetaned an' disloyalty punished, an' I think this a case wher the mos' extream penerlty ov the lor should be sarved out.

" ' I hav some witnesses hear, but if there needs any evidence to show that the brown setter dorg Ned consorted with the wust kind ov rebbils, I recomommen' that a kullerd gentleman by name ov Marcus Aurelius Washington Buggs, now on his way North in the Gin'ral Lion, may be suppeeneyed. If Mr. Buggs should pass thro' Moun Citty without your nollege, he can be found at Newport, Rode Iland, where he an' his famly propose to taik up there residunce in ether the Biddle cottage or Bennet manshun.

" ' I hav the honnor to remane
" ' CORPORAL FOSTER,
" ' Major Gin'ral commandin' this diocees.'

"The admiral larfed harty you bet wen he red Foster's letter an' heered the hull story. He sent another ossifer to releeve the corporal, ' for,' says he, ' I must hav him neer me, for I shall liv twice as long if I kin hav the corporal to maik me larf.'

"I have lots ov good things to tell you, Jim Blazes, which will keep until you heer from me agin.

"I remane your ole shipmait in the grane bizness,
"JACK TILLER."

THE END.

By ADMIRAL PORTER.

Allan Dare and Robert le Diable.

A ROMANCE. By ADMIRAL PORTER. Illustrated by Alfred Fredericks. Two volumes, 8vo. Paper, $2.00; cloth, $3.00.

"Admiral Porter is the latest distinguished accession to the list of authors. He produces not a work on navigation but—a novel. Men of all professions are trying their hands at romancing nowadays. Admiral Porter need not be afraid of comparing his work with that of some professional novelists. The admiral excites the curiosity of the reader with a great deal of artfulness. The story has a mystery to which the author is leading up with much skill; he displays humor, touches of pathos, and a knack of sketching characters."—*New York Journal of Commerce.*

"All wonderfully vivid, exciting, and picturesque, with enough plot and incident already to furnish out some half-dozen ordinary novels. Admiral Porter has surprising vigor and freshness of style in narration, of picturesqueness in description of scenes and incidents, and of vividness in character-sketching. His story is wildly improbable, but it rivets the attention, nevertheless, and holds it steadily by its force, originality, and daring."—*Boston Gazette.*

"Since the Earl of Beaconsfield's time, no famous man in public affairs has written a novel that could excite public interest more than this one."—*Philadelphia Bulletin.*

The Adventures of Harry Marline;

OR NOTES FROM AN AMERICAN MIDSHIPMAN'S LUCKY BAG. By ADMIRAL PORTER. With Illustrations. 8vo, 378 pages. Paper, $1.00; cloth, $1.50.

These life-like and stirring adventures were written by the admiral for the amusement of his boys; and, thinking it better for people to laugh than to cry, the author has put them into book-form. The picture of the midshipmen in the olden times will delight our middies of the present day.

"'Harry Marline' is written in the racy manner that ought to characterize every account of doings at sea. In reading it one is brought face to face with the stern and humorous reality of a midshipman's life. The descriptions are most exhaustive; the humor of the driest; the cock-and-bull stories—'yarns' we believe they be called aboardship—the cockiest-and-bulliest afloat; the satires upon the green Secretaries of the Navy (of those old days) the keenest and most satisfactory. There is hardly a page that does not excite the risibilities involuntarily, and after one closes the volume delightful memories remain. The admiral deserves the title of 'our later Cooper' or perhaps, by reason of his deep stratum of humor, that of the Marryat of America. There are several illustrations, well designed and executed."—*Hartford Evening Post.*

New York: D. APPLETON & CO., 1, 3, & 5 Bond Street.

ANECDOTES OF THE CIVIL WAR
IN THE UNITED STATES.

By Brevet Major-General E. D. TOWNSEND,
Late Adjutant-General U. S. Army.

12mo. . . . . Cloth, $1.25.

"The work treats in a very pleasant conversational way of various events and incidents, around which our interest lingers, and of which much is here said that has hitherto been unsaid. Among the topics upon which the author dwells, and which may be cited as giving an idea of the scope and nature of his work, are General Scott's loyalty, the defense of Washington, the neutrality of Kentucky, Early's invasion, service in the Adjutant-General's office, President Lincoln's funeral, Fort Sumter, origin of military commissions, Army of the Potomac commanders, etc."—*Washington Daily Post.*

"General E. D. Townsend, who was Assistant Adjutant-General on the staff of General Scott at the outbreak of the rebellion, and who continued to discharge the same functions during the civil war, had of course opportunities of acquiring much curious information. Some of the facts thus brought to his knowledge he may never feel at liberty to divulge, but there is, on the other hand, a good deal which the lapse of time has made it proper to publish. Such of his recollections as belong to the latter category are now set forth in a medium-sized volume called "Anecdotes of the Civil War." General Townsend's stories are related in an entertaining way, and, even where they bear somewhat severely on the character or motives of the persons named, seem free from any propensity to exaggerate or taint of malice. The personal reminiscences of a man holding confidential relations to men in high authority might be expected to throw light on several obscure transactions, and this will be found to be the case."—*New York Sun.*

"General Townsend's book is all interesting."—*New York Army and Navy Journal.*

"An agreeable intermingling of personal anecdotes and historical statements. Full of useful information."—*New York Home Journal.*

"The General bore an important and honorable part in the struggle, and has the rare gift of telling briefly, humorously, and pathetically of what he saw and heard during all the eventful years."—*New York Journal of Commerce.*

"General Townsend has much to say of individuals, and a kindly spirit animates all his comments. Numerous incidents are related that are wholly new to the reader, though he be an inveterate newspaper peruser or reporter, and they can not fail to interest the most casual reader. The old soldiers of the great contest will enjoy these recitals."—*Boston Commonwealth.*

"Another of those contributions to the inner history of the war which are not only interesting to the curious reader, but form valuable material for the future historian. Much is told of General Scott which is interesting; we get some new anecdotes concerning President Lincoln, and there is an account of Secretary Stanton which will be likely to modify the harsh criticism of him, of late more prevalent than ever. The book abounds in quotable material, which we regret that our space does not permit us to transfer to our columns."—*Boston Gazette.*

"No man in the United States is better qualified to gossip pleasantly upon the great events which twenty years ago were in everybody's mouth than Brevet Major-General E. D. Townsend. His anecdotes are not only remarkably entertaining, but they throw a light upon many vexed questions which will prove of infinite value to the military historian."—*New York Commercial Advertiser.*

"The author writes in a charitable spirit of Scott, Stone, Lee, Buckner, Burke, McClellan, Blair, Sheridan, Stanton, Lincoln, and many others. General Townsend fully disposes of the malicious rumor that Stanton committed suicide. These anecdotes are well worth buying and reading from beginning to end."—*New York Christian Advocate.*

New York: D. APPLETON & CO., 1, 3, & 5 Bond Street.

www.ingramcontent.com/pod-product-compliance
Lightning Source LLC
Chambersburg PA
CBHW021726110726
47902CB00005B/1359